S0-CFT-148

FROST OF HEAVEN

JUNIUS PODRUG

A TOM DOHERTY ASSOCIATES BOOK
NEW YORK

This is a work of fiction. All the characters and events portrayed in this book are either products of the author's imagination or are used fictitiously.

FROST OF HEAVEN

Copyright © 1992 by Junius Podrug

This book was first published in Great Britain in 1993 by Headline Book Publishing PLC.

A Forge Book
Published by Tom Doherty Associates, LLC
175 Fifth Avenue
New York, NY 10010

www.tor.com

Forge is a registered trademark of Tom Doherty Associates, LLC.

ISBN: 0-812-55505-8
Library of Congress Catalog Card Number: 98-18904

First edition: November 1998
First mass market edition: April 2000

Printed in the United States of America

0 9 8 7 6 5 4 3 2 1

For
Paul Mikol and Scott Stadalsky,
harvesters of dreams

PROLOGUE

Out of whose womb came the ice?
and the hoary frost of heaven, who hath gendered it?

Job 38.29

The plane sped toward the pass like a dog running for a closing gate. Avalanches triggered by the rasp of its engine rushed down the sides of mountains as he steered toward the opening. Racing between Titanic peaks, the plane had no more significance than a fly in the Grand Canyon.

Suddenly he was at the right altitude, and he nursed the joystick to keep the nose up as the plane shot into the pass.

The engine coughed and the nose turned down. He fought the control stick as the plane dived for the bottom of the icy jaw. With thoughts of love and hate—the girl he left behind, the bastards who sent him to nowhere in a crippled plane—he was a drowning man seeing himself in that slippery moment between life and death. The plane turned up reluctantly, the metal fuselage trembling as if it had tasted the fear and sweat of the hands directing it.

The plane broke out of the pass and a gasp of relief escaped from him. The plunge had raised the hair on his soul.

He gritted his teeth. Bloody bastards. Risking his life without even letting him in on the secret. They were all puffed up with self-importance about the mission. They even had a priest at the briefing. Whoever heard of a priest at a top-secret briefing?

At the end of the briefing the priest had hurried to

him and started talking about how important the mission was to God. He had almost laughed. The man reeked of holy fervor and moldy wine. The priest had started to tell him something about a skull when a security officer pulled the man away.

Smoke and flames burst from the engine and the controls shook in his grip. He started losing altitude, limping like a wounded bird. In the distance was a great peak, a snowcapped giant, utterly majestic with lines as dramatic as the facets of a diamond. The big mountain—*he couldn't keep the plane's nose up. He'd never clear it!* The plane shuddered again, the death rattle of the Phoenix, as he stoked the burning engine. He screamed as the mountain rushed at him.

Driven by nervous energy, he crawled away from the crash, a rush of adrenaline fooling him into thinking he had survived when all he had probably achieved was a prelude to death. He was injured, hurt badly, his path in the snow marked by his blood. Places where his flight suit had been torn were not just rips in cloth but tears to his body. The wounds quickly froze. It was the bitter chill that would kill him.

He made one more mindless effort to get on his feet but managed only to roll over onto his back. His brain still functioned, but the ice pack was freezing his life's blood, creating rigor mortis while he still had a few breaths left.

He saw the movement out of the corner of his eye, what appeared to be an animal coming toward him, but he was too weak, too frozen, to turn his head. As it got closer he realized it was walking erect, like something human, and he imagined it to be a yeti, the legendary abominable snow creature said to haunt the mountains.

He wanted to get up and run but the joints of his arms and legs were frozen and his brain was slowly closing down. His mind screamed as the creature knelt beside him. He couldn't see what it was doing but sensed that hands were examining him.

It began taking off his clothes!

Soon he lay naked in the snow, his numbed brain reeling in the horror that the thing had undressed him.

Then the creature stood up and slipped out of its own furry coat. It was a *woman*, not an animal but a woman wearing a red robe under the hooded coat. She had dark-honey skin, black hair and molasses eyes, and an almost otherworldliness about her that transcended race. A silver pendant carved in the image of a snow leopard hung from a chain around her neck.

She tucked the furry coat under him and stood and slipped off her red robe. Her body was smooth and firm and seemed impervious to the bitter cold. She pressed her naked body against his, her breasts pushing on his bare chest, her legs wrapping around his, drawing them together, sealed by the warmth of her thighs, the fire in her blood flowing from her flesh to his . . .

LONDON

CHAPTER I

*Who were you before your mother
and father conceived you?*

Fog had settled on Whitehall, a weeping shroud
chillwet and unstirred as the breath of the dead.
Peter shivered and pulled up the collar on his coat.
He knew they were back there, knew he was being
followed, that the thick night hid the men behind him.

*What would it feel like to get a bullet in the back?
Ripping through me, exploding my lungs out of my
chest?*

He kept walking, trying to listen to the night, but
the fog seemed to distort every sound. Somewhere in
the distance the bells of a church tolled. As if in answer a foghorn whispered on the River Thames, the
coarse song suspended for a moment, melancholy,
like the mort played on a hunting horn heralding that
a kill had been made.

What in God's name was he supposed to know?

He was threatened by the ghost of a man he had
never met.

What could his father have seen in a plane over the
Himalayas that was still important thirty years later?

Reaching a corner where a street lamp glowed, he
stepped away from the light and listened for sounds.
A car started up and accelerated somewhere ...
streets away? *Would they come for him in a car? Pick
him off the sidewalk, getting rid of him as quick and
easy as spitting on a slate and wiping it clean?*

He walked in a direction where he thought he'd

find the Thames and the tube station near Victoria Embankment. *Keep moving. Harder to hit. The fog works both ways.*

He was in the heart of government row, surrounded by the citadels of British history—the Admiralty, the old War Office, Whitehall Palace where Charles I lost his head for high treason and other crimes.

A few hours ago the area was bustling with people and cars and taxis. Now the night was thick, the streets deserted. He'd left freak tornadoes and violent rainstorms behind in sunny California—and stumbled into a near whiteout by the Thames in a city that hadn't seen peasoupers in decades. The fog was scary. That's why they let him off in the middle of it. To scare him. To kill him?

Fuck them. They weren't going to scare him away. They would have to kill him.

It had all seemed so simple in the beginning.

Down the River Thames, not far from where he was walking, was Waterloo Bridge. His mother, a young woman from California on vacation in Britain, had met a Scotsman named Duncan MacKinzie on that bridge over three decades ago. She was forced to return home pregnant and unwed after the handsome RAF officer disappeared in a forgotten flight over the loneliest place on earth—the Himalayas.

"You look like your father," his mother told him a thousand times, which told him nothing because he didn't know what his father looked like.

When he was twelve and other kids were out fishing with their dads, he stood in front of a mirror and mentally subtracted his mother's looks from his own to construct his father from the leftovers. His brown hair was darker and thicker than his mother's, his eyes greener than her hazel ones; he was tall as a kid and sprouted up over six one as an adult, muscular in a willowy way, lacking that pumped look many muscular men cultivate. He never knew if the image of his father he conjured up was accurate because there was no one to compare it with. ⁓

His mother never lost her hope, her hopeless dream, that her handsome young RAF pilot would come back to her, to rekindle their love and claim his son. Married to a nice, solid, boring man, she committed emotional suicide and withered inside like a forgotten rose pressed between the pages of a book.

Her unfulfilled romantic yearnings became part of the makeup of her child, passed along like a genetic defect.

Peter left his job, his way of life, at the age of thirty, to find a missing piece of himself.

And walked into what?

His father's last mission—what the hell had happened thirty years ago that seemed to be putting his own life in jeopardy today?

He had gone to the government building where personnel files of British war dead and MIAs were stored, "the paper graveyard," he heard a clerk call it. Accessing his father's service file was the quickest way to get a lead on his family, to let them know Duncan MacKinzie had a son and to get a peek at his own roots.

It was his tenth trip to the paper graveyard to wade through red tape in an attempt to see the file, but this time two men burst into the room with a show of authority and muscle, shoving him up against the counter and cuffing him. The pretty file clerk went from being flirtatious to gawking as they hustled him out the back door.

On the rear loading dock one of the men tripped him, sending him down the concrete ramp with his hands cuffed behind. They jerked him off the ground, ignoring his curses, and shoved him onto the backseat of a waiting car. Blindfolded, he was taken a few blocks, through more doors and up stairs. He counted the steps, thirty-nine, with two landings in between.

All because he wanted to see the file of a dead man.

What was so important about his father's flight? Had he been flying a spy plane? The geography was right: The Himalayas are between India and China, two nations rattling sabers at each other three decades ago. The time was right, too, an era that saw Gary Powers shot down while piloting a U2.

But what could Duncan MacKinzie have seen in a spy plane over the icy world of the Himalayas that would be so important thirty years later that British Intelligence would haul his son in and batter him with hours of relentless questions and accusations?

Cops is how he thought of them. Peter was a reporter, an investigative reporter, and had scrapped with the cops before. They told him they were MI5, but the men who interrogated him were pricks, more likely to spend an evening putting a bullet behind the ear of an IRA terrorist than enjoying high tea and scotch with foreign spies at the Dorchester.

In the shabby interrogation room the two agents had taken turns at him like jackals ripping the flesh from a carcass while a third man hid and listened.

"What's the worst thing that could happen to you?" the chief thug asked, a boozer who talked with a slight lisp, leaning close with Johnny Walker breath, staring at him with bloodshot eyes glazed with an unhealthy yellow film. Fine veins had pushed to the surface of his nose like tiny blue worms wiggling out.

What's the worst thing that could happen to you?

"Everyone has fears, their worst nightmares," the lisper told him, staring through the slits of Venetian blinds, talking to the gray night.

They told him what he feared and it hit him like a kick in the balls.

They had been watching him, had dug into his background, got under his skin and passed his life under a microscope.

Because he wanted to see his father's military file?

He choked on his own laughter. They knew who he was but *he couldn't prove he was Peter Mac-Kinzie*. His driver's license said Novak, his passport said Novak, hell, he didn't know how to sign his name *except* as Peter Novak. But what's in a name? A good man named Novak married a pregnant woman and allowed his name to be written on a birth certificate to keep a child from being labeled a bastard. The only evidence he had that he was Duncan MacKinzie's son was the word of his mother. And she had been dead for five years.

Footsteps shuffled somewhere behind him and he swung around, straining to see. There were *things* in the fog—like the images on a Rorschach ink blot, what the eye didn't see, the mind imagined.

The fog was getting to him. He picked up his pace, his ear tuned to the sounds of the night.

No damn taxis. On a clear day the area was crawling with them. Nights like this, the gray damp of winterkill settling on the city, the streets reading like a Gothic novel, must have been what fed the Ripper and drove Poe to madness.

Charming thoughts. "Keep it up, Peter," he said aloud.

He tried to get the dreary night off his mind by thinking of his hurts. His right shoulder ached from the tumble down the ramp, his head hurt from bouncing off the floor, but questions swirling in his head like bats in an attic kept him from focusing on the pain.

Who was the third man? One side of the room had been partitioned off. He sensed someone behind the divider, someone listening as the other two took turns at him. He made a deliberately clumsy attempt to get off the chair with his hands still cuffed, turning it over, bouncing his nose off the floor to get a look under the divider at a pair of scuffed black shoes and black pants.

Was he the one, the killer sent to put a bullet in his back in the fog or run him down with a car, another victim of big-city violence? The other two had dropped him off several streets back and stood by their car, a look passing between them as they told him to start walking.

Maybe they're just trying to intimidate me. Scare me a little. He shivered and tugged his coat collar higher. They sure as hell chose a fine night if they wanted to get under his skin. Nothing like a dark and dreary night with angry gargoyles glaring down from shadowy buildings. The British were civilized, weren't they? Hell, he was *half* British. They probably just wanted to scare him off. Thought he was nothing but a nosy newspaper reporter, digging out dirt and putting it on the front pages like he did before he traded in a California tan for gray London. He thought about what an ugly bastard Lisper was and lost confidence in his "scare-off" theory. Lisper liked to hurt people.

What the hell is it about that file that gets these bastards seemingly kill crazy? And who the hell was the guy behind the partition, the third man?

He heard footsteps again, running steps, and he swung around. Nothing, just shadows in the fog, but now he was pissed. He was tired of being scared, finished with being bullied. *Fuck 'em.* He wasn't going to turn his back again and worry that someone was going to slip it to him.

He stepped off the street and into the doorway of a building, losing himself in the shadows, listening to the night. Tense. Nerves on fire. He hadn't thought about what he would do when his stalker showed up. But running wasn't one of the options.

He rubbed his cold hands. *Where's the best place to hit some son of a bitch with a gun before he blows my face off? Balls? Throat? Solar plexus? Grab the gun and butt the bastard in the nose with his head? Shit, that was all movie crap!*

Something touched his leg and he almost jumped out of his pants.

A cat, *a goddamn black cat!*

It brushed against his pants leg again and he stared down at it. He slowly took a breath and let his tensed muscles relax. He felt like laughing.

Nothing but a damn cat.

He had had it with lurking in doorways. He stepped out and bumped into someone.

"What—!"

A woman stepped back, startled. He thought she was going to run but instead she stared at him with searching eyes, as if she had been expecting someone whose face she didn't know. Her face was partly cloaked by the hood of her coat, exposing only dark eyes and lovely cheeks.

He got his own breathing under control and tried to smile. "Sorry, I didn't see you."

She clutched a bag he thought at first was a large carryall but then realized it was an old-fashioned carpetbag.

Surprise registered on her features as her eyes met his and he stared back, puzzled. He didn't know her, but she struck a chord deep within him as if he *should.*

"Do I know you?" he asked.

"I—"

Footsteps sounded from an alley to his left. She looked to the alley and tensed, as if ready to bolt. He fought back his own panic. "Is something wrong?"

She backed away from him slowly.

"Miss . . ."

She turned and dashed into the street.

"Watch out!"

Headlights of an oncoming car bore down on her. He leaped after her, getting a handhold on her coat and jerking her back as the car screeched to a stop beside him.

"Christ! You almost got killed."

A taxi sign glowed on the roof of the car and an anxious English face poked out of the window on the driver's side. "Anybody 'urt?"

"Are you all right?" Peter asked the woman.

"I . . . I'm fine."

The footsteps sounded again, heavy steps, that of a man or possibly more than one. Peter still had a hold of her arm and he felt tension spring through it—she was ready to run again.

"We're coming aboard," he told the driver. He steered her to the back door, opening it for her. She hurried in and he climbed in behind her, slamming the door. The driver peered back at them through the open glass partition. "Let's go," Peter snapped. As the taxi pulled away he got a glimpse of someone running toward it, a threatening shadow screened by the fog. The image faded as the taxi moved down the street.

The cabbie glanced back at his passengers. "Nearly got me in an accident. Destination?"

Peter was too intent on watching the woman to be interested in the cabbie's track record. The hood had fallen to her shoulders, exposing long, wavy black hair that glowed with the midnight sheen of Poe's raven. Light and shadow caressed her face as the taxi passed street lamps; her eyelashes curved dramatically above brown eyes that took his measure with the dangerous intensity of a jungle cat.

"Where you goin'?" the cabbie asked insistently.

Peter raised his eyebrows to the woman.

"Where are *you* going?" she countered.

"Soho."

The cabbie reached up and slammed the glass screen shut.

"I don't think he's happy with us," Peter said.

Her features were different in a way that fascinated him. The cast of her eyes, the curve of her high cheekbones, hinted of the exotic Orient, but there was an elusive quality about her features—she could have been born in a suburb of Birmingham or a tent on the steppes of Asia.

A mystic quality about her fed his imagination. He remembered a trip to Stonehenge and a story told to him by a farmer he met in a pub, a tale of a Druid princess whom the farmer insisted visited the bleak plains at night to walk among the silent sentinels of the past.

"Have you ever been to Stonehenge?" he asked.

The question startled her. "Stonehenge?" Large brown eyes searched his face, looking for hidden meaning behind the question.

"I just—have we met before?"

"Not in this life." She treated him with the hint of a smile as if her remark was retaliation for his disarming question about Stonehenge.

"Are you—"

"I'm not from London," she said.

"That's a coincidence, I'm not from London, either."

"Perhaps that's why we seem to know each other."

He had tried to keep a straight face but broke off into a soft smile. "There's a certain amount of perverse logic to that."

"You're an American."

"I'm an American. Peter Novak."

She didn't volunteer her name, leaving a blank in

the conversation that grew pregnant. He was struck again by that haunting sense of familiarity, as if they had met but he knew they had not. This was not a woman he would forget.

"What happened back there?"

"A man . . . a mugger tried to attack me." She looked out the back window as if she expected she was being followed.

Her English was Received Standard, the archaic dialect of Oxford and Cambridge, underlined by a touch of foreign accent that added to the aura of mystery that surrounded her.

He didn't believe her story about the mugger. He tried a bluff. "I'll have the cabbie take us to the nearest police station to report the matter."

"I appreciate your concern." He loved the sound of her voice, the rich English accent laced with foreign intrigue. "But it won't be necessary. I'm not even certain anyone was following me. The darkness, the fog, my imagination got the best of me."

"Are you in some sort of trouble?" He could have asked the question about himself.

"I don't know what you mean."

She avoided his eyes and glanced back at the window. Her hooded coat—almost a cape—was Russian sable; a snow leopard delicately wrought in silver hung from a chain around her slender neck. Her only other jewelry was a white-gold watch sprinkled with diamonds. Peter liked the effect; jewelry would distract from her beauty.

"Worried about being followed?"

"I told you, there was a man—"

"Muggers don't hop into cars and follow their victims. Not even ones as lovely as you."

Her eyes swept his face, scanning his green eyes, brown hair, the line of his jaw, her expression one of curiosity, even puzzlement, as if she were searching for someone hidden under the features. "Who are you, Peter Novak? Who were you before this life?"

What was she talking about?

Her hand touched his knee, a casual intimacy that seemed to be offered unconsciously, as if she had touched him to see if he was real.

Her touch—it was so familiar. He stared at her lips, wondering what it would be like to kiss her, and at the same time he was struck by the sensation that he already knew.

It didn't make sense—she wasn't someone he would forget. And she sure as hell wasn't the type he could ask, "Excuse me, lady, but have we ever fucked?"

Tashi took her hand from Peter's knee and stared out the window on her side to hide the storm of emotions assaulting her. Their meeting had not been an accident—she felt lured to him as inexorably as a moth batting its wings on the rim of a volcano, drawn to the inferno even in the face of doom.

She had watched the priest follow Peter. As the priest came down the dark street, she stepped out of a doorway and grabbed the bag. After she lost the priest in the fog, she waited, certain the footfalls she heard were Peter's, experiencing again the emotions that had electrified her when she saw him for the first time.

She was not a Druid princess but a woman of worldly flesh and human desires. Her background and training made her different from most women: She was a product of the Orient, the "mysterious East," raised in a lamasery by Tibetan monks and trained to bring mind and body into a universe of *awareness*.

Her instincts about people were exceptional. There was nothing mystical about her abilities—she had been trained to see each blade of grass, each flower

in a meadow. By opening herself up to people—to
the motives revealed by the way they walked and
talked, the secrets in their smile, the desire in their
eyes—she was able to leaf quickly through a person's
mind like someone flipping through the pages of a
book.

She had been trained from childhood also to listen
to her own emotions, to stand within herself and experience her subconscious, an area of self that few
Westerners ever probe.

But Peter Novak scrambled her fine-honed senses.
Her eyes told her he was a stranger, but her heart told
her something else.

A strange sense of intimacy teased her like the
sweet warmth that lingered after stepping from a hot
bath; she imagined herself naked in bed with him, his
hands softly caressing her breasts, down her flat stomach, moving up her thighs like a burning ember igniting desire that started between her legs and spread
through her body like blood-fire.

"Are you all right?" he asked.

He wanted her to turn to him, to look into his eyes
again. When their eyes had met before he hadn't seen
glamour wrapped in sable but a real woman, tender,
caring, yet fiercely defiant. He had never experienced
emotions like the ones now talking to him from some
inner recess of his mind. He felt an intense bond with
her, not fascination, not infatuation, but something
simple, natural, as if running, laughing with her in the
rain, or holding her in his arms before a roaring fireplace were not just to be desired but expected.

He slowly raised his hand to her cheek and touched
it.

"Who are you?" he whispered.

She turned to face him, her cheeks hot, her eyes
exposing her desire. The desire he saw was not lust

but burning innocence, the wonderful sensation of two lovers long apart seeing each other across the crowded ramp of a train station, racing for each other's arms. He felt her in the beat of his heart, felt the fire in his own body.

She leaned closer to him, soft tears in her eyes. Her fingers traced the curve of his jaw, the warmth of his cheeks, and pushed gently into his hair. She pulled his face to hers until her sweet breath brushed his lips.

He wanted her, now, on a white satin bed, his body bonded with hers; he wanted her *now*, in the backseat of a taxi in foggy Londontown.

He slipped open her coat and pulled her to him.

Her fingers dug deeper in his hair and pulled him closer until their lips met, cautiously, unsure, slowly folding together and then opening until he could taste her essence and she his, a tiny flame uniting them until it exploded and they pressed hungrily at each other, her breasts eager against his chest, her hands pulling at his hair.

This wasn't the way she dealt with men, but her body hungered for this stranger, and she lost herself to her desires as his hand slid into the warmth under her dress—

"Shit!" The taxi suddenly swerved in the roadway and the driver laid on the horn. "Bleedin' idiot on a bike with no lights!"

She pulled away from him, breathless, and scooted down the seat, straightening her clothing.

Peter cleared his throat and combed his hair with his hand. *Jesus H. Christ!*

He turned to her to say something and the words snagged in his throat. She was staring at him with the angry shock of a woman who had just been pinched by a total stranger.

Her hand moved in a blur, the slap wiping away

the rest of his words, leaving his cheek stinging and his jaw hanging.

"What did I do?"

The rear window of the taxi glowed blue, startling both of them.

"The Old Bill," the cabbie cursed.

Peter twisted in the seat and rubbed steam off the window to get a look at the police car with its flashing blue light as the cabbie steered to the curb. "I—I wonder why they're stopping us." He stammered a little, his nerves still on fire.

She opened the door and slipped out of the taxi as it came to a stop.

"Wait!" He scooted across the seat to the closing door, his leg hitting the bag she left on the floor.

"Oi! What about the fare?" The cabbie twisted in his seat and glared at him.

Peter ignored him and stared out the window. *Why were they being stopped?* Something Lisper cooked up?

The woman was gone, vanished into the fog as abruptly as she had appeared. He didn't even know her name. His leg touched the carryall again and he picked it up and put it on his lap. "She left her bag," he said, more to himself than the cabbie. The bag was old and well worn, its wooden handle scarred, the seams frayed. Not an imitation but the genuine article, an old-fashioned carpetbag used as an overnighter in the leisurely days of trains and carriages. He squeezed the sides and felt something solid inside, half the size of a loaf of bread. He hoped it was her purse with her name and address in it.

The cabbie grumbled as he rolled down the window for the policeman who appeared beside the taxi. Peter was relieved to see the policeman had a notebook in hand. "Maybe it's full of dosh," the cabbie said, glancing in the rearview mirror as he handed his license to the policeman. " 'eard about a fella in Liverpool, his fare left a briefcase on the backseat that . . ."

Peter wasn't listening. Two worn leather straps slipped into tarnished brass buckles held the carryall closed. He undid the two straps and pulled open the bag. Something white at the bottom glowed in the dim light. He reached for it, a rough, hard object that felt like a piece of unfinished porcelain. He pulled it out and held it up to the dome light.

"What the hell?"

A *human skull* stared back at him.

CHAPTER 2

Tashi was a couple of streets away from where she had fled the taxi when a black Mercedes limousine pulled to the curb beside her. The back door opened and she got in.

A man was waiting in the backseat for her. He had the cold, handsome face of an emperor's death mask, as if his features had been sculpted by a plastic surgeon with an eye for the classics. His age was late forties or fifties, but he could have been older or younger—the rigidity of his features gave him an ageless quality. His hair was brown streaked with slivers of gray; ice-green eyes were set like emeralds in the mask.

The name on his passport said Zhdanov, but he had no more right to the name than to his stolen face.

"What happened?" His English was internationalized; his tone betrayed no emotion.

She took off her coat to gain time to get her thoughts together. "I grabbed the bag from the priest, but I got confused in the fog and ran the wrong way."

"Where's the bag?"

"It's in a taxi."

"A taxi!"

"I . . . I ran into a man and he helped me into a taxi." The lies were sticking in her throat. "Everything went insane. The police stopped the taxi for something. I slipped out and forgot the bag."

"You forgot the bag?"

"I was frightened."

"Why did the police stop the taxi? Was the priest with them?"

"I'm not sure." His anger seethed on the edge of a violent explosion. *He'd kill me if he knew I was lying.*

"We have to locate the taxi," he said. The words came out like chips of ice. "And the man, if he removed the bag. Do you know anything about him?"

She turned away from the cold fury in his voice. "Only his name. Peter Novak. The priest was following him."

"Novak, Peter Novak. The name means nothing to me. I don't know why the priest was following him. Describe him."

"About my age, maybe a couple years older, thirty, thirty-two, brown hair—"

"Height?"

"I'm not sure. Tall, a little taller than you—"

"How much taller?"

"A little. An inch or two. He was . . . slender. I'm sorry. I only saw him briefly and in bad light at that."

"He fits the description of half the men in London." Green-ice eyes examined her, burning at layers of deceit. She met his eyes with a power of her own. "You're usually so incredibly observant, to the point of psychic. You've chosen a bad time to have a memory loss."

She had deliberately made the description accurate—and vague. She could have drawn a picture of Peter Novak from mind's eye, a portrait of a young man a little tan in pale London, not good-looking in the sense of men selected to puff on a Marlboro or wear the newest fad jeans on camera, but sensuously attractive, sensitivity and inquisitiveness reflected in his searching eyes, etched into the firm line of his jaw, signaling strength of character and an almost stubborn integrity.

His smile was reserved, a little cautious, and didn't relax the sharp lines of his face. He smiled too easily, and she recognized him as one of those slightly reserved people who unconsciously use a smile as a defense mechanism. No one would mistake him for an absentminded professor, but there was an air of introspection about him, as if he were looking out at the world while standing within himself, an intellectual intensity not entirely foreign to the heady madness that inflicts drunken poets.

More than anything else, his intense eyes separated him from the crowd—eyes that probed, eyes that could speak to a woman across a crowded room.

The gallant way he took her arm and made sure she entered the taxi first when he thought there was danger, the almost *casual* manner in which he accepted the fact she was in danger, as if damsels in distress were part of his normal routine, told her that Peter Novak was a very special person, a romantic in an age when too many men expended their passions on football and the Dow Jones average.

She gave minimal detail about Peter because she didn't want to sign his death warrant.

"We were supposed to grab the bag," the man beside her said. "You were told to wait in the car."

"I'm sorry. I became anxious and followed. I bumped into the priest in that dreadful fog and grabbed the bag on impulse." This was the crucial moment. She met his eye without flinching, a storm of emotions within her hidden behind the mask she'd chosen for the role. Grabbing the bag had been premeditated, a desperate move to keep the skull out of his hands. She knew the man beside her loved her, as much as a man could who had had his emotions cut out of him with shears as sharp as a lobotomy needle.

But she also knew he was driven by demons stronger than love, demons that could rip her throat before he got his emotions under control.

"We have to retrieve the skull. If your friend from the taxi gets in the way . . ."

He let her imagination finish the threat.

What had happened to her in the taxi? Her cheeks burned with embarrassment, and she turned away from Zhdanov again to hide her emotions. She stared at her own reflection in the dark window and touched her face, asking herself how she could have acted so . . . so unrestrained. She had been all over Peter Novak, clawing at him like a bitch in heat. She had never been that way with a man—*any man.* Zhdanov's friends called her the "Ice Princess" because of the cold shoulder she gave to their advances.

Thoughts of Peter evoked that deep sense of *intimacy with a stranger.*

Kismet is what they call it in the East, that mysterious feeling of having been destined to meet.

Like an amnesia victim returning to normal, every thought of Peter brought on whispers of memories, visions that stayed just out of reach, fading like mirages on desert highways as she reached for them. But another emotion had crawled into her thoughts like a black spider.

Shame.

Why shame? she wondered.

She sensed that they had been lovers in a life past. That they would be lovers again.

But why did her feelings evoke a terrible sense of shame within her?

What was forbidden about her desire for Peter?

CHAPTER 3

It's old," Peter told the policeman. Blood pounded in his temples. He had been left holding the bag. Literally.

"Get out of the taxi."

He stepped out onto the pavement, carrying the piece of skull with him.

The policeman waiting for him had traded his notebook for a nightstick. "Put the skull on the bonnet, hands on the car."

"Look—"

"Now!"

Peter leaned up against the taxi hood while the policeman quickly frisked him.

The officer's backup was standing next to the police car, nightstick in hand. Peter heard most British cops didn't carry guns openly but somehow managed to produce them when the need arose.

"Stand up straight."

Peter pushed away from the taxi and turned to face the officer.

The taxi driver shoved his head and half his shoulders out the window. "Somebody's been murdered and chopped up!"

"It's old, for Christ's sake. Look at it," Peter told the policeman. "The woman left it."

"Woman?" The policeman glanced at the empty backseat.

The cabbie cranked his neck a little more and squinted up to get a good look at the homicidal maniac. "Where'd the bird go, mate?"

"I don't know. I don't even know her."

"Got in together, didn't you?"

"I bumped into her back on the Embankment and we shared the taxi. She hopped out when you stopped us. Leaving that bag behind with . . . that in it," he finished lamely.

"It's a *human* skull," the policeman said.

"It's obviously old, a collector's item or something," Peter said. The bone was granite gray with dark pockmarks and chips. *Don't sound so damn anxious.*

The cabbie's eyes lit up. " 'Ere, maybe the British Museum's been ripped off!"

Peter almost groaned aloud. *Mouthy bastard couldn't leave well enough alone.* If there had been a heist, he'd been caught red-handed with the stolen goods.

"I think you had better step over to the police car, sir."

"This is ridiculous—"

"Move it!"

The backup officer opened the car door and gestured with his nightstick for Peter to get in.

He climbed in and the officer shut the door. *Jesus Christ, I'm being arrested.* He was all alone, nobody to call, no way to set bail. He'd never make it in prison. Being cooped up in the rear cell of a police car gave him instant trapped-animal panic. He had been arrested once, in L.A., when he refused to back off questioning a witness at the scene of a police shooting. Rather than putting him in a holding tank with drunks and muggers as he waited for his editor to bail him out, they threw him in the hard-ass detention cell with six East L.A. gangbangers for company, figuring the street punks would play music on the bars with the head of the geek wearing a suit and tie.

He quickly identified himself as a newsman and said he was looking for a front-page story. "Who wants to be famous?" All six answered the call for media glory, and he spent the night listening to gang stories.

That was L.A.

He watched tight-jawed as the two cops examined the skull closely by flashlight, the cabbie leaning out the window blabbing God knows what to them.

What the hell did I get myself into now? It stank of setup. They really knew their pigeon. Put a pretty girl on a dark street, a frightened glance over her shoulder, big brown pleading eyes, and Peter Novak to the rescue.

They said they would get him, but he would have been less surprised if he had found dope in the bag than a *skull*. Hell, maybe they'll find dope. One of the officers was checking out the carpetbag. He pulled out another piece of bone. Peter wondered if this one had fresh meat on it.

The backup pulled a microphone off his coat lapel and spoke into it while the second officer examined the bones. The cabbie shot a glance back at the police car, no doubt drilling all the details into his head to tell his wife, kids, and the morning news.

The rear holding compartment smelled of puke and piss. He didn't know if that was from previous occupants or if he was smelling his own fear.

Dumb bastard, letting a woman set me up.

The two policemen kept looking back in Peter's direction as the one jabbered on the phone. Finally the backup returned the microphone to his coat and the two officers walked to the patrol car. The backup opened the rear door and the other officer bent down and told Peter, "Step out, sir."

Peter got out of the police car, the bitter night air biting at the sweat on his face.

The officer was holding the two pieces of bone. The specimen Peter pulled out of the bag was the cranium, the top half of the head down to the eye sockets and temples. The piece the officer had pulled out was a jaw, with part of the right side broken off. The jaw was as chipped and pockmarked as the other piece.

Frowning at the bones, the policeman said, "They do look old, might be fossils or the like. There's no report of missing bones. I suggest you take 'em to your local station in the morning."

Peter walked back to the taxi clutching the bones like a man staggering away from the gallows with a pardon in hand. He climbed into the backseat where the carpetbag was waiting for him and shoved the bones into it, out of sight, out of mind, as the cop who started the ticket was back at the cabbie's window to finish up.

"You say you don't know the girl?" The cabbie squinted back at Peter, his voice reeking with doubt.

"I don't know her." He wondered what else might come out of the man's mouth to get him into trouble.

"Friendly for strangers," the cabbie muttered.

Who was she? The thought that he had been set up nagged him again. Maybe the traffic stop wasn't part of the setup. Maybe they were waiting for bigger and better things, and the beautiful woman and the bones were just the opening gambit.

The policeman left and the cabbie got the taxi moving. "Went through a red light. Have to work overtime to pay for the violation." He glared at Peter in the rearview mirror.

Peter suddenly realized why the man was so venomous toward him—he probably ran the light because he was catching the action in the backseat instead of watching the road.

"Bugger didn't want to do the paperwork, that's why he didn't take them bones into custody. Know what I think? Probably the cranium of a great ape, stolen from old Doc Leakey himself in Africa."

"Good theory. You should have told the cops." *You told them everything else.* He cut off another comment about to erupt from the cabbie's mouth. "Do you know the Seri Sushi restaurant? Soho, somewhere above Shaftesbury Avenue. In an alley?" He had got vague instructions from Sheila, the date he was meeting at the restaurant, but the events of the past few hours had pushed them out of his mind.

"Seri Sushi," the cabbie muttered. "S'pose that's in one of them alleys only cats and muggers hang around."

"Wonderful. Being mugged would nicely top off the evening." *What does a mugger do when he finds out the bag he grabbed has a human skull inside?*

"Have to ride around a bit to find the place seeing as you don't know where this gaff is."

"Ride around a bit" was no doubt the cabbie's way of telling him he was going to run up the meter to help pay for the traffic ticket. Peter let it pass—a more urgent thought had occurred to him. The woman's story about a mugger had sounded like a fabrication. But she had been afraid she was being followed. Why would she be followed? The bones were the obvious candidate, and now he had them. If someone had followed her, *they might be following him now.*

He looked at the traffic to the rear. He was being followed by a long line of headlights.

The taxi was approaching Cambridge Circus, a much better lit district at night than government row, but the fog was still there, casting a blurry film on the night.

"Sorry, Guv, can't get you right up to the door. That part of Soho's roped off. They're 'aving a Guy Fawkes celebration, least that's what they call it. Took a butcher's earlier, there's tables of food and carnival games all down the street, fortune tellers and the sort. Bleedin' nuts if you ask me, all those Gypsies and what 'ave you, and it's s'posed to be Guy Fawkes night. Not keen on that Soho bunch meself. Frogs and Dagos and slanty-eyes . . ."

"Took a butcher's." Peter tried to remember what he had been told about Cockney speech. Butcher's hook rhymes with look. He tuned out the cabbie and thought again about the woman. Had she left the bag deliberately? Or forgotten it in a panic? Who did the bones belong to? One bit of deductive reasoning had excluded her as the owner: The bag had a musty *masculine* odor to it, the smell of clothes that belonged to an older man, a bachelor or widower, who didn't air out his clothing. And he got a faint whiff of something ninety proof when he opened the bag. The owner had carried a bottle of booze in the bag, more than once.

The Mercedes carrying Tashi and the man called Zhdanov raced through Trafalgar Square and sped up Charing Cross Road, pausing briefly beside each taxi it passed to give its passengers an opportunity to check out the cab's occupants.

Zhdanov cursed. "The damn city is full of black taxis and they all look alike."

Tashi stared out the window at passing traffic, avoiding eye contact with him.

"I don't understand why you grabbed the bag from the priest," Zhdanov said. "You were told to stay in the limo."

His anger was building again. She put her hand on his arm. "I was trying to help," she murmured.

As the limousine pulled up to a traffic light, she saw a man and a woman embracing in a taxi coming from the opposite direction and she gave a start. *It's him*. The couple broke the embrace and the man turned. No, it wasn't him. She felt a sense of relief and a little wonder. Was that jealousy? That sudden tightening of the chest muscles, the shortness of breath, the pinching of the heart? She had never experienced jealousy before. Can you be jealous of a man you had only known for minutes? Or had it just been for minutes? She wanted to see him again, to feel the touch of his lips against hers—

"Is that him?" Zhdanov asked.

"What?"

"The man in the taxi."

A taxi had pulled up beside them. A man in his early thirties was the only passenger.

"No, that's not him."

Zhdanov grabbed her wrist. "Are you sure?" His grip tightened. *He knows I'm lying*. It frightened her. He had been close to obtaining the skull, and she had lost it for him. It was the first time she had interfered with his quest, and it had exposed a frightening side of him. She knew he loved her, but the skull in the bag was his blind side, stirring unspeakable horror and pain that drove him with maniacal force.

"It's not him."

She was torn between her empathy for Zhdanov— she knew his pain as her own—and her fear of him. She had walked a thousand miles, asked a thousand questions, to find him, but even now she hardly knew him better than the enigma she had searched for. He hid behind plastic surgery and all the façade money could buy. She wanted so much to know him, not the mysterious too-handsome millionaire so many women had tried—and failed—to possess but the man behind the mask.

He had rained clothes and jewels upon her but gave nothing of himself.

Bagora, Zhdanov's assistant, twisted in the front seat of the limousine and glared at her through the glass that created privacy for the rear compartment. Tashi glanced to the communication button; it was on. Bagora and Ma, the driver, could hear everything that was being said by her and Zhdanov. He had wanted his creature to hear her. He knew Bagora was insanely jealous of her, and he used it to play him off against her.

She didn't fear the little man. At first she had felt sorry for him, for the bad luck of the genetic draw that gave him a short body, broad flat nose, and wrinkled skin that hung so loosely it looked like his face was ready to slip off. But the swarthy little man's ugliness was not an accident of birth but a reflection of the slime of his soul.

If danger came to Peter, it would be from Bagora.

She leaned over and flicked off the communication switch.

"This is impossible!" Zhdanov snapped. "There's not even a dent on any of these taxis to tell them apart. You should have taken the number of the taxi."

He was right about the lack of dents. London's licensed taxis were almost all black and had not a scratch on them.

As they approached Leicester Square, Zhdanov instructed the driver to pull over. He spoke curtly to Tashi. "Take a taxi back to the hotel. I'll call in fifteen minutes to make sure you're there."

"What are you going to do?"

"You said this man Novak was on his way to Soho. We'll drive around the area and try to spot him."

"But you need me to identify him."

"I have his name and description. I'm going to telephone one of my London contacts to see if he can get a lead on the man, in case we miss him in Soho."

"I should stay and help."

Zhdanov nodded at the car telephone. "In fifteen minutes you had better be in your room."

"You're not going to harm him?"

"Fifteen minutes."

She stood on the street corner and watched the Mercedes pull away. *They wouldn't hurt him. They'd just grab the carryall and leave.* But what if he resisted? Peter Novak didn't seem like the type to let someone push him around.

She signaled an approaching taxi. "Palace Club Hotel," she told the driver through the side window. She opened the back door and got in, settling back on the rear seat, feeling a little lonely in the huge passenger area.

She couldn't shake the sense of apprehension. She had created a dangerous situation for an innocent man. She stared out the window, wondering what she should do as the driver whipped the taxi down gray streets. She wanted to tell him to turn around, to take her to Soho, but she knew she would only make things worse if she wasn't in her room to receive Zhdanov's call.

Leaving the bag in the taxi had been foolish. She should have thrown it in a waste bin and told Zhdanov someone had grabbed it from her.

She stared at the dark night. He was out there somewhere in the city. With a bag of bones. And ruthless men in pursuit. She wanted to reach out to him, to warn him of the danger.

The taxi dropped Tashi off at the front door of the Palace Club Hotel. The hotel was not listed in any guidebook or even in the telephone directory. At hotels like the Dorchester and the Ritz, *anybody* with enough money could rent a room; at the Palace Club, only people who were *somebody* had the unlisted number. Being a wealthy somebody was also mandatory; the daily rate for suites began in the low four digits and went up to five digits for a penthouse. The dark mahogany and brass of the hotel lobby created the ambience of a lounge aboard a great ship of yesteryear.

The phone was ringing as she entered her bedroom in the suite.

"Hello."

"Fine."

Zhdanov hung up. She listened to the dial tone for a moment before putting the receiver back.

Her fear for Peter Novak welled up again. It had been a mistake to give Zhdanov Peter's name, but she had wondered herself if Peter was mixed up in the business with the priest and had given the name to see if Zhdanov recognized it.

She had to locate him. He had said he was an American, but he didn't strike her as a tourist. If he had been in London any length of time, he might have a telephone.

She dialed the telephone on the desk. "Please check the telephone directory for a Peter Novak," she told the hotel operator. "I want his address."

She opened the French doors to the balcony and stepped out into the cold and misty night, carrying the telephone with her. He was out there somewhere, in foggy London town, unaware a pack of wolves was chasing him.

Who are you, Peter Novak? Who were you before your mother and father conceived you?

The taxi with Peter inside moved up Charing Cross, past the Palace Theatre, and turned left above Old Compton Street. Peter was lost immediately. Soho was crawling with restaurants on lighted, crowded streets, and Sheila had chosen one hidden in a back alley. He glanced to the rear again, using his coat sleeve to clean the steamy window.

A black Mercedes turned the corner behind them. Had he seen it before? Behind them earlier?

" 'Ere, been thinking about them bones . . ."

"What?"

"Them bones," the cabbie said. "I'll bet they were taken from a university as a prank. Tell you what I'll do, mate. I'll have me youngest take 'em into school tomorrow to 'er science class and give 'em to the teacher."

"Uh, we'll see." He glanced again at the rear window. The Mercedes was still back there. It maintained the same distance between them, block after block.

"Slow down," he told the cabbie.

"What?"

"Slow down a little. I want to see something."

The taxi driver eased up on the accelerator. *The Mercedes slowed.*

"Speed up," Peter said.

The cabbie put his foot down. "What's the game, mate?"

"I think someone's following us."

" 'Ere, maybe it's the mate of that bird you 'ad in the backseat."

Peter leaned toward the cab's inside window. "Lose that Mercedes behind us and I'll pay your traffic ticket."

The cabbie eyed him in the rearview mirror. "Will ya pay if I get another ticket?"

"You're on."

The cabbie jerked the wheel to the right, turning at an intersection at the last moment, sending Peter over sideways on the backseat. He kept the wheel cranked, creating a U turn from what had started as a right turn, bringing the taxi around, almost broadsiding the Mercedes entering the turning. Cutting a left and gun-ning it, the cabbie headed back up the street with a grin on his face.

"We're 'eading back to Cambridge Circus now. Nice thing about London cabs—'cept for them with no class, they're all black and all look the same."

Five minutes later the taxi pulled up to sawhorse barricades blocking traffic from entering a street. Beyond the barricades, the entire area was filled with tables and booths, part of the Guy Fawkes celebration. "Close as I can get, Guv. That slanty-eye restaurant is just up the street, alley to your right."

Peter checked his watch and groaned. He was nearly two hours late for his date with Sheila. "Can you wait for me?"

"Wait for ya?"

"I'm late for my date. If she's not there, I want you to take me home." There were no taxis in sight, and he didn't feel like another stroll down a dark street to find one.

The driver squinted suspiciously at him. "Pay the fare, mate, and me bonus, and I'll wait for ya."

Peter handed him exactly enough for the fare and the traffic ticket. "You'll get the tip when I come back." *If* you wait for me, he thought. He opened the door and started to slide out, leaving the carryall on the seat, but reached back and grabbed it. The man might decide the bones were worth more than a tip. "Be back in a minute."

The cabbie opened his own door as Peter got out. "D'ya turn off the light back there, mate?"

"No."

"It's that bleedin' switch again. It's always sticking." The man climbed into the backseat to test the light as Peter walked away.

Peter did another check to the rear as he walked toward the barricades. No black Mercedes. They hadn't seen the car since Toad's Wild Ride had nearly

sliced it in two at the intersection where the cabbie
made the U turn. Probably innocent people on their
way to a play. What the hell—they'd have something
to talk about at dinner afterward.

The carnival tried to be merry but did little more
than create a glowing bubble in the dark night. Flashing lights of the Ferris wheel and carousel glowed a
little fuzzy, not bright and cheerful, Peter thought, but
a ghost of the real thing.

A Chinese rocket burst over the bubble, red and
white and yellow tinting the fog.

Food smells coming from the booths aroused his
stomach juices. He was caught in a cross-fire between
a booth selling baked potatoes with butter and
cheese—jacket potatoes the British called them—and
another hustling meat sausages called bangers.

Sheila wouldn't be at the restaurant waiting for
him. Knowing her, she would give him fifteen
minutes before she grabbed somebody more available. He had known her for just a few weeks, and
they had only progressed to the intimate dinner stage.
She sure as hell wouldn't be calling the local hospitals
and having the Thames dragged because he stood her
up. If she wasn't there he'd pass up the sushi for
jacket potatoes and some of the baked beans and sausages that were sending signals to his stomach.

A gang of kids wearing grotesque masks came tearing by pushing a shopping cart with a guy in it, one
of those effigies of Guy Fawkes British kids create
with old clothes stuffed with straw and rags. He tried
to remember who Guy Fawkes was. Some sort of
early terrorist, he thought. A Catholic extremist who
tried to blow up Parliament back during the days of
religious turmoil. Nowadays the kids hang 'em and
burn 'em.

One of the pint-size counterrevolutionaries spotted

him and charged. "A penny for the guy! A penny for the guy!"

Peter dug change out of his pocket, separated out pound coins, and gave the rest to the kid.

The pint-size bandit yelled "Thank you!" over his shoulder on his way to his next victim. Peter didn't know if there was a trick if he didn't treat and wasn't going to find out. He was having enough problems with the British Establishment without pissing off the kids, too.

A chilling thought struck him, and he stopped smiling and looked behind him.

What's the worst thing that could happen to you?

The bastard had had the right answer.

Poked his wormy nose in a private life.

But they weren't going to send him back to L.A. with his ass kicked. He wouldn't have backed off from the devil to get a story, and this time *he* was part of the story. Besides, he had cleverly burned all his bridges before leaving L.A., quitting his job, selling everything that couldn't be shoved into suitcases, antagonizing friends who told him he was crazy to throw everything away on a journey to find himself—pissing them off because they would have liked to do the same thing and didn't have the guts.

Now someone was stepping on his roots.

Thinking about Worm Nose and his buddy got his adrenaline pumping, his mind churning.

What about the third man? Why was he hiding behind the divider?

Someone grabbed his arm and he jerked away, fists cocked.

It was a Gypsy woman, no more than a girl. Dark hair fluffed out of a scarf that covered her head and most of her face, leaving a pretty brown face marred by a gold ring poking through a hole on the side of her nose.

"I can tell you about the woman," she said.

The hair on the back of his neck rose. "How—what do you know about her?"

"I can reveal many secrets about her. Secrets of love and desire." A diamond in her front tooth flashed as she smiled. "Secrets about your job, money. I can reveal the future to you."

His breathing came back. "You're sweet but I'm afraid I have such a bleak future hearing the gory details would scare the crap out of me."

The cabbie was tinkering with the dome light when the back door was opened by Bagora.

"Sorry, mate," the cabbie said. "Occupied."

A knife in the short man's right hand flicked open as he climbed into the taxi, closing the door behind him.

He spotted the restaurant where the taxi driver said it would be. A sign halfway down the alley blinked SERI SUSHI, and he headed for it. The place had been Sheila's idea. She was on a health kick, and things like raw fish and seaweed sounded healthy to her. He liked raw fish about as much as having his teeth drilled. Where he came from, tuna grew in a can that was thrown away if dented.

He entered the restaurant, letting the door swing shut, and went up to the cashier, an elderly woman with the dignified serenity and coal-black hair that follow Japanese women into the golden years.

"I'm looking for—"

"Young woman say send handsome man back when he come."

Peter blushed a little at the compliment.

The woman shook her finger at him. "But you third handsome man that come. She leave with number two."

"She's gone?"

"She gone. You very late. Young woman be old lady if she wait for you."

He didn't blame Sheila. He was lucky she hadn't hung around to give him a piece of her mind. It was a relief she had left. He couldn't shake his paranoia about the Mercedes, and he didn't want to drag her into any trouble.

"Young woman say give handsome man message."

She handed him a note written in a hurried, feminine script on a napkin.

In case you haven't got the hint, I've left. Don't call, don't write. If I see those big green eyes again I'll scratch them out.

                                        SHEILA

P.S. The cashier has something for you!

Peter chuckled. He liked Sheila. There was nothing serious between them, not of a permanent nature, but she was a good person and fun to be with. He'd invite her to dinner next week and she'd forgive him. "You have something for me?" he asked the cashier.

Smiling and bowing, she handed Peter a slip of paper with a bunch of chicken-scratches on it.

"What's this?"

"Raw oyster, octopus, eel, sea urchin with seaweed. Ten pound six."

"Ten pound six? You mean money? This is her dinner tab? She left it for me to pay?"

The old woman shook her finger at Peter again. "You very late. You pay."

"But she left with another man!"

The serene Japanese features went firm, and she nodded meaningfully toward the sushi counter where a couple of Japanese cooks the size of Moby Dick were hacking at raw fish, employing knives with a speed and efficiency that would have made Jack the Ripper envious. Hands and knives were blurred into one. Some of the things being chopped looked like fingers. "You pay," she said.

"I pay." He got an inspiration as he fished through his wallet. "Would you mind if I left this with you for a few minutes?" He put the carryall on the counter. "I need to run an errand."

"Yes. Very good." The bag was whipped off the counter top with true Japanese efficiency and disappeared somewhere below. He started to walk away and she shook her finger at him again. "No late next time. Handsome only handsome do."

He went back to the taxi to give the cabbie a tip. With Sheila and the bag taken care of, he decided to stick around for dinner à la carnival. And maybe hunt up that fortune-telling girl with the gold ring in her nose. Maybe get his fortune told. "You're going to have a mad love affair with a beautiful woman who runs into your arms from out of the night . . . *if the bogeyman doesn't get you!*"

How does one blow their nose with a ring in it? How many diamonds does she swallow in a year? He wondered about such monumental mysteries and what other parts of her anatomy were jeweled as he headed back for the taxi.

It was still parked where he left it. As he approached, he spotted the driver in the backseat. Must still be fiddling with the light, Peter thought. A woman on the other side of the cab was hurrying for it. He'd tip the driver and let her have it. He took ten pounds out of his wallet, a big tip considering his financial state, but the man deserved it despite his rabid mouth.

Peter opened the back door and slid in. The dome light didn't come on. "I've changed my mind. I won't be needing you." The driver was asleep, his chin resting on his chest. Peter lightly touched his shoulder and the man fell sideways against him.

"Sir, you're . . ." He felt something wet as he pushed the man back against the seat. His skin crawled. The whole front of the man's coat was soaked in blood. *The man's throat had been cut!* Peter froze, his mind numbed by the horror. The door next to the driver opened and a woman stuck her head in.

"Is this taxi—" She stopped and gaped. Peter stared wide-eyed at her, bloody money in hand. The driver slipped sideways toward the woman, falling across the seat, his head hanging over the edge of the seat, exposing the ugly slit in the neck.

The woman recoiled and screamed.

Peter snapped out of his stupor and backed out of the taxi. He started around to the other side to explain, but she was already running toward the barricades. Peter stared around in utter confusion and spotted the *black Mercedes*. It was fifty yards away, hanging back like a waiting vulture.

The lights of the Mercedes went on, spotlighting him, and two men standing beside the car started toward him. A thought hit him with a magnum punch— *he was being framed*. He ran, darting into a dark passageway between buildings to the left, knowing he had been set up and the two men were going to perform the coup de grâce.

The passageway filled with light behind him as he reached the end—the Mercedes, too wide to enter, had stopped at the head of the alley. He shot around the corner and came out on a street that was a mixture of business and residential buildings, dark and gloomy after the well-lit festival, the night thickened by the fog, street lamps glowing only at the far corners. He ran across the street and down to the left, looking for an alley, a crack between buildings, anything to get him out of sight before the Mercedes or the men came around the corner. He darted into a driveway between a closed restaurant and a hardware store; it opened into a parking lot behind the restaurant.

He went round the back of the restaurant and stopped at the rear corner, breathing heavily; he peeked cautiously around the corner. The Mercedes streaked through the intersection to the right.

He ran down the street, away from the intersection, past wall-to-wall storefronts, all closed and dark. Apartment buildings lined the other side of the street. He crossed the street and ran down an alley between the buildings. A dog shot out of a hole in a fence and yapped at his heels. He kicked at it and cursed as he hurried away, trying to get his breathing under control so he could run again.

What the hell had he gotten himself into?

The taxi driver with his throat cut kept flashing in his mind. *Poor bastard.* The man might have been hacked by a robber who had nothing to do with the woman in the fog and the bones, but Peter didn't believe it. Someone was after her. The men in the black Mercedes. If he hadn't run, he'd be lying on the ground beside the taxi, framed for killing the cabbie, a bullet in his head from an anonymous "good Samaritan."

He increased his pace and tried to keep his breathing under control. Going to the police for help was out of the question. He had no money, no friends; worse, he had a black mark against his name with the authorities for poking his nose into government secrets. He'd be arrested and slammed in jail, unable to prove his innocence. Was he going to be arrested anyway? There was nothing with his name on it back in the taxi. The woman who screamed had got only a brief look at him, and in the dark at that. But what about the policemen who'd stopped the taxi earlier?

They hadn't asked his name when they lost interest in the bones, but they had got a good look at him.

Don't panic. London is one of the largest cities in the world. There must be unsolved killings every day. Soho had its fair share of violence. The police would put it down to a thief, not a respectable newspaper reporter. He had one ace in the hole—no motive. But the attitude of the M15 agents kept coming to mind; they'd burn him if they could. Innocent or not, he'd spend months in jail waiting for justice to take its course, waking each morning with the threat of a murder conviction over him.

If it hadn't been a thief who killed the cabbie, one thing was clear: *He had been the intended victim.* The cabbie had been sitting in the backseat where he would have been if he hadn't got out to go into the café. What was so important about an old skull that someone would murder for it?

He came out of an alley and turned to his right. Someone came around the corner half a block up the street, walking slowly, a black figure against the fuzzy glow of the streetlight on the corner. Size, shape, made the figure masculine, a short man, very short, not a little person, but short and stocky like a tree stump. Peter heard footsteps to the rear and swung around. *There was another man at the other end of the street,* silhouetted black on the gray in front of the light, a fine mist hanging between them like a silken screen; this one was big with the trunk and limbs of a massive tree.

The two men who had come at him from the Mercedes.

He was in a squeeze play. *The big man's hands went into his coat pockets.* Going for a gun? Half a block between them; a bullet could travel farther in the span of a heartbeat.

He darted into the street. Car lights came on, catching him halfway across the street. He heard the engine accelerating, heard the pound of footsteps to the rear. He didn't look. He kept his eye on an alley almost directly in front of him. He hit the alley with car lights running him down. The car followed him into the alley, the driver realizing too late that trash cans made the passageway too narrow to negotiate. The Mercedes hit the cans, sending lids and trash flying like shrapnel.

He shot out of the alley, flying around the corner. The car came onto the street, trash cans flying in front of it, tires screeching, engine roaring. It spun around in the street and came at him again, the engine breathing at the back of his neck. The car jumped the curb, the undercarriage screaming as it scraped on the pavement, skidding out of control, coming at him sideways, sparks flying from underneath, glass and wood exploding as the bumper smashed a storefront. He threw himself on top of the hood and tumbled over it, flopping down to the pavement as the car swept by and careened to a halt. He rolled on the pavement and got to his feet, dodging into an alley to his right. The car's engine roared, tires burned, and the undercarriage screeched painfully as the driver backed the Mercedes off the pavement.

Running past trash bins and Dumpsters, he saw a barricade ahead—*a goddamn wall*—ten, maybe twelve feet tall, too high for him to climb. *A dead end*—he was trapped. A fire escape was to the left, a Dumpster beneath it, but his mind was too frosted with confusion to react. Someone out on the street yelled, "Hurry" and he heard the word "alley." It shook him out of his stupor. He leaped up, both hands going on the Dumpster, levering his right knee up, then his left. He reached the fire escape ladder on tiptoes, pulling it down. It came down well greased, and he scrambled up to the first level, letting the ladder swing back up, using his foot to keep it from banging shut.

The black Mercedes appeared at the head of the alley and stopped. The right front of the car had been ripped open; only the left headlight shone, but it was enough to spotlight the alley. Big and Little entered cautiously, car light reflecting off the blued barrel of the gun each man carried. Peter squeezed into the dark corner at the rear of the fire escape, his back to the brick wall of the building, right arm against the outside molding of a window, heart ricocheting in his throat.

The two men below spread out like a SWAT team, weapons at the ready, ready to blast anything that moved. Peter saw lights in a third-floor apartment across the alley come on and a window go up; a woman with rainbow-colored pin curls poked her head out. "What's going on down there?"

"Shut up! Go back inside!" The little man spoke with a foreign twang, Indian or Pakistani, Peter thought. *The man looked up, staring at the shadowy area where Peter was hiding.* Peter didn't move, didn't breathe. The word "dwarf" came to mind as Peter stared at the man, even though he was merely short. His lips were thick and cruel, his brow low, the skin around his eyes folded; there was an East Indian cast to his features, but his build and dwarflike features gave him more kinship to an ape.

"I'm gonna call the police," the woman across the way yelled.

Little turned and snarled, "Get inside!"

The other man was a big, heavy brute with twelve-ply arms and legs, perhaps only six feet tall, but so broad and muscular he looked like a giant troll. He was also foreign. Chinese? Mongolian? Something Asian, Peter thought.

The window beside him went up. A tiny head with

golden locks poked out, looking first at the men below
and then at Peter's shoes, slowly moving up his pants
and coat until a peachy seven-year-old face peered at
him, big blue eyes wide, mouth open, ready to cry
out. Peter put a finger to his lips, signaling the little
girl to silence. She looked to the men searching the
alley and back to him, concern etched on her little
features. In another ten years she would be a beauty
stopping men in their tracks as she walked down the
street, but right now she had Peter's skin crawling as
he waited to see if she would scream. She looked
again at the two men in the alley, the small creature
with the simian form and the big man with hands like
trashcan lids, and back to Peter, his eyes talking to
her, *pleading with her*

A police siren pulsated in the distance and the horn
of the Mercedes sounded. Big and Little ran for the
car, climbing in as the vehicle was backing up. Peter
started off the fire escape as soon as the car shot out
of sight. He went down the ladder backward, pausing
to look up before he jumped the last couple of feet
down to the Dumpster. Big blue eyes set in an angelic
face expressed concern for him; he smiled and blew
her a kiss.

He walked two blocks before cutting into a narrow
passageway between buildings. He leaned against a
wall, shaking, chills crawling over him. With more
mental reserve than he realized he had, he got his
nerves under control. It was a simple matter of survival. He couldn't afford to fold in the clinch. Whatever the woman in the fog was caught up in, he was
now ensnarled. He didn't resent her. In a strange way,
it felt natural for his life to be entwined with hers.

Shaftesbury Avenue and a big red bus came along
at the same time. He fumbled with change as half a
dozen people went aboard ahead of him, then stepped

up, paying the conductor and taking the corkscrew stairway to the second level.

He settled into a window seat and tensed as he caught a quick look at a man in a dark overcoat hurriedly boarding at the last minute. *They'd found him.* Footsteps sounded on the stairs as the bus pulled from the curb. He dropped his wallet as a pretense to crouch down in the seat and saw the man's shoes and pants first—black shoes, black pants. *The third man.* He slowly sat up, ready to come out of the seat at the man.

The man came down the narrow passageway, paying no attention to Peter. It was a *priest*, a thin, elderly cleric with bad skin, rusty blotches on his face and neck. The wiry old man was bundled in a black coat that looked old enough—and warm enough—to have made a trip to the Pole with Peary.

Peter relaxed a little and stared out the window. If you can't trust a priest, who can you trust?

CHAPTER 4

The priest sat behind Peter on the bus, his eyes boring into the back of Peter's head as if he were drilling for answers. He had followed the Mercedes to Soho and witnessed the attempt to run Peter down. The action near the barricades had spread out too fast for him to keep up with, and it was pure luck that he had spotted Peter boarding the bus on Shaftesbury Avenue.

He knew who the young man was. Peter Novak, an American newspaper reporter. The British authorities thought he was looking for a story. The priest didn't know what he was looking for, but despite the skepticism of his contacts at MI5, he didn't doubt that the young man was who he claimed to be: the son of Duncan MacKinzie. He had met Duncan MacKinzie at the final briefing for an ill-fated Himalayan flight, and something about Peter jogged that three-decades-old memory.

But what did the son of Duncan MacKinzie have to do with Zhdanov's woman? It was to Novak-MacKinzie that the woman fled after she grabbed the bag.

Even stranger was the question of why Zhdanov was pursuing the young man.

Zhdanov. Curious name. The man who used the name could be Russian—or any one of a dozen personalities. He had a manufactured identity that went even deeper than the passports of the four different nations that he carried.

Rich. Powerful. "Merchant of Death" was an old expression for the business Zhdanov was in, supplying guns and other munitions to warring factions. When the price was right, he supplied both sides to a dispute. Business was business—morality was never an issue. The priest's MI5 contacts told him Zhdanov was reputed to have sold guns to five different groups in Lebanon.

He was many things to many people but one thing the priest knew: He was not the man he claimed to be.

Not unless the dead could walk.

I was there when the man died, the priest thought. Over thirty years ago, while searching for that mysterious valley Tibetans call Shambala. Westerners called the valley Shangri-La because that was the name given the valley in the book and movie *Lost Horizon.* To the Asian, the Vale of Shambala was not literary fiction but the place where life itself began.

In those days there had been three of them searching, each a wanderer who had crossed doomed desert and pathless jungle, scaled the Himalayas and walked on the Roof of the World in Bod, the Land Behind the Snows, the place Westerners called Tibet.

TIBET

The priest was tall, a lean man who allowed his body no pity. A decade of exploring, searching, under burning sun sweated the fat from his bones and fried the freckles brown on his face until he looked as if he had been left out in the rain to rust.

While his brethren built concrete and glass temples in metropolitan jungles, hoping God would be guided to them by flashing neon crosses, the priest sought

God in the Wilderness, cutting paths where no Westerner had trod.

He was a bullet fired by the hand of God.

Central Asia was his cathedral.

Central Asia. Long thought to be the birthplace of Man. The priest had come to find that birthplace. With him were two other men, each following his own god, *avaricious gods that demanded treachery and greed*, the priest thought. He had not banded together with the other two men out of faith, hope, or charity but opportunity and expediency. He knew that when his usefulness was gone, he could expect a knife in his back despite their common goal: each was a treasure hunter lured by something more precious than gold, piecing together a million-year-old puzzle, chasing the truths, half truths, and myths until they met in Calcutta, pooled their resources, and set out to find a silver box in an ancient holy cave in Tibet, a box no man living had seen but many told tales about.

Their quest had brought them to the Roof of the World, the foot of a cave, in a race for the ultimate prize: *the bones of God.*

As they rested their horses in sight of the cave, Zhdanov, the scientist, came up beside the priest and spoke, his voice muffled by the scarf protecting his face from the bitter cold.

"You think it's up there, don't you, priest? A little box you'll open to let God pop out. The only thing we'll find in that cave is another link in the chain of evolution strangling Mother Church."

The priest ignored him and scratched ice from his frozen beard. Exertion made him sweat; the windchill factor turned the sweat into ice. There was nothing to smile about, and he tried not to frown—both made the ice crack and cut.

He had contempt for the scientist, a man who sought God in a test tube, who thought he could find a man's soul by dissecting him like a frog. He was also suspicious of the man's loyalties. Zhdanov claimed to be White Russian, the son of nobility that fled to the Orient during the Russian Revolution. A paleontologist, he was a member of the scientific discipline that traced the roots of man through fossilized remains, piecing together the chain of human evolution, believing that when the last link—the *missing link*—was found, it would prove that man was created in the image of science, not God.

His short, stocky frame and bullet head were ethnically vague enough to have been fathered by the United Nations. His contempt of God made him a Communist in the priest's mind. A dangerous man. But the priest had handled many dangerous men during his quest.

The third man came up behind them and pointed to a ridge above them. "Look."

Sunlight struck the ridge and a great cat, an Ice Age beast with long gray hair and black spots, stood on the edge of the cliff with the majesty of a monarch surveying his domain.

"A snow leopard," the priest said. "We are privileged. Few Westerners have seen a snow leopard in the wild."

Dr. Poc, the man who had spotted the beast, was more alchemist than scientist, more comfortable delving in the black arts than the precise arts. Doctor of Theology, Master of Skulduggery, he had wisdom's great white beard and reptilian black eyes. The priest wasn't accustomed to thinking of people in racial terms, but the name used by others fitted the man, the *Chinaman.*

The Chinaman brushed ice from his beard as he gazed up at the great cat. "There is said to be a queen of snow leopards who rules this forbidden region, a creature that can change shape, taking the form of a man or beast, exacting vengeance on any who enter its territory."

"The animal's flesh and bone," Zhdanov scoffed. "If we had the time I'd bag it for a winter coat."

The Chinaman smiled. His eyes remained cold and dead. "Is it so certain all that walks on this earth is of flesh and bone?"

The man sweats evil, the priest thought. He knew he could never let either man gain possession of the prize they sought. The scientist sought the prize for acclaim and recognition. And no doubt to serve his Godless masters. To the Chinaman the prize was a treasure to be sold to the highest bidder, a whore-master selling his wares.

The priest sought neither fame nor fortune. A man of the cloth and a learned paleontologist himself, he was tortured by inner conflict that drove him on a decades-long quest to reconcile evolution with creation, angels with apes.

To the priest there had to be more to the creation of man than chemicals merging in a primeval sea, wading ashore, bruising knuckles on the ground until learning to walk erect, evolving from fish to monkey to Homo sapiens. There had to be the miracle of Genesis, of Adam, the Garden, and the rib. His heart told him so.

In search of miracles, and apes, the priest became a wanderer in the wilderness, chasing a legend, pushing himself relentlessly, beyond pain, beyond companionship.

Zhdanov unwrapped his face scarf and spat. The spit turned into ice and shattered as it hit the ground. It was so cold even the hair in their noses froze. "This isn't Shambala," he growled.

"No, it's not Shambala," the priest said.

Shambala. A name whispered the breadth of Asia, a land of milk and honey, of myth and magic. James

Hilton heard the tales and wrote of the enchanted valley of Shangri-La. But to the Asian it was Shambala. Eden. The birthplace of man. A green valley lost in the snow and ice of the Tibetan Himalayas.

The priest had not expected the valley to be the magic land. He had been searching longer than the others and had only come for another clue, another piece in a kaleidoscope that still had to be twisted to see what new shape the puzzle took.

Tibet was a forgotten pool along the river of time, an eddy that flowed in circles while the main current swept civilization from medieval to megalopolis. Isolated by its topography, ringed by the world's highest mountains, the ancient kingdom was a vast, three-mile-high plateau twice the size of Texas and colder than Poe's misty mid-regions of Weir.

Somewhere to the east was Lhasa, the enchanting capital of the frozen empire where the Dalai Lama, worshipped as a god, obeyed as a king, had ruled both the heavens and earth from a golden-roofed palace, a sight beheld by only a handful of Westerners right up to the middle of the twentieth century.

The Chinese Communists had invaded Tibet, but not even China's billion could conquer the savage weather and the limitless twisted terrain on the Roof of the World. They stayed in Lhasa and a few of the larger settlements, driving out the monks so they could billet their troops in ancient monasteries, unaware that three men were treading dangerously close to unlocking the mystery of the ages and unleashing a power that could decide the future.

They rode as close to the cave as their mounts could take them. A rocky gully, too steep for the horses, led to the opening.

The cave was in the V formed by the breasts of two hills. No trail led there; it appeared on no map, was not at the beginning or end of anywhere. The surrounding terrain was a place of desert, the highest in the world, 16,000 feet above sea level, a moonscape badland filled with mocking rock formations carved by razor-sharp winds.

Two Hindu baggage handlers tended the horses and short-legged Tibetan ponies loaded with supplies and cooked the evening meal. Ever increasing the size of the *baksheesh* and letting them supplement their income with whatever they could steal kept the two baggage handlers "loyal." Sherpa bearers who had led them over the great Himalayan las, some passes so high not even birds could fly over, had all returned to the hearth as the explorers trekked deeper into uncharted regions.

They left one baggage handler to tend the horses and set up camp. Taking the other Hindu with them to carry equipment, they slowly scaled the rocky incline.

The opening to the cave was an icy dragon's jaw, a narrow hole filled with jagged icicle stalactites and stalagmites. Inside the cave they gasped in amazement as their flashlights lit up the interior.

The cavern they had entered was a netherworld of ice, a forest of wild and beautiful ice formations, a sky of ice crystals glittering with the fire of an emperor's crown.

"A miracle," the priest whispered.

Zhdanov snorted. "Underground springs and subzero temperatures."

They moved deeper into the cavern, threading their way through the ice forest, the priest leading the way. Fifty yards into the cavern he stopped and shone his light on the cave wall.

"What is it? The box?" the Chinaman asked.

The priest walked closer to the wall. "Three men," he said. The remains of three men, dried, cracked skin stretched over bone, were chained to the wall and covered with a transparent layer of ice. The men wore uniforms; they were warriors from another age.

"Incredible," Zhdanov said. "The markings on their breastplates look Roman."

The priest examined the markings closer with his flashlight. "Not Roman . . . I would say Greek, third or fourth century B.C. That would make them soldiers of the great Alexander." He peered closer at the markings. "Yes, that would be right. The legends about Shambala were being told in India thousands of years before Alexander conquered the subcontinent. These men must have been treasure seekers who deserted and followed the stories."

"And met their end in battle with Tibetans."

"No," the Chinaman said. He moved along the wall, adding his light to the priest's. "These men did not die in battle. There are no marks on their bones." He chuckled. "They were chained here and allowed to freeze to death."

"I doubt if they found it as amusing as you do," Zhadanov said. "It certainly tells us we have been on the right track, but the trail has ended. We've reached the end of the cave." He shone his light on the opposite walls.

The Chinaman made a clicking noise with his teeth and stroked his beard. "Perhaps not," he muttered, "perhaps not. Would it not be a fine example of Oriental torture to chain thieves within sight of the treasure they desire . . . and let them die with the glint of that very treasure in their eyes?"

The Chinaman walked around the cave, examining the walls. The priest felt the ache of disappointment but watched the Chinaman with hope. If the silver box was there, the man's greed would lead him like the nose of a bloodhound to it.

As the Chinaman walked he lightly tapped the walls of the cave with his ice pick.

The priest shone his light at the ceiling. For a moment he had the impression that the ceiling had moved. Each time the Chinaman hit a wall, a movement like a wave moving through water swept across the ceiling.

"Stop!" The priest's voice was hoarse and full of fear, but he didn't shout the word.

Zhdanov frowned at him. "What—"

"Quiet," the priest said. He pointed his light to the ceiling. "Bats. Tibetan cave bats. They're smaller than hummingbirds and suck little more than a mosquito, but when they swarm by the thousands they're as dangerous as a school of piranha. *They're vampire bats*."

He spoke very quietly as he started backing away. "We have to leave—"

An ice pick struck a wall with a low whack. The Hindu was chopping through the ice to get at the remains of the uniforms of the Greek warriors.

"Stop, you fool!" The priest started for the Hindu. The man ignored him and hit the wall harder.

A high-pitched whine erupted overhead and a cloud of furry white suddenly dropped on them, nearly knocking the priest off his feet. He struck out blindly but it was like trying to hold back an ocean wave. They went for the exposed flesh on his face. He covered his eyes with his hands and dropped to the floor, burying his face and hands between his knees. As he bent over the back of his neck was exposed and dozens of tiny teeth picked at it.

Dr. Poc pulled a long-barreled .44 from underneath his coat and fired blindly. The gunfire resounded off the cavern walls, throwing the bats' sensitive echolocation system into chaos. They went berserk, flying into walls, ceiling, people, each other, insanely, mindlessly, until the floor was carpeted with dead, dazed, and writhing white creatures.

The explosion of gunfire in the cave brought a

storm of ice crashing down from the ceiling. The Hindu went down, crushed by a block of ice that filled half the passageway.

And then the priest saw it. Ice raining from the ceiling, exploding like artillery shells, blew a hole in the wall opposite from where the warriors had been chained. Through the opening the priest could see the box sitting on an altar.

Carved from ice, the altar was as pure as a windowpane and etched with gold-filled scroll patterns. Seven ice steps led up to the holy place; on each step was a golden vase that the ancients burned yak butter oil in to light their ceremonies.

On the altar was a silver box. The box of the legend.

He went for it, mindless of the cave disintegrating around him. Inside the altar room a wall of ice collapsed beside him, knocking him off his feet. In a daze he saw feet move by him. It was the scientist, Zhdanov. Fire erupted in the priest, the fury of the zealot, and he struggled to his feet and surged on.

As the scientist reached the top of the steps the floor beneath him suddenly gave way and he stumbled waist deep into the wide crack in the ice. The priest was suddenly there, the silver box an arm's length away, the scientist screaming for help, reaching out with his hands for the priest to grab and pull him from the ice that was moving together and crushing him.

The box or the man? The priest reached out.

The priest sat on the ground outside the cave and stared numbly at the desolate valley before him. He had crawled through the dragon's teeth opening as the entrance to the cave was being sealed forever by millions of tons of collapsing ice and snow.

He saw a movement out of the corner of his eye.

The Chinaman lay on the ground, his breath coming in deep gulps.

It was a moment before the priest realized he was clutching the silver box.

He couldn't have saved both, he thought, the box and the man.

God had guided his hand, he told himself.

They sat around the campfire watching the flames, watching the treasure, watching each other.

The priest sat in the lotus position, the box resting on his legs. The skull inside was visible through openings between the elaborate figures carved on the box. No attempt had been made to open it—the box had to be examined, analyzed for booby traps before the attempt was made. That examination would come later, in the light of day. *Once ownership of it had been decided.*

Firelight danced with shadows on the Chinaman's face. The priest looked across the fire and saw greed and hate flashing across the man's face like the changing message on a Times Square sign.

The baggage handler, offering no remorse over the loss of his coworker, kept back from the fire. Waiting. The priest had seen the Chinaman talking to the man earlier and knew the man had sold his soul.

Chill night winds swept across the plains as the priest carefully wrapped the silver box in a towel and retired to his tent, leaving the yellow coiled snake still sitting by the campfire, firelight reflecting in his dark eyes like fire on pools of oil.

The loneliest hour of night is just before twilight when the moon has passed and the sun has yet to give hint of its coming.

When empty darkness shrouded the land, someone

crept across the camp, paused at the priest's tent, and pointed a pistol.

Shots rang through the night. From the distant hills, echoing an answer, came the blood-chilling cry of wolves.

The Chinaman jerked back the flaps of the tent to claim the fruits of murder.

The priest was gone.

The Chinaman and the baggage handler had no difficulty tracking the priest; there was only one way back. Any deviation from the known path led to the most remote and savage wilderness on earth, with perils of subzero weather, starvation, and wolves.

On the third day of the chase the baggage handler noticed a change in the hoofprints left by the priest's horse. "Horse lame. Hoof cut by rock."

Two days later they found the carcass. The horse had been brought down by wolves. Vultures picked through the leftovers.

They caught up with the priest near a rope bridge spanning a narrow gorge. The priest was at the foot of the bridge when the Chinaman fired.

The priest stumbled and the box slipped from his hands and went over the edge, into the river canyon. The Chinaman cursed and whipped his mount riding for the edge of the gorge, ignoring the priest escaping across the bridge. The box had landed on a ledge halfway down the gorge.

The Hindu pointed across the river. "The holy man escapes!"

"Leave him. The wolves will finish him. We have to get the box."

"Cliff too much."

The Chinaman stroked his beard and looked thoughtfully at the rope bridge.

"I can lower you with rope from the bridge."

The baggage handler stared wide-eyed at the slender Chinaman. "You have no power. I lower you."

"I'm too old to play monkey. I can use the bridge posts as leverage and lower you. You tie the rope to the box and I'll haul it up, then lower the rope so you can climb up."

"No—"

The Chinaman pointed the gun at him. "Cut the rope."

The baggage handler was lowered down the cliff, his face as gray as the granite. When the Hindu had his footing on the ledge and the rope untied from his waist, the Chinaman yelled down. "Tie the rope to the box!"

The Hindu looked fearfully up to where the Chinaman stood with gun in hand.

"Hurry, you fool! Tie the box."

He dropped the rope and hurried along the ledge, clutching the box to his chest.

The Chinaman fired until the gun was empty and the man had disappeared around a bend. He cursed to himself. There was no honor among thieves. Even in Tibet.

The night sky was heavy, brooding. Moon shadows turned the land forbidding. High above the desert floor a snow leopard perched on the edge of a cliff, a sovereign surveying its realm.

Watching.

Waiting.

CHAPTER 5

Peter got off the bus two blocks from his East End flat. It was nearly midnight. He walked quickly after checking behind him to make sure he wasn't being followed. The only other person who got off was the priest, and the man set out in the opposite direction.

A little rain had started falling, just enough to wet the chill already gripping him. The warmth in the bus had defrosted some of his aches and now his right knee hurt more than his shoulder, probably from the dive he took over the Mercedes' hood. Right about now he had had it with London. He wished the hell he was back in L.A. It never rained in Southern California. And none of the weirdos, creeps, and freaks in L.A., not even the ones that were cops, had tried to leave his teethmarks on their bumpers.

He was shaking by the time he made it a block down the street. He told himself it was just the goddamn chill, but he knew it was the trauma.

The taxi driver hadn't left his thoughts during the bus ride home. *Poor bastard.* Said he had kids. What the hell were his wife and kids thinking now? *What the hell were the cops thinking?* Had they marked it down to a robber? Had the woman screaming out her lungs got a good look at him? Who the hell were the hatchetmen in the Mercedes? And the bones, *them bones.* Still back at the restaurant. They could dump them in their eel soup for all he cared. Right now all he wanted was to get to his apartment, bolt the door, crawl under his blankets, and hide.

Even with the drizzle there was still a little fog, but it wouldn't have stopped the action on the street if people had had to swim through murk. It was a tenderloin district: blighted apartment buildings and chipped storefronts, but at night it erupted with people, cars, and hole-in-the-wall restaurants. The little restaurants sold pasta, curry, beef, and ale, all the food underspiced to please the peculiar tastebuds of the British.

His love affair with the city was over. Splattered with the blood in the backseat of a taxi. It was no longer a game—the woman, the bones, the queer attitude about his father's military file. This wasn't about a news story. They were out to kill him. Three men. Not Lisper, Pal, and Black Shoes, but a couple weird dudes, Big and Little, and somebody at the helm of a Mercedes.

If there was a connection between Lisper and the Mercedes, he didn't know what the hell it was. The woman on the street had been too surprised, too emotional with him, to have been a plant. *I was in the wrong place at the wrong time*. That's what crime is all about. Walking into a convenience store late at night to pick up a quart of milk and getting your guts blown out the small of your back by some junkie with a shaky hand on a rusty shotgun.

Or maybe he was just fucking stupid and Lisper, the woman, and the bones were all playing the same game.

Right now he didn't care if the plot had been hatched in a cloakroom at Buckingham Palace. The shakes that began around the exposed nape of his neck had worked their way down his back and into his legs. He needed to get out of the chill night air and into his miserable but warm little flat.

A black limo pulled to the curb ahead of him and he tensed, but it was just a couple of happy drunks checking out some prostitutes. He veered around the action but caught some of the dialogue. Americans, of course. Not that the British weren't out trolling. They just weren't as loud about it.

The neighborhood was one of those tarnished pockets of the nineteenth-century East End that had been a receiving station for immigrants for centuries, beginning with the Hugenot invasion from France following the revocation of some edict or another from the French Catholics that sent the Protestants packing. Waves of persecuted Eastern European Jews, potato famine Irish, West Indians with lyrical British accents, and most recently East Indians, Pakistanis, and Vietnamese left their imprint on the neighborhood. Now it was abandoned to the street people as it waited for the ultimate symbol of progress, redevelopment funds and the Acme Demolition Company wrecking ball.

One of his neighbors told him the street had the dubious distinction of having been the location of one of Jack the Ripper's atrocities and an early police experiment in "scientific" detection: Scotland Yard detectives had the victim's eyes photographed under the belief that the murderer's image would be recorded on the retinas.

Wonderful world we live in. Jack killed five women and made history. Today he could kill *fifty* and not even get honorable mention in *Guinness*.

A rusty iron railing ran along the pavement in front of his building, guarding the short stairwell down to his flat. Oliver was there, perched on the railing.

The cat belonged to Sally, a woman on the second floor. He liked to sit on the railing and "speak" to people as they walked by, occasionally slicing open the hand of a poor dupe who stopped to pet kitty.

Oliver fit right into the neighborhood.

Peter hurried by the cat, keeping his hands in his pocket, and took the worn stone steps down to his basement flat two at a time.

He got inside and shut and bolted the door behind him, then leaned back against the door, waves of warmth and nausea sweeping over him.

He pushed himself away from the door, took off his overcoat, and pasted his back against the warm sheetmetal duct on the wall to the left of the front door. Some enterprising slumlord had partitioned off a small apartment from what had been the building's coal storage area, leaving the duct on the wall with the building's furnace on the other side of it. It looked like hell but it kept his place toasty warm and cost him nothing for heat, not a bad arrangement on his frayed shoestring budget.

His unmade bed, a frumpy old horsehair chair left behind by a previous tenant, a battered coffee table with hot cup circles burned into the top, and walls of books, mostly used, mostly bought at street sales, made up the rest of the living-sleeping area. A standing-room-only bathroom—toilet with cracked seat, rust-stained white porcelain sink, and cheap cement shower stall so narrow you couldn't save water by bathing with a friend—was between the furnace duct and the doorway to the kitchen. The narrow kitchen came equipped with blackened walls, peeling linoleum, and a gas stove that had been converted from woodburning. The back door to the flat was through the kitchen and led into an alley behind the building.

Sheila thought the place had all the subtle charm of a cell in Dartmoor Prison. The only bad thing about it to Peter was the landlady. Mrs. Murdstone wrapped herself in sloppy robes and ill wind. She took a dislike to him the moment he showed up at her door with a note from the rental agent that the flat had been let to him. One of the neighbors said Murdstone had been saving it for a nephew planning to move to London. Whatever the reason, her flat was above his, and any noise he emitted louder than a deep sigh boiled her blood. He kept his mouth shut to her because the rent was cheap.

He toasted his front side on the heater duct and then kicked off his shoes, stripped down to shorts, and stretched out on the bed. He was still shaky. *Calm down,* he told himself. *You're not responsible for that poor man's death.*

He thought about Lisper, about the threat that chilled his blood, and told himself he'd been put under the microscope.

What's the worst thing that could happen to you? Lisper asked. And then he leaned down, his nose close enough for the blue worms to crawl off and burrow into Peter's, his breath stinking of stomach acid and curdled scotch.

"Nobody knows you, Novak, nobody *cares* about you. You could disappear and no one would ever ask why. Be walkin' down the street one day when a car pulls up and a couple gents invite you in. Take you to a mossy bog and put a bullet in your ear."

He fired a bullet in Peter's ear with his index finger.

"And then it's all over, my friend. You'll sink into the bog, facedown, and you'll stay there forever, no one even remembering, no one caring. In that fuckin' bog with no one giving a gnat's ass."

They had gotten to a woman in his past, a woman he thought he loved, *tried* to love, before he gave up a way of life that wasn't working for him and left L.A. He had told her how he felt about his life: no causes that fired his blood, he was bored with his job, bored with love; and more than anything there was the feeling that there was no real meaning to life.

"I don't understand what you're talking about," she had said. "You have a good job, friends. What else is there?"

There was something else, but he didn't know how to define it. Maybe it was a person, the kind of woman a man meets once in a life, the kind you see across a crowded room and it makes time stand still. Or a place, somewhere, without its quota of takers and noisemakers and crazies.

"Do you know," he told her the last time they were together, "I've got nothing, nobody, to give my life for. I mean, I can't even throw away my life for some cause or on a battlefield for my buddies. There's nothing I'd give my life for because I don't believe in anything." He didn't say it, but there was no one he *loved* enough to throw away his life for.

Back in L.A., thinking about it, thinking about *dying unfulfilled*, without having found some meaning in life, formed a ball of panic at the back of his throat.

It was private stuff, thoughts and feelings he bared to the woman because he wanted her to understand why he had to walk away from their relationship, sell everything he could, throw away, give away everything else.

But somebody had gotten to her, talked to her.

"Tell us about this guy Peter Novak. What kind of fuck is he?"

Private stuff. And that snoopy bastard with the Lisp & Liquor had poked his wormy nose in it. Peter always played by the rules: It's okay to dig into a person's public life, to find the graft and greed that feed politicians and their hangers-on, but he never stepped on the person's private life, never gave a damn about who was sleeping with whom.

For some reason his father's mission, the one that would be the man's last for Queen and Country, still dredged up enough concern at Whitehall that they turned that sick bullying bastard on to him just for brushing close to it.

The murder of the cabbie came back and hit him between the eyes. Where did that fit in?

"For Christ's sake, what have I got myself into?"

He should go to the police, tell the whole story. The truth never hurt an innocent man.

Bullshit. Lisper and Company were out there, waiting to bust him, break him, on anything they could. Guilt or innocence wasn't the issue: If they didn't bury him in a mossy bog they'd do it in a bureaucratic mire. A foreigner in Britain who couldn't make bail, couldn't afford to hire a lawyer, he'd spend the next decade in a jail cell just trying to unwrap the red tape.

Get on a plane, get back to L.A. *now.*

He shot up from the bed then lay back down. No, he couldn't run. Running was an admission of guilt to the cops. They'd catch him or extradite him and the worms on Lisper's nose would wriggle with pleasure.

Could they trace him to the cabbie? He doubted the woman trying to get into the taxi got much of a look at him. But the cops who stopped the cab for the ticket had. They hadn't taken his name but they had ticketed the cabbie. But hell, he could have got out anywhere, and the cabbie had had enough time to have picked up and let off a couple fares.

Besides, damn it, he was innocent.

And had no motive.

No motive. That gave him some peace of mind.

Nuts. *I'm kidding myself.* The danger wasn't in being found guilty but in just being snagged up in the mess. Even if Lisper had no connection to the killing of the cabbie, eventually the local cops would connect Peter to the killing and find him. He'd be a fool to figure otherwise.

He couldn't run. He couldn't go to the police. He had one option: get out and find the killers.

The killer's motive had to be the bones. If it wasn't just a robber. *Wrong place, wrong fare.*

Hell, they'd probably come to him; he had the bait. They might be out looking for him right now, for the wise-ass that ripped off their bones.

Comforting thought.

He'd have to go back to get the bones from the restaurant. He didn't know what significance the bones had, but they were his only ace. The rest of his hand was pure bluff.

A strange sense of comfort came with the resolution that he was going to fight back. And that he had something to fight with. The only person he trusted with his life was himself.

And if he ran he'd never see *her* again.

The woman. He thought about the woman in the fog, replaying the scene in his mind, seeing her again, the puzzled look on her face as if she recognized him. His own strange sense of having known her before . . .

God, she excited him!

With all his aches and raw nerves, thinking of her still sent tingling down his bare thighs.

He reached over and turned on the tape player of the boom box he kept next to the bed. In L.A. he had a stereo system that could have filled a closet and was capable of shattering windows. A little craziness later and he had a cheap radio/tape player that he didn't dare turn up past a whisper for fear Mrs. Murdstone would rag on him.

Great. The Righteous Brothers and the Unchained Melody. One of his favorite tear-jerking oldies about love lost. Just what he needed when he was already miserable. Wait, your love will return, don't give up hope, the song seemed to say.

One in a lifetime, that's what his mother told him

about love. You can love a lot, live a lot, but no matter how many times you marry, no matter how many times you mate, there's only one *true* love in a lifetime.

After Peter's stepfather died, she used to sit on the front porch and watch the street for hours, lost in her thoughts. And memories. Waiting, hoping, that her RAF pilot lover would come back, returned to her arms by a miracle. She ruined her life for the memory of her one love. He knew that, knew it was stupid, could have sat down and written a story for a magazine about the second (or third or fourth) time around the love game and how it got better every time.

But it was in his blood, the true-love syndrome. And he never found her among the California Girls the Beach Boys told the world about. He found sex, occasional infatuation, but he never found that one woman his mother told him would be his *true* love.

His mother's romanticism had been a destructive disease in her life, and he worried that it blurred his own actions. The concern made him standoffish with women, holding himself back for fear he'd be hurt.

He questioned his feelings, *motives*, about the woman in the fog. Was he drawn to her because of whimsical romantic notions—the Harlequin variety? He remembered the taste of her lips against his, the feel of her body . . .

He awoke at three o'clock in the morning with cold feet on his chest.

A hairy face nuzzled him and sharp claws dug into his skin. He groaned and rolled over, but the creature wouldn't give up. It climbed on again and massaged its claws on his back.

It was Oliver. Sometimes when he was out carousing the back streets and alleys of the neighborhood till the wee hours and ended up locked out, Oliver would come scratching on Peter's back door for a bowl of milk before curling up against the warm heater duct.

"You little shit."

He pushed him off and got up. Oliver wasn't going to leave him alone until he was fed.

A cold draft greeted his ankles as he approached the kitchen door. He stopped; every nerve in his body snapped to attention. *He hadn't let Oliver into the house.*

The back door leading into the kitchen from the alley must be open.

He heard a squeak, the sound of a footstep on the linoleum floor in the kitchen.

Someone was in the kitchen.

He took the lamp off the stand next to the stuffed chair and set it on the chair, then picked up the lampstand, holding it by the legs like a club.

Light from the street windows spread a gray shadow to the kitchen door, leaving the rest of the room in utter darkness. Peter kept to the side of the light, waiting in the darkness by the foot of the bed; he heard the crunch of kitchen linoleum again—*the person was just behind the kitchen door.*

He adjusted his grip on the lampstand and cocked it back, a batter waiting for the pitch.

I'm a fool, he thought. There are three of them, Big and Little and the driver. *And they're armed.* Not that it mattered. The Mongol was big enough to catch the lampstand with his teeth. He was insane to think he could handle the killers with guns. It was too late to get out the front door. They'd blow him away while he was still fumbling with the lock.

The kitchen door started to open slowly. He held his breath. He had only heard the steps of one person in the kitchen, but one with a gun was enough.

"I've got a gun." He spoke loudly, but he didn't

sound convincing, at least not to himself. "The police are on their way."

The kitchen door moved back. Running steps, not the pound of a heavy man, but light footsteps, sounded on the linoleum. *It might be her.*

He shoved open the door—the kitchen was empty. The door to the alley was cocked open. He ran for it, flying out into the foggy night without a thought of what he could be running into.

A car down the alley started up and pulled away. It was too foggy to make out anything but the hazy glow of retreating taillights.

Barefoot, bare-assed except for a pair of Jockey shorts, he suddenly realized how cold it was. After taking one more look around in the hope that she would materialize out of the fog, he went back into the house.

He shut the back door and wedged a chair under the door knob. He wasn't that sure his visitor had been his mystery woman. For all he knew his mystery woman had been the driver of the Mercedes that chased him. It wasn't a pleasant thought. He almost left teethmarks on the bumper of the car. And that would associate her with the murder of the cabbie.

He double-checked the lock on the front door and wedged a chair under the doorknob. Oliver was asleep next to the warm furnace duct and Peter joined him, wrapping himself in blankets from the bed and leaning back to feel the warmth of the metal. He leaned back too hard and the aluminium buckled, the air inside letting out a *boom!* that vibrated up the duct. "Damn!" He looked up to the ceiling. The pounding came almost immediately—Mrs. Murdstone banging a shoe on the floor of her flat.

Bitch. He felt like giving the duct a kick that would send a shock wave upstairs and knock the old hag out of bed, but he wasn't that stupid. He couldn't afford to move. Besides, she'd have the police on to him for disturbing the peace.

Just what he needed, to draw the attention of the police to himself before he had a chance to prove his innocence.

Could he risk picking up the carryall at the restaurant? He couldn't risk *not* picking it up. But somebody might have checked the contents and the cops could be waiting for him. Would the old woman behind the cashier's counter be a good witness for him, corroborating that he had acted "normal" when he came in? "Yes, yes, handsome young man very normal . . . until I tell him that pretty girl leave with other man, then he storm out in murderous rage . . ."

Jesus. He was letting his imagination run wild. Too many books and movies. He definitely would go back and get the bag, whatever the risk. The bones seemed to be the key to the killing of the taxi driver and the assault on himself. And they were his only link to *her.*

The intrigue was tailor-made for someone nurtured on books and movies and tales of love lost. It would spoil things if the woman turned out to be a villain. Or if he got killed. The latter would especially put a damper on things.

Seri Sushi didn't open until five o'clock in the afternoon. Peter was waiting by the door when a younger version of the elegant Japanese woman cashier unlocked it.

He retrieved the bag from the cashier's counter, assuring the young woman that it was his. He was glad she didn't ask him to identify the contents.

As he walked back to catch a bus, he worried about the woman who had spotted him in the taxi. What if she lived in the neighborhood? Stepped out of a store as he came down the street? Sat next to him on a bus? Started screaming, "Murderer!"

The morning papers had not said much about the killing: A witness had seen a "dark-haired man in his late twenties" in the taxi with the dead man. "Police speculate that the witness scared the killer off before the killer was able to remove the dead man's valuables . . ."

Wonderful. He was the chief suspect. He probably could explain everything—except why he hadn't gone to the authorities immediately. There was no mention of a car crashing into a storefront. Probably attributed it to a drunken driver, Peter thought.

It was dark by the time he got home.

He examined the two pieces that made up the skull. He wasn't sure what the difference was between a fossil and a bone, but he realized the weathered, pitted skull belonged to someone dead hundreds, perhaps thousands, of years. Which was why the police who stopped the taxi hadn't been excited about it.

The brain case had chicken scratches all over the top and a small hole on the left side. "Blunt instrument," he muttered without scientific basis. He wondered if it was evidence of a murder that took place a thousand years ago.

The carpetbag had an airline identification tag attached to the handle. The name and address of the owner was blank, but the issuing airline was Trans-India Air Lines, Dum Dum Airport, Calcutta, India.

Calcutta.

His father had flown out of Calcutta on his last mission. That was about all Peter's mother knew about the mission, that and the fact the plane had been lost in the Himalayas, information his mother received from one of his father's fellow officers who telephoned the terrible news to her at the London hotel where she had been staying.

The coincidence bothered him, but it was too much even for someone with his vivid imagination to make a connection between his father's RAF mission and an ancient skull.

But . . . how could he have two *unconnected* Calcutta incidences in his short lifetime?

Alarm bells ran in his head but he switched them off. No way could the two be connected.

He wrapped the bones in newspaper, turned off the kitchen light, and crept into the alley, leaving the empty carpetbag on his bed.

Mist haunted the alley. Somewhere in the night an ambulance wailed; neighborhood dogs howled to the tune.

He unlatched the gate to the weed and vegetable patch that was Mrs. Murdstone's pride and joy, grabbed a shovel from the tools leaning against the fence, and dug a hole. He put the bones in the hole and covered them, spreading the dirt to remove traces of the digging.

He left the garden and carefully latched the gate behind him. Catching a movement out of the corner of his eye, he swung around. Nothing took shape in the gloom. He hurried back inside the apartment, locking the kitchen door securely.

An hour later he left the house for beer and a sandwich, boarding a bus down the street, taking a seat in the rear. As the bus was pulling away from the curb he saw an elderly priest standing on the corner, watching the bus. The man was vaguely familiar. Had a priest moved into the neighborhood? He'll have his hands full if he did, Peter thought.

Cocks had originally been a cockpit. When the brutal sport was outlawed, the owners split the arena and made a pub out of one of the half-moons.

Too many London pubs had gone the way of Formica bars, noisy jukeboxes and flashing neon beer signs. Cocks stayed traditional, keeping yesteryear's furniture: dark wormwood walls, stained glass windows, and a roaring fire in a stone hearth big enough to roast whole pigs.

Steve Jones, an advertising executive he met doing a story, introduced Peter to Cocks. "It's like a private club," Steve told him. "Once the crowd gets to know you, the same type of camaraderie develops that you find at the hobnob clubs."

Steve was there and hailed him as he came through the door. "Peter! Over here."

Steve detached himself from a group at the bar and steered Peter to a table. "How's life been treating you, Pete?"

Peter suddenly felt the need to confide in someone. Maybe not everything, but enough to have an ally if he got arrested. "Steve, I'm going to tell you a bizarre story. If I'm found floating facedown in the Thames, I want you to cry foul play to the papers."

"Sounds like bloody good fun. I can see myself running down Fleet Street crying, 'Foul play! Foul play!' "

They sipped beer as Peter told Steve about the mystery of the bag with the skull in it, omitting reference to the taxi and Soho. Steve wasn't the sort of friend who would hesitate to call the cops if he thought he was sharing a beer with the Soho Cabbie Killer.

Steve goggled when Peter told him about the invasion of his flat. "Ha! The plot thickens."

"What plot?" The question came from one of the men at the bar. It was Bremer, one of Steve's drinking buddies.

"Haven't you heard?" Steve's voice carried across the room. "Peter had a bag dumped in his lap by a woman of mystery!"

"Steve, don't . . ."

It was too late. Steve's proclamation attracted half a dozen men. Peter sank deeper into his chair, wishing the hell he hadn't started the ball rolling.

"It happened this way," Steve told them. "Peter here was walking along one dark and dreary night . . ."

"A long time ago," Peter interjected.

"Last night, when out of the misty fog comes a woman of mystery, of beauty, Mata Hari, *mon amour*! She rushes into Peter's arms, says she's in danger, gives him a bag, and tells him to safeguard it with his life. If it falls into the wrong hands the kingdom will fall. Then she disappears into the night with killers stalking her."

"What did Peter do when the killers chased the girl?"

"He fought them hand and foot—"

"Tooth and nail," Peter corrected. He was sweating blood but trying to act nonchalant. He'd been crazy to confide in a drunk. Everyone was treating the thing as a joke, and he prayed it would stay that way. The morning papers hadn't made a connection between the bag of bones the cops saw and the murdered cabbie, but he hadn't checked the evening paper. If the papers had mentioned it, someone was bound to remember.

"But it was six to one. They left Peter bloody and battered on the street, but with a dead man's grip on the mysterious bag!"

"What's in the bag?" Bremer asked.

"Are you ready for this, gentlemen?" Steve took a long swig of ale. He set the glass down and wiped his mouth with the back of his hand. "Bones," he whispered.

"What'd he say?"

"Bones, the man said."

"Bones!"

"What kind of bones were they, Peter?"

Peter cleared his throat. "Uh, the kind you can buy for your—"

"That's the mystery," Steve said, grabbing back the spotlight. "Men, it's up to us to save the kingdom. Our lovely isles will crash upon the rocks of ill fortune unless we can decipher the mystery of the bones."

"What do the bones look like?" Bremer asked.

"There's a skull, a big jaw, an arm, a leg, and a foot."

"Don't forget the rib cage and ring finger," Peter said.

"All right, gents, now we have here one solicitor, one, two businessmen, a psychiatrist—"

"Psychologist!"

"Or whatever, plus a couple whoevers. Now tell me, gents: Whose bones are they?"

"They're the remains of the queen's paramour," the solicitor said. "Poisoned and buried in Buckingham gardens. The Russians have dug him up and are blackmailing the queen, demanding the battle plans of the kingdom in exchange for the *corpus delicti*."

Steve lifted his glass in a salute. "Gentlemen. How vote ye on the queen's paramour?"

There were universal groans and thumbs down.

"I've got it," Bremer said. "It's the mortal remains of Sir Isaac Newton. They're gonna scrape some cells from the bone and grow a clone."

"Why?" Peter asked.

"Don't you see? Newton was Britain's greatest scientific mind. If we had old Isaac back, he'd figure out some way to beat the Arabs by running our factories on good English gin and Britannia would still rule the waves!"

A cheer went up, but Bremer only managed three votes.

"I have the solution to the bag of bones," the psychiatrist-psychologist-whatever said.

"He's gonna tell us it's Freud's mother," Steve said.

"There are no bones, no damsel in distress, no battle with the Forces of Darkness. The entire episode was invented by our friend here. Bored, insecure, lacking the friends and admiration his little ego feeds upon, he invented a fantasy adventure to attract attention to himself!"

The jury loved it. Peter laughed with them.

"I've seen dozens of sick cases like this one," the solicitor said. "Every time some poor girl gets sliced up in Soho, they line up at the police stations to confess. Pathetic creatures."

Steve motioned for silence. "How vote ye on the theory the mysterious affair is all a figment of Mr. Novak's imagination?"

The vote was unanimous.

Somebody slammed Peter on the back. "If you can't get a real woman, Peter, don't invent one. I'll give you my wife!"

The crowd roared with laughter. The solicitor pounded on the table to get attention. "Gentlemen. Gentlemen of the jury. After a fair and impartial trial—"

"Here, here!"

"By his betters, the defendant was found guilty of fraudulently fantasizing. We have passed judgment. Now justice must be served. We must administer punishment!"

"Here, here!"

"But first the thirst of justice must be wetted!" Bremer yelled.

The front door opened and a woman entered, letting the door swing fully open, fog rolling in at her feet like a white carpet. She moved with the smoothness and ease of someone who knew her own body, like a yoga master whose mind touches every part of the body.

She was a woman of the night, of beauty; she wore the same sable coat she'd had on when she had slipped out of the taxi and disappeared in the fog. The hood was bunched on her shoulders and diamonds of mist glistened in her hair. She came into the pub as if for a brief respite while a coach waited outside to carry her though the dark night along cobblestone roads to a secret rendezvous.

Every eye in the pub was drawn to her as she slowly walked to the table where Peter was sitting. The good-natured group jostling Peter one by one grew silent and stared.

She paused in front of Peter. She looked into his eyes, and he felt the hair rise on the back of his neck.

"Have you been taking good care of my bones, Peter?"

CHAPTER 6

Quoth the Raven, "Nevermore."

They walked along the footpath in a public garden across from the pub, their way lined with lamp-posts. Fog turned the innocent park into a realm of eerie forms and threatening shadows. Hazy moonlight reflected off the snow leopard pendant hanging from the chain around her neck. It suited her, he thought. Great cats were exotic. Dangerous.

She seemed unbothered by the fact they were walking in a dark park on a cold, miserable night where muggers and God knows what might be lurking. He seemed unbothered, too, but it was an act on his part. He pulled up the collar of his coat and stuck his hands in his pockets to keep them from freezing and breaking off at the wrist.

"You must have many questions," she said.

He shrugged. "Not really. I'm a foreign correspondent. It's all part of my work day to have beautiful women drop mysterious packages in my lap, shots in the dark—"

"You were shot at?"

"Not yet." He deliberately didn't mention the cabbie, waiting to see if she'd mention it. "But the night's young."

"I like your sense of humor."

"You do?" That warmed the cockles of his heart and he had to remind himself that the woman turning him on was involved in murder.

"Yes. You're a little reserved and you hide it behind a little humor."

"Are you a psychiatrist, by chance?"

"Why? Do you need one?"

"Maybe. If you hadn't shown up, my drinking buddies were planning to have me hauled away in a straitjacket."

"Why did you leave America?" she asked.

He thought for a moment. "Songs without words."

"Songs without words?"

"That's how it started. I'm from L.A. I was going down Sunset, on my way home one night, usual jam-up, everybody crazy, jockeying for car lengths, teeth-marks on our bumpers. You know what I mean? Anyway, I stopped for a light and cars on each side of me had their radios shooting out pop music. People like to share their noise in L.A. The one with the loudest radio wins." He smiled. She probably thought he was nuts.

"I had my windows rolled up because I was listening to an oldies station, the Beatles telling a girl they wanted to hold her hand. As the decibels from the other cars ricocheted off my windows I realized that so much of the music of my generation doesn't *say* anything. I'm always listening to stuff from the fifties and sixties because the songs had meaning—boy breaks girl's heart, cops break boy's head, flowers gone to graveyards every one." He stopped. He was nuts. "I'm sorry. It's hard to explain."

"I understand. Please. Go on."

"It wasn't just the music. Everywhere I looked I saw a void in my life. I didn't vote because the politicians all seemed so generic, you know, mass produced from the same mold. People were still talking about the Kennedys, Camelot, and the New Frontier, the War on Poverty. Those were songs with words."

He glanced sideways at her. "You sure you want to hear this?"

"Very much."

"Okay. Then let's talk about the movies. Actors today. They need a billion bucks' worth of special effects to carry a movie because they're generic, too. Pumped bodies. Magazine-cover faces. But I couldn't stand going to movies because those people on the screen couldn't make me forget they were *acting*. I found myself renting old movies at the video store or watching the Classic Channel. Bogie and Bacall and *Key Largo* and shit, how the hell can you compare the look Gable gave Scarlett the first time he saw her with the jack-offs today who confuse making love with making sex."

He took time out to breathe. "By the way. Will you make love to me!"

"Are you a jack-off?"

"Uh, let's talk about McDonaldism."

"McDonaldism?"

"Yeah, the hamburger people. They drove the mama-papa stands and corner sweet shops out of business. Fast food designed by accountants, not chefs. Fast, efficient, faceless." He threw up his hands. "Generics. McDonaldism has infected everything. Look at our cars. Fast, efficient—but they're harder to tell apart than hamburgers. Buildings? As aerodynamic as a BMW. But when you twist glass and steel you give shape, not character. The problem is craftsmanship. You need human hands to make cars and buildings and hamburgers interesting. But today's hands are trained only to press buttons on machines that shape the steel and mold the patties."

He stuck his hands back in his pockets and looked at her out of the corner of his eye. "Well, that's it. What makes Peter run. Why I gave up the pursuit of fame and fortune and came to Merry Ole England to search for my roots."

"What about her?"

"Her?"

"There has to be a woman in among the cars, the movies, and the hamburgers."

"*Women*. Fast food is efficient."

She didn't accept his answer. He shrugged. "Okay. One woman in particular. When she thought I was getting weird she took a walk. It's easy to do. People don't get married today—they take a lease on love and shack up. Something called a 'relationship.' "

He stopped walking and faced her. "Okay, it was me, all me. She was sweet as hell and I was a dick. I just couldn't get married and get a family and get a mortgage and the other L.A. gets. I had to *get* out. She thought I was chasing windmills. I tried to tell her that steel, glass, concrete, and BMWs weren't reality. We made that crap. I had to get away from it if I was ever going to find the real world. But first I had to find myself."

She continued to walk and he took quick steps to catch her. "Okay, now tell me the truth. You think I'm crazy."

"You're crazy."

"Fine. Now, since you have this impulse to be frank and truthful, why don't you tell me why you dumped those bones in my lap?"

The footpath led to a wooden bridge arched over a duck pond. Pausing at the foot of the bridge, she turned to him, her eyes intently scanning his face, searching.

"What are you thinking about, now, as we walk together?"

"What am I thinking about? Trains."

"Trains?"

"And a train station. Did you ever see the old

Hitchcock movie, *Foreign Correspondent*, with Joel McCrea?"

She shook her head.

"It's one of my favorites. When I was a kid, I used to daydream about being a foreign correspondent, traveling around the world, covering dangerous assignments. Somehow I always ended up at the railroad station in Paris with a mysterious woman in a trench coat running up to me and saying something like, 'Help me, I'm in danger.' " He laughed, a little embarrassed.

"Have you been to the train station in Paris in search of your damsel in distress?"

He followed her as she slowly walked up the arched bridge. "I haven't made it to Paris yet. I've been shying away from the trip. I don't think there are many *innocent* damsels in distress left."

Leaning back against the railing, she stared out at the deserted pond and lonesome lily pads before meeting his eye. Hair on the back of his neck rose again. Her eyes were deep pools of mystery, shaded by Oriental eyelids, temple doors guarding a treasure.

"Why do you seem so familiar to me?" he asked.

"Perhaps we have met. In a life past. And our kismet has brought us back together."

"Lives past? That's a strange expression. You mean . . . reincarnation?"

"Your Occidental upbringing rejects the notion of reincarnation. You were raised in a world where the only truth is that seen by the eye."

"True. And you of the Orient practice wisdom, not science. That's why the West dominates the world."

"In machines, not minds," she said. "There are many truths in this world that can't be seen under a microscope. How do you explain the sensation we experience when we're together? We've never met."

"Maybe we have and just didn't realize it. In a tube

station, on the street, at the soda fountain at Harrod's. Walking past or sitting next to each other and not realizing. Ships passing in the night."

"It sounds like a theory one of those scientists of yours who torment mice in mazes would dream up."

He stared at her, his look full of questions. "Who are you?"

"I'm a thief," she said.

She had a way of starting conversations that left him speechless.

"I'm entangled in schemes I have no control over. I assure you I'm not a secret agent from some cheap spy story."

He didn't think she was the product of a *cheap* spy story. She was definitely Somerset Maugham material.

"I'm a paleontologist with the British Museum."

"Come again?"

"Paleontology is the study of prehistoric man through fossils."

"Like Leakey in Africa?" Educated by a London cabbie.

"That sort of thing. I . . . I did something very stupid. I'm ashamed even to admit I managed to put myself in a position where I could be so easily compromised. I committed a crime. An act of theft." She paused as if she expected him to say something and continued when he didn't respond. "Rare fossils are extremely valuable. The fossils of early Homo species like Cro-Magnon and Neanderthal are priceless because they are irreplaceable. There are more Gutenberg Bibles and paintings by Rembrandt in museums than most species of prehistoric man."

"Are you telling me they're worth millions?"

"The rarer ones, yes. Are you familiar with the Piltdown Man scandal?"

"Piltdown Man?"

"It's the most sensational scientific fraud in English history. Around 1912 an amateur paleontologist named Dawson, a solicitor by trade, allegedly found fossils of early man in a remote quarry in Sussex. The find stunned the British scientific community.

"Darwin's theory of evolution was a hotly debated topic. While fossil evidence of prehistoric man had been found in other areas of the world, none had been found in the British Isles. A group of scientists examined the bones, ignored some rather obvious discrepancies, and hailed the fossils as the missing link in the evolution of the English-speaking people.

"The fossils of Piltdown Man sat in an honored place in the British Museum for over forty years. Finally, in 1953, unable to reconcile the mounting contradictions between Piltdown and later finds, like Homo erectus, Piltdown Man was reexamined and discovered to be a fraud.

"Someone, perhaps Dawson, doctored the bones to make them appear prehistoric. Anthropology, paleontology were infant sciences. The scientists of that day lacked testing equipment for age dating. And they were eager to prove Darwin's theory, thus substantiating their own premises."

"If it's fraud, where's the value?"

"The notoriety alone made the fossils priceless."

"The skull in the bag is like Piltdown Man?"

"It *is* Piltdown Man."

"How did this, uh, priceless skull make its way from the hallowed halls of the British Museum to a walk along Whitehall?"

"I was duped. I've been examining the errors made with Piltdown Man as part of a research project analyzing fallacies in the evolution theory due to misinterpretation of data. A man contacted me who claimed he was a researcher for a noted Canadian paleontologist and convinced me his credentials were genuine. He said he could prove the Piltdown Man fraud was part of a much larger scientific conspiracy and talked me into removing the fossil from the museum. He asked me to bring it to a government building on Whitehall for a series of tests he claimed would be conducted as part of an official investigation.

"I was looking for evidence of scientific malfeasance and he dangled a first-class conspiracy in front of me. I put the skull in a bag after I finished at the museum yesterday and went to the appointed place on Whitehall. The building was closed. I found myself standing on a deserted street late at night with a bag containing a British scientific treasure that I had removed from the museum with no more authority than a common thief. I started walking down the street, confused. The fog was thick and I became frightened. I saw you walking on the street and fell into step behind you."

"Taillights in the fog."

"What?"

"When you're traveling in a car in low visibility, the safest thing to do is follow the taillights of a car ahead. If there's any trouble in the roadway, the other car will run into it first."

"I suppose that's what I was doing, but I was the one who hit obstacles. Someone tried to grab the bag from me and I ran."

"How did you find me tonight?"

"I obtained the address from your telephone listing. A woman sitting on the front steps of your building told me you frequented that pub."

He tried to remember if anyone at the building knew he went to Cocks.

"Peter, you must help me. I'll be ruined if I don't return the skull to the museum." She looked close to tears.

She didn't strike him as a scientist, though there was nothing inconsistent about digging up old bones and being beautiful. It was her body language, her aura, that was unscientific. She was more Kim Novak in *Bell, Book, and Candle* than Margaret Mead in the jungle. And her story struck him as rehearsed.

She suddenly tensed. "Someone's coming!"

He spun around. A shadowy figure cloaked by the mist and drizzle was approaching the bridge.

"Stay here," he said. He went down to the foot of the bridge. It was only a couple dozen feet, but it would give her a chance to run if there was trouble.

He had nothing to use as a weapon. If it was a mugger, his only chance would be to beat the man to a pulp with his wallet.

The person came into sight, a policeman. "Good evening, sir."

"Good evening, officer."

"See you're out for a stroll. If you don't mind me saying so, sir, you ought not to spend too much time in the park at night. Not that safe even on clear nights."

"Good advice. My friend and I were just . . ." He turned and looked up at the bridge.

She was gone.

He started to call for her but realized he didn't know her name.

Harry Browne's was the biggest, most disorganized and untidy bookshop on earth. It attracted poets, scholars, and winos. The store had books with pictures for perverts, big type for the elderly, Braille for the blind, and even small print for lawyers.

Peter loved the place.

He found a book on Piltdown Man in the science room, a dingy cubbyhole in a dark corner of the third floor. It took less than a minute to skim the dust jacket blurb and leaf through the pictures in the heart of the book to confirm she had not lied about the Piltdown Man fraud.

And *had* lied about everything else.

The Piltdown Man scandal was a blow to British science and the theory of evolution. But the skull in the bag was different from the one in the pictures.

"The plot thickens," he told the cashier on the way out.

A block from the bookshop he picked up a city bus and settled back in his seat. Why had she lied to him? Obviously, to keep the truth from him, but he wondered how bad the truth could be. He had good instincts about people, and his gut told him that she was not a bad person, but he had to question his own motives. Was he judging her for what she was—or what he wanted her to be? She had lied to him and obviously was up to her neck in some shady deal. Yet . . .

The building was dark by the time he reached home. The tenants were hardworking people who went to bed early on Sunday nights to make sure they were fresh for the start of the work week. He took the steps down to his door lightly, giving Oliver a "Shhhhhh . . ." when the cat tried to talk to him. He didn't want any more trouble with Mudface Murdstone; his meager savings were almost depleted, and he couldn't afford to move or attract the cops to his door.

He opened the door quietly and slipped in, turning on the light after he closed the door.

His apartment was a shambles—the bed ripped apart, every book in the place dumped onto the floor, furniture overturned, his clothing tossed from the closet and into a pile just outside the closet door. His crack about it being ransacked had come true. He kicked a cotton sack at his feet to get it out of the way—it was his shoe-shining stuff, usually kept in a corner of the closet.

"Son of a bitch!" The carpetbag was gone.

"They can have it," he said aloud. The bones were buried in the garden. Let 'em find them there.

He felt a cold draft. The kitchen door was closed, but moved a fraction on its swing hinges, as if teased by a flow of air. *The back door was open.* It was the only thing that would make that door move; the kitchen window wasn't open—it was sealed shut by fifty years of paint and grime.

Had Big and Little come back for another try?

He stuck his right hand in his coat pocket. "Come out," he said. "I've got a gun."

No one came out.

Had they come and gone? He hoped the hell so.

A squeak came from the kitchen, the sound of a footstep on old linoleum. *Christ, here we go again.*

The kitchen door slowly swung open; he held his breath until he saw her. She stood in the open doorway and stared at him for a long moment before stepping in, letting the kitchen door swing shut. She leaned back against the wall and put her hands inside her coat pockets.

"How did you get in?" he asked. "Kick open the back door?"

"It was open."

He nodded at the mess. "I'm going to have to nail it shut. And brick it up. This place is becoming a freeway. I don't suppose you had anything to do with this?"

She shook her head.

"Why did you come?" he asked softly. He didn't give a damn if she told him she came to burn the place.

"The bones. I want them."

"I was hoping you had come because you found me so irresistible. That was a clever story you told me in the park, but I stopped at a bookstore on the way home."

"Give me the bones."

"Is that all you came for?"

He noticed the hesitation in her body before she answered, "Yes."

"I don't believe you."

He approached slowly, his eyes on hers.

"Do you really have a gun?" she asked.

"Just bluffing."

"I'm not." Her right hand came out of her pocket, clutching a snub-nosed automatic, a little black one, the kind they call a woman's purse gun, cute and lethal. "Stay where you are."

"You've lied about everything."

"This gun isn't a lie."

"You wouldn't use it." He smiled. "Remember me—I'm the guy you met in a past life."

"We'll meet next in lives to come if you take another step."

"What about trains?"

"Trains?"

"Trains passing in the night." He edged closer. "You and me and that sense of familiarity. How are you going to live with your karma if you shoot me?"

He was almost in grabbing range.

"One more step and I'll shoot."

He stopped. The velvet was gone—her voice was a steel hammer. He recognized a quality in her, a willingness to shrug off unimportant things but to be a rock when she took a stand. He recognized it because it was a quality he shared. *She wasn't bluffing.*

"Give me the bones, Peter, and I'll get out of your life forever."

"Is that what you want? The bones and out of my life?"

"That's the way it has to be."

He shrugged. "Okay, I was only saving them for you." He stepped over to where he had kicked the sack of shoe-shine stuff. "Whoever searched the place found the carpetbag and missed the bones. They had 'em right in their hands." He picked up the sack and turned to her. "I'll be happy to get my life back to nor—" He half handed, half tossed the sack to her, letting it fall just a little short. She reached for it with both hands, and he grabbed her wrists and jerked them down, spreading her arms out and slamming her back against the wall, pinning her with his body.

"I knew you wouldn't shoot me," he said. His lips brushed hers, kissing her lightly.

She tried to kick him and he jerked her around, away from the wall, and moved her backward, keeping her feet in motion. She fell backward onto the bed with him on top of her. She tried to point the gun at him and he stretched her arm out, pointing it away from him, at the wall where the furnace duct jutted out.

He spread himself over her, more from survival than lust, and stared down at her, their lips a kiss apart. "Lethal little bitch, aren't you."

"Peter, stop this, give me the bones. You don't understand." She tried to push him off.

He pressed her back down. "Tell me . . . tell me about the bones and the Mercedes and the dwarf and the big guy."

"Please . . ."

He lost himself in the dreamy pools of her eyes. "What is it about you?" he asked. "Why do I feel I know you?"

"We were lovers in a life past," she whispered.

The fiery chemistry he felt in the taxi was igniting.

"I don't understand . . ." But it didn't matter whether he did or not. He kissed her, his lips melting into hers. She twisted her hand free, the one without the gun, and put it around his neck, pulling him hard onto her lips. When he came up for air she was searching his features again. "What is it?" he asked.

"I wanted to see if you evoked a memory," she said.

"Did I?"

She pulled him down again and kissed him.

"Oh, God," he breathed. He was getting aroused, and the sensation was spreading like an oil fire through his system. He softly kissed her cheeks and nose and eyes and chin while his hand clumsily opened the top of her dress, exposing her breasts. He caressed her taut nipples with his tongue as his hand slipped inside her dress, over silk panties and be-tween—*a shot exploded in the room.*

They gawked at each other, wide-eyed, stunned. Peter's ears rang, his mind was numb. She held up the gun. "It went off," she said, "*it went off.*"

The furnace duct was screaming. The bullet had punched a neat little hole in the duct and steam was escaping with a horrible screech. He pushed himself off of her and onto his feet. "It'll wake the whole building!"

He grabbed the first thing handy, a stray sock atop a pile of clothing on the floor near the dresser. He jammed the sock into the hole, pushing it in with his fingers. The noise stopped but he knew it was too late. Footsteps pounded above.

"I'll head her off," Peter said.

He jerked open the door and flew out. Mrs. Murd-stone was charging to the head of the stairs, her purple mules flapping. He stopped as she spotted him at the bottom of the stairs, pointing an accusatory finger up at her. "That damn furnace of yours is going to blow up this whole building some day!"

"Wha—what?" Her double chins quivered. "We've never had any—"

"I'm going to call the fire department if there's any more trouble. And the building owners. That furnace makes one more noise and there'll be trouble. And a change of management!"

He stepped back inside, shutting the door firmly and locking it. He leaned back against it, taking a deep breath.

"The old bitch is—" He realized he was talking to an empty room. He hurried into the kitchen and found the back door open, air-conditioning the house with 40-degree London air. He ran out the back door, into the fog-shrouded alley.

She was gone.

Again.

CHAPTER 7

Dogs barking and Mrs. Murdstone yelling in her garden awoke him the next morning. He rolled over and put a pillow over his head to tune out the commotion, then bolted up in bed. *The bones were in the garden!*

He grabbed a pair of pants and hopped into them. Mrs. Murdstone was coming out of the garden swinging a broom at a pack of mongrel dogs as he came into the alley. The dogs ran down the alley barking.

Blood vessels in her cheeks were purple. "If I find out who left me garden gate open——"

Peter rushed by her and ran into the garden. "Oh, no!" A hole occupied the spot where he had buried the bones. He kicked at pieces of newspaper, hoping to find the bones underneath.

Mrs. Murdstone followed him into the garden, her purple robe dragging in the dirt. "You're stepping on me cabbage!"

"Those damn dogs stole my bones!"

Wide-eyed, she drew aside to let him pass. "Whose bones did ya bury in me garden?"

He went inside, slamming the back door. He cared about the bones not only because they were a tie to *her*, but his clue to the killing. First the carpetbag, then the bones, and he still didn't know her name or have the slightest clue to finding her or the damn killer.

Almost eight o'clock. He was going to be late for work. He didn't want to go to work but forced himself into the bathroom to shave. He had to keep acting normal. Waltz into work as if nothing had happened. A murder in Soho? Never go near the place. Don't care much for slanty-eyed restaurants myself. Bones buried in the garden? Why, everyone knows Mrs. Murdstone is a wee bit touched . . .

He cut himself three times. A fine Monday morning.

Stepping out the front door of the flat, he found a Notice to Quit Premises tacked to the door. Murdstone had struck again. No doubt she would have the police exhume her garden.

In his mailbox was a "final" demand from American Express for the long-overdue payment on a great ski trip to St. Moritz. Qualifying for the AMEX card with his small income had been a fluke: he'd met an AMEX credit rep at a party, she got him the card, he took her to St. Moritz. Now American Express was threatening to repossess his life for not paying.

There was a string attached to everything.

The AMEX people wanted their card, the security people wanted him deported, the cops wanted to pin a murder on him, his landlady wanted him evicted, a dog ate his bones, his mystery woman disappeared. And Rex Silvernale wanted the price of pig bellies.

Silvernale was editor, London office, *Manchester Financial Standard*. He'd hired Peter as a "foreign news consultant." The title gave Peter an extended visitor's visa that permitted him to stay in the country. And it gave Silvernale an excuse to pay him just enough to survive in a slum apartment, entertain himself in used bookshops, and have his shoes periodically resoled.

Chicken Lips was waiting as he came through the office door. Silvernale's secretary had a proper name, but it was long forgotten by the staff to whom her

thin lipped, puckered sneer, and sour disposition answered the ancient riddle of whether chickens had
lips.

"Report to Mr. Silvernale *immediately!*"

Peter leered on his way by. "Get any lately?"

An office girl giggled and buried her head in paperwork as Chicken Lips whipped around.

He should learn to keep his mouth shut. He had
already pissed off too many people. It was a small
country and he might need allies. Or friends on a jury.

Silvernale was on the phone when Peter entered.
The man had tarnished silver hair, bushy black eyebrows, and blue-veined Richard Nixon jowls. He
hung up and glared at Peter. "What kind of trouble
are you stirring up for the paper, Novak?"

Peter blinked in surprise. "Trouble for the paper?"

"Two months you've been employed by this paper
and at three o'clock this morning I received a telephone call. Three o'clock in the morning!" Silvernale
raised his eyebrows in mock surprise. "Do you want
to know *whoommm* I received a telephone call from
at *three o'clock this morning?*"

Peter's whole life seemed a little out of kilter, a
little warped. Terrified that he could be arrested at any
moment for a murder he didn't commit, he had to sit
in his boss's office like a cub reporter and get chewed
out because someone didn't like what he said in a
story. *"Whoommm?"* he asked.

"Mr. Anthony Burgess in Manchester, *the* Anthony
Burgess, who is managing editor of the *Financial
Standard.*"

"Mr. Silvernale—"

Silvernale rose from his chair. "Two months with
the paper and I receive a call at three o'clock in the
morning about you. Mund has been with the paper
sixteen years and I've *never* received a call about
him!" He collapsed back in his chair. His Nixon jowls

were inflamed and quivering. "And do you know why Burgess called me? Because a cabinet minister telephoned Burgess at two-thirty this morning!"

Peter's jaw dropped. "A cabinet minister called about me? The plane crash. It must be because of the plane crash."

"What plane crash? What are you talking about?"

Peter scooted to the edge of his chair. "My father was an RAF officer killed in a plane that took off from Calcutta in the sixties and crashed in the Himalayas. I came to Britain to trace his family. I've been trying to get a peek at his RAF personnel file and the government's been putting roadblocks in my way. A couple days ago, two MI5 men grilled me and threatened to have my visa pulled. They won't believe I'm the man's illegitimate son."

Silvernale didn't appear excited by the revelations. He looked even more annoyed.

Peter swallowed hard, restraining the urge to grab the bastard by the throat and shake some common sense into him. "Mr. Silvernale, I'm talking about a conspiracy, a cover-up, maybe something as big as Watergate and Profumo."

"Poppycock. Whitehall is annoyed because you lied on an application to see a file."

"Since when do cabinet ministers get involved with such trivialities? You don't understand—"

"Correction! *You* do not understand. The *Manchester Financial Standard* is an eighty-six-year-old institution. Not a newspaper, an institution! And do you know who our biggest advertiser is? Not those cancer stick manufacturers, not grocery market coupons, not even feminine hygiene deodorant sprays, thank God, but legal printing for the government. Do you understand what I am getting at, young man?"

Peter shook his head. The air was thick with sinister plots and the toad wanted to talk about advertising.

"It's obvious the shoddy handling of your personal affairs has reflected upon the *Financial Standard*. I have been informed by private sources at Whitehall that you have been trying to exploit the matter to embarrass the government."

"I'm telling you there's a cover-up. If we break the story we might topple the whole bloody government."

Silvernale gasped. "Topple the government? The *Financial Standard*? In eighty-six years we have not toppled a single government. We are *pro-government!*"

"This could be the story of the century. We owe it to the public to protect freedom of the press, to—"

"Horse shit!"

Peter blinked. "What did you say?"

Silvernale smacked his lips appreciatively. "I said . . . horse shit. To the people. To the freedom of the press."

"To the people? To freedom of the press?"

"Horse shit."

Peter stood up and leaned across the editor's desk. "You are the biggest asshole I've ever met."

"There you go, ducky, down to the last penny."

Peter stared at the check the payroll clerk handed him. "Penny is right."

"Sorry, you weren't 'ere long enough for severance pay. Any idea 'bout findin' another job?"

"Not in the least."

"Well, we all wish you luck. Maybe you should ask your priest friend to pray for one."

"Priest friend?"

"The one who was 'ere earlier looking for you. The old one. Said he'd be back later. So did that other fellow."

"Other fellow?"

"You know, love, the one with all them blue things on his nose. Speaks kind of funny, doesn't he? I mean, I'm not one to—"

Peter's guts retched. "Where's he at? The man with the lisp."

"Saw him just a minute ago going into Mr. Silvernale's office with Chic—Dear me, where are you going in such an 'urry?"

Peter left the building and walked quickly down Fleet Street, ducking into the first alley he came to. He had tight jaws and weak knees. His luck was running out. The next papers he'd get would be an arrest warrant. He'd been sacked, evicted, and was about to be arrested, all on the same morning. Now he could anticipate being gang-raped and whatever other joys go with spending time in a British slammer. All because of a plane crash that *should* have been ancient history and bones that *were* ancient history. He even had a priest looking for him. Maybe he was in trouble with heaven, too.

There aren't any coincidences, not when cabinet ministers were phoning his boss in the wee hours and a man was murdered merely for having driven a taxi carrying the bag of bones. There was a connection among the bones, his father, and the woman in the fog.

His father flew out of Calcutta. The bones flew out of Calcutta.

On the spur of the moment he made one of those decisions that should have been contemplated and weighed. And rejected.

He counted the money in his wallet. Less than two hundred American dollars and a couple of dozen British pounds. Plus a paycheck he couldn't take the time or risk to cash.

He couldn't run far on two hundred bucks and some pounds.

He fingered his American Express card. A passport to the world. If they were looking for him, they'd have the flights to America staked out.

He stepped into a corner phone booth. "British Airways? Do you fly to Calcutta?"

SHAMBALA

CHAPTER 8

There were times of hazy, dreamy consciousness with blurry movement of people around him, and times of mindless sleep. During the moments of consciousness he experienced the pain of having his wounds cleansed, the biting sting of hot, moist, green leaves laid across raw flesh while chills racked his body.

What measure of time passed while he had lain in the gray-walled room he had neither knowledge of nor interest in. He had suffered greatly and some inner clock had tuned out his senses to reserve all bodily energy for the healing process.

He knew a woman had been with him, had caressed his cheeks and whispered softly as short brown men in red robes tried to put him back together.

His dreams were surrealistic nightmares with a recurring theme: He was a World War II pilot pulled half frozen out of the North Sea and taken to a Nazi hospital where innocent young Jewish girls used their hot, naked bodies to defrost him. Hovering over him and the girls was a leering Nazi doctor in a white smock. The doctor had wire-rimmed glasses and a German death's head grin but looked familiar; the face was his own, but twisted and marred, a reflection in a fun house mirror.

He woke once to find the woman standing next to

the window to the left of the bed. Shallow light spread into the room from the breaking dawn. He lay very still, staring at her, not speaking, not really sure she wasn't an illusion, not caring as long as the enchantment remained unbroken. She seemed tall because she was slender and held herself proudly erect. Her neck was long and graceful, her cheekbones delicate. He wondered how old she was. Young, he guessed, perhaps no more than her late teens, but an aura of dignity and serenity gave an older presence, even a royal presence.

He had no memory of the plane crash except the engine dying, a mountain rushing at him. He didn't know how he'd survived the crash, how he'd made it to the gray-walled room. Nor did he know who the woman and the red-robed men who helped him were.

She sat at the edge of the bed and returned his stare, her features revealing nothing, but her fingers exposing her nervousness as they rubbed the snow leopard pendant hanging from a chain around her neck. Her eyes were curious, intent, and something else. Sad? he wondered.

"Am I that ugly?" he asked. She didn't seem to understand his words. He had spoken in English, and now he repeated the question in Tibetan, the language he had been trained in for the mission.

She didn't answer and he wondered if he had actually spoken the words or merely thought them. Then she said in Tibetan, "You are not ugly. You are . . . broken."

He tried to laugh, but it stuck in his throat and he choked, pain splintering his body.

She caressed his forehead and cheeks with a cool, wet cloth taken from a bowl on a stand next to the bed. The cloth smelled of the minty green leaves that had been placed on his open wounds.

"I was looking at your eyes," she told him gravely.

"They are the color of the moss on river rocks."

He felt himself drifting off, away from the enchanted moment, back to the place of dreams and nightmares.

"Where am I?" he asked.

"You are in the Lamasery of Shambala."

Shambala. They had drilled into him what little was known about the region, and there had been no Shambala.

His flight plan had taken him northwest after leaving Calcutta, crossing the swampy Ganges River delta and the smoke-green Bengal jungle, a primeval kingdom of vine and tiger. An hour into the flight he had veered east, toward the most awesome physical obstacle on earth, the Great Himalayan Barrier.

When the plane crossed the Himalayas, leaving behind the lush, warm Indian subcontinent, it had ventured into a political and physical no-man's-land.

Forbidden territory.

Few of the mountains had been climbed by Europeans; many were unnamed, some were sacred, the lofty thrones of the gods of Hindustan and Buddhism.

"Diamonds, that's what's shiny on those peaks," Dilly, the plane's mechanic, told him before the flight. "Diamonds as big as an elephant's arse. They're guarded by snow snakes and big hairy snowmen so ugly they're called abominable. And you know what else? There are places up there so isolated they're lost from history and the people are still hiding their gold and women from bloody old Genghis Khan. Places where a white man can go and they think he's a god just 'cause his skin ain't the color of mud.

"I heard a story, the truth so help me, 'bout two Englishmen who whipped a whole army of natives in some forgotten kingdom tucked in the Himalayas. Now they sit on thrones of solid gold and each night they get a fresh virgin to screw, never more than thirteen years old . . ."

Dilly was right. There were forgotten places high in the netherworld of snow and ice, pockets of civilization so ancient and so isolated history did not acknowledge them. He might even be right about the gold and thirteen-year-old virgins.

He edged closer to sleep and his voice slipped into a whisper, hardly more than a murmur. "Where is . . . Shambala?"

She gently tucked the blankets around him, careful not to disturb his sleep. She wiped his face with the refreshing cloth, then quietly sat beside him, taking his hand in hers.

"Some say you can find Shambala only in your heart," she whispered.

She was still sitting on the edge of the bed, holding his hand, when the High Lama came into the room. The head of the priesthood of Shambala was old and moved slowly.

She quickly let go of his hand and moved away from the bed as the High Lama approached, his look expressing disapproval.

As the High Lama paused beside the bed and stared down at the sleeping man, the young woman asked the urgent question that was beating inside her.

"Can it be, holy father? Is he . . . the *One?*"

He sat at the window and watched flashes of brilliant light in the dawn sky, flaming rubies, sparkling diamonds, green-fire emeralds, and topaz so dazzling it appeared fired by the sun itself.

In flights over the Arctic region he had seen colorful flashes of light called diamond dust created by rays of the sun spearing the countless ice crystals floating in air, but the celestial fireworks over Shambala were more dazzling. He understood the reason why: Warm air in the form of a silver mist rising from the valley collided explosively with the subzero temperatures above, turning the sky overhead into a prism as the sun's brilliant rays struck.

At dusk when the last rays of the setting sun speared the ice crystals, the phenomena occurred again.

The monks of Shambala had a more profound explanation than ice crystals and light rays: The silver mist was the crown of Buddha, and the sparkling lights the precious gems set within the crown. They called the phenomena the frost of heaven.

It was part of the mystery of the enchanted valley he had fallen into, half dead, his body torn and battered.

He struggled his sore body off the bed and into a chair by the window each morning to watch the silver mist rising. He was in a Tibetan "lamasery," the name given to monasteries in the land where some ranks of monks were called lamas.

He whittled a cane as he sat before the window. He didn't know if he had stumbled into a Shangri-La, didn't know if, like Shangri-La, the lamasery had a library filled with classics penned in the hand of authors and musical scores penciled by masters.

The single window in the room defined his world, giving him a limited view of the valley, the lake near the lamasery, and the mountains beyond. It had been weeks or months since the crash. He had lost track of time. Time didn't seem important to the monks who tended him; he wasn't sure they even understood the concept of time "passing." As far as he could tell, there were no clocks in Shambala except the internal "clock" each person was born with.

He paused in his task of whittling to take a sip of barley tea, a thick, steamy concoction as much like gruel as tea. His right knee was still stiff and weak, and he needed the cane to escape the confines of the room. He had not been out of the room since he had been carried in more dead than alive. The solitary confinement was driving him crazy, but he couldn't get anyone to understand that he wanted to leave the room and get a look at the lamasery. The monks who tended him suddenly couldn't understand his rough Tibetan whenever he mentioned seeing the rest of the lamasery.

With its dark, rough-hewn stone walls and sparse furnishings, small, Spartan-hard bed and an end table sturdy enough for an elephant to stand upon, the room reminded him of a monk's cell in a medieval monastery. Perhaps that was exactly what it was. Only one door led into the room, a solid slab of wood too short for him to walk under without ducking, but perfect for the monks, few of whom appeared to be more than five foot five or six.

The bed was on the right entering the room, with a fireplace against the left wall; the fireplace mantel—a shaved log half buried in the stone wall—was lined with yak-butter candles, crude clay-looking clumps with wicks sticking out. Centuries of black soot and melted wax coated the mantel and the wall beside it.

Another batch of yak-butter candles sat on the table next to the bed.

On the wall opposite the door was the window, with its view that defined his world. Next to it was the end table and the bed. On the other side of the bed hung an ancient tapestry, worn and venerable, the finely spun cloth depicting a woman with long black hair and flowing red robes riding a great snow leopard, the long hair, prehistoric-looking Himalayan cousin to the jungle leopard. He had stared at the tapestry for endless hours before he had progressed from lying flat on his back on the bed to sitting up by the window.

The blanket on his bed was woven from yak hair, the wicks in the candles came from the tails of yaks, and he had discovered by close examination that even the elegant tapestry had been finely crafted from the hair of yak.

He had seen the yak herd from his window, great Stone Age beasts that looked like a cross between a buffalo and a Texas longhorn with a little long-haired mastodon thrown in.

There were no yak steaks in Shambala—the people were vegetarians, like most Buddhists—but the yak seemed to supply everything from candlelight to shoes—the leather from the hide of animals that died a natural death. Yak butter seemed to be an ingredient in almost everything the monks cooked. They even threw a clump of it into the barley tea, the more rancid the butter the better.

He took another break from whittling, warming his hands with the big clay teacup as he stared out the window.

Tibet. The Forbidden Kingdom, a savage realm of lamaistic Buddhism, a three-mile-high Tibetan plateau sparsely populated, with some villages so remote little contact existed with the outside world. Savage warrior tribes, the Khampas, spiritual brothers of the Bedouin and Cossack, still roamed some of the great badlands in horse troops much like the barbaric horde of Genghis Khan that spewed out of nearby Mongolia to plunder half the world, ejaculating Mongol bloodlines into Tibet through rape and torture.

A twelfth-century relic in a twentieth-century world, the country had no roads, no wheeled vehicles, and for all he knew, no radio transmitters. Not that he was sure Shambala was part of Tibet. The valley was just one of thousands of wrinkles in the vast Himalayas, a region so inaccessible it had never been completely mapped or politically contained.

He had owed the air force one last mission and they had come up with something incredible. "You're the man for the job," his wing commander had said. He had experience flying high-altitude recon flights over the Arctic, a camera in the cold belly of the plane mapping that frozen hell, but those flights were over open air space no one gave a damn about. This one had smacked of something dreamed up by the cloak and dagger boys.

His gut reaction to the mission had been bad from the moment they hustled him out of London and packed him off to a secret landing field chopped out of the jungle near Calcutta. They couldn't use a regular airport because they had to keep his spy plane out of sight—shit would have hit the fan if the Red Chinese found out Nehru was letting the Western allies use India as a base for a peek at the mountains.

They risked his life but kept him in the dark about the importance of reconning five-mile-high mountains. The only clue he got was from his wing commander as the man walked him to the plane. "There's something up there," he had said, "bigger than the bloody bomb! We've got to find it before the Chinks grab it."

Bigger than the bomb . . .

The mountains surrounding the valley sure as hell fit that description. They were big even by the standards of the mountain range that made up the Roof of the World. The biggest of the Titans, the ones the monks referred to as the "great mountain," was the one he buried the nose of the plane in. The remains of the primeval glacier that carved the valley still clung to the mountain. Where the glacier ended, sharp ridges began that soon tapered into rolling hills blanketed with white flowers that created an impression of frosting on the hills.

Between the lamasery and the rolling hills was the

Lake of Celestial Reflection, its pure waters mirroring the snowcapped mountains and gold-roofed lamasery in form and color no artist living or dead could match. On nights of the full moon, he sat by the window and watched the ghostly reflection of the lamasery and mountains dance on the wind ripples of the lake.

In the early dawn, while the mist was rising and spreading across the sky, the land stirred and women entered the waist-high fields of barley on the other side of the lake and sang as they worked, the whisper of their melody floating down the hills and across the water, carried on the cool breeze that drifted off the glacier and flowed down to the valley floor.

Shambala was a blind man's vision, pure imagination unprejudiced by nature's imperfections.

And of all the incredible luck—he had fallen into the valley he had been sent to find. It had to be the place. There couldn't be two *green* valleys on top of the Himalayas. The only things that grew that high were snow and misery.

More than that, he had fallen into a lost world, a lush, green paradise untouched by the evils of modern "civilization."

The only mar was his battered body. He touched his face with his fingertips, feeling the scars, the jagged edges. He had to find a mirror. The flesh had healed, but he suspected some of the pieces of his face didn't fit back the same as they had been before the crash. The rest of his body hadn't fared too well, either. An ugly scar ran from his bad knee to his groin. That wound worried the hell out of him. Not so much the knee, it would be okay as soon as he shook the stiffness out, but his manhood. He'd heard of men who got their nuts shot off and were shipped home no better than eunuchs. Hadn't Hemingway written about a guy like that? All of his own plumbing seemed to be there, but he worried that the raging

infection that had set into the wounds could have
damaged his . . .

He didn't want to think about it. He diverted his
thoughts to the bastards who'd organized the mission.
It had become a habit to stop worrying and direct
some hate toward the brass. They had sent him in a
defective plane over the highest mountains in the
world. On his last mission. *Last mission*. The thought
haunted him.

If his body hadn't taken such a savage beating in
the crash, he would have been thrilled to have discovered Shambala. He felt like a guy who on the
same day was told he had inherited a fortune and had
terminal cancer. He was constantly feeling his face,
trying to determine if there were any scars. If he just
had a mirror he could get it off his mind. He had
improved upon his Tibetan by speaking to the monks
and reading a dusty volume of the *Tibetan Book of
the Dead* he found under the bed, but he had not been
able to communicate the fact he needed a mirror to
see his face. He didn't know if the lamasery lacked
mirrors—or if the monks were hiding his face from
him.

He knew he'd feel better about Shambala when he
had his full strength back and could make the trip
back over the mountains. How long would it take to
make it back to India on foot? Weeks? Months? It
didn't matter, he had to do it. Shambala was a charming place, ascetics and anthropologists would love the
valley, but it wasn't for him. He had to get home. He
had a girl waiting for him and a new life to begin.

Amy.

He had never believed in love, not until he met her.
There hadn't been anyone in his life to love or be
loved. Raised in an orphanage, he had lied about his
age to enter the air force and in eight years worked
his way from washing the tires of airplanes to flying

one. He had a knack, not just for flying—anyone could *fly* a plane—but that rare sensitivity of eye and hand that wartime aces were gifted with.

Amy. Damn. She came to London on vacation from a small town in America, somewhere out west in California where gold was discovered, Mother Lode country, she called it.

They met on Waterloo Bridge on a glorious May morning that was unseasonably warm and bright. He was on a ten-day leave, wandering a bit aimlessly about the town, wondering if he was going to re-up after his last mission or get a job jockeying airliners. He was crossing the bridge, mulling over his future, when he saw her standing at the railing, her long, amber hair dancing in the salty breeze. He leaned near her on the railing and pretended to be interested in the river traffic as he watched her out of the corner of his eye. At first she averted her eyes shyly, then turned to him with girlish boldness and asked if his blue uniform meant he was in the navy.

Within minutes they were joking and laughing like old friends. She had walked to the middle of the bridge to watch the traffic on the Thames. "I cried for Vivian Leigh in *Waterloo Bridge*," she told him. She loved the movies and had been affected by the romanticism.

Hours later they sat shyly across from each other, separated by candlelight and breadsticks in the corner of a cozy Italian café. The days that followed were spent together. He rented a car and showed her the heart of England, Roman ruins in Bath and thatched cottages in the Cotswolds, Stow-on-the-Wold and Shakespeare's house near the Avon. They fell in love quickly, impulsively, and he made up his mind to leave the service and build a life with her.

He never told her he was an orphan. It started as a joke. Americans are so enthralled when they come from their young country and discover how "old" everything is in Britain. Farmhouses older than Mayan temples, Roman ruins predating Christ, and Druid ruins predating Romans. She asked eager questions about his "heritage" and he told her tales of his "family," a lineage of hearty Scots farmers who shaped plowshares into swords to fight beside Bonnie Prince Charlie and Robert the Bruce, of the big old house where he was raised, a fireplace in every room, even the bathrooms, and the meadows where he ran as a boy, the creek he fished and the forest beyond that he explored and built a fort in to defend against the Krauts.

The lies put a lump in his throat. The boyhood was the one he had fantasized a thousand times as he lay awake on a bunk bed in the institution's dormitory and wondered what it would be like to have a real family. With Amy he could make his dreams come true.

On his last night in London they went to a movie, and she cried when Audrey Hepburn as the errant princess left somber newspaperman Gregory Peck to return to the palace after her *Roman Holiday*. "I would have married a prince and kept Gregory Peck as my lover on the sly," she told him, leaving the theater.

They stopped at a little wine shop near the bed-and-breakfast place where she was staying. A cheap bottle of bubbling domestic was all they were able to buy, but to them it was champagne.

"When you're in love it's all champagne," he told her.

She laughed. She laughed at everything he said.

When they reached the hotel, he carried her up the last flight of stairs as she nibbled his ear and kissed his neck.

They grabbed a blanket, two paper cups, a candle

and her radio, and went up to the roof. While he set out the picnic blanket, she tuned in romantic music. They popped the cork and toasted the moon, the stars, and each other.

The wine was more bubble than grape, the radio squeaked, the candle was a little crooked, and gray ghosts sneaking in from the North Sea threatened to put a wet damper on the precious moment, but not even Fred Astaire and Ginger Rogers felt more enchantment than he and Amy waltzing on the rooftop, intoxicated with the night, with each other.

She pressed deeper against him, losing herself in his arms as a cold, wet breeze rattled across the roof. *Rain, rain, go away, come again some other day*, she whispered against his cheek.

He touched his cheek, remembering the warmth of her cheek against his, the exciting press of her body.

Rain, Rain, go away.

It came down despite the plea, and they grabbed the blanket and ran laughing for the door to the stairs. Amy fumbled with the doorknob, but it wouldn't budge. He tried it and they burst out laughing again. They had locked themselves out.

They squeezed together under the eave of the stairwell cover, holding each other close, wrapped in the blanket, hidden by the rainfall.

She trembled as thunder shook the sky and he held her tighter. Their lips touched, softly, tenderly, then with the impatience of new love; unafraid, their bodies melted into one.

He remembered the smell of her hair, the taste of rain and wine on her lips, the beat of her heart in his palm as he caressed her breast. His hand searched private places, slipping into her panties; she opened like a flower cup kissed by the sun, and they loved until he exploded and she cried out from joy, from innocence lost.

They exchanged eternal vows, promising not only love and fidelity but an exciting new life together . . .

Would Amy wait? She said she would, but he had been due home in a few weeks. What would Amy think when the news came that he was missing—presumed dead? Go on with her life, that's what she'd do. She'd mourn for him, but she was young and someday soon she'd meet another man, maybe another man in uniform on a bridge somewhere. But she was such a romantic, maybe . . . no, that's stupid, he thought. She wouldn't throw herself on the funeral pyres for him. She'd do what everyone else would do—cry and then find solace in another man's arms.

Thoughts of her in the arms of another man sent poison shooting through his system.

He rejected the idea that a rescue mission would find him. The odds were too great. He had lost radio contact at least a couple of hundred miles before the crash. Besides, there was that mist, a fine layer of ice crystals, the building blocks of clouds hovering over the valley like a dome, trapping in the heat and obscuring the valley from aerial view because the crystals magnified the glare from the sun and snowy mountains. From the valley floor the mist was hardly noticeable, just a light haze slightly filtering an incredibly blue Himalayan sky and bright amber sun. But he hadn't seen the valley from the air until he lost altitude; the reflected glare made the region appear as just another part of the whiteout of snow and ice clinging to the sky-high mountains.

The Himalayas were the most uncharted region on the face of the earth. The camera in the belly of his plane had been destroyed in the crash, but even if he had completed the mission and returned to the landing field near Calcutta, the film wouldn't have shown the brass anything about Shambala.

The mist was an inversion layer that trapped the

heat of the sun, creating a greenhouse effect that kept the valley warm and lush in the heart of a frozen wasteland. He remembered something from the Bible, something about God putting a mist over Eden to create a paradise for Adam and Eve. He had fallen into the Tibetan Eden.

He felt his face again. What if he was scarred? Ugly? Impotent? What if Amy took one look and—

Hell, he couldn't be that bad. He got burned, sure, and his face felt funny, numblike, but he was all there. Except for facial hair. He didn't need to shave because he was getting just a little facial hair, just a couple of patches. A guy with a scar on his chin in his RAF wing once told him he couldn't grow a beard because hair doesn't grow through scar tissue. But his own face couldn't be that bad. Probably something in those minty leaves that the monks laid across the wounds on his face retarded the growth of facial hair. The thought was intriguing. He could make a fortune back home selling it not just to men but to women for their legs.

He might not get rich selling hair remover, but famous he'd be for sure. He'd found a lost world. He'd make the front page of the Sunday papers and the telly, too. Probably give him a medal. Honors list? Not likely, though he went through a hell of a lot more than Hillary did climbing Everest. He'd tackle climbing a mountain any day over riding a burning plane into the side of one.

He thought about Amy again, in the railway station saying good-bye. *Don't think about it.* Think about Shambala. Think about the bastards that did this to you. Think about anything but Amy with tears in her eyes telling him to hurry home. Amy in another man's arms.

He took deep breaths, trying to shake off the gloom. Sticking around Shambala for a while could be interesting, he told himself. Like Dilly said, there were places lost in the vast Himalayas where the natives thought white men were gods just because of the color of their skin. He had to be the first white-skinned, green-eyed person they'd ever seen in Shambala. Monks who brought him food stared at him as if he'd just stepped in from another planet. More than respect, more than curiosity, the monks treated him with fear—as if he had the power to strike them dead with a stare.

The woman intrigued him, too. She had stopped coming to his room as soon as he had regained full consciousness and was able to sit up in bed. From what he observed from his window, the monks carried her in a palanquin whenever she left the lamasery. Like a queen. The only time he saw her by herself was at night as she walked along the shore of the lake in the moonlight.

His instincts told him he'd get more information about Shambala in a few minutes alone with her than he had during the weeks he had tried to wheedle information from the monks who brought his food.

He stopped whittling and examined the cane. A bit rough, slightly crooked. Like my leg, he thought. Using the cane for support, he hobbled around the room, a little clumsily but he had his feet back under him! Tonight he would leave the room while the monks were at dinner. To speak to the woman when she was walking around the lake.

And get a closer look at his lost world.

CHAPTER 9

After the fall of dark he saw her walking toward the lake and he left his room, limping with the cane.

The corridor was lit by yak-butter lamps. The walls and ceiling were composed of a strange, dark-green marble thickly veined with gold. Rich tapestries and elaborate murals were placed on the walls like gems in a setting. The woman in red robes, snow leopards, and dragons seemed to be the main artistic theme. The tapestries were finer in color and detail than the one in his monk's cell. Thoughts of monetary value popped into his mind as he wondered what such ancient treasures could be worth, but he realized that the artwork that adorned the corridor was priceless, sacred richness one imagines can be found only in the inner sanctum of the Vatican and the most powerful citadels of Islam.

He crept along, trying to make as little noise as possible with his cane, a snail that had wiggled out of its protective shell.

At the end of the corridor he came out on a landing above a courtyard that filled the center of the lamasery. He could make out only large detail in the moonlight—ponds, statues, and shrubs. He went down the stairway slowly, leaning on his cane for support. No one was around. Chanting came from the communal dining room somewhere below.

Om Mani Padme Hum!

"O Jewel in the Heart of the Lotus!"

The mystical mantra was chanted daily by the mountain people in the belief that the words created a spiritual bond between them and the very heavens.

While he had been confined to bed, half conscious, his body raw, the hypnotic chant had flowed into his room twice a day when the monks sat down to meals; he imagined the mystical sounds entering his wounds, hurrying the healing process. He remembered, too, a woman's sweet voice, whispering the mantra to him . . .

The main gate was wide open and unguarded. No guard was necessary, he thought. This was paradise.

Walking softly, he approached the woman, not wanting to disturb the magic of the moment. She was utterly mystifying in a white silken sari that flowed from her shoulders to her ankles, a forest nymph, picking the petals of lotus blossoms and casting them into the waters. Blue moonlight turned the lake the color of dark mountain wine.

The scent of the lotus blossoms rode the gentle breeze. The ancients believed the fruit of the lotus created a dreamy languor when eaten. Ulysses was bewitched by a lotus queen during his travels. Duncan walked slowly toward the lake, bewitched by the moonlight, the lotus, the woman.

She turned to face him, expressing no surprise, as if she had sensed his presence long before she heard the fall of his steps.

"I saw you from my window," he said.

She looked away shyly. "I come here at night. The lake is my . . . mentor, my guru. I talk to it."

"I'll go back upstairs if you want to be alone."

"No, please, share my walk this night."

He walked beside her along the shore of the lake, conscious of a perfection about her and the lake that made him feel like a pebble among gems.

"The lake is beautiful." And so are you, he thought.

"It is the loveliest beneath heaven. The Lord Buddha walked along these very shores over two thousand years ago. The cups of water he drew from the lake turned to tea to refresh him."

Across the lake was the great mountain. His plane was up there, buried under snow and ice. A wave of anger shot through him. She looked at him with concern and he shook his head. "I'm sorry. I've stared at that mountain for weeks and it hasn't bothered me. I looked up this time and got hit with memories."

"Memories of your people in the Western Heaven?"

"The Western Heaven. That's an interesting name for where I'm from. In comparison with Shambala, some people might say I come from the Western Hell."

"I . . . I do not understand."

"What I mean is that things are so crowded and hectic where I come from, people there would call this valley God's country. How much do you know about the . . . Western Heaven?"

"You are the first person that has come to Shambala from that strange land. Pathfinders, monks who have been trained in the secret ways of the mountains, occasionally cross and bring us word of the valleys beyond Shambala, but in truth we know little of the Western Heaven. Is it a place like Shambala?"

"Hardly. It's vast, a million Shambalas."

"What are the people like?"

He shrugged. "I suppose people everywhere are more or less the same. They have jobs, family, friends—" He stopped. There were no Tibetan words to describe cars and planes, cities of concrete and glass, movies, television, mortgages. Shambala probably didn't even have books other than the musty old volumes of the *Tibetan Book of the Dead* used in the religion.

"You've never been out of this valley, have you?"

She avoided his eyes and dropped the last of the lotus blossoms she was holding into the water. She stared for a moment at the petals floating on the dark waters. "In truth, I was born in a valley many days' journey from here. Monks of Shambala found me there, guided to me by the signs that said the spirit of the Tashivaana had come to rest in me after the thirty-first Tashivaana had passed beyond sorrow."

A "Tashivaana" must be some sort of Incarnate, Duncan thought. What had the Oriental history expert who briefed him said? Lamaism, the particular variety of Buddhism practiced in Tibet, had many Incarnates, with the Dalai Lama, the "Great Lama," held in the highest esteem. An Incarnate was the living spirit of an Enlightened One, a person who had obtained *nirvana,* the state of perfect blessedness achieved by the extinction of individual existence, all desires and passions gone. The spirit occupies the body of a living person through a process of reincarnation, usually entering the mother's womb at the time of the person's birth.

"Reincarnation is what we call it," Duncan said. "Not many people from where I'm from believe in it. It's more common here in the Orient."

"The Orient?"

"That's what people in the Western Heaven call the, uh, Eastern Heaven. How old were you when the monks found you?"

"I was seven."

"Then you must remember something of what it's like beyond Shambala."

She glanced back at the lamasery. "I remember a little. A farm . . ." She stared out at the lake. "Sometimes at night my mother held me in her arms and sang to me."

"Do you miss that life?" he asked.

"I am Tashivaana. My spirit is not of this world but of the Other."

The monks probably had her say that over and over, he thought. Brainwashing her since she was a kid.

"What exactly is a . . . Tashivaana?"

"Tashivaana is the She-Demon." She smiled at the look on his face. "A good demon. A long time ago, before the race of people who populated the earth came to be, this valley was ruled by a She-Demon called Tashivaana. The She-Demon was powerful, but an even more powerful demon, a bad demon, a red dragon with seven heads, came to the valley. Tashivaana sent a message on all the winds of the world, a call for help from a hero who could conquer the red dragon. The call was answered by the Monkey-King, a great warrior who came to the valley from beyond the western mountains."

"From India?"

"Beyond India, from a land without a name. The Monkey-King flew to the valley on the back of a great snow leopard and battled the red dragon from the leopard's back. The leopard fell during the battle, and Tashivaana became one with the beast." She fingered the snow leopard pendant hanging from the chain she wore around her neck. "The leopard rose and carried the Monkey-King to victory against the red dragon."

"I remember a legend," he said, "in my studies about Tibet. Tibetans believe they and all mankind are the product of a mating between a Monkey-King and a She-Demon."

"Yes. After the battle was won the She-Demon changed shape and took the womanly form of Tashivaana again. She became the mate of the Monkey-

King and from their loins came the race of people that walk upon the earth."

"And now you bear the title?"

"I *am* Tashivaana."

"Do other woman live in the lamasery?"

The question caught her by surprise. "Other women?"

"I've only seen you. And the monks."

"I am the only woman in the lamasery."

"It is lonely for you?"

"I . . . I am Tashivaana. I am never alone. I share my soul with a thousand women who have come before me."

Up to that moment she had been a porcelain doll to him, pretty but not quite real. Now he saw the woman struggling underneath the glaze and instantly felt sorry for her. The monks had turned her into a piece of stone to worship—at the price of her womanhood.

"When it came time for the Monkey-King to leave this life and pass beyond sorrow, he built a great tomb for his mortal body. Tashivaana swore an oath to protect and defend that tomb until it became time for the Monkey-King to once again rise. Before he entered the tomb he placed the Frost of Heaven over the valley to keep the valley warm and lush, for the dragon's breath had made the rest of the world barren."

"When is the Monkey-King supposed to rise?"

"When the dragon returns and the Vale of Shambala is again threatened. Until that time the soul of Tashivaana will occupy the body of mortal women. I am the thirty-second Tashivaana. After the death of the thirty-first Tashivaana, the monks searched the valley and the valleys beyond our mountains for the girl-child in whom the spirit came to rest. I was that girl-child and, like the women before me, I became

Tashivaana and will defend the land and the tomb
with my life."

The body of mortal women. Reincarnation. She
was a living goddess, but what about the mortal
woman? What about love and family and being a
woman to a man? Could she really be happy as an
object of worship to a bunch of dusty monks? If that
was the only life she knew, she would accept it without question. Did she know what was going on in the
outside world? That the Chinese ambitions to annex
Tibet, held in check for thousands of years by Tibet's
savage mountains, could now become a reality in an
age of air travel?

"Strange," he said, "about your legend. Tibetans
call the Chinese, their ancient enemy, the 'dragon
people' and the dragon is the symbol of China. I suppose now that the Communists are running the country, it's a red dragon. Are you aware that the Red
Chinese are making threatening moves against Tibet?
To us, in the West, it seems a forgone conclusion that
the Chinese will invade Tibet sometime in the near
future. That's why . . ."

He almost told her that was the reason he had been
sent in a spy plane. There was something in Tibet that
the Western allies didn't want the Chinese to get their
hands on, but then he remembered—*that something
was Shambala!* It couldn't just be curiosity about a
valley lost in time. There had to be a military angle.

"I know not of the things you speak of but if a red
dragon threatens Shambala, the Monkey-King will
rise and drive it from the valley."

Not unless he's packing thermonuclear weapons,
Duncan thought.

She hesitated, as if she were reluctant to say something, then plunged into it. "You caused great excitement when you flew into the valley on the back of a
creature with silver wings. Many monks thought the

Monkey-King had risen. We have waited a thousand-thousand years for the return of the champion."

No wonder the monks treated him so strangely. There must have been mass hysteria when his plane shot out of the haze and did a nosedive into the mountain.

"How do you know I'm not the Monkey-King?" He said it as a joke and instantly regretted it when she responded with a look of fright and awe.

She shot a glance in the direction of the lamasery. "The High Lama and the council decreed that you are not."

"Almost a legend," he said with a wry smile. "Do you remember anything of what life was like outside the valley?"

"I remember," she said almost in a whisper, as if the lake beside them had ears and memories were a sin, "the day the monks came to our farm. There was much excitement. It is a great honor for the family when an Incarnate is discovered within it. My family were poor farmers, and none had even suspected that the spirit of the Tashivaana had come to rest in one of its daughters."

"Seven years old," Duncan said. Their Incarnate died and the monks waited for clues, the "signs" that would lead them to the person in whom the spirit of the Tashivaana had entered. The Oriental history expert said the "signs" usually led to a bright, healthy child of three or four. Duncan hadn't thought of it when he was listening to the lectures on Tibetan history at the briefing, but there was probably a good reason the kids were selected at that age. They were weaned and out of diapers, but not filled with memories of family that might stay with them and haunt them. At seven she was old enough to remember.

The Shambalan monks probably didn't have as many "candidates" to choose from as a less isolated region would. They'd first look in the valley and when they couldn't find a suitable female-child, they'd have to make the hazardous trip outside. And be forced to take a seven-year-old that might retain memories of family when a suitable three- or four-year-old could not be found. "It must have been hard on you, seven years old and taken from your mother."

"I did not belong to my mother. The spirit of the Tashivaana flows within me. It entered my mother's womb and became one with the child growing there." Her words were a rehearsed speech and she stared beyond him, in mind's eye, to a farm and a family she once knew. "I remember the day the monks came for me. People laughed and danced with joy after the High Lama tested me and proclaimed that I was the Incarnate. I looked back as the monks carried me away . . . looked back and saw my mother as the others danced and sang with joy. She was crying and I wondered why she would cry. I thought it was only a game, that the monks would tire of playing and send me back to my mother. But I . . . I never saw her again."

"Your mother cried because she had lost someone she loved. You must have cried, too."

"I cried. At so young an age great honors are not so easily understood. And you," she said, heading off another question from him, "have you ever lost someone you loved?"

Memories welled up inside, choking him: the girl he'd left behind in London, their arms desperately around each other as they said good-bye at Victoria Station. He touched his cheek, remembering the softness of her cheek against his, her warm, tender tears. His fingers crawled over the scars on his face and he flinched.

The woman saw his pain and reached out and touched him, only to quickly glance back at the lamasery and step back from him, averting her eyes.

"We're sort of in the same boat," he said.

She shook her head, confused.

"Life has treated us the same. The monks"—he nodded in the direction of the lamasery—"took you away from your loved ones without ever asking if that's what you wanted. The brass—my superiors back home—treated me the same way. They needed a pilot good at hopping over mountaintops and volunteered me. No one gave a damn about our feelings, about yanking us out of our niche, as long as they got what they wanted."

"I am here because it is my duty."

"Duty?" He ran his fingers over the jagged edges. "I suppose I got these because it was my duty."

"The scars that make men ugly are on their souls, not their faces."

He laughed harshly. "Not in the Western Heaven." He struggled to get control of himself. *The poison.* Hate threatened to take control of him, spreading through his system like an oil fire.

"You must not think of the crash."

"I can't think of anything else. I had a girl. We were in love. She probably thinks I'm dead now."

"Love. It is a strange word. The feeling of a man and woman for each other. I am full of love, but not for any one person. Tashivaana must love all. And be loved by all."

"That's not love, it's worship. Haven't you ever been in love with a man?"

"No. That would be sacrilege." She hesitated again and looked beyond him, remembering. "Once, long ago, I treated the wounds of another man, a young monk new to the lamasery. He was injured in a fall and I came to his bedside and helped heal his wounds just as I came to your bedside. We . . . we grew to be very . . . close."

"Did you love him?"

"Tashivaana loves all."

"*Did you love him?*"

"He . . . he went away. He tried to cross the mountains." She looked up at the mountain, the great sentinel guarding—imprisoning—the valley. "Storms rage in the mountains. Only the Pathfinders know the secret ways and can survive. No one else can cross."

The mountains, so beautiful, he thought. So dangerous. Guarding a valley older than time. Guarding it or holding it captive? She did have a lover. The Monkey-King. A lover dead for an eon worshipped by virgin queens.

The mountain was the secret to the valley. Not just a religious secret of musty old monks. A secret coveted by world powers. Whatever the top brass was after, it must be in the mountain.

"What's in the mountain?"

Her reaction surprised him. For a second her composure broke and she looked frightened. Had his question scared her—or *was she frightened of what was in the mountain?*

. "The tomb of the Monkey-King is in the mountain," she said.

"The tomb of the Monkey-King," he said, aloud, but more to himself than to her. "That's what it's all about . . . this valley, the lamasery. What's in the tomb that keeps it all ticking?"

She walked away as he stared hypnotically at the mountain. He started to call after her and stopped. Dark figures lined the wall of the lamasery like crows on a fence—monks watching them. It gave him cold chills. What's the word for a bunch of crows? *A murder.*

CHAPTER 10

Duncan left his room at midmorning the next day. His leg hurt and he limped a little, but the walk along the lake had limbered it up. He could have navigated without the cane and carried it more for security than need.

Sleep had not come easily after he returned from the lake. Memories boiled in his mind after he closed his eyes, flashes of a girl he'd left behind in London, his flight over the Himalayas, and the woman he walked with along the lake. No matter where his thoughts began, they always took him to flames licking at his face in a burning cockpit and to terrible pain that started in his groin and spread through the rest of his body.

He paused on the landing at the end of the corridor and blinked in the bright sunlight.

The entire lamasery was made of a gold-veined green marble. At the bottom was the courtyard he had seen by the light of the moon. The lamasery was built like an inverted Mayan temple: great stairways led from the courtyard up to the second level, then to the next level and the next.

The courtyard was a lush garden with pathways, ponds, and fountains. Vines laced with colorful flowers flowed beside each of the stairways, adding life to the richness no other garden has seen since Nebuchadnezzar's Hanging Gardens of Babylon. This was ice-bitter Tibet, he thought, yet before him was a tropical garden as green and moist as a rain forest.

He spotted her in the gardens below.

She was seated on a throne, a huge chunk of silver sculpted into the shape of a snow leopard and set beneath an arch of white lotus flowers. Half a dozen red-robed monks were standing around her. Her back was to him, and she did not turn and look even when the attention of the monks was drawn to him at the top of the stairs. A large golden bird cage sat next to the throne, and she was feeding the bird inside by hand.

He went down the stairs slowly, taking in the sights and sounds of the strange environment.

The lamasery wasn't medieval; it was older than that, older than the lofty worlds of Rome and Greece, already ancient when the Egyptians were planning their pyramids. There was an otherworldliness about the structure, shapes and forms that were not familiar, as if Shambala had developed entirely on its own, totally free of the influence of other civilizations.

He realized there was a pattern to the ten ponds in the garden. The center pond where the woman was seated had a wide band of gold around it; the other nine ponds were of varying size and distance from the central one. It was the solar system, the sun and nine planets. The rings of Saturn were presented as a rainbow of flowers circling a pond, little Pluto was a frigid white puddle.

He reached the bottom of the stairs and limped along a pathway toward the arch of lotus blossoms. Flocks of butterflies burst into flight in his path.

The monks around the woman moved back at his approach, butter fading from a hot knife. They were afraid of him; the thought gave him a shot of adrenaline.

She didn't rise and turn until he was nearly beside her.

He bowed his head slightly and spoke a greeting in Tibetan.

"You carry your cane as a stick," she said. Her manner was stiff and formal. "Your wounds heal well. It is said that the very air of Shambala is a healing loam that speeds recovery from ailments."

"I feel better."

She turned her attention back to the bird in the cage as she spoke. "You are free to go wherever you desire in the lamasery or the grounds outside. There are no restraints in Shambala."

"Thank you." He sensed more was coming and he waited as she fed the bird with grains in her palm. The bird was a delicate white with a green twist of feathers on its head.

"You are free to wander wherever you desire in the lamasery, but I regret that we shall not be able to speak again. My duties are such that this must be our last meeting. I . . . I must devote most of each day to meditation and prayer."

Duncan's jaws tightened. The group of monks were hanging back just within earshot, red-robed, bald men with wrinkled, ancient faces and dead eyes. He recognized the one with the richest robes and most precious jewels as the High Lama. The man had visited him in the early stages of recuperation in his room.

"Is that your preference," he asked her, "or orders from them?" He nodded at the monks.

"In Shambala, Tashivaana speaks for all. You must understand, our customs here are not the same as those in the Western Heaven. No one may speak to Tashivaana unless permission is granted. That permission comes from the High Lama."

They had got to her. Afraid I'll mess up their little game, he thought. He could play games, too. He was the stuff of legend in a land that thrived on legends.

He spoke slowly to make sure the High Lama and the monks nearby would catch his words. "The Red Chinese will be moving into Tibet any time now. When they do, it'll just be a matter of time until they stumble onto this place."

She looked past him, refusing to meet his eye. "It is written that the Monkey-King will rise when Shambala is in danger—"

"Your religion says that the She-Demon is to guard the tomb of the Monkey-King until he returns to claim his kingdom. I flew here over the mountains from the west on the wings of a silver beast."

"When the danger comes," she said, still avoiding his eyes, "it is written that the She-Demon will recognize the Monkey-King by the fact that he is the man to whom she will give her love. I am the thirty-second Tashivaana, She-Demon of Shambala, and none but the first Tashivaana, who gave her love to the Monkey-King, has ever given her love to a man. And none will until it is time for the return of the Monkey-King."

"I don't understand what you mean about recognizing the man you will love."

"He will have Shambala in his heart."

"Shambala in his heart?"

"He . . . he will be pure of heart and soul, strong, but filled with love for all. The High Lama has decreed that the spirit of the Monkey-King will occupy the body of a man perfect in mind and form. He . . . he will not be . . . broken." She avoided his eyes. "I am sorry. I must be alone to meditate."

He left in a daze, hot flashes of rage and humiliation shearing through him. *Broken*. He had tried to intimidate them and had it thrown back in his face. His reflection stared back at him as he passed a silver-bottomed pool. He gasped and cried out, touching his face with his hands.

It wasn't just the face of a stranger; it was burned and twisted and scarred beyond what he considered humanly recognizable. *He was a monster.*

The High Lama approached the woman as Duncan walked away. She stared at the caged bird as she spoke. "That was cruel."

"It was necessary."

"He is lonely."

"And you, Tashivaana, are you lonely?"

I am Tashivaana. I am never alone. The words had been ingrained into her, but they wouldn't come this time. Opening the door of the bird cage, she reached in with both hands, gently grasping the bird, careful not to injure its fluttering wings. She brought the bird out and kissed it, then opened her hands and let it fly.

The bird flew around the garden before zooming up, over the lamasery wall, disappearing from sight in the direction of the lake.

The High Lama shook his head. "The bird is a stranger to the land. It has been hand fed and will not survive in the wild."

"Better dead than caged."

Duncan stood at the window as the celestial fireworks of the Frost of Heaven exploded in the night sky.

He wasn't watching the dazzling light show, wasn't enchanted by the magic. He stared at the great mountain and the glacier that hugged it like a parasitic leech. Why hadn't they left him to die in the burning wreckage? It would have been *his* tomb.

He could never go home. He was a monster. *Monster.* The word rotted his mind. His thoughts went to a pretty girl he had danced with on a rooftop. He imagined her in another man's arms, and it sent another jolt of poison through him. She would never be in his arms again. No woman would. He was not a whole man.

The words spoken to him by the woman had reopened his wounds and the fever that had racked his body for weeks had come back. He ached from fires within and shivered from the cold draft from the window.

They had made him a monster, the machinations of men and nations, greedy bastards coveting the secret of the ages. The prize was there, in the tomb of the Monkey-King. The power source sought by nations. The ponds in the courtyard had given him the clue that had solved the mystery.

He understood the secret the brass had not made him privy to at the briefing. Something in the mountains was producing the mist that hovered over the valley and locked in the heat, an energy source so incredibly powerful it had been operating since time immemorial. "Bigger than the bloody Bomb!" the wing commander had said. Bigger than the Bomb for sure, Duncan thought. Bigger than anything on earth. Power that was a spark from the sun.

He knew what the power source was, knew who the Monkey-King was.

He had found the secret that the world powers coveted.

He staggered to the bed and collapsed on it, tangling himself in the heap of blankets to smother the chills.

He awoke in the middle of the night to find someone beside his bed. He shot up, sitting erect.

"Shhh."

It was the woman.

"I must not be found here. I came to warn you."

"Warn me?" He tried to shake sleep from his head;

fuzziness stuffed his head ear to ear. His bones ached and he shivered. The yak-butter candle next to the bed was almost spent.

"You must not talk to me again. Ever."

"Today—"

"I know. That is why I came. They made me say those terrible things. I am so sorry." Her fingers touched the scars on his face.

"Broken," he said. His voice cracked as he spoke the word. "Not just my face. My body, my manhood."

"They made me say those words. They are afraid of you, afraid of what you will tell me about the world beyond Shambala."

He pulled the blankets higher. She was dressed in a simple woolen nightgown and showed no sign that the freezing temperature in the room affected her.

"Someday a plane without a bad engine is going to make it through the mist layer and find this valley. When it does and the power source in that mountain is discovered, the superpowers will fight over Shambala like dogs scrapping over a bone."

Alarm registered on her face. "That must not happen!"

"It's . . . going . . . to . . . happen." His teeth chattered, breaking his sentence into chips. He started to say something and she sealed his lips with her fingers.

"Shhh."

Footsteps sounded in the corridor, not hurried steps, but more of a shuffle. Someone on a call of nature in the middle of the night.

"I came to tell you I was sorry about my words. And to warn you not to approach me again. The young monk I told you about, the one whose wounds I treated, he was forced to leave the valley because I befriended him. They took him up the mountain."

"That doesn't sound so harsh."

"No one can leave the valley. All the paths across

They don't kill people in Shambala. *The mountain killed!*

He started to shout to her as the door to his room burst open. He grabbed the chair next to the window as monks poured into the room, swinging at the first man before he went down.

They pinned him to the floor and tied his hands behind his back. They turned him over onto his back as a monk lugged a stone urn filled with red-hot coals into the room and set it on the floor beside Duncan. A steel poker stuck out of the ashen pile.

The High Lama came into the room and stood over Duncan.

"The Council of Elders have made their decision. What you have done . . . the sin you committed . . . no man had ever dared before. You have brought into Shambala the poison from your own world. Better you had died when you fell from the sky. Now you cannot be sent back up the mountain. You survived the mountain once; the council will not risk you surviving again, to carry tales of Shambala back to your own world.

"Punishment by death is forbidden in Shambala, even for one who has committed the greatest sin," the High Lama whispered. "Your eyes must be darkened so you can never again see a treasure you want to steal or a tradition you want to violate, and you must be hidden away, in the bowels of the earth where no man will ever look upon you again and be reminded of your sin."

A scream came from the lamasery. The woman swung around and stared at the window to Duncan's room.

"What . . . what are they doing to him?"

Neither monk would meet her eye. She started back for the lamasery and they stopped her.

She spoke to the shorter of the two monks. "Hying,

I cared for you when you were ill." The purple thread on the collar of his robe identified him as a Pathfinder, one of the select few who knew the secret to crossing the mountains. "Please, I must go back. I must help him. They do not understand."

Hying looked away.

The other monk took her by the arm and turned her back toward the mountain.

Tears flowed down her cheeks as they led her away.

CALCUTTA

CHAPTER 11

*In the middle of the journey of life, I found myself
in a dark wood, having lost the straight path.*
                                                —Dante

Peter stood spellbound in the middle of the Calcutta
air terminal, experiencing the same fascination as
a young boy seeing a naked woman for the first time.

Dum Dum Airport was a kaleidoscope of personalities and a clash of cultures. Rich European and
Eastern women moved quickly in their painted-on
jeans, silk blouses, and high heels; Japanese businessmen walked with extreme efficiency, allowing
their briefcases to polish their appearance, while tall,
East African males with bushy hair moved through
the crowds with the rhythm of pure soul, their women
in stunning peacock clothing, flaunting their wealth
with layers of gold earrings, often showing more gold
than ear. Muslim women with their faces covered,
exposing only their deep-secret eyes, kept their distance from Hindu women with delicate stars painted
on their foreheads.

The Indians knew the best way to dress and keep
cool; white linen or cotton material, loosely draped
over their bodies. Peter's dark suit stood out like a
black toadstool in a field of white flowers.

He stepped outside and the air smacked him in the
face; it was oven hot, stale and wet, with the salty
taste of a steam room.

The fear that he was being followed suddenly
struck him and he swung around. People glanced cu-
riously at him as they shouldered by. You're as dum

dum as the airport, he told himself. But the feeling of being watched stayed with him.

He passed up the first taxi in line and the second, remembering Sherlock Holmes's tactic for avoiding traps by taking the third in line. The cabbies he passed over each seemed to know enough English to damn him, his mother, and several generations past. A pamphlet he found in the seat pocket on the plane told him that Indians involved in commerce or government usually spoke some degree of English if for no other reason than there were so many native tongues in the country that English became the unofficial-official language by default.

The chosen taxi was a battered Datsun that looked as if it had made a stop at the Gulf War. Even the dents had dents.

"Downtown Calcutta," he told the driver, a gum-chewing, long-haired Indian youth wearing a baseball cap, tie-dyed jeans, and a Delhi University T-shirt. He needed a haircut, a shave, and a bath. A roach clip was on the dashboard; a cultural import from the American 1960s, no doubt. But the baseball cap told a different story to the roach clip: it was Japanese.

The dusty backseat was as comfortable as the rack of an oven. And as dirty. It looked like people had died on it. Or maybe they just melted from the heat. It smelled like well-done flesh, too.

After the taxi got moving, Peter exercised his paranoia again and glanced out the dirty back window. He was being followed all right, by a hundred other taxis and cars in a kamikaze race into the city.

"Know a good hotel?" he asked the driver.

The kid popped his gum and tilted the baseball cap back a little before he answered. "Sleep as Indian with rats, good hotel, six rupee." He smirked at Peter in the rearview mirror. "English sahib sleep no rats, six hundred rupee."

At the current exchange rate, Peter calculated the range at from $2 to $200 a day.

"How about something a little more than Indian and a lot less than English?"

It occurred to him how amazing it was that he had been in the country only minutes and had already discovered that a taxi driver knew enough English to cuss him or recommend a hotel. Christ, what would happen to some poor Indian who climbed into a cab at LAX or JFK and asked directions to the nearest Hilton in Hindi? Americans were smug and spoiled, he thought. Yeah, the kid could speak a little English, but the car and the hat were Japanese . . .

The India he whizzed through wasn't the one romanticized by Hollywood. Instead of the exotic East, he got the emerging Third World. He hung onto the dusty seat with sweaty hands as the Delhi U. kid made an end run around a battered old Rover, then shot by a battered new Japanese compact, nearly clipping an ox and cart as he swerved to avoid a hole in the road big enough to swallow the ox.

The city flying by was everything Peter expected and nothing he imagined: chrome-and-glass skyscrapers housing international banks nudged dingy cardboard stalls where potions were sold to ward off evil spells, while high-rise apartment complexes towered over slums so squalid they looked like a pit stop before hell.

The taxi jerked to a stop in front of a seven-story pink stucco, Mediterranean-style building.

"Royal Bengal," the driver said. "Sixty rupee for ride."

Sixty sounded like he was being ripped off. The thought flashed but he was too embarrassed to act like an Ugly American and confront the kid over money. He gave him eighty rupees. The driver pocketed the inflated fare and overgenerous tip and flipped Peter a smirking "Thanks, Sahib!"

Peter stepped out of the taxi and into the arms of a horde of dirty beggars. An old man with half his jaw eaten away from cancer led the pack, shoving the last two fingers of a rotted hand in Peter's face.

"Baksheesh! Baksheesh!"

Oh, God! Poor bastards!

He spread money around eager hands until the pack retreated as the hotel doorman came running, screaming Bengali curses at them.

"Beggars are lice of Calcutta," the doorman told Peter as he opened the front door for him. "Feed them and they multiply."

He didn't say anything. He was so shook up he had not even looked at the denominations of the money he passed out. Poverty, disease, and misery had a hell of a lot more impact hands-on than it had had from the backseat of a taxi.

He caught the reflection of a passing car in the plate glass and swung around as a black limo slowly rolled by the hotel. The driver was a huge man with pudgy, Mongol features, the passenger a short creature with cruel lips.

His old friends from London.

They knew he was in Calcutta, knew where he was staying. He wondered if they had reserved a room for him at the Royal Bengal. Maybe an adjoining suite to Lisper and pals.

His paranoia suddenly became reality.

Between the front doors and the dark, cool lobby was a courtyard restaurant, lush with banana and date palms shading scattered wicker tables and chairs; white-coated waiters served fruit juices and booze to guests lounging in the shade of the palms. The Royal Bengal was a charmer, the sort of place he'd expect

Ingrid Bergman to stay in Casablanca when she went to see Bogie.

A patronizing clerk with a twenty-four-carat smile imprinted his AMEX card. The gold teeth were amazing; Peter could image thieves going after them with a pair of pliers.

"There usually that many beggars outside?" Peter asked.

The gold smile widened. "Two hundred thousand people sleep on the streets of Calcutta each night. Not everyone is so fortunate as to have an American Express card."

He almost told the clerk that American Express wanted the card back, and when they took it he'd be as prosperous as the people sleeping on the street, but he prudently kept his mouth shut and followed a porter to a cage elevator, smiling tightly as the tarnished brass cage shuddered up five stories.

The porter led him into his room and pointed at the two shaded windows. "No open till sun go. Two hours more."

He had no idea as to how much he was supposed to tip. He realized he had overtipped when he gave the porter ten rupees and the man gawked at it. He shut the door and told himself he was going to have to watch his money.

The room was wicker, wicker, and wicker, from bed to dresser to chair and nightstand. A rheumatoid ceiling fan achingly stirred the warm, moist air trapped in the room. Peter could appreciate the need for wicker—no doubt wood rusts in a climate wet enough to drink with a straw.

He had jet lag and culture shock but was too excited to sleep. He peeled off the suit that had molded to his skin, took a shower in tepid water that smelled of rotten eggs, then dressed in a cool pair of beige, lightweight cotton pants, and a dark blue shirt made out of the same casual material.

He left the room, passing up the quaint brass cage in favor of a solid set of stairs down to the lobby.

As he went across the courtyard, a man sipping a cool tropical drink at a shaded table watched him. The man had brown blotches on his face and wore the white collar of a priest. A carpetbag was at his feet.

Outside the entrance, Peter, by now a hardened veteran, quickly shot by the beggars. It was early dusk, and the heat that the porter had warned him not to let into his room was pressing heavy on the streets as he walked up the block and turned the corner, heading in the direction where the doorman told him decent restaurants were located.

The block was crowded with people camped out on the pavement—whole families, eating, sleeping, and no doubt excreting and copulating. A line from Kipling flew into his mind; the "sheeted dead" was what the poet had called them, the poor of Calcutta who wrapped thin blankets around themselves at night as they claimed a few feet of pavement as their only home.

He hurried, keeping his eyes straight ahead, a lump in his throat, embarrassed by the accident of birth that gave him an American Express card and a room at the Royal Bengal.

Something brushed his leg and he kicked out, thinking it was a dog. He looked down and choked. A beggar boy about ten or eleven was crawling beside him. The boy's bare arms and legs were stunted and grotesquely twisted; he crawled on all fours like a dog, with a tin begging cup hanging from a piece of rope around his neck.

"Baksheesh!" the child squealed.

Peter pushed a wad of rupee notes into the cup and dashed into the street, dodging traffic until he reached the other side with his heart pumping madly.

A well-fed Indian wearing a white linen suit and carrying a $500 briefcase spoke to Peter in English with an Oxford accent. "It is shocking, is it not? Would it shock you more to know that the child was probably purchased or stolen as a baby by a king of beggars who bound the child's limbs to stunt the growth?" The man nodded and clicked his tongue at the expression of disgust on Peter's face. "Crippling them, you see, makes for appealing beggars and keeps them at the mercy of the beggar king. It is good for business."

He stopped looking back to see if he was being followed by a black Mercedes as the Calcutta heat, which Mark Twain claimed could turn brass door-knobs mushy, fried his brains and made the rubber soles of his shoes squish like wet sponges.

He was a people watcher and Calcutta was a voyeur's wet dream. The city raped his senses as he staggered down pavements crowded with fierce-looking, black-bearded Sikhs with daggers in their belts, Bengalis wearing turbans and loincloths, dark-eyed women in flowing silk saris, businessmen in suits and ties, and gangs of kids splashing in the gutters flowing with brown water from fire hydrants and toilets.

Every few blocks a policeman wearing a pith helmet and white uniform stood under an umbrella in the middle of the intersection, somehow instilling order in the chaos of cars, trucks, ox carts, and rickshaws that scrambled down the street like Indy drivers jockeying for position. Sleigh bells on rickshaw wheels jingled, adding a touch of White Christmas to grimy Calcutta.

He watched a rickshaw moving away in the distance, carrying a dark-haired woman. Heat waves rose from the pavement, distorting the vision, bending reality; he imagined himself with a raven-haired beauty on a damp midnight walk in a London park.

Night had fallen and a timid breeze started flowing through the hot canyons of the city by the time he reached Park Street, the honkytonk bar and restaurant drag of the city. The sweat stains that appeared under the arms of his shirt the moment he'd left the hotel had spread down to his socks and he was ready for a light dinner and a lot of something cool to drink. He passed up street vendors selling lemon and lime juices from open jugs on carts after he noticed that flies were the vendors' best customers.

Park Street really brought home the incredible dichotomy between rich and poor that he saw everywhere in the city. He walked by a fancy restaurant where limousines and horse-drawn tongas unloaded glittering passengers; a few feet down the gutter an old man in a turban and loincloth sweated beside a pot of rice and vegetables cooking over hot coals. On the dirty curb next to the old man was a stack of banana tree leaves. Peter watched him take a leaf from the stack, flop a mound of the steaming concoction from the pot on it, and hand it to a customer in exchange for a fraction of a rupee.

What the hell—if it was good enough for the locals and cheap, why not try it? He was tired of being a tourist in exotic India. He smiled at the gutter gourmet. "I'll take one."

The old man said something in Bengali. Peter replied, "Thank you, sir," as he gave him five rupees and walked away without the change.

The leaf was burning a hole in his hand and he hurriedly shoved some of the filling into his mouth.

Oh shit!

He had a fire storm in his mouth. Dog poo seasoned with red hot peppers. He dumped the concoction in the gutter and wiped tears from his eyes. Too embarrassed to spit on the street, he spit what was left of the crap into his handkerchief and shoved the rag into his back pocket.

Teary-eyed, he brushed by a tall, handsome Hindu in black tuxedo and white turban escorting a platinum blonde with cherry lips and big tits into a fancy restaurant. The ritzy pair made him feel like scuffed shoe leather in his sweat-wrinkled shirt and pants.

It occurred to him that they would spend more money on dinner that night than the gutter entrepreneur earned in a year.

Of course, they would survive the dinner.

No doubt some of the "sheeted dead" got there from dining at the Gutter Gourmet.

He needed something cold and *clean* to drink, and he started looking for a restaurant in earnest, smiling and murmuring "Sorry" to a sari-clad Indian girl he nearly bumped into. She had soft brown skin, delicate features, and enigmatic markings painted on her forehead. She turned her head away shyly as she walked by. He sighed, wondering if he looked as horny as he felt.

He had planned to celebrate his first night in the exotic East with a terrific dinner, compliments of American Express, but he had lost his appetite for splurging when he saw the little boy crawling like a dog with a begging cup around his neck. Now he was sure he had burned away his taste buds. He took a right off of Park Street, cutting down a side street to find a restaurant where his conscience—and good sense—would let him eat. He found a place where all the flies on the window were dead and went in, taking a table by the door to pick up a little of the stingy breeze coming from the street.

The menu was handwritten on brown cardboard in English and Bengali. He ordered curried rice, mutton, and Bengali beer from a shriveled waiter who looked ancient enough to be the father of the old man selling rice in the gutter. The only English the old man seemed to know was "Yes, yes," but the language barrier was overcome by Peter pointing to items on the menu.

The place was full of people speaking languages he couldn't understand, but his ear was good enough to recognize that several languages were bouncing off the walls and ceiling. He shook his head. India was an incredible country.

The beer was warm but it cleared his mouth and prepared him for the curry that burned all the way down, gathering in his stomach and smoldering like embers in a waning fire. The mutton was juicy, but the butter holding it all together tasted a little rancid. He hoped the slow burn in his stomach would kill anything that shouldn't be swimming around his digestive juices.

In a corner of the restaurant a youth was pedaling a stationary bike that had been rigged with cables so three ceiling fans turned as he pedaled. An incredibly old and battered record player next to the bike was playing a scratchy recording of sitar music. When the needle got to the end, the kid reached over and reset it back at the beginning without missing a stroke on the pedals.

Peter sipped warm beer and listened to the twang of scratchy sitar as he mulled over his next move. He had leaped to Calcutta without any real game plan. Seeing the two goons he had run into in London pass by on the street had clinched the fact that all roads led to Calcutta. But the road to what? Was she in Calcutta? Thinking about her sent his pulse racing.

An ugly thought occurred to him. It had been easy to slip out of London and onto a plane to Calcutta. Too easy. He wondered if he was being led around by a string tied to his nose. What if Lisper's visit to the newspaper office had been made to spook him, to send him packing off to Calcutta? His father's flight had taken off from Calcutta. So had the bones in the carpetbag. London had just been a rehearsal. They— whoever the hell *they* were—wanted him in Calcutta for Act I.

He took a sip of warm beer and almost spit it on the table.

She was standing in the doorway!

She was an eye stopper, in a pub in rainy London, in a café in sultry Calcutta. For a moment the hubbub in the café died and every eye went to her. Even the pedaler stopped and the fans groaned to a halt. She wore a cool white cotton blouse and skirt, with her long black hair falling out of a wide-brimmed white hat that had a girlish black ribbon hanging from it.

As she came to his table the people went back to their rancid butter and rice, the kid started pedaling again, and the sitar scratched along.

He nodded coolly as she sat down, but his heart was pounding in his throat.

"Can I buy you a warm beer?" he asked.

She smiled, not friendly, not aloof, but with a certain gravity, as if she hadn't been sure of her welcome and had been waiting for a clue. Her large brown eyes were bright and intense. "Hello, Peter."

He leaned back in his chair a little, taking in the wide-brimmed hat, the thin cotton blouse, following the curve of her breasts, her hips, the contours of the natural copper sheen of her shapely legs.

"White gives you a deceptively innocent look."

She looked away for a moment, then met his eyes again. "You're right. White is for little girls and puppy dogs. Would you prefer I wear black?"

"I'd prefer you wore nothing."

"I'm not sure you could handle the naked truth, Mr.

Novak. Last time we were together you became over-
ly . . . excited."

"It must have been the gun in my stomach."

Her cool, dark eyes raked him. "I thought you were
an innocent bystander on the street at the wrong place,
wrong time, but now that you've shown up in Calcutta your status as a nonbelligerent is in jeopardy.
What did you do with the skull?"

"I buried it in a cabbage patch. Dogs dug it up and
ate it."

"There are people interested in that skull who
would kill for that sort of humor."

"It's the naked truth," he said. "What were you
doing on the street with a bag of bones?"

"Trying to keep them away from your friends."

"Who are my friends?" he asked.

"The people after the skull."

"What skull?"

"The one in the cabbage patch."

"Who's on first?"

That one stopped her. She blinked. "First?"

"An old Abbott and Costello line." He took a sip
of beer.

"If your interest in the skull is money," she said,
"you'll find me a generous bidder."

"I wasn't joking about the dogs and the cabbage
patch."

Her dark eyes probed him again. "You're serious."

"I spotted your two playmates cruising by my hotel
earlier. I, uh, hope all the airfare and hotel expenses
aren't just because of me."

"I'm afraid we were here first. You are the one who
incurred the unnecessary expense of coming to Calcutta . . . just to leave so soon."

He had hoped she would deny being linked with
the two creatures in the limo. His stomach knotted at

the thought of what she might be mixed up in. "Do you have a name?"

"Tashi."

"Tashi. I like it. Somehow it fits. And what's Mr. Big's name?"

She raised her eyebrows. "Mr. Big?"

"The guy behind it all. The one with enough money to let goons run around in limos and pay for that beautiful manicure job on your nails."

"How do you know it's not a woman?"

"No woman would let someone like you hang around."

She stared at him thoughtfully for a moment before she answered. "The name of the man who pays for the limousine and manicures is Zhdanov. Have you heard of him?"

Was she deliberately giving him the name to see what his reaction would be? He shook his head. "Sounds Polish. Or Russian. Do any of you have second names?"

"No, I'm afraid not."

"You people must be rich. I thought only rock stars get away with one name."

The door to the restaurant opened and she glanced behind her. A man and woman with two small children entered.

"Expecting company?" Peter asked.

"You were insane to come here. You've placed yourself in danger. You have to leave Calcutta. Immediately."

"Or I'll get the same treatment as the cabbie?"

"Cabbie?"

"The one in London. The one your friends took care of."

"I don't know what you're talking about."

"I'm talking about the cabbie that picked us up on Whitehall. His throat was cut." He watched her closely as he spoke. She seemed genuinely startled.

"I . . . I don't understand."

"Neither do I." His hands shot across the table and grabbed hers. He leaned forward and stared into her eyes. She tried to pull her hands away but he held onto them. 'Why'd you come here? What do you want?'

"I came to warn you," she said, softly.

"Warn me about what?"

"Go home, Peter, wherever home is. Leave Calcutta. Tonight, first thing in the morning, as soon as you can."

"Your friend Zhdanov send you to tell me that?"

"Nobody sent me. I came to convince you to leave before it's too late."

He slowly relaxed the tight grip on her hands and gently cupped them in his own. "Why would you want to warn me?"

She refused to meet his eyes. "I . . . I can't explain." She pulled her hands away and picked up her purse, as if she were getting ready to leave. But she didn't get up. She stared at him for a long moment. "Why did you come to Calcutta?"

"For my own reasons."

"It's hard to believe. If that's true, go home. Leave before something terrible happens."

He sipped his beer. The fizz was gone, but the wetness felt good on his dry throat. "I'm not going home. I don't really have any place called home. I came to Calcutta for answers and I'm going to follow wherever they take me." He lost himself in the deep pools of her eyes. "I haven't been able to get you off my mind. Something about you . . ."

For a moment her features softened, and he thought she was going to reach out and touch him; she struggled with herself and suddenly stood up.

"Don't go."

"Please. I may have been followed. It would be bad for both of us if we're seen together."

"When will I see you again?"

She left without answering. He sat for ten minutes and listened to the scratchy sitar and watched the kid pedal, resisting the temptation to follow her out of concern for her safety. He believed her when she said no one had sent her. She had lied to him in London, and here he sat in a dingy café in Calcutta and believed every word she said.

Before he left the restaurant he gave ten rupees to the kid pedaling. The surprised kid asked Peter a question in Bengali. Peter shook his head. He didn't know why he tipped him, either. Maybe it's because you always tip the piano player.

The streets had cooled down to the temperature of warm Bengali beer by the time he left the restaurant. As he walked down the dark street, back toward Park, he decided the tepid night air in Calcutta tasted a little like beer.

Sleigh bells jingled beside him as a rickshaw came down the gutter and paced him. Instead of a Hindu in a loincloth, a Chinese in black pajamas was pulling it.

The rickshaw driver stopped beside him and pulled a chit, a hand-delivered message, out of his sleeve and handed the piece of paper to Peter.

> *Mr. Novak*
> *I must see you. My man will guide you.*
> > *Dr. Poc*

Peter looked at the impassive Chinese face. "Who the hell is Dr. Poc?"

The man bowed and smiled, then spoke with a heavy Chinese accent. "You come. We go."

"You go. I don't need any teeth pulled or bones set."

Peter tossed the chit in the gutter and started to walk off as another Chinese in black pajamas stepped out of the shadows with his hands tucked in the long sleeves of his smock.

He bowed to Peter. "We go."

The man pulled his right hand out of his sleeve just enough for the street light to reflect off the rusted blue barrel of an old Indian Army issue.

CHAPTER 12

Peter had never met a Chinese he didn't like. He was probably prejudiced by movies and books that portrayed "old world" Chinese as wise, honorable people. As he rode through the streets of Calcutta, a hostage in a rickshaw, he wondered if it wasn't time he reassessed his feelings.

The Chinese beside him was a jaundiced weasel with a small, shaved head, sloped-shouldered frame, and spoiled skin. A mole on his cheek had long, black hairs hanging from it. The mole fascinated Peter. He was tempted to tell the man it wasn't polite to let hair grow from a mole. Worse than hair growing out of a man's nose.

Calcutta's Chinatown was on Bowbazar between Lower Chitpore Road and Chittarangan Avenue. The area looked like a pocket of old China transplanted to Calcutta; elderly men sat on the pavements playing mah-jongg, women squatted in the gutter with babies strapped to their backs while they cooked vegetables in woks over open fires. During a pause in traffic Peter watched a mother softening a banana in her mouth and use her tongue to slide the food into her baby's mouth.

The driver turned onto Chatawallah Gully and trotted into a dark alley where the rickshaw came to a halt before a door without a light or sign over it.

Two more black-pajamaed chips off the old block

crawled out of the cracks, each carrying a brutal Chinese hatchet. They led him down a dingy hallway thick with a sickening sweet smell and past a gambling room pressed with excited men crowded around fan-tan tables. Young Chinese girls in brocade silk dresses mingled, supplying drinks and encouragement.

The revolting sweet smell grew heavier as they passed a dark chamber where men lounged on cushions and shared opium pipes, bringing a cheap ecstasy into their lives. Peter stopped and watched a girl kneeling on a red satin cushion in front of a wicker basket in the center of the opium room. She was naked, melon-teated, baby-ass naked, with glittering tassels linked to the nipples of her breasts defying nature's laws by spinning in opposite directions. A king cobra slowly rose from the wicker basket, its head fanning with anger as it came erect.

Peter shuddered as the snake swayed before the woman, slowly, fluidly, moving in a reptilian mimicry of her bouncing breasts as if it were attracted sexually.

Dr. Poc definitely wasn't in the business of jerking teeth or mending bones. The place was an opium den that would have put to shame the infamous dens of iniquity of Hong Kong and Macao.

The Chinese weasel poked him in the shoulder with the rusty cannon and directed him to a small office where an elderly Chinese rose from behind a desk and bowed. The man had a long white beard and a flowing white and gold brocade robe. Peter's first impression was that of an elder statesman or college professor, but when the man looked him in the eye Peter had the sensation of staring into a black cesspool.

"Welcome to the House of the Three Perfections, Mr. Novak. I am Dr. Poc. I believe you have already met your guide, Lo Fat." Lo Fat was the Chinese with the big .44. He stood stoically by the door, hand tucked back up his sleeve to keep the .44 warm. "And this is my honorable cousin, the proprietor of this establishment."

Honorable Cousin was a creature behind a haze of cigar smoke, to Poc's right. His face was a Stephen King horror story; a scar splitting his nose was just the opening paragraph. He seemed to be constructed of rings of fat that began under his nose and got bigger going down his torso. He looked like a stack of yellow tire tubes.

"Please sit down," Dr. Poc said.

Peter took a chair in front of the desk and locked eyes with Dr. Poc. "Why did you bring me here?"

"Word has come to me that your foes are, shall we say, foes of mine."

"Foes over what?"

"It is said that you came into possession of a certain skull in London."

"In and out of possession. Someone tossed it to me in the rain, I buried it, dogs dug it up and ate it. Period. Open and shut. Ancient history."

Poc stroked his beard as he eyed Peter. "Perhaps not as ancient as one might imagine," he mused, "but we can leave that matter with, shall we say, the dogs. My concern is over another object that is, shall we say, related to that mysterious skull dogs found surprisingly nourishing. It is a small object of little value to anyone but scholars of antiquity like myself."

"That doesn't tell me anything."

"Precisely. And for you to enjoy continued good health, that is for the best."

Peter started out of the chair. "Well, now that we've got that settled . . ."

Dr. Poc motioned him to sit back. "I need assistance in a small business matter that could prove profitable to you. And let me assure you that the small

deed I wish you to perform will be handsomely rewarded and"—Poc wrapped his words in sincerity—
"involves no illegalities."

Peter choked but kept a straight face, reminding
himself there was a yellow weasel with a .44 behind
him and a dozen hatchet men between him and the
nearest exit. "Why don't you send one of your, uh,
crew?"

"My crew, as you put it, are all Chinese and would
be easily recognized as my emissaries."

"Hire an Indian. The town's crawling with them
and they're all dirt poor."

"And all equally untrustworthy. No, Mr. Novak,
fate has cast our hands together. I need a small deed
performed, you are alone in a foreign city and need
friends . . . and information."

"Information?" What the hell was the man up to?
"What information do you have that would interest
me?"

"For much of my life I have traveled that icy wilderness of the Himalayas called the Roof of the
World," the yellow spider whispered, "and have heard
many tales, including a story told of an English pilot
and a plane crash. I might be induced to share such
knowledge with a man who, shall we say, performs
a small task for me."

Peter tried to keep his face blank, but he knew the
man was reading him. "What do you know about my
father?"

"I seek a small silver box. I was once in possession
of this very box," Dr. Poc said dreamily, "at a time
and place very distant from here. I lost the box to
treachery and have spent more years than your lifetime in tracking it down." The Chinaman stroked his
beard and stared gravely at Peter. "I am a scientist
and a scholar and it is my duty to protect this irreplaceable historical relic. I am, shall we say, a man

more versed in the world of books and antiquities than the practical world of dollars and cents and as such am penniless. However, in the interest of science, my honorable cousin has agreed to finance my endeavors."

Peter shot a glance at the Yellow Peril behind the haze of cigar smoke. Honorable Cousin and his hatchet men didn't strike him as advance men for the Metropolitan Museum.

Poc stared at Peter through half-closed eyes, a lizard eyeing a juicy fly. "No *sacrifice* is too great to preserve this relic for science." He paused to let his words sink in.

The skull in London, a silver box in Calcutta, his father. The Himalayas. Pieces to the same puzzle. A beautiful girl hands him a skull; Fu Manchu wants a silver box. Where did his father fit in? "You haven't answered my question. What information do you have about my father?"

"That answer is subject, shall we say, to *reciprocity*."

It could be a ploy. The man might have no information, but he wasn't in a position to call a bluff, not unless he wanted to end up with his throat cut and hanging by his feet from a meat hook in a shop window along Bowbazar. Peter cleared his throat. "What exactly do you want me to do?"

"Merely take possession of the silver box. One of my emissaries will give it to you."

"What's in the box?"

"Let us say it's a clue to the mystery of the ages. You merely bring it to me and I will exchange it for, shall we say, a piece to the mystery you are unraveling."

He was being baited, but there was nothing he could do but bite. It sounded like a setup. Why would the man need him to run an errand? "Sounds too easy. There's a catch."

Dr. Poc chuckled. "There is another man, an acquaintance of the young woman who had the skull in London. Zhdanov. This man also desires the box, as does his consort. I will lead him on a false trail, leaving the path clear for you."

"What if I tell you it's no dice?"

Dr. Poc sighed and gently stroked his beard, gazing up at the ceiling as if he was looking beyond the cracked plaster to Chinese heaven.

Peter cleared his throat again. "That bad, huh."

"Precisely."

"I bring you the box and you're going to tell me about my father."

Dr. Poc smiled, the toothy grin of the sharks hanging by the tail in the windows of the fish joints on Bowbazar. "Precisely."

They sealed the deal with a shot of velvety Chinese whiskey.

Poc showed him out through the kitchen of a restaurant that smelled of warm almonds and fried fish. On Bowbazar the Chinaman insisted on flagging down a rickshaw and giving the driver instructions to Peter's hotel.

Peter settled back in the rickshaw, thinking it foolish of Poc to be seen on a public street with him if he wanted Peter kept neutral. The "if" bothered him. The nefarious old devil had shown a surprising lack of interest in the skull.

The skull and a silver box. Somewhere in between was his father's mysterious flight.

Poc's instructions were merely that Peter was to meet a man at a temple in the Kalighat District the next evening and take possession of the silver box. It was all so simple . . .

By the time he got back to his hotel the doorman

was curled up asleep on a rug in front of the entrance and the beggars were gone, taking their place with the rest of the living dead sleeping on the streets. He stepped over the doorman and padded his way across the deserted lobby, too tired to be sensibly scared about the bird cage elevator.

An old friend was waiting for him in his room.

The carpetbag sat on his bed, as welcome as a grinning cobra. Unless it had sprouted wings and flown in, someone had access to his room. They'd turned his London flat into a freeway, now they were doing it in Calcutta.

He opened the bag and took out Mr. Skull. The bones came wrapped in a recent issue of the London *Daily Mail.* Dogs had not gotten the bones.

The newspaper's lead article was a breakthrough in the Soho cabbie murder case.

An American named Peter Novak was being sought for questioning about the killer. U.S. authorities had been advised.

Someone wanted him to know he couldn't go home.

Tashi stayed hidden in the shadows of a narrow alley half a block down the street from the Chinese restaurant Peter and Dr. Poc had come out of. She remained frozen in place, no movement giving hint of her concealment, even after Peter left in the rickshaw and Poc went back inside.

A moment later another rickshaw moved down the street in the direction Peter's had taken, only instead of a Chinese or Indian, it was pulled by a big Mongol sweating like a draught horse. A veil draped in front of the seat roof shielded the passenger, but short, stubby legs stuck out from under the veil.

Bagora was using Ma as a draft horse. The little

man would be reborn a gnat in a rubbish bin for the way he treated Ma.

She left the alley, making her way back to where she had left her car, her mind buzzing. *Peter Novak and Poc!* Zhdanov had been right. Every fiber of her soul rebelled against the notion that Peter was scheming with Poc, but she had seen them together. Poc had even hailed a rickshaw for Peter.

Her instincts about people were exceptional, but Peter Novak kept scrambling her fine-honed senses. Her heart told her one thing, her eyes another.

One thing her senses had not lied about was the danger to him.

Her car, parked three blocks from the alley, was being watched over by two youths she had hired off the street—one to watch the car, the other to watch the watcher. The average Indian was honest, but there was nothing average about anything in Calcutta.

CHAPTER 13

Tashi paid off the youths and maneuvered the yellow convertible through Calcutta's pulsating night traffic with the skill of a kamikaze taxi driver. Born and raised in a society devoid of mechanical devices, she'd handled the powerful car with ease from the moment she sat behind the steering wheel, not fighting the steel monster, but as if she were riding a horse bareback, feeling the power and flowing with it.

The car was a restored Cord worth a maharajah's ransom, a canary-yellow convertible with pearl-buttoned, ostrich-leather seat covers, rosewood dash, and mink floor rugs. Zhdanov had first opposed her having a car and she knew why—lack of an automobile increased her dependency on him. He capitulated after she began running around the city on a battered old motor scooter she obtained by barter with a hotel porter. She preferred the rusty motor scooter over the handsome Cord, because the scooter came with a sense of her own accomplishment, but took the Cord to keep peace. The first vehicle he bought for her had been a new Mercedes, but she had refused to accept it. The Mercedes was like thousands of other Mercedes, while the Cord was a rare jewel. Only two others like it existed in all the world: one in a billionaire's collection in Denver, Colorado, the other in the basement at the summer palace of the King of Denmark.

She drove by the front entrance to the Royal Bengal Hotel and turned into a gated driveway beside it.

The gate guard lifted the barrier, saluting her as she passed. She pressed a button hidden under the dash and the door to Zhdanov's private garage opened. An armed attendant was waiting inside the garage. She surrendered the Cord to the guard and took the private elevator to the top. Zhdanov owned the hotel and reserved the top two floors for himself and his entourage.

Another armed guard and a porter bowed respectfully as she stepped out of the elevator on the fifteenth floor. Her reception had changed since the day she had come to the hotel as a mudlark wearing rags, her bare feet black from road tar, searching for a man with a borrowed name and a strange past. The air-conditioning and soft carpets had made the hotel lobby feel like a cool meadow compared to the lava streets.

She tossed her white linen jacket on a chair in her dressing room and sat down at the vanity to remove the foul touch of Calcutta's polluted atmosphere with facial cream. Zhadanov knocked softly and entered. He came up behind her and rested his hands on her bare shoulders.

"You've been gone most of the day," he said.

"I took a ride down the delta."

"You enjoy the night air, don't you?"

"Darkness hides some of the ugliness of Calcutta." She met his eye in the mirror. "Earlier I went to Peter Novak to warn him about you."

He chuckled. "I would admire your disarming honesty if I didn't know you suspect I have your activities monitored." His hands gently massaged the area between her neck and shoulders. "You're tense. Are you disturbed about something?"

"Peter Novak told me a taxicab driver was murdered in London, the driver who had picked us up on Whitehall."

"That's unfortunate, but surely you don't think I would have anything to do with the killing of a cabbie."

"I don't know what to think."

"Taxi drivers are found murdered all the time. It's a hazard of the trade. But if anyone had a motive to kill the cabbie, I would say your friend Mr. Novak heads the list. Has it occurred to you that he may have eliminated the cabbie to remove a witness to the fact he had come into possession of the skull?"

"I don't believe that."

"You don't want to believe it because you've become infatuated with Mr. Novak." His voice got harder. "Novak is an emissary of Poc's. That makes him our enemy. *Your* enemy. Have you forgotten what cruelty Dr. Poc is capable of inflicting in his mad drive to find Shambala?"

"I haven't forgotten," she whispered. She wiped cream off her face, avoiding his eyes in the mirror.

"Bagora followed Novak to the House of the Three Perfections and later saw Poc and Novak on the street together. Now do you understand why Peter Novak came to Calcutta? Why he was on Whitehall that night? He's after the secret to Shambala, and he's allied with a snake you wouldn't want in paradise."

"I . . . I've been around Peter Novak. He doesn't seem to have malice toward anyone."

"Strange, you're so willing to protect Mr. Novak, no matter how strong the evidence is, and just as willing to indict me for every imaginable sin without an iota of proof. Now that you've found a young man you can relate to, why don't you tell him the way to

Shambala? He can let Poc know and the Red Chinese can move in."

"I don't know the way to Shambala."

"I wish I could be sure of that. I know the general region of the Himalayas where the valley is located, but we wouldn't be able to spot it from the air, not with that mist concealing it. But I suspect that if I got you close, your instincts would guide you to the valley."

"My instincts? You think I'm a witch or a seer. My instincts would be no better than anyone else's in the mountains."

"I wonder. Sometimes you are so perceptive about people that I suspect you crawled into their minds."

"I sense things about people because I listen to their emotions, their feelings." Peter flashed through her mind. Nobody had ever confused her like Peter. She could read people, understand them very quickly, but Peter . . .

His hands had tightened on her shoulders. She met his cold stare in the mirror.

"What were you just thinking about?"

She couldn't answer his question; discussing Peter would only infuriate him.

"You're not the only one who can read minds." His voice was icy. "You were thinking about Peter Novak. Novak is our enemy. Help me find Shambala before he and Poc loot it."

"I can't."

"You mean you won't."

"Shambala is a dream. You'll find it when your heart is full of love."

He touched his face. "You're young and your mind is full of foolish ideas. You don't understand love. It brings nothing but pain and misery."

She stood up and faced him. "Why don't we forget Shambala, leave all this and go somewhere no one knows us. Don't you understand, I don't want the clothes and furs you've given me, the jewelry, none of those things makes me happy. What would make me happy, and you refuse to give, is yourself."

His features remained stiff and cold as she talked. She wanted so much to break through the wall he put between them.

"I'll give up Shambala if you give up Peter Novak." Not waiting for her reply, he turned and left the room.

She stripped and showered, letting the cold water run full blast. *Peter had met with Dr. Poc.* Tonight was the first time she had seen the Doctor of Death since he killed a man in the Sinkiang and tried to torture secrets from her, but the thought of him made her cringe. The crafty Chinese is probably using Peter, she thought. And he would dispose of Peter when he was through with him.

She lay naked on the bed, thinking of Peter. Imagining him beside her. For the hundredth time since she stared into his eyes in a taxi in London, she wondered, *Is he the One?*

The One. A strange, mystical phrase for a woman who was now as much West as East. Once the phrase had not seemed so strange to her, but that was a different time, a different place.

A different world.

Shambala. To millions of downtrodden Asians who had never seen the fabled land but grew up hearing tales about it, Shambala was heaven on earth, as lush as the Garden of Allah, as fruitful as Eden.

Shambala was not a myth to her any more than it was to the man who called himself Zhdanov.

She had first seen the valley with the eyes and heart of a frightened child ...

TASHI

DAUGHTER OF THE SEVENTH MOON

CHAPTER 14

Three wise men followed the star in the east.

They were truly Kings of Orient, these three old men on white donkeys. Each was a venerable lama of Buddhism; the eldest and the wisest was the High Lama of Shambala. They were tired and cold and hungry, their bones old and chipped, their skin weathered, their discipline supreme. They carried treasure in their saddle bags: a rosary, a pair of earrings, and a simple wooden bowl, to them every bit as valuable as gold and frankincense and myrrh.

They had journeyed across winter-bitter mountains, assaulted by knifing winds that slapped and cut their faces, howling furies that caused their donkeys to stagger like drunken men.

A disastrous invasion of Tibet had occurred since the last time any lama had ventured out of the green vale of Shambala: the Red Chinese dragon sat in Lhasa, the Dalai Lama had fled the holy city and was reigning in exile on the Indian side of the Himalayas. The Red Chinese presence in Lhasa and the few other areas of Tibet with a large enough population to attract the Beijing regime had little effect on the tiny hamlets and settlements pocketed in the innumerable valleys and mountain wrinkles of the vast Himalayan region; it would be decades before the Red Chinese could explore most of the regions, never mind map them and bring them under control. Nomadic Tibetan tribes, the Khampas, kept control of much of the wilderness plateau with savage attacks on any Chinese patrols that dared leave city compounds.

The quest of the three lamas of Shambala had actually begun four years ago when the thirty-second Tashivaana had passed beyond sorrow in the mountains ringing the Vale of Shambala. The passing had not been witnessed—it was said the Tashivaana became lost in a terrible storm in the mountains and perished. Word of another incredible event had also slowly crept among the scattered settlements in the region of Shambala, a rumor carried by a snail, a tale of man from the Western Heaven flying into Shambala on silver wings, raising hope of the rise of the Monkey-King among villagers who had never heard of, much less seen, an airplane.

Since the passing of the Tashivaana of Shambala had been sudden, unexpected, the woman who had been queen and deity of the tiny mountain region left no clue as to where her successor was to be found. Because no word had been left by the thirty-second Tashivaana, those whose duty it was to seek out the thirty-third Incarnate had waited for a sign to lead them to the female child into whom the spirit of the Tashivaana had come to dwell.

The doctrines of Tibetan Buddhism hold that when a person dies the spirit enters Bardo, the Buddhist purgatory, before it passes into the body of a living being.

A year passed before word came from an oracle at the temple at Lake Manasarvar, the sacred lake in the heart of Tibet, that a vision had been seen in the reflection of the moon on the holy waters. The oracle's vision was that the spirit of the Tashivaana had passed to a child born on the day of the full moon in the seventh month of the year of the Stone Dragon.

There were many female children born in Tibet on that day, but soon another clue came, this time from a lowly monk of Shambala, Hying, a Pathfinder trained in the secret of crossing the mountains that ringed Shambala.

Hying reported a vision he had one lonely night sleeping in a snow cave during a mountain crossing: the Incarnate of the Tashivaana was to be found in the Valley of Po, many days' journey from Shambala. In his vision Hying saw a mountain shaped like a camel's hump and a giant yak that swam a river with many people on its back.

Two monks went to the area to quietly conduct an investigation. To ensure against fraud, no one was told of the mission. Prestige and the opportunity for great rewards can fall to the family of a high-ranking Incarnate. There are those who temper their religious zeal with worldly greed.

The two scouts found the camel's hump, a bald hill near the banks of a river; a village was on the opposite shore.

A yak large enough to carry many people across water had puzzled those who weighed Hying's vision, and it was with pure astonishment that they watched the "yak" come toward them. It was a ferryboat made of yak skins stretched across a wood frame, the skins sewn together and the seams sealed with tree pitch.

The excited monks inquired at the village about girl-children born on the day of the full moon in the seventh month three years before. There was only one child, the daughter of a local merchant.

After the monks returned, the High Lama of Shambala and two of his elder lamas set out upon the final Quest, a quest similar to the ones that had led to the discovery of every Incarnate. With them were other clues: the rosary, the gold earrings, and the wooden bowl. The child, the candidate, was to be tested to

ensure that she was the One and True Incarnation of
the Spirit of the queen-goddess.

All the people in the small hamlet and those for
miles around gathered to greet the seekers. Prayer
flags fluttered in the breeze and electric excitement
ran through the crowd. Red Chinese troops occupied
Lhasa, but the disturbance in the land was far from
this remote village.

The people in the valley had known for days of the
Coming and had prepared a feast, as great and plentiful
a banquet as these poor people could muster. Tea, with
butter and salt, for all and because this was a great oc-
casion, chang, the Tibetan barley beer, was served
along with black bread, tsampa, and vegetables. There
were no plates because each person carried a wooden
bowl in a pocket formed by the fold of their robes.
Utensils they also carried, five on each hand.

The procession stopped in the village square, the
common people leaving a respectful space so the holy
men and the village elders could gather in the middle.
The excited but restrained crowd—men, women, children of all ages—looked on in quiet awe. The discovery of the Tashivaana in their midst would bring
great prestige to their village, and the events of this
day would be legend.

Drink was consumed, bread broken, and sacred
kata scarfs exchanged, before the High Lama spoke.

"There was a girl-child born in this village on the
day of the Full Moon during the time of the Seventh
Month in the year of the Stone Dragon. Where is that
child?"

The headman and the village elders conferred. The
child and her anxious parents were waiting on the
sidelines, the child scrubbed till her cheeks shone like
apples, but a certain protocol had to be satisfied.

The three weary holy men waited, each with the
same thought, the same hope.

After much discussion, head scratching, and consultation of the scrolls that all births, deaths, and land transactions were recorded upon, the headman rose and called a name. The crowd parted and the nervous parents stepped forward pulling a girl-child of three years between them.

The child was stocky, with a moon-shaped, peasant face, pug nose, and sunken eyes. There was a sore in the corner of the right eye with yellow pus in its heart. Despite the parents' best efforts, at the last moment a drop of fluid had slipped down from the child's nose and rolled over her upper lip. The child sniffed and pulled her hand out of her father's grasp to wipe her nose.

No expression other than mild interest was revealed in the features of any of the holy men, but all three were instantly disappointed at the candidate's appearance. The child was sickly. The spirit of the Tashivaana was a powerful force in the metaphysical world of Tibet. It was highly improbable to the holy men that its spiritual power would not heal the disorders.

The High Lama spoke to the parents. "Were there any happenings at the time of birth of this girl-child?"

"Yes, your holiness." The father spoke quickly, eagerly. "At the moment of birth my wife heard a sound like a thunderbolt from the sky and a flash of light came at her. She felt a spiritual being enter her womb."

An excited murmur rippled through the crowd, but the holy men showed no sign they were impressed by the story. The story of a spirit entering the womb at birth was a common tale among mothers whose children were candidates for sainthood.

"Let the test begin," the High Lama said.

The two lamas moved between the table and the candidate. One of them spread a red silk scarf on the ground and the other placed on it a rosary necklace containing 108 pieces of carved ivory, a pair of golden earrings, and a wooden bowl, a simple tsampa bowl similar to all the others that had been used at the feast.

The High Lama spoke to the parents. "The child is to choose from the offerings."

The father urged the child forward. She looked confused for a moment. One of the lamas smiled and gestured at the three items on the scarf.

The shiny gold earrings caught her fancy and with a cry of delight she swooped down and picked them up. Then she picked up the rosary and placed it around her neck. A roar went up from the crowd.

The excitement extinguished as quickly as it had erupted as the people realized that the three holy men did not share their joy.

The High Lama sighed deeply. "The child is not the Incarnate."

A groan escaped from the crowd. The mother of the candidate took the rosary and the earrings from the child's hands and placed them back on the scarf.

The village headman rushed forward with apologies. He was interrupted by a little girl who slipped out of the crowd and went directly to the red scarf on the ground. She picked up the wooden bowl and waved it at the holy men. "Tsampa," she said, "tsampa." Food.

The headman stared at the girl in horror. He lunged to get the bowl out of her hand but was stopped by a sharp command from the High Lama. The crowd picked up on the drama and grew silent.

"Who is this child?"

"My apologies, your holiness. The child is an orphan in the care of a farmer's wife."

"Tsampa," the child said, waving the bowl.

"She's probably hungry, your holiness."

"Who cares for the child?"

The headman pointed at an old woman in the crowd. The High Lama gestured to her and the old woman came forward nervously.

"Did the child eat during the feast?"

The old woman was terrified at the prospect that the child had offended the holy tribunal. "She is not my child," she wailed. "She is a worthless orphan I care for out of holy charity!"

"Did the child eat during the feast?"

"I filled her bowl myself, your holiness. She is a worthless child," the woman whined.

The three holy men exchanged looks. The child had passed up the decoys, the shiny earrings and tantalizing necklace, and picked up the simple wooden bowl, a bowl so common there would be no temptation to reach for it. Especially if her stomach was full.

The tribunal studied the little girl. She was about the same age and height as the candidate, but she was thinner and there were no obvious signs of ill health. Her ears were large and tapered a little toward the top, pixielike; her thin eyebrows were slightly arched. Body marks pointing upward were signs of celestial favor.

There was something familiar about the child; all three holy men felt a sense of uneasiness.

"When was this child born?" the High Lama asked.

There was a pause before the old woman answered with a quiver in her voice. "On the day of the full moon during the time of the Seventh Month."

"Of what year?" The question was barely whispered.

"The year of the Stone Dragon."

The High Lama's eyes shot to the headman. "Why were we not told about this child?"

The headman looked confused. "But, your holiness, we were asked only about girl-children born in the village. This child was not born in the village."

"Where was the child born?"

The headman looked helplessly at the old woman.

"At the farm of my husband's," the old woman said.

"Where?"

"There!" The old woman pointed at the camel hump hill. "Beyond the river, beyond the hills. A woman came to the farm heavy with child and sick with fever. The woman died giving birth and I have raised the child out of the goodness of my heart."

The two lamas drew the High Lama aside. They maintained a dignified presence, but panic showed in their eyes.

"The child," one of them whispered, "look at her features. She is to the thirty-second Tashivaana what one lotus petal is to another."

"There is no doubt," the High Lama said. "The child carries the spirit of the thirty-second Tashivaana. And the flesh."

"But it is forbidden! You yourself ordered the thirty-second Tashivaana taken to the mountain. She must have made it over the mountain and to this valley. The child is a product of the greatest sin!"

The High Lama smiled gravely. Bitterly. "Is there a more appropriate place for the spirit of the thirty-second Tashivaana to come to rest than the daughter of her own womb?"

The two lamas started to protest and the High Lama commanded their silence. "It is not for us to judge. We must follow the Signs. There is a final test," he told the village elders.

He set three small chips of wood facedown so that a word written on only one of them could be seen.

"Bring the child forward."

The old woman brought the little girl up to the table and the High Lama took the bowl from her, the bowl that had belonged to the thirty-second Incarnate Tashivaana.

"Child, look at me."

The child looked solemnly up at the elderly churchman, the High Lama of Shambala. He gestured at the three chips of wood. "Take one."

The child unhesitantly picked up one of the chips.

The High Lama slowly turned the chip over. There was a single word written on the face of the wood.

. *Tashivaana.*

The procession came over the pass and into the milk-and-honey contours of the Valley of Shambala.

People gathered along the route to wave prayer flags and throw petals of wild roses in the path of the palanquin carrying the three-year-old girl-child to the lamasery beside the Lake of the Celestial Reflection.

As the procession marched down the mountain, golden rays of sun broke through a crack in the clouds and a rainbow burst into full glory.

Monks wept openly at the sight of the heavenly omen.

In the great courtyard of the lamasery five hundred monks stood shoulder to shoulder with blazing torches creating a sea of fire. At the top of the steps, surrounded by lamas and monks fanned out by rank and age, the girl-child sat on a silver throne.

While the throng roared its admiration and adulation, the little girl sat quietly. She wasn't quite sure what was happening, but there was no uncertainty about the fact her new position was a vast improvement over the status of homeless orphan. At first she had been confused, then excited, and now she was tired and hungry. The religious throng had been so busy praising her since her arrival in Shambala that they had forgotten to feed her. Her little stomach growled with displeasure at the error.

Of even greater significance, as she received the praise of hundreds, the thirty-third Incarnate Tashi-vaana had an uncontrollable urge to pee.

CHAPTER 15

TWO YEARS LATER

Lsong heard the girl-child's voice coming from the balcony. When she stepped out onto the dark balcony, the little girl was clapping her hands with delight.

"Who are you talking to, little Tashi?"

She picked Tashi up and carried her back inside. It was past the child's bedtime. The contours of the valley were lost in darkness, even from the vantage of the balcony to the suite of rooms high in the Lamasery of Shambala. Only the white jackets of the great mountains ringing the valley were visible, glowing ghostly.

Tashi laughed. "Djinni."

She held up the silver medallion from the chain around her neck. The image was that of a snow leopard, a great mountain beast Tibetan folklore imbued with the power of djinnis, creatures of the spirit world.

"There was no djinni on the balcony," Lsong, her nurse, scolded. "They are in the mountains, guarding the Tomb."

"Djinni is there, on the balcony."

"Hush now. Don't speak disrespectfully or the djinnis will sneak down from the mountains and eat you." Lsong tucked her in bed, then sat at the edge and fondly brushed hair from her ward's forehead. "The

snow leopard is the friend and protector of the Tashivaana, but there are none here at the lamasery. They
are all in the mountains, watching over the tomb of
the Monkey-King."

The child was uncommonly beautiful, with large,
brown eyes and angelic smile. Those big eyes now
studied Lsong's face inquisitively. "Are you my
mother?"

Lsong cringed. There are so many things that have
to be explained to a growing child; so many things
that could *never* be explained to this child.

Lsong was the child's nurse and the only other female in the all-male lamasery. She loved the child as
her own.

Earlier that day Lsong had taken Tashi to mingle
with village children for a few hours. There had been
resistance to the outing by the elder lamas; the thirty-
third Tashivaana was not an ordinary child, and there
was no purpose in exposing her to the village children, they said. But the High Lama had approved; the
child's horizons had to be broadened beyond the lamasery walls.

The experience filled the child's mind with questions.

"Your mother passed beyond sorrow at the moment
of your birth."

"Did my father pass beyond sorrow, too?"

Lsong hesitated. This was the most difficult question she would ever face from the child. Not even the
High Lama, in all his venerable wisdom, had been
able to prepare her to answer it.

"Yes," she said, not meeting the child's eye. "Your
father is gone. Gone beyond sorrow."

Lsong adjusted the covers. It was the bed of a
queen, and the little girl was almost lost in its sheer
scope.

"Go to sleep, little Tashi."

Lsong affectionately brushed her fingers across the child's cheek. She was not allowed to kiss the child, not even good night. She would have been severely reprimanded if anyone had heard her call the child Tashi; the child had no personal name. Tashivaana was the name of the She-Demon, and a Tashivaana bore no other name.

Lsong put out the yak-butter lamps in the room and paused at the door to say good night.

During the child's first months at the lamasery Lsong had slept on the floor at the foot of the bed. The lamas had put a stop to the practice; the child was not permitted even token reliance on human companionship. She was different from other children. Children need family and playmates. A Tashivaana was not permitted to be a child.

After Lsong closed the door, Tashi looked over at the doorway to the balcony. A great cat with long gray hair and coal spots sat in the doorway.

Tashi smiled with pleasure.

"Djinni," she whispered.

"Her hands don't reach the saddle but she reaches for the sky." Tsaral, her teacher, shook his head.

She was ten years old and had spent the last six years in strenuous training. Philosophy, meditation, and religious history were heavy subjects for a ten-year-old girl, even one that was respected and worshipped as a living goddess.

On this particular morning, bored with the rote ritual she had to make of the seven stages to Enlightenment, she had strained her tutor's patience by showing off, repeating the stages forward and backward.

Tsaral knelt and bowed deeply. He got back on his feet and picked up a wooden rod.

"Prepare for punishment," he told her.

She closed her eyes and held out her hands, chanting to herself the mantra of Tibetan Buddhism, *Om Mani Padme Hum!* "O Jewel in the Heart of the Lotus!" The rod struck fingers of her right hand and then the left. The pain was quickly extinguished by the anesthetic meditation. She opened her eyes, careful to keep her features stone. The slightest expression and there would have been a repeat of the punishment.

Tsaral got down on his knees and bowed again. He told her apologetically, "Teaching the Tashivaana discipline is like shaping a statue; the image must be hammered to obtain the correct form."

She received the same bows, blows, and speech each time she was punished. Her punishment was mild in comparison to that applied to the lowly monk novices, many of them no older than she. Of the over five hundred monks in the lamasery, the youngest were boys of six and seven and the oldest spry individuals over ninety.

"We will end the lessons early today," the tutor said. "Lsong needs time to prepare you for the ceremonies tonight. When the ceremonies are completed go to the chapel and meditate for three hours. To teach you humility, you are to kneel on these." He laid pebbles in her lap.

She groaned inwardly but displayed no change in expression. The ceremony would not end till after midnight. It was going to be a long night.

"Lsong says some day I am to leave the lamasery and go to the place of *another* great teacher. Is that true, teacher?"

Tsaral nodded. "You will travel to the Forest of Lam to be tutored in the Tantric arts by the Great Gomchen."

The Tantric arts. The name gave her a shiver of excitement even though she knew little of the mystic art form.

Tsaral went on. "You must be prepared, just as each Tashivaana before you was prepared, and that is why you must be trained by the Great Gomchen. The Tantric arts will protect you and give you strength during the perilous Journey."

The Journey. The search for the Monkey-King if the land is threatened. She knew the legend by heart, but it was all just words to her. She couldn't conceive of leaving Shambala, could hardly conceive of a world beyond Shambala.

"Will I travel to the Forest of Lam soon?"

Tsaral shook his head. "Such impatience. You have merely scratched the skin of the melon of knowledge. The sweet juices and rich pulp are still untasted. You are indeed a fast learner, but you must be well armed before you venture to the Forest of Lam and become a disciple to the Great Gomchen."

"The Great Gomchen?"

"A gomchen is a hermit-wizard. Lam is a place famous for the power of its wizards and the ferocity of its demons and forest spirits. The Great Gomchen is the most powerful wizard in all of Tibet. It is said he can send messages carried on the wind and that he can kill a man with words alone. The Great Gomchen knows all the magic of this world and has gone to the netherworld that lies beneath and learned the magic of the King of the World. Like a djinni, he can take the shape of any person or animal."

"Will I learn to send messages upon the wind, strike a man dead with words, and change into an animal?"

The tutor rolled up the scrolls that had been the basis for the day's study. The sunlight that beamed through the only window in the tower room was falling and the shadows in the corners of the room were rising.

"You will learn many things when you dwell with

the Great Gomchen in the Cave of Spiritual Light."

She grinned maliciously. "Perhaps the Great Gomchen will teach me how to change into a tiger."

He asked without turning to her, "And what will you do once you are a tiger, little holy one?"

"Eat you!" she shouted, running for the door.

She sat restlessly on a pillow in the middle of her private chamber while Lsong braided her long hair.

"Will I ever be able to cut my hair, Lsong?"

"Your hair will not be cut until the time of the snows after your twelfth birthday. That is when the next Ceremony of the Goddess will take place at the temple, little Tashi."

A bond had arisen between the two women that would be frowned upon by the religious order. The girl was the only daughter Lsong would ever have, and Lsong was the only mother Tashi could remember. "Do you not remember the first ceremony?"

The ceremony took place soon after Tashi had been discovered. Tashi remembered little except that the temple had been cold and she had been sleepy.

"There will be a great magician at the ritual tonight. He will conduct the Dance of the Demons," Lsong said.

"Is it the Great Gomchen?"

"No, child, the Great Gomchen never leaves the Cave of Spiritual Light in the forest of Lam, although it is said his spirit can fly from one end of the world to the other on wings of birds. The magician here tonight is a ngagspa, a Bon sorcerer, said to be the most powerful sorcerer of the Old Religion."

The "Old Religion" was the name given to the Bon religion, which was older than Buddhism in Tibet. The Old Religion had been displaced by Buddhism, yet it remained active, with its gods, forest spirits, and sorcerers respected as defenders of Buddhism. The

Lamasery of Shambala predated both religions and had adopted part of each over the centuries. The teachings of the monks of Shambala were not a branch of Buddhism but the trunk. Buddha himself journeyed to Shambala as a young man to learn from the wisest at the lamasery.

"Lubo will dance with an evil demon tonight."

Tashi twisted on the pillow and looked up at the nun. "Lubo will dance with a demon?"

Lubo was a young monk-novice. The son of poor farmers, he earned his keep at the lamasery as a helper to Tashi and Lsong.

"He was chosen by the High Lama. It is a great honor. The Dance with the Demon is very dangerous. Lubo is very brave to attempt it."

Tashi looked wide-eyed at the nun. "Will I see the demon tonight? Is it horrible to behold?"

"No one can behold the demon and live. Not unless they know the magic words provided by the ngagspa that keep the demon imprisoned. Perhaps after you are taught by the Great Gomchen in the forest of Lam you will be able to behold an evil demon and strike it down. It is said the Great Gomchen's power is greater than even the Bon ngagspas."

"How will Lubo dance with the demon if he will be struck dead when he beholds it?"

"He will use the magic words provided by the ngagspa. You saw the big wooden box brought into the courtyard today?"

Tashi nodded. The "box" was big enough for six men to stand in.

"The demon is inside that box, the corpse of an evil man, a brigand who murdered many people and violated many wives and daughters before Khampas warriors slew him.

"Lubo will lay on the body with his mouth over the mouth of the demon-corpse. He must keep repeating magic words in his mind. If he hesitates even for a moment, the demon will enter him and kill him. The demon will struggle, but Lubo must keep his arms tightly around the corpse and his mouth over the mouth until the tongue of the corpse protrudes."

"Until the tongue protrudes," Tashi whispered, horrified.

"At the moment the tongue protrudes, snap! Lubo must bite off the tongue. The tongue is then dried and becomes a great charm of magic."

Tears welled in Tashi's eyes. She tried to hold them back but they burst out and rolled down her cheeks. "I'm scared for Lubo."

Lsong stared at her, astonished. "Hush, child. The Tashivaana cannot cry. It is a great honor for Lubo."

Tashi sat on the throne on top of the stairs overlooking the courtyard. Wrapped in warm robes, she sipped buttered tea, holding the mug in both hands as she watched the ritual in the courtyard.

Monks wearing wooden masks marched in a wide circle around the courtyard. The masks were horror stories depicting demons and devils. In the center of the courtyard a tall box stood like a black tomb. The Bon sorcerer pranced around the box, drawing mysterious signs in the air.

The ngagspa's face was blotched on both sides with self-inflicted cheek scars that gave a sinister cast to his features. His robes were mouse brown with black fur trim. Around his neck was a rosary of knuckle bones from 108 corpses. His dagger was carved from a human leg bone.

She worried about her friend Lubo. What would it be like to kiss a corpse? She had never seen a demon-corpse, and the image she conjured up resembled the ngagspa prancing in the courtyard.

It was nearly midnight when the box began to

shake. Lsong told her the corpse would struggle, dance, in the arms of Lubo as the demon tried to escape the taunt of the magic words. When that happened the box would quake from the battle until the demon's tongue protruded and Lubo bit it off. Once the tongue was bitten off, the demon would die and the corpse would collapse. If Lubo failed to keep repeating the magic words until he bit off the tongue, the demon would overwhelm and kill him.

The box shook with a frenzy. Then came a scream, a horrible cry full of pain and terror. The scream slowly faded and the box stopped shaking. For a brief moment all was still in the courtyard. Then the ngagspa rushed inside the box with his dagger.

Lubo was brought out of the box after the ngagspa did his mysterious work to slay the demon. The boy's face was a map of terror. It took four strong men to pry his arms from around the corpse.

Tashi dropped the stones she was supposed to kneel upon. They rolled down the steps as she went to her chamber to pray for the soul of her friend.

She was eleven years old when she found the secret passageway behind the tapestry hanging on the wall at the head of the bed. A section of the wall behind her bed was composed of loose stones.

She removed stones until she was able to squeeze through the opening. She felt no fear; her mind was unpolluted by fear of things that lurk in the night. She lived in an animistic world, a culture in which the stones in the ground, the mountains, the wind, the water, the very earth itself were believed to shelter spirits. In the Western world children are taught evil things hide in dark places. In Shambala the world is believed to be full of spirits, good and evil, and dark places were no less threatening than where the sun shines.

The passageway ran parallel with the wall of her chamber for a dozen feet, then became a narrow, twisting stairway. The walls and floor were rough stone, musty and dank with cobwebs to leap over and crawl under.

The stairway suddenly fanned into a secret room lit by butter lamps. She had found the treasure room of the lamasery.

The "treasure" most valued by the religious order was not gold and silver, though she saw stacks of gold plates and silver bowls she recognized as the ones used during very special religious holdings and festivals, but the priceless, ancient scrolls, books, and artifacts that preserved the wisdom and glory of the religion.

Covering an entire wall was a great tapestry of brocaded gold and silver, an image of the seventeenth Tashivaana, the saint and martyr who blocked the gate to the Lamasery of Shambala with her own body, barring Mongol brigands who had stumbled into the valley and taking the point of 108 arrows in her body.

As Tashi stared up at the sainted image she felt a cold draft on her feet. The bottom of the tapestry fluffed a little. She got down on her hands and knees and wiggled under it.

She had found a secret passageway hidden in a secret passageway.

Before her was a creature whose legend predated the lamasery and whose glory overshadowed even the glory of the great seventeenth Tashivaana: the Snow Leopard.

She knew the legend; it was as much a part of her as the mantra chanted daily. The tale was of Shambala when there were tribes in the valley of a race of life that no longer exists. Their ruler was a good demon, the She-Demon called Tashivaana.

The She-Demon ruled the valley wisely and peacefully until an evil descended upon the land, a great Red Dragon, a Thing of Darkness whose shadow chilled the land. The spirit of the She-Demon left the valley in search of a savior. In answer to the call came a great warrior with a flaming sword and astride a winged Snow Leopard: the Money-King.

During the battle the Snow Leopard was slain by the fierce dragon. The spirit of the Tashivaana entered the Snow Leopard and the beast rose, carrying the Monkey-King to victory. After the battle, the She-Demon and Monkey-King were conquered by each other's love. From their loins came the race called Man.

The Snow Leopard before her was fearsome, a snarling beast of chiseled silver with huge clawed feet, wide wings, and a single great eye. As she moved in front of the tall statue the eye seemed to follow her. She ran from the room, racing down another steep stairway. At the bottom of the stairs she found a dungeon and Shambala's darkest secret.

Behind the steel bars of a cell was a shaggy animal. Her first thought was that the creature was a yeti, the legendary beast that walks upright like a man and is spoken of in the legends of the mountains. But then the creature spoke.

"Someone's here! They can't fool me. I can hear a cockroach scratch its back."

It was a man dressed in rags, his shaggy beard and hair falling below his shoulders. His eyes were huge and milky white. He was blind.

"It's not one of the monks. The footfall is too light. It must be a small person."

Her voice quivered a little but the words came out strong and clear. "I . . . I am the Tashivaana!"

The man flinched as if he had been hit. When he spoke again, the words dribbled out of his private thoughts. "The Tashivaana is dead. She's dead and they took away my eyes."

"In time we shall all pass beyond sorrow," Tashi said, not knowing what else to say to the mad creature who spoke aloud his own thoughts. She started to back out of the dungeon, sure she was confronting a demon.

The blind man perked up. "She's leaving!" He gripped the bars tighter. "She can't leave me. I've spoken to no one but roaches and spiders for so long."

Tashi hesitated at the foot of the stairs, her little knees trembling. The creature had twisted, ugly features and a strange, pale skin tone, as if all the color had drained from his face. He had to be a demon imprisoned by the monks, but something kept her from running up the steps, fleeing this filthy, blind creature that spoke its thoughts aloud.

"Who are you?" she asked.

The man cranked his head as if he could see about the room. "Who am I? Doesn't this child see before her the Monkey-King?"

The Monkey-King! She flinched at the words. But no, he couldn't be. Tsaral told her the Lord Master sat on a throne of gold in an Underworld palace.

"If you are the Monkey-King, why are you a prisoner in this dungeon?"

The man held his hands to his ears and groaned, as if the words hurt. "I can't hear her! It's been too long since I heard the sound of a voice. If she'd come closer . . ."

Tashi took two steps forward. "There. Can you hear me now?"

He groaned. "She has to come closer. I can't hear her."

Tashi shook her head. She shouted, "I will not come closer. Can you hear me now?"

The man coughed and his body shook with spasms.

"Water! Water!" He coughed again, deep in his lungs, his whole body contorting.

A bucket of water with a dipper was sitting next to the cell. She ran to the bucket and scooped up a dipper of water, stepping close to hand it to him.

His hand flashed between the bars and grabbed her robes. He jerked her to him and she struck the bars. She dropped the dipper and cried out. The jagged nails of his fingers pierced her robes, cutting into her soft flesh. She could smell his dungeon-rotted flesh.

"I have you," the creature whispered.

Strong hands jerked her out of his clutches. She looked up at the stern countenance of the High Lama.

"Is he really the Monkey-King?"

The High Lama did not laugh at the question. They were in his chamber drinking tea and eating honey cakes. The fact she had got a sweet treat instead of punishment had come as a surprise to her. It was the first time she had been in the High Lama's chambers and the first time she had shared food with the stern old man.

"He is King of Rats and Roaches." The High Lama frowned. "Your tutor complains that you have not acquired the jewel of patience. There are many things you are to know, but they must come slowly. Wisdom is not sucked into the mind with a straw, but is soaked in slowly, *patiently*."

Tashi looked at her lap.

"You advance in your studies at astounding speed. Your ability with languages is such that we wonder if you could not walk into the forest and speak to the birds and animals. Perhaps we are trying to teach you at the pace of a snail when you race through knowledge like a hare."

"Who is the man in the dungeon?"

The High Lama sighed. "The second fault your

teacher finds is your unrelenting curiosity. You can learn more about faith with the heart than the mind. You must learn to accept, not question."

She waited while the High Lama sipped tea. "There are many things you must know," he said. "Many secrets that not even I, nor the eldest lamas of Shambala, share. You are still young, and the mysteries of life will unfold for you when the spirit of the She-Demon blooms fully within you. It's said Shambala can be found only in the heart, and that is where you will find the answers to your questions."

The High Lama got up and stood by the window, looking out at the lake and mountains as he spoke. "I cannot explain the man in the dungeon." He turned back to her. "It is the Tashivaana who knows the answers in her heart, and it is you who will someday reveal the answers to us."

"If he is not a demon, why must he be kept alone and filthy in the dungeon?"

The High Lama shifted uncomfortably in his chair. "The man in the dungeon has a sickness in his head, a malady of pain and rage and revenge that not even the healing loam of Shambala can cure. We know not what to do with this creature." He stared at Tashi. "What would you do, child? What would you do with a mad creature that craves Shambala's secrets?"

She gravely pondered the question before answering. "Tsaral says that each of us walks in the path set for us by the Universal Plan, guided only by our kismet. I do not know what path the creature is to walk, but I . . . I . . ."

"Yes, child?"

"I do not know if I can explain, Holy Father. I . . . I felt something when I saw the man in the dungeon, an urge . . . to . . . set him free, as if some part of me was trapped behind the bars with the madman."

The High Lama turned back to the window. His

face had paled. He spoke in a whisper. "He must be set free. To walk the Path."

He returned to his chair, his shoulders stooped from burden. He gave a great sigh. "Many women have carried the spirit of the Tashivaana and many men have held the mantle of High Lama of Shambala. To our sorrow and glory have fallen the last days. The Oracles of the Lake have seen the signs."

"I don't understand, Holy Father."

"I know, child. But you will, you will. Your heart will tell you and guide you to the truth and the perilous Journey you must take." He took her hand and squeezed it gently. "Word of the outside world comes into the valley, carried by the Pathfinders, our order of monks who have passed the secret of crossing the mountains from one to another for thousands of years.

"Evil demons plague the world, spreading their evil to the lands that lie beyond the snows of our mountains. The demons of war and avarice and fear stalk the many lands while demons called machines suck life's very nectar from the good earth itself and fill the sky and waters with their foul excretions.

"Shambala alone remains untouched, unfouled by the demons, protected by our vast mountains, hidden from even the demons that fly over the mist that hovers over the valley." A shadow passed over the High Lama's face. "Shambala is a jewel in a festering sore, but the day grows near when the eye of the demon will spot us, just as the Red Dragon descended upon the land before the Beginning. The time grows near," he whispered, "when Shambala must again shine the light that rids the earth of demons and breathes life back into the soul."

"What is the light, Great Father?"

"That, my child, is the secret of Shambala. The secret coveted by the madman in the dungeon and . . . others. That, my child," he whispered, "is the secret known to Tashivaana, the good demon."

"But I am Tashivaana!"

"And you will know the secret. When the time is right." He held up his hand to stop her questions. "Patience, child, patience. The burden of the secret, of the land, is a terrible one. Perhaps it is the most terrible demon of all, for the price of sheltering it is all that you are . . . and all that you will ever be."

"I don't understand."

"It is good that you do not. Heed those words: You are no ordinary child, nor will you be an ordinary woman. In your soul flows the spirit of Ones who walked the earth before this race called Man. You have been put on this earth for a purpose, a mission."

"What is my mission?"

"To walk side by side with the Monkey-King, together to shine the Light that rids the world of darkness."

"But if the Tomb of the Monkey-King is in the mountain, why must I leave Shambala to seek him?"

"You seek the spirit, child, the mortal man in whom the spirit has come to possess, just as the spirit of the She-Demon came to possess you."

His features softened. "It is time your knowledge and virtues be expanded. I will send a message to the Great Gomchen and ask him to accept you as his disciple at the time of your twelfth year."

"Will I learn how to strike a man dead, send messages on the wind, and change into a tiger?"

The High Lama smiled. "You will learn many things. Perhaps even patience."

CHAPTER 16

They carried her to the Forest of Lam on a palanquin, guided over the mountains by Pathfinders. The forest of Lam was between Shambala and the sub-Himalayan range that stood as a wall to the great deserts of the Sinkiang and Mongolia. The region was one of rugged, twisted contours with paths that led to dead ends and bridges to nowhere. Shambala was lost in the puzzlement, and only the map carried by one of the Pathfinders—a skull with scratches on it—showed the secret way, and then only to one who could interpret the bewildering scratches.

Lsong walked beside the palanquin. Tashi asked to get down and walk, too, but Lsong met the request with a look of horror. "The Tashivaana cannot walk like a commoner! You would lose face."

Lsong told her the Forest of Lam was haunted by brigands, thieves, and spirits.

"Does the Great Gomchen dwell in a mighty fortress?" Tashi asked.

"The Great Gomchen needs no walls to protect him. Not the most powerful brigand knight or evil demon would dare to violate his realm."

They journeyed three days in the forest before they stopped and Lsong told her she had to go the rest of the way alone.

"Alone! But how . . . ?"

Lsong pointed to a path that led up the mountain.

"That is the way to the Cave of Spiritual Light. You must not leave the path. If you do, you will get lost and be devoured by wolves or demons. When you come to the Lake of the Crescent Moon, keep the lake on your right. The path will lead you to the cave and the Great Gomchen will be waiting."

"But, Lsong, why must I go alone?"

"I am sorry, little princess. The Great Gomchen is an ascetic. He would be greatly angered if anyone accompanied you. Here. This bundle of clothes is all you are permitted to take." Lsong leaned closer and whispered. "I put some honey cakes inside."

Tashi left the group and started up the trail.

"Do not worry, little princess. You are under the shadow of the Great Gomchen. He will protect you!" Lsong shouted after her.

The trail was narrow, crowded by heavy brush; towering trees cast long shadows in her path. In two hours she reached the Lake of the Crescent Moon and dutifully followed the path that kept the lake on her right.

The snowline began at the foot of the lake.

At a meadow in front of a cave she paused, knee deep in snow, shivering. Near the mouth of the cave a man was sitting in the snow.

She walked slowly toward him, not certain if she was beholding the Great Gomchen or a forest demon in human form. The man had a great beard and hair that fell to his waist, hair as white and pure as frost glistening in the sunlight.

He was naked. She had been taught to know the body and the sight of a nude male aroused neither curiosity nor embarrassment.

The man was in a trance, his face blank, his eyes dazed. He showed no sign of chill; his naked flesh was blushed, as if tinted by a fever.

The heat from his body was melting the snow

around him. She was curious about the phenomenon but not awestruck—Tibet was a land of many mysteries, a land where men danced with corpses and cast magic spells.

His muscles slowly relaxed and life returned to his eyes. Without looking at her, he spoke.

"Go into the cave and prepare a warm fire, child."

"What will I learn from that, Great Gomchen?"

"How to light a fire, child."

"Breathing is the horse; the mind is the rider."

They were walking through the forest. With his great mane of hair, long beard, and flowing white robe, he looked like a king of forest spirits.

"First you expand the abdomen, bringing air into the bottom of the lungs, then fill the chest cavity, bringing air into the center, then raise your shoulders and fill the upper lungs," he told her, "breathing slowly, noiselessly. Proper breathing, absolute concentration and meditation are all necessary for physical and mental well-being. You must learn how to control and direct the waves of energy available when you rid the mind of the physical world, the distractions, passions, and other vices that rob you of psychic energy."

"Will I be able to perform magic with this energy?"

"What magic do you wish to perform, child?"

"Send messages upon the wind?"

"To whom do you wish to send a message?"

She hadn't considered that question. She groped. "To Lsong, the nun who cares for me."

"Why send it upon the wind when you know not all the ways the wind blows between here and the Lamasery of Shambala? Write it and I will have it delivered by messenger."

"Will I learn how to kill a man from a distance?"

"Whom do you wish to kill, child?"

"No one!"

"Then you have no need for this talent. There is a story about the Enlightened One, a tale of the Great Buddha when He walked these mountains. He came to the cave of an ascetic, a hermit who lived near the river. The hermit proudly told Buddha that he had spent twenty years in diligent study to develop the ability to walk upon the waters of the river. The Enlightened One scoffed. Why waste a lifetime to learn how to walk upon the waters of this river when for a few coppers a ferryman will take you across in his boat?"

She tried another tack. "What will I learn, Great Gomchen?"

"Whatever it is that you need to learn."

"How long will it take?"

"As long as it need be."

She thought for a moment, then changed tack again. "It is very cold in these mountains. I need the knowledge of staying warm when I lack proper clothing."

"If that is your need, I will teach you."

"I must walk an hour to obtain the milk the shepherds leave. If I had wings on my feet, I could fetch the milk quickly so I can serve you better and have more time for my studies."

"If that is your need, I will teach you."

She grinned with success. "I need the power to destroy the type of demon that killed my friend Lubo so I can protect the land from such evils."

"You have many needs, most of which neither you nor I can define and which will reveal themselves only in time. The solution to all is the same: proper breathing, concentration, directing your psychic forces. I can do no more than plant the seed. In time, with *patience*, hard work, the seed will bloom and bear fruit."

*   *   *

They sat in the lotus position, facing each other across the fire in the center of the Cave of Spiritual Light.

Next to the cave a small waterfall cascaded down the mountain and into a pond. A submerged opening brought part of the pond inside the cave. When sunlight struck the pond, blue light spread in the cave like the burst of a nova, slowly fading as the day drew to a close.

At night, with a fire roaring, crystalline specks glittered inside the dome like tiny tears in a midnight sky.

"The mind, child, that is where the most powerful forces of the universe lie. The antelope runs faster, the ox carries a greater load, but they lack the power of the mind. Few people use the full force of their mind. Most men carry greater loads on their back than in their mind, travel farther on their feet than with their imagination. You must learn to bring forth the power hidden within you."

His voice was distant thunder. She had been meditating for hours, silently chanting *Om Mani Padme Hum!* She was in a state of a perfect concentration and had left open a window for her master's words.

"There are men in India, the Land of Monkeys, who are able to walk on hot coals by putting mind over matter.

"I will take a hot coal from the fire and place it in the palm of your hand. It will not burn your hand. It will leave a red mark, but the skin will not blister."

Om Mani Padme Hum! "O Jewel in the Heart of the Lotus!"

She felt the hot coal in her hand. There was no pain, just a tingling, no more than the brush of a feather.

Later, they sat before the fire and drank tea.

She looked at the small red mark in the palm of

her hand. "How long did I have the hot coal in my hand, Great Gomchen?"

"You never had a coal in your hand, child. I touched the palm of your hand with my finger."

"Your finger burned my palm!"

"Your *mind* created the red mark. Have you not heard of people breaking out with a rash from fear? There are men who make sores in their stomach from worry. That is the mind affecting the body. You *thought* the coal would leave a red mark and created one with the power of your mind."

"That is strong magic."

"No, child, it is the power of the mind directed by the power of suggestion. I once witnessed a frail woman lift a large tree trunk that had rolled upon her child. Six strong men couldn't have lifted that log, but the power generated by her love and panic gave her the strength.

"Your friend Lubo was told there was a demon in the corpse and his own fears gave life to the demon. You believe there was a hot coal in your hand. They are fruit from the same tree."

"But there are evil demons in the world," she protested. "The monks at the lamasery have all seen one or more."

"Let me tell you a tale of demons, child. A traveler was coming down a mountain path to a village when his hat blew off and became tangled in tree branches far from the trail. Other travelers imagined from its unusual shape that it was a strange forest creature.

"Word spread that a demon was living in a tree outside the village. The frightened villagers began to leave food near the trail to appease the demon. Wolves attracted by the food killed a goat, and the attack was attributed to the demon. One day, when the winds were stronger than usual, the hat was blown out of the tree and tumbled toward the village. The terrified villagers fled their homes."

"Are you saying the only evils are those in our own mind?"

"Do not say *only*, child, as if evil demons are not real. Personal demons such as fear, hate, and jealousy destroy as effectively as knives and arrows. The demons that rage in this world, evils like war, tyranny, and hate, kill millions and are all born in the mind.

"You asked how to kill a man with words. It can be done by planting the seed of self-destruction in his mind and letting it grow, nourished by fear and apprehension, until the person is devoured by his own emotions. If you convince a man there is a tiger on his heels, he will feel the hot breath on the back of his neck and run until his heart bursts.

"Heed this warning: When you use the power of your mind, you are opening new channels, tunnels to the subconscious. Who knows what may pour forth from the Unknown? *Beware!*"

As she had astonished Tsaral with her ability to learn, so she amazed the Great Gomchen. In months she learned the art of lun-gom, walking at high speed over great distances, a feat few men mastered even after years of effort. Speed-walking required that a person breathe, step, and chant in unison, creating a trance that blocked all distractions, remaining cognizant only of physical obstacles such as rocks and trees along the way.

The movement began slowly, the chant coordinating breath and step like the drum on a slave galley setting the pace for the rowers. The person concentrates on a single distant object, eyes wide open, mind blank, body moving in a fluid rhythm. Soon the weight of the body evaporates, slowly lifting up, up, until the feet no longer seem to touch the ground.

As a practical matter, lun-gom cut in half the time it took her to fetch the daily milk.

One night, as they walked the shore of the Lake of the Crescent Moon, she said, "This lake is lovely, but the Lake of Celestial Reflection is even lovelier."

"That is true. The lake next to the Lamasery of Shambala is truly a rare jewel. It is said that Buddha Himself walked around the lake, meditating, exploring the corridors of mind and soul. He refreshed himself with water from the lake and the water turned to tea in his cup."

"If he thought it was tea, it became tea."

"No, child, it *was* tea, not water. It was a miracle, not self-suggestion."

"What is the difference between a man who drinks water and tastes tea because he thinks it is tea and a man whose cup of water turns to tea as a miracle? Are they both not drinking tea?"

"No, child. There is tea in one cup and self-deceit in the other. Self-deceit leads to destruction. One cannot live on handfuls of dirt under the delusion that dirt is rice. Rice sustains the body. Dirt starves it."

Each night she worked toward mastering thumo, the generation of internal body heat to withstand the cold.

"It is a method of staying warm that hermits in the mountains discovered long ago. Perhaps they learned it from the bee, for when the land freezes and no living creature can exist without shelter, the bee is able to generate internal heat and survive the cold. In the power of meditation, chanting, breathing in harmony, in that state of concentration, you generate a fire in your blood."

She began by wearing fewer garments each day. By the tenth month of the Tibetan year, with snow fresh on the ground, she was able to remain naked in the holy cave with no fire lit day or night. It was on a winter night filled with soft flakes of snow that he decided to test her.

"From the time the sun sets this night to the time it rises tomorrow you are to sit in the snow outside the entrance of the cave. You are to wear a single robe, which I will remove from your body when I am satisfied you are able to generate internal heat."

When she stepped out of the cave, cold air wrapped around her. She sat in the snow and the chill attacked her like knives.

She began to chant, to pace her breathing until each breath was full and held a long time. "Imagine your lungs to be a bellows, your throat the neck of the bellows, your mouth, the mouth of the bellows, a fire all around you. With each breath the wind of the bellows fans the flames and they roar with delight!"

A spark in the deep recess of her mind glowed brighter, hotter, until the heat generated in her mind's eye sent hot liquid coursing through her veins. The fire grew, tiny flames coached by the bellows until they shot up, roaring all around her. She sat in the snow, wrapped snugly in the fires of her imagination.

At sunrise she walked slowly back into the cave. She was tired but exhilarated. Three robes were lying on her straw bedding.

"Three times I wrapped wet robes around you last night. Each time the heat of your body dried them." He suddenly smiled. It was the first time she had seen him smile. "You are the youngest thumo master in Tibet!"

She smiled happily. "I am a good student, Master?"

"You are the best pupil I have had. Only one ever came close to matching you at thumo and that was your . . ." The Great Gomchen lost his smile. "That was your predecessor, the thirty-second Tashivaana."

"I have heard little of the thirty-second Tashivaana, Master. No stories are told of her feats as they are of the other Tashivaana. What was she like, Master?"

"Like you, a good student," he said gruffly. "But curiosity was her downfall. Learn from her disgrace and see you do not stray from the Path."

"I do not understand. What disgrace?"

"It is not for me or any other to explain. Someday your mind will open wide enough for you to understand without being told. Enough of talk about the thirty-second Tashivaana. She is beyond sorrow and rests in peace. Come, let us take a walk in the forest while there is still light."

They walked side by side in the forest, the master and his disciple.

She expressed her pleasure at the knowledge and training she was receiving.

"You will need all that I can teach you and more on the journey you will take."

"When will I begin my journey, Great Gomchen?"

"When your heart directs it" was all that he would say.

She pointed to a ledge high above them. "Yesterday when I was returning with the milk I saw a snow leopard on that ledge."

"That is unusual. The snow leopards usually do not come this far down from the great mountains."

"Truly I saw it, Great Gomchen."

He raised his eyebrows. "Why do you falter when you say that, as if you do not think I will believe you?"

She stared down at the ground. "When I was younger I used to imagine that a snow leopard stood guard in my room at night. My nurse, Lsong, scolded me for telling such stories."

He glanced sideways at her. "The snow leopard is said to be the most powerful djinni in the spirit world, a shape-changer that can take the form of man or beast. It is said to be the She-Demon, Tashivaana, that gave it this power when she became One with the flesh and spirit of the great Snow Leopard that carried the Monkey-King to victory. That is why the snow leopard is now protector of Shambala."

They are wild berries beside a tumbling brook. She could see mountains in the distance and wondered what was beyond.

"Have you traveled far, Great Gomchen?"

"My feet have not left this forest in many times your years."

"The High Lama says that beyond our mountains evil demons run amuck. Have you seen these demons, Great Gomchen?"

"We have all seen some of the demons but don't recognize them because many are almost invisible." He pointed to a snowcapped mountain. "When I was a boy-child no older than you, the snow on those mountains was purer than mothers' milk. From here the snow looks the same, but it is not. A demon called technology has fouled the air in places far from here and the wind has carried the poison to the tops of our mountains. Someday the snow on our mountains will be the color of the ash in our fires if the demon cannot be stopped."

"The Light will clear the darkness," she said, remembering the High Lama's words.

"Yes. You will seek out the One and follow the Light."

She asked him what he meant, but he never answered.

That night in bed she tried to send a message carried on the wind.

She drew herself into a state of deep concentration, balancing her breathing and chant, then tried to reach out, to "touch" Lsong with a flow of psychic energy. Instead of an image of Lsong she experienced a vision of the snow leopard she saw on the ledge.

She didn't try to shake the vision. Instead she probed deeper, into that unknown region the Great Gomchen warned her about.

She felt dizzy and numb.

Her mind swirled. When it cleared she realized she *had drawn out of her own body* and was ascending toward the top of the cave.

There was no sensation of leaving the cave, of flying up the mountain; she was suddenly on the mountain, racing across the top, leaping, climbing. She felt the coils of muscles in her haunches that allowed her to powerfully spring up, the great claws that gave her traction even on slippery rock.

She never thought about who she was. Or what she had become.

She woke exhausted the next morning. She decided not to tell the Great Gomchen about her dream. If Lsong scolded her for imaging a snow leopard in her room, what would be said if it was revealed she had dreamed she had become a snow leopard?

In the early spring, when over a year had passed since she had come to live with the hermit, she hurried back up the mountain with a pail of milk, breaking out of a lun-gom trance she came into the clearing.

As she approached the cave the Great Gomchen came out. He was dressed as she had never seen him. His long white robes were heavily laced with silver thread, around his waist was a sash of precious Chinese red silk; hanging from his neck was a rosary of gold.

Excited, she asked, "Are we going somewhere, Master?"

"I am going on a long journey, child, a journey from which I shall return but not in this body nor perhaps this time or place. You are to stay here at the cave no matter what happens. Do you understand?"

"Yes . . . yes, Master. But . . ."

He held up a hand to silence her. "Last night I dreamed of an eclipse of the sun. This morning when I awoke the waters of the pond were murky and the sun did not shine into the Cave of Spiritual Light. A vulture sat in the hole at the top of the cave, filling the cave with its shadow. It was waiting for its dinner."

Lsong had told her that a dream in which there is an eclipse of the sun is an omen foretelling the demise of an Incarnate. The Great Gomchen was dying.

For three days and three nights he sat in the meadow in a trance. On the morning of the fourth day his eyes were closed, his skin bleached by death.

She was praying for his soul when a group of people broke out of the trees. Lsong saw her and shouted.

Tashi ran to Lsong and hugged her and wept. "The Great Gomchen has gone beyond sorrow, Lsong."

"Yes, little princess. The High Lama received the message and sent us to fetch you."

Tashi wiped tears from her face and stared up at the nun. "What message, Lsong? I sent no message."

"The message was sent by the Great Gomchen."

"He sent no message. He never left the place in the meadow from where he passed beyond sorrow."

"He did not have to leave, little princess. The message was carried on the wind."

Tashi refused to ride in the palanquin. She had walked step for step with the Great Gomchen and would walk back to Shambala. Lsong started to object, but stopped. Her little Tashi had been trained in the Tantric arts by the greatest wizard in Tibet.

A Pathfinder, with a skull-map that revealed the secret way to Shambala, and three monks as an escort made up the rest of the party.

"We must keep a sharp lookout and hurry in our

travels," Lsong told her. "Mongol brigands have been reported in the area. The brigands have been forced into the rural areas because the Chinese army patrols the main roads. The Chinese soldiers are little more than brigands themselves. We must avoid both."

Mongols. Tashi was familiar with the language of the Mongolian people, as she was of the Chinese, but she had never set eyes upon a person of either race.

"I would like to see a Mongolian and a Chinese," Tashi said. "Do they look like us?"

"In truth I have never seen either race, but a Pathfinder who has seen both tells me the races are truly similar to Tibetans. Did not Tsaral teach you how the three great races, Tibetan, Mongolian, and Chinese, came to be?"

Tashi shook her head.

"In the beginning there was but a single man on earth. This man had three children. When the man died, the three children quarreled over their father's remains. They finally decided to cut the body into three pieces, each to take a piece and go upon their separate way.

"One took the head and the arms and he became the ancestor of the Chinese people. That is why the Chinese have become versed in the arts and are known for their intelligence.

"Another took the lower half of the body; from him descended the peoples of Tartary, the simple Mongols who are without head and heart and whose only merit is in keeping themselves in the saddle.

"The third took the chest and stomach and from him came the Tibetan people who are full of heart and courage."

On the second night they camped beside a river gorge. They had come across no other travelers, and the monks risked a small fire to heat water for their tea.

Tashi and Lsong squeezed through the heavy brush lining the edge of the river gorge. They sat on rocks and ate tsampa and drank tea as they watched the cascading waters.

Lsong refused to call her Tashi even in private and referred to her as "your holiness." Tashi tried to re-kindle the simple warmth of their relationship, but it had been replaced by something new: reverence. Tashi was no longer a little girl and was soon to be a queen. There had been a conversation between them that ached Tashi's soul. She had forced Lsong into telling her the truth behind the man that had been in Shambala's dungeon. Tashi had wanted the truth, but the conversation had left her with more questions than when it began and had driven Lsong to tears.

"All rivers in our mountains flow to the Land of the Rains," Lsong said, nodding down at the river.

Tashi frowned. "I do not know where the Land of the Rains lies, but I have seen rivers flow in many different directions." Tashi had once heard a Path-finder use another name for the Land of the Rains: India.

"But it is so. This I was told by an elder lama who was told by his elder when he was a boy."

They heard shouts behind them and the pound of horses' hooves.

Six riders stormed into the camp. They were like no other men Tashi had ever seen and one word instantly came to mind: demons!

"Mongols!" Lsong cried.

The raiders were part of a horde that had come over the mountains to the north, from the Sinkiang and Inner Mongolia, that vast desert wilderness that the Chinese claimed but had never tamed.

They were plunderers, thieves, rapists and killers, brigands and mad dogs who preyed on the hapless without mercy, cowards who never stood ground to fight, but roamed, picking the weak and helpless as their prey. They struck swiftly and deadly, leaving pain and confusion in their wake, never returning upon the same trail for fear they'd meet old enemies and recent victims better prepared for a fight.

They rode into the camp, cutting down the monks in their path. The Pathfinder ran before a horseman and threw the silver box containing the skull-map over the ledge and into the river gorge before the Mongol cut him down.

Lsong shoved Tashi into the bushes and ran into the open to lure them away from where Tashi was concealed. The horsemen gave chase, running Lsong to ground like a pack of dogs after a rabbit. Two men held Lsong while a third man ripped open her clothes. Once her flesh was showing, the Mongol opened his pants and dropped between her legs.

Lsong screamed and Tashi felt the pain as her own. Trembling with fear but wanting to help, Tashi came out of the bushes.

"Stop!" she cried.

The startled Mongols swung around. The man on Lsong scrambled to his feet. As Tashi drew the Mongols' attention, Lsong reached up and grabbed at a knife on the man's belt. A Mongol on horseback leaned in the saddle as he came by Lsong. His sword clashed and Lsong's head separated from her body. The head bounced on the ground.

Tashi stared in frozen horror at the rolling head. "No, no, *Lsong!*"

The rider turned his horse and charged Tashi, roaring a battle cry, bloody sword held high.

She stumbled backward. Rocks gave way underfoot and she fell over the cliff. A scream stuck in her throat as she felt herself freefalling. She hit hard, as if her whole body had been punched, and blacked out as raging waters carried her downriver.

CALCUTTA

CHAPTER 17

Peter left the hotel while the streets were dizzy from the heat. He wanted to check out, while it was still day, the location Dr. Poc said the exchange would take place.

He left the carpetbag with Mr. Skull in it sitting in plain sight on his dresser. He didn't want his room demolished if someone came looking for it.

The rendezvous point designated by Dr. Poc was the courtyard at the Temple of Kali in the Kalighat District. Peter squatted in a shady spot along the wall surrounding the temple. The courtyard statue portrayed the Hindu goddess as a hideous hag smeared with blood, teeth bared and tongue protruding. In her four hands, respectively, were a sword, a shield, a severed hand, and a strangling noose. She was naked except for a necklace of skulls and a belt of severed hands.

Dr. Poc couldn't have chosen a more appropriate place for the exchange. Even graveyards pale in comparison with the Temple of Kali.

A boy about twelve came running over and squatted by him. "Welcome, great sahib. I show you temple. One rupee. Very good guided tour!"

"No tour," he told the kid.

He was spotted by half a dozen ragged mudlarks like the one squatting beside him, and they came running toward him like the front line of Notre Dame.

Peter hastily changed his mind; he didn't want an army of waifs calling attention to him.

"Okay. One rupee. Now get rid of your friends."

The boy ran to meet the pack and in a flurry of Bengali and hand signals told the ragged army that he had already staked a claim on Peter. Then he strutted back and squatted by Peter.

"Okay, sahib. Very good tour now."

The exchange was set for midnight outside the temple, and after seeing the exterior he had no intention of going inside. "Just relax, kid. Your English is pretty good. Learn it in school?"

"No school. Learn from tourist."

"What's, uh, that temple about?"

"Okay, sahib. Kali very powerful goddess." The kid acted out his little spiel with hand gestures and rolling eyes. "Kali the Black, Kali the Terrible, Kali most powerful goddess in all India. Goddess of Death and Destruction. Calcutta her home."

"Kali a Hindu goddess?"

The boy was a pathetic little creature, barefoot, all skin and bones with rags for shirt and shorts.

"Kali biggest Hindu goddess. Kali also worshipped by Thuggie."

"Thuggie?" Peter pondered the word. "Thugs. Some sort of murder cult, wasn't it?"

Sweat dripped from the boy's chin. "Thuggie bad. Kill people as sacrifice to Kali."

"The Thugs are gone now, aren't they?"

The boy shrugged and rolled his eyes.

Peter noticed a large block of stone near the temple. It had dark red stains and flies swarming it. "What's that?"

"That where sacrifices made."

"What kind of sacrifices?"

"Each day priests sacrifice virgin to Kali."

"What?"

The boy broke out laughing. Realizing his little joke might cost him a fee, he got serious again. "Virgin goat or lamb, Sahib. You see later." He eyed Peter shrewdly. "Sahib ask many questions. Price of tour now two rupee."

Peter grinned. "All right, you little bandit. You live around here?"

The boy didn't quite understand the question. "Where I go, I live. Me Kangalis."

Peter understood. He had come across a story about the tragedy of Kangalis children when he was reading a local newspaper at breakfast. A Kangalis was a child of the streets, an orphan who was abandoned at an early age or whose parents were wiped out in one of the epidemics that periodically raged in the city. They attach themselves to other street children, banding together for protection and territorial rights. They eat, sleep, and die on the streets. He had seen Kangalis kids rummaging through the garbage piles for food scraps the night before when he walked along Park Street.

The kids must be streetwise and smart because the dumb ones die in the gutter, he thought, or get picked up by a beggar king and have their limbs broken to make them appealing beggars.

"What's your name, kid?"

"Saru."

"Okay, Saru. I'm Peter."

"Okay, Peter."

"I'm meeting a man here tonight. He's going to give me something. I want to make sure the meeting is private. Understand?"

"You no want men to take what man give you."

The kid was no dummy. "You've got it. You hang around the temple tonight and watch my back, whistle if anyone shows up, and I'll pay you three rupees."

The kid put back on his shrewd mask. "If Saru

watch back, Saru bodyguard. Saru charge five rupees!" Less than two dollars.

"Sold!"

The boy sat next to Peter and stretched out his
toothpick legs. Bits and pieces were missing from
several toes. Peter made the mistake of asking what
caused the damage.

"Rats."

When night fell, flaming torches lit the temple
grounds and a trembling lamb was carried to the sacrificial block. Peter decided it was time to take a walk.

Crowds of people, many of them wearing costumes, were converging on the street behind the
temple, as Peter and Saru stopped to buy dinner off
a street vendor selling steamy vegetables rolled in a
large, flat bread that looked like a Mexican tortilla.

"What's going on?" Peter asked the boy.

"Monsoon festival. Tonight people make noise
to frighten away rain clouds. Dress as gods"—he
pointed at people wearing masks and costumes depicting Vishnu, Brahma, and Ganesha, the son of Kali
who wore an elephant's head because his wicked
mother sliced his head off—"to make storm clouds
believe gods no want clouds to come to Calcutta."
Some of the masks had death's head grins and devil
horns. "They dress as Thuggie," the boy said. "Even
clouds frighten of Thuggie."

Peter and the boy carried their food down the steps
of the Kalighat and walked along the shore of Tolly's
Nullah, the river that flowed through the district.
Tolly's Nullah was holy water, an extension of the
Hooghly River, which in turn fed from the mother of
holy rivers, the Ganges. The "sheeted dead" had already staked out much of the riverbank. "Cool by
river," Saru told him. "Better than sleeping in street."

They sat on rocks beside the water and watched

night fishermen in dhows, the Indian Ocean fishing craft with a single mast and triangular sail.

A strange full moon sailed the gloomy night sky, a swollen amber ball with shadowy stripes. "Tiger moon," Saru told him. "Before monsoon, King of Tigers ride moon across sky."

"He doesn't want to get wet?"

"He seeking peace. Tiger most feared of all jungle beasts. Once friend of all animals. Then he taste forbidden flesh of other animals, taste blood in his mouth, and all-powerful Brahma punish him, make him be alone, always hunted and hunter.

"But Brahma merciful and once each year let King of Tigers leap up to moon and ride around world in search of place where he find peace and happiness. But he never find peace. Everyone know tiger is bad and word fly faster than moon. Who want tiger for neighbor?"

By the time the witching hour approached, the temple grounds were dark and deserted. The torches had burned down to smoldering embers, and the blood had dried on the sacrificial block. Even the flies had moved on to fresher prey.

Peter could hear the clamor of the monsoon festival taking place in the streets to the rear of the temple grounds as he and the boy returned. The grim statue of Kali in the courtyard had grown more venomous as moon rays cast her in pale glows and dark shadows. Saru told him the heads in Kali's necklace were those of her sons. Sweet mother.

Dr. Poc's instructions were for Peter to hang around the statue and wait to be contacted by a man carrying a parcel. Peter staked out Saru behind a fountain where the kid would have a good view in all directions and took his own position by the statue. The suspicion that Poc was setting him up nagged at him.

*   *   *

Tashi sat behind the steering wheel of the yellow Cord convertible parked two blocks from the Temple of Kali.

A parade of merrymakers in masks flowed by the car. A man who had had too much to drink spotted the young woman alone in the car and staggered over, noisily boasting of his sexual prowess. Tashi's hand went to the small black automatic in the open purse beside her. The drunk was three feet from the car when big hands grabbed him from behind and turned him back in the direction of the flow of merrymakers. A big foot sent him on his way.

After disposing of the drunk, Ma paused by the car and stared impassively down at Tashi. He never spoke without first having been spoken to. It was a characteristic of the Mongol race, a people who once conquered most of the known world through sheer savagery. She had lived among Ma's people in the Sinkiang and knew the language and ways of the quiet yet fierce Mongols. Her knowledge of his language and customs had created a bond between them that neither Zhdanov nor Bagora could sever.

"Did you find him?" she asked.

Ma nodded. "He waits at the temple for the messenger."

"What else did you see?"

"Man with gun. On rooftop. There." He pointed down the street at a two-story building. The building was across from the back side of the temple.

"What's the man doing on the roof?"

Ma shrugged. "He waits."

"Waits for what?"

He said nothing. His eyes, his face betrayed nothing. She stared down the street, toward the temple. She was certain Peter had been sent on a mission by Poc. A rendezvous with death.

*   *   *

As the minutes ticked off past midnight Peter grew more uneasy, extending his pacing farther from the statue. He was about to call off his vigil when he heard Saru's whistle.

A man had entered the temple ground and was walking toward Peter. He wasn't carrying a box. Peter tensed. The man might be a pilgrim straggler who came for a bit of late-night meditating. Or something might be wrong. In any case, he didn't particularly want to mingle with the type of person who came to worship the bloodthirsty goddess by the light of a full moon.

"Hi. Nice night," Peter said as the man paused in front of him.

"Very nice night, good friend." The man smiled, exposing sparkling white teeth that glowed in the dark, unusual for a land of betelnut chewers. Smiley pointed up to the moon. "The King of Tigers is riding the moon out of Bengal tonight so he does not get his feet wet when the rain comes."

"Smart tiger," Peter said.

White teeth flashed again. "It is good you seek the blessing of Kali under cover of night. Kali the Black is Kali of the Darkness. Her strength and thirst for blood grows at night."

"That's nice." He cleared his throat. "Well, have a nice night."

"I can be of some small assistance to you," Smiley said. "You are to meet someone. I am his friend."

"Go on."

"The one you seek is waiting in back of the temple. I will guide you."

"No dice. He can come out here."

"He will not. There is more privacy in back of the temple."

"Yeah. That's what I'm afraid of."

Saru whistled again. Peter took his eyes off Smiley long enough to glance around. A man wearing a grinning Thuggie mask had entered the courtyard to Peter's right. Smiley's grin got wider until it looked like the death's head grin of the Thuggie masks.

The boy whistled frantically. Another man in a Thuggie mask had entered the courtyard. Peter started to turn back to Smiley and caught the flash of metal out of the corner of his eye; he jumped back as Smiley swung at him with a dagger. Half off balance, Peter threw a wild punch, catching the man's mouth half open, feeling the flesh rip on his knuckles as his fist shattered beautiful white teeth. Smiley was flying backward as Saru came running by, shouting "Thuggie!"

Peter lost sight of the kid as he followed him around the back of the temple.

On a rooftop a block away from the temple a man knelt at the edge, resting a high-powered rifle on the guard rail. The man was focusing the rifle's night scope at the rear of the temple as a little Hindu boy darted around a corner.

The sniper on the roof frowned. He had been told to expect a man, a Westerner. A second later the man he was waiting for came running around the corner behind the boy. The sniper smiled as he adjusted his aim to bring the cross bars of the night scope center to the man's chest. His concentration was interrupted by a movement behind him. As the sniper started to turn around, Ma grabbed him by the neck in a paralyzing grip.

Peter ran across the dark courtyard at the rear of the temple and out the open back gate. The street in back was crowded with masked people having fun raising hell to scare off the monsoon. People scattered in panic as a yellow convertible came down the gutter lane. The car screeched to a stop beside him.

"Get in!" Tashi yelled.

He threw himself over the window rail and she gunned the car down the lane with the gods and monsters of Hindu mythology jumping out of the way. Someone with a Thuggie mask and a big knife didn't move fast enough, and the Cord's front bumper gave him a nudge as it roared by.

Beyond the temple she kept a heavy foot on the throttle, maneuvering the powerful car through the light vehicle traffic, whipping around ox carts and taxis, ignoring the angry whistle of an umbrella cop in the middle of an intersection.

Peter was still a little breathless from the foray at the temple and her driving didn't help his blood pressure. "I thought for a minute you were going to leave that cop's teethmarks on your bumper," he said.

"Teethmarks?"

"To go with the tire marks on his chest." He took a couple of deep breaths. "That was interesting."

"What was interesting?"

"Being chased by homicidal maniacs around an ancient temple." He cleared his throat and leaned toward her in mock seriousness. "I don't want to stick my nose into your personal business, but how is it you knew there were plans afoot to murder me tonight?"

"I'm a mind reader."

"That's good. For a moment I was worried. I thought you were going to tell me you hang around with Thugs and dwarfs and oversize Mongols with murderous appetites." He took a closer look at the car and ran his hand over the rosewood dash. "Nice car. Did you, uh, have to do much to earn it?"

No response.

"I know," he said, "I'm supposed to be grateful that you saved me. I am grateful, but it would be nice to get a few answers, too." She was heading the car south out of the city. "Where are we going?"

"Somewhere safe."

"I should have been clever and thought of that myself." He leaned toward her. "You know what I like about the way you answer questions?"

"Nothing," she said.

"Jesus. You *do* read minds."

A gun was poking out of the open purse on the seat beside her. It had a familiar look. He didn't doubt she was capable of using it.

Outside the city, she opened the Cord up on a long, flat roadway that followed the river delta toward the sea. Oxen and chickens were under the impression that the pockmarked ribbon of roadway was built for them to sleep on at night; she expertly maneuvered the car around them, occasionally veering off onto the grassy shoulder when both sides of the road were blocked by sleeping animals.

With the convertible top down, moonlight and a breeze from the balmy night bathed them. The breeze felt good, antiseptic, washing away some of the terrible social grime Calcutta had left on him.

He studied her profile in the moonlight. She had flawless physical beauty, but he was a people watcher and looked for more, reading faces the way other people read books. There was character to her features, character shaped by pride and passion, but he knew that he had only barely scratched the surface. She was an enigma wrapped in a mystery, like a gift box one unwraps only to find another box inside. He sensed an incredible reservoir of strength and will beneath the delicate beauty; she would step around a butterfly in her path but not flinch if she came upon a snake.

He wondered if the "safe" place she was taking him was also private. There were so many questions he had, so many things he wanted to find out. And share.

He leaned over and kissed her on the cheek, startling her.

"Why did you do that?"

He kissed her cheek again and again, caressing her cheek and the nape of her neck with his lips, tasting her flesh with his tongue.

She almost drove off the road. "Peter!"

"Pull over."

"What?"

"Pull over. I want you."

His lips inched down the front of her low-cut dress. He unbuttoned the top and put his face into the lush flesh between her breasts, sneaking around the side of one, softly nibbling at the firm mound until he found the nipple.

She groaned. "Stop it."

He tasted her nipple with his lips and tongue and it grew hard in his mouth as he ran his hand slowly, gently, up her soft, warm thigh, her legs spreading at his touch.

"Nooooo!"

The Cord flew off the road, barreling across a ditch and into the hanging garden of a banyan tree before it stopped. Tashi was in his arms when the car came to a halt. He unbuttoned her dress and frantically pulled it off. She threw her arms around his neck and squeezed him, her teeth biting into his neck and shoulders as she pulled at his clothes.

"Crazy," she whispered breathlessly, "you're crazy."

She pulled off his shirt and rubbed her breasts across his firm chest and kissed him, her mouth and tongue frantically exploring his. Peter fell back on the seat with her on top of him. She spread her legs and captured him in the softness between, rubbing herself over the hardness until he slipped inside her.

They both felt the magic, the memory, of lovers

long apart, passions long smothered; they were one, meant for each other, destined by their kismet to find each other across mountains, seas, and time itself . . .

Peter drove with Tashi's head on his lap, his hand on her bare shoulder. He wasn't tired; he was at peace. For the first time in his life he felt fulfilled. It wasn't just sexual satisfaction; his soul had found peace.

He used both hands on the steering wheel to avoid a pair of oxen in the road. She stirred in his lap and he put his hand back on her shoulder, running his fingers over the delicate curve of her neck. He felt the silver pendant she always wore.

"The snow leopard, it's more than a piece of jewelry, isn't it?"

She sat up and snuggled against his shoulder, her warm breath on his neck sending pleasure signals all the way down to his toes.

"It reminds me of my home. In the mountains."

"Is Zhdanov your lover?"

The question popped out and he regretted it instantly. She sat up, brushing back her hair, bathing her face in the breeze.

"I'm sorry," he said. He put his free hand on her leg. "It doesn't matter. Nothing matters but you and me."

They reached the sea at dawn. She directed him off the main road and through a small, sleeping village. Several miles past the village the dirt road turned into sand and finally ended at the foot of palm trees lining a white, sandy beach.

They got out of the car and walked through the palm trees.

"This is my secret place," she said. It was a bamboo hut in the grove of palms, a simple place with a floor of sand, palm fronds on the roof to keep off tropical showers, open windows to let in the sea breeze, a hammock hanging inside, and a fire pit outside.

He had expected an elaborate beach house, glass and chrome and driftwood furniture, but he should have known better. She was in tune with nature, not material things.

They kicked off their shoes and walked barefoot in the sand. He took off his shirt and threw it to the side. It was a good feeling to know he could have dropped his wallet on the beach and it would have been there when he got back.

"I love the ocean," she said. "It has the peace and tranquility of my mountains."

"Which mountains?"

"The Himalayas. The Roof of the World."

"The Roof of the World," he said. The place where his father's plane went down. "The highest mountains in the world. Many of them still unclimbed. That high up, they must be the cleanest place on earth, too."

"They're the closest thing to heaven," she said. "White and pure and clean. I feel sorry for the people who live and die in the filth of Calcutta, never knowing that there is a place that man has not polluted."

"Maybe it's better that they don't know," he murmured. He glanced sideways at her. "Where exactly are you from? Who are you? What do you want to be when you grow up?"

She laughed and put her arm around him and rested her head against his shoulder as they walked.

"Who am I? I am . . . me. Whoever that is. I am the sum total of cells that swam in the sea of my mother's womb until they reached land and walked erect."

"That explains a lot. Who were your parents? Descartes and Darwin?"

"My mother was Tibetan, my father Swiss. Both have passed beyond sorrow."

Passed beyond sorrow. He liked the expression. Death was permanent. Passing beyond sorrow must be just one step in birth and rebirth.

He also realized she was lying. She had spoken the word "Swiss" as if she wasn't completely comfortable with it. Swiss was a good choice, he thought. Multinational, multilingual, it was perfect for someone who wanted a vague, neutral background. No one disliked the Swiss—not even terrorists picked on them.

The Tibetan half gave her fascinating dimensions. He had never met a Tibetan and knew little about the ancient kingdom, other than the fact it was the site of Hilton's lost utopia, Shangri-La, and a few news stories. "Tibet was taken over by Red China, wasn't it? Back in the early sixties." She nodded. "Were your family refugees?"

"Yes," she said.

Another lie, he thought.

"I remember reading about Tibet when I was a kid," he said. "Quite a mysterious place. It wasn't opened up to the West until a few years ago."

"Most of it is still not open to the West or the Red Chinese. Chinese troops occupy the half-dozen population centers, but most of the region is still independent because not even the Communists can conquer Mother Nature. There are valleys no plane has ever flown over, villages so remote the language they speak is different from that spoken at the next village.

"But time is running out." Bitterness crept into her voice. "If the world does not destroy itself with bombs or pollution, someday the Red Chinese will reach every crevice of the great plateau. By accident, if nothing else." She changed the subject. "Your last question, what I plan to do when I grow up, is very

American. The question suggests a choice, and choice is totally alien to my culture."

"Doctor, lawyer, Indian chief," he said. "Those are the choices young Americans thought about in the past. Since *Star Wars*, Indians are out and space cadets are in."

She shook her head. "The society I was raised in presumes one's path in life has already been set out at birth."

"By family, caste, mores—"

"All of those. And most of all, the Universal Plan."

"The Universal Plan?"

"Predestination. Destiny, is another way of putting it."

He stopped and pulled her close. "Kismet?"

"Yes, kismet."

He nuzzled her nose with his lips. "What does our kismet say? Will I fight duels for your honor? Will we live happily ever after?"

She kissed him tenderly. "We won't know until the plan unfolds."

"To hell with the plan. Let's you and I go off together. Or stay here at your hideaway. We'll live off bananas and breadfruit and fish from the sea."

She put her arms around his waist and held him tight, pressing her head against his chest, listening to the miracle of heartbeat.

He gently cupped her chin in his hand and lifted it until her eyes met his.

"There is one secret you have to tell me," he said, "one part of yourself you have to reveal. What's your relationship with the man called Zhdanov?"

She looked deeply into his eyes before she spoke, probing, again leaving him with the sensation that she was searching for a part of him that was buried so deep not even he had reached it.

"Have you ever heard of Shambala?" she asked. She studied his face as he answered.

"Shambala?" He shook his head. "No. Where is it?"

"Some say you can only find Shambala in the heart," she murmured. She looked away, at the endless ocean. "It's in the mountains."

"I've never heard of Shambala, but I know there are a lot of little postage-stamp kingdoms in the Himalayas that India and Red China squabble over. Places like Nepal, Bhutan, Mustang. Is Shambala one of them?"

"Yes. It's hard for a Westerner to imagine, but the Tibetan plateau is not one big place but thousands of little places, each utterly desolate. Ninety-nine percent of the country has no roads, has never seen a car, a television, or even an airplane."

"What about Zhdanov? What's his connection to this empire of ice and rock?"

"Zhdanov is a rich and powerful man. He is . . . a benefactor of Shambala, a man with worldwide contacts who will help keep it from the hands of the Red Chinese."

She wasn't at all comfortable describing Zhdanov as a humanitarian. This time he didn't let it pass. "You're not telling me the truth."

She caressed his cheek with her hand. "I'm sorry, but there are some things that I can't reveal even to you."

"Damn." He hugged her tightly to him. "What I'm willing to take from you is incredible."

She whispered in his ear, "Do you know what I want?"

"What?"

"A bath!"

She dropped her dress on the sand and ran laughing into the surf. He hopped out of his pants and tossed them behind him as he splashed in after her.

God, he felt good!

She disappeared for a moment as a wave swallowed her, then reappeared and waded toward him in waist-deep water, a sea nymph shadowed by the mist from the burst of powerful waves at her back.

They kissed, standing in a shower of spray as the surf exploded around them. He lifted her to him and they came together as one, her legs around him, his love inside her, the showering surf hiding them from the world.

They slept wrapped in each other's arms in the shade of a palm tree. Peter awoke before noon to find her gone and scrambled to his feet, his heart pounding, until he spotted her coming back from the hut carrying a sack. She knelt in the sand and turned the sack upside down, spilling bananas, melon, and a coconut.

"It's from the village," she said. "They know I'm here when the car passes through. They bring food a couple of times a day and leave it discreetly by the hut. They never disturb me."

"That's nice of them."

"They're good people. And poor. I bring them medical supplies from the city. I didn't have a chance to pick up anything this time, but I'll send something back after we return."

The coconut had already been breached and a piece of cork shoved in the hole.

They sat side by side under the palm, a naked Adam and Eve in Paradise, drinking milk from the coconut and eating fresh-picked fruit. Their clothes, the sand brushed off, were draped over a bush.

He ate his fill and stretched out on warm sand, utterly content. She laid her head on his chest, her ear to his heartbeat, and doodled in the hair of his chest with a piece of palm leaf.

He purred with contentment. "I don't want this moment to ever end," he told her.

She sighed. "We must return to the city sometime."

"Why can't we stay here? Let the world go on without us?"

"Choices," she said. "I don't have the option to be an Indian chief. I have duties, not choices."

"We only have to do what we want to, Tashi. There are no set paths of life. You start out in one direction and something happens and you go off in another. Life isn't predestined. I came to Calcutta for one purpose, met you, and now I'm off in another direction."

She sat up and rested her elbows on his chest. She stared, puzzled, at him. "I thought you came to Calcutta because you traced me here."

"I couldn't trace you. I didn't even know your name. I came to Calcutta because of some strange responses I got in London when I was looking into my father's plane crash."

"Your father's plane crash?"

Peter put his hands behind his head and closed his eyes. He wished she would drop the subject. He wanted the here and now with her, not ancient bones and military secrets.

"I went to London to trace my father's family. He was an RAF pilot back in the late fifties. He disappeared in a flight over the Himalayas before I was born. The flight originated in Calcutta, but I'm sure it wasn't made public. There was something secret about the flight. I ran into roadblocks trying—"

"What was your father's name?" She got to her feet. She turned from him, brushing sand off as she asked the question.

"MacKinzie," he said, sitting up, yawning. "Duncan MacKinzie. I was given my stepfather's name of Novak."

She took her dress off the bush and picked up her shoes.

"Why are you getting dressed?"

"I have to go," she said. Her voice was cold.

He got to his feet, concerned. "Are you okay?"

Tashi didn't answer. She disappeared into the palm grove without saying a word.

Going where? he wondered. She didn't need her dress or shoes for a call of nature.

Peter grabbed his pants and pulled them on. He heard the car start before he was halfway through the grove of palms. He broke into a run, but the yellow Cord was already leaving a trail of dust behind it as it raced away. He stared at the car in shock and bewilderment.

She had abandoned him. Left him stranded. Pumped him for whatever he knew and dumped him.

He went back to find his shoes. It was going to be a long walk to the village. And then what the hell would he do? Hitch a ride on an ox?

The only transportation back to the city was a smoking, overcrowded wreck of a bus he caught on the highway.

He rode back to Calcutta wedged between a woman with live chickens in her lap and a man holding a baby pig.

CHAPTER 18

It took five long, miserable hours for the chugging, smoking, crowded bus to crawl, jerk, and bump its way to the outskirts of Calcutta where Peter caught a taxi back to his hotel.

It was nearly six, still daylight and hot enough to stir the asphalt street with a spoon by the time he reached the hotel. The horde of beggars staking out the hotel started for Peter and then backed off. He was hot, disgusted, and angry; he looked mad enough to bite off the hand held out for baksheesh.

He spotted Smiley loitering in front of a tobacco stand a couple of doors down the street. Smiley was holding a Thuggie mask like the ones worn by monsoon celebrants—and assassins—at the temple. He quickly put it on and disappeared into an alley next to the tobacco shop.

Peter's free-flowing anger turned to cold fury. He was tired of people playing games with him. He went after Smiley, beggars and pedestrians scrambling out of his way as he charged down the sidewalk.

The alley was a long stretch of cardboard stalls with curtains. Smiley had almost reached the other end. The assassin glanced back just before turning the corner. He was still wearing his Thuggie mask.

Peter raced down the alley, the corners of his eyes picking up the action in the makeshift stalls. It was a street of prostitutes. Each stall with an open curtain had a girl displayed on a bed. The ones with closed curtains were doing business. Jesus. What a city.

He took the corner wide coming out of the alley, just in case Smiley was waiting with a knife. He wasn't. Peter spotted him at the entrance to a marketplace down the street. It looked like half the population of Calcutta was surging into the market wearing a variety of monsoon masks. The Indians were still trying to scare off the rain clouds.

Smiley paused and looked back to Peter before melting into the crowd flowing into the market. He realized Smiley wasn't checking to see if he was following; *he was making sure he followed.*

Good! He'd rather have it out in a public marketplace with a thousand people around than wait for the bastards to sneak into his room and cut his throat while he was sleeping.

He went after Smiley, following the crowd into the market, trying to keep an eye on the man's bobbing head among the sea of bobbing heads.

The people around him were dancing, singing, chanting, shaking rattles, banging tin drums, creating enough noise to scare off a hurricane. Shades of Rudyard Kipling. Man trespassed on the moon, built concrete cities, encircled the world with golden arches, and put Adidas on *real* camel jockeys, but the pulsating heart of the Asian marketplace had remained the same from Sinbad to Sputnik. Even the Timex watches and Japanese cameras smacked of antiquity.

Peter stepped by fly-infested piles of fruit and vegetables, overripe papayas and bananas with ugly black spiders crawling on the stacks, hairy coconuts, dirt-encrusted sweet potatoes, and mounds of unshelled rice. There were baskets of aromatic spices next to racks of Swiss watches, strings of garlic and French postcards, musty piles of hemp alongside light bulbs and can openers. Intermingled with the wares was a press of people speaking a babel of languages and dressed in costumes from the Arabian Nights. The smell of fermenting fruit hung in the air.

There was magic in the marketplace: jugglers with rhythm in their fingers, medicine men with potions to cure sore feet and sick love affairs, fortune tellers who painted their bodies with gray ash and read life's passages from splinters of human bones. Small children in ragged clothes intercepted him, clamoring "Baksheesh, sahib, baksheesh." Money, master, money. "A penny for the guy."

He cursed. The army of mudlarks cost him sight of Smiley. Worse, there were dozens of men in the crowd wearing Thuggie masks. He couldn't tell one from the other. Now he realized why Smiley had lured him into the marketplace. His white face and six-foot-plus frame poked out like a white sail on a brown ocean.

Any one of the people around him could be an assassin, ready to stick a knife in his back.

The only policeman he spotted was a hundred yards across the sea of people, a cop in a pith helmet standing under an umbrella on a platform that elevated him slightly above the crowd.

The kids begging for money had left him for fresher bait and Peter yelled for them.

"Hey, kids!" He grabbed a handful of change and threw it in the air. A dozen waifs came running.

They might not have understood him, but the money he was flashing got across the message. They surrounded him, clamoring for more. He threw them a little and flashed more as he moved toward the policeman's platform, the dirty dozen around him.

A short man in a Thuggie mask suddenly dashed into the crowd of kids behind Peter. Peter swung around and lashed out with a karate kick he hadn't used since college. The blow caught the man in the chest and stopped him in his tracks. Peter ripped off the Thuggie mask—it was Smiley, with a swollen lip and gap in his smile. Peter hit him with the right cross again, putting all his anger behind the punch, feeling the welcome crunch of the man's nose under his fist, blood squirting, the bastard falling backward into the dirt. Another Thuggie charged; Peter sidestepped and sent him sprawling with an elbow to the back of the head.

Peter spotted a flight of wooden stairs leading up to tenements and went for the stairway, cursing himself for being so damned stupid. He hit the steps and took them two at a time. There was a woman ahead of him who had reached the top before he was halfway up. She opened a door and he yelled as she started to close it.

"Wait!"

She gave him a startled look and slammed the door. He heard footsteps behind him and charged up the stairs with everything he had. Just as he reached the top, he heard a latch dropping. He hit the door with his shoulder and bounced off.

"Son of a bitch!"

A dagger breezed by his head and bit into the door. He swung around. A grinning, masked Thuggie rushed up the steps at him. Peter kicked at the face, experiencing the satisfaction of his toe catching the dagger thrower neatly under the chin. Another Thuggie reached the bottom of the steps, pulling out a dagger as his friend tumbled down.

The thatched roof of a shop was only a few feet from the top step. He didn't think it would hold him.

He leaped onto the roof and took two stumbling steps before it gave under his weight. "Akkkk!!" He crashed through, taking a big hunk of the thatch with him. He hit a table of clay pots in the stall below and the table collapsed, sending him to the dirt floor with pottery flying and breaking all around him.

He crawled out of the wreckage, his breath gone, adrenaline keeping him moving, and ran from the shop, knocking over another table of pottery.

People scattered in confusion, yelling in six different languages as he shot into the crowd with men brandishing daggers in hot pursuit. He ran into a coolie with a mile-high stack of baskets balanced on his head, sending the coolie sprawling into cages of chickens. Chickens burst from the cages, feathers flying everywhere.

A Thuggie came at him with a dagger. He dodged the thrust, grabbed the man's knife hand, and hit him in the chest with his shoulder, sending him backward over the stone wall of a water well. Peter stumbled off balance and fell to his knees by the well. He heard the crunch of footsteps behind him and started to turn, fists cocked, when something whacked him across the head. Just before he kissed the ground, he had a vision of the white helmet worn by the man who hit him. It reminded him of the pith helmets Indian policemen wear.

CHAPTER 19

Assistant Police Commissioner E. M. S. Jinnah had a dry, barbed, warped sense of humor. "It's a good thing you Americans have hard heads."

The inflection in his voice suggested he wouldn't have been displeased if Peter's brains had been splattered in the dirt of the bazaar. Peter had woken up in the Calcutta jail, which was something like awakening from a bad dream and finding himself in a nightmare. He had spent two days in the hellish jail before being brought to Jinnah's office.

"If it helps any, I'm only half American."

" 'Fraid not. Not when the other half's British and you've caused a riot in a busy marketplace."

Peter started to defend himself and Jinnah held up his hand to forestall the alibiing. "I've read the report. Thieves with knives suddenly attacked you in the marketplace. A young woman, a tourist, witnessed the incident and her word has got you released from jail, but I still don't like the smell of it. You created havoc in the marketplace and caused one of our citizens to nearly drown in a well."

Peter had to clench his teeth to keep from telling Jinnah the good citizen was probably a hired assassin. He hadn't told Jinnah about Poc, the silver box, or the rendezvous at the Temple of Kali for fear it would earn him more time in the stinking jail.

Jinnah jabbed a long, slender finger at Peter. "I

have a feeling about you. Call it Eastern hocus-pocus if you like. You have bad karma. And I'm not talking about that foul stench of jail I smell on you." He stood and glared at Peter, a hanging judge looking down at the prisoner in the dock. "Evil acts in a man's previous lives determine the nature of his present one. Karma, Mr. Novak. Bad acts create bad karma. You wear it like a badge. You can't see it or taste it, but it's affecting every step you take. Stay out of trouble in my city or you'll end up a permanent resident in that jail you call a pest hole."

The assistant police commissioner started to turn away, then swung back and glared at Peter. "I don't know what you did in past lives to deserve this one, but you must have pissed off someone."

Peter left the police building and walked along the Maidan, the greenbelt the British left undeveloped in the heart of the city to give the guns of Fort Williams a clear shot at the Indians they stole the land from.

He was broke.

Baksheesh. Money. When kids and beggars clamored for it on the street, it was a handout; to a jail guard it was a bribe. The word of an anonymous woman had cleared his name, but it had been baksheesh that unlocked the door.

Thank God he still had his American Express card. He could live like a king in the city, and it was his ticket home.

The Royal Bengal Hotel looked like the Taj Mahal compared to the Calcutta jail. He felt reborn as he padded across the plush carpeting and handed his credit card to thè clerk with the gold smile.

"I'm back. Give me a room with the biggest bath in the hotel. And air conditioning. And a view. And send up room service."

Gold Tooth's smile got bigger as he checked a list

of numbers in a booklet. He took a pair of scissors out of a drawer.

"Your card is on the bad credit list."

He clipped the card in half with the scissors and gave Peter a 24-carat smile. "You'll never leave home with it again."

A porter came to the desk and dropped at Peter's feet his suitcase and the carpetbag. Peter left the hotel in a daze, carrying the two pieces of luggage.

The elderly priest with rusty features sipped a cool tropical drink in the shady courtyard as Peter staggered by.

Peter went to a moneylender's shack pressing against the towering Bank of Calcutta skyscraper. He showed the man the gold watch his mother had bought him for graduation. The man frowned at it for a while before making a bid.

"Fifty rupee."

"The watch is a family heirloom. My father gave it to me on his deathbed."

"Forty rupee." The moneylender sneered. "Two owner. More wear."

The man knew he was completely at his mercy. Destitute people must put out the same sort of panic vibes that swimmers tip off sharks with. No doubt moneylenders and sharks share a common ancestor.

"I'll take the fifty." About fifteen dollars. Enough for a fleabag hotel and a starvation diet for a couple of days. After that he'd have to sell off his other possessions—like his shoes and soul.

He put the carpetbag on the counter. He leaned across and whispered. "In this bag is a priceless fossil that a museum would pay a fortune for. A hundred rupees and its yours."

"Ten rupees for bag. You keep bone."

"I'm serious. It's part of the mortal remains of the

Father of the English People. Seventy-five rupees."

"Seven rupee for bag. You pay me ten rupee I poison my dog with bone of English father."

The Hooghly Hotel was near the river. The hotel stank of piss and curry. The river breeze smelled like a sewer.

He had the skull stuffed in his shirt when he checked into the fleabag. The clerk learned his trade from moneylenders and taxi drivers; he would have charged for a double had he known Peter was sharing the room with Mr. Skull.

His stomach growled; he planned one meal for the day. Being broke was frightening. For the first time he realized how alone he was in the world.

The next morning someone slipped a note under the door of his room.

Mr. Novak—
Please honor me by attending a party at my home
this evening. My car will call for you at five.
                              —Zhdanov

Peter had not been sure what his next move should be. He was grateful someone had made the decision for him. He put in a call to Jinnah at Calcutta police headquarters.

Jinnah came across a little fuzzy through the static. "Hope you're not calling from the holding tank of our jail."

"You haven't got phones in your jail. The rats ate them. I've called for a favor, Commissioner."

"If you want to know the schedule of the next plane out of Calcutta, I'll be glad to tell you. If you promise to be on it."

Charming bastard.

"Have you ever heard of someone named Zhda-nov?"

"Zhdanov? What business do you have with Cal-cutta's shadow man?"

"Nothing. It's just a name someone dropped on me. The man's supposed to be superrich. I was wondering what kind of business he was in."

"We keep dossiers on, uh, interesting foreigners, regardless of whether they're rich robber barons or rioters in the marketplace."

"Zhdanov's a robber baron?"

"I don't know what Zhdanov is and it's not because I haven't tried. I know he's rich, that he has the sort of influence only great wealth can buy, and that this rich, influential man has some of the worse Calcutta scum hanging around. Looking for a job, Mr. No-vak?" Jinnah laughed. "He has his own island, upriver in the delta. It's guarded by a private army."

"I get the impression you're interested in the man."

"Fascinated is a better word. Like looking at snakes through glass at the zoo, wondering what it would be like if you stuck your hand inside to pet one. Let me tell you a little story I heard. Zhdanov was blind when he came to Calcutta years ago, but he had an opera-tion that restored his sight. There were dirty rumors on the streets about that operation."

"Such as?"

"A young man, an acid-headed Australian youth was passing through Calcutta about that time. Hitch-hiking to Katmandu or some nonsense. We found his body floating in the Hooghly."

"And?"

"He had green eyes. They were gone when we pulled him out of the river."

"Zhdanov has green eyes?"

"Clever of you to deduce that."

"Why don't you ask his eye doctor about it?"

"Can't. He disappeared. Along with a noted plastic surgeon."

"Jesus." He thought of Tashi in Zhdanov's arms and shuddered.

Jinnah chuckled. "Why the sudden interest in one of Calcutta's less desirable characters?"

"I'm writing a book about your charming city. I'm going to devote a whole chapter to the efficiency of your street-cleaning crews."

Jinnah laughed and Peter decided to push his luck. "Ever hear of a Chinese named Dr. Poc? White beard, scholarly."

"Dr. Poc? What kind of doctor is he?"

"I'm not sure. Witch doctor for all I know."

"I've never heard of him. Maybe he hasn't been in Calcutta long or keeps a low profile. That's not hard to do if he's Chinese. We've got a big yellow population, and they're the most clannish group in Calcutta. One thing for sure: If he has anything to do with the Ho Sing Yee, stay clear of him."

"The Ho . . . what?"

"Ho Sing Yee, the biggest tong in Chinatown. Has most of the rackets and collects the biggest pot of protection money. They run around in black pajamas and carry hatchets. I'd rather tangle with a gang of Thugs than those yellow devils."

"If they're so bad, why don't you move in and clean them out?"

"Why don't you Americans clean up Chicago? We have an agreement with them: We don't bother them as long as they earn their protection money by keeping the streets of Chinatown quiet. Our policemen want nothing to do with the place. You know, I just remembered something. This ought to give you shivers."

"What?"

"*You* have green eyes."

                    *   *   *

At five o'clock there was only one car parked in front
of the hotel, a twelve-cylinder Hispano-Suiza, a sleek,
kingly masterpiece of yesterday. The limo looked a
little embarrassed to be parked in front of the fleabag
hotel.

The chauffeur got out of the car and held the door
for Peter. It was the big Mongol from London. The
man had a twelve-cylinder torso and eight-ply arms
and legs.

"You leave your toady little friend at the zoo?"
Peter asked.

Ma didn't reply but gave Peter the look a person
gives an insect before squashing it. Peter got into the
car, vowing to keep his mouth shut.

He thought about why he had got the invitation and
came up with a blank. A lamb to the slaughter. He
kicked himself for not telling Jinnah about the invitation. Not that it really mattered. He would have
walked on burning coals for a chance to see Tashi.

The limo took him to a boat ramp an hour's drive
upriver from Calcutta where he boarded a high-speed
hydrojet that carried him and another guest into a
maze of tropical river islands. Standing by the helms-
man was a guard wearing a black uniform and armed
with an automatic weapon. "For crocodiles," the other
guest told Peter with a wink. The man identified himself as a German factory rep. He didn't say what kind
of merchandise his factory produced, but he didn't
look like a widget salesman.

Another black-uniformed guard waited at the boat
ramp to Zhdanov's private island, and Peter spotted
others off to the side. The island had more guns than
palm trees.

The river island was several hundred yards long
and almost that wide. Dominating the center, surrounded by jungle flora and thick walls, was a ram-

bling stucco villa large enough for a maharajah and fortified for a robber baron. Two gunmetal-black helicopters were on a landing pad near the dock. They were armored—and armed.

A tall blonde wrapped in a slinky red silk sari and heavy Swedish accent was playing hostess at the front door. "Enjoy," she said, gesturing for him to join the other guests. "Mr. Zhdanov will be with you shortly."

The guests were grouped into one large room dominated by a crystal and gold chandelier and spiraling marble staircase. Costly paintings and tapestries crowded the walls. The only style to the room was the School of Opulence.

Servants in white turbans and black tuxedos circulated with champagne and hors d'oeuvres. He noticed the guest list was composed almost exclusively of two types: well-dressed, middle-age men and professionally pleasant women.

Peter took a glass of champagne and was staring blankly at an etching hanging on the wall when someone came up beside him.

"Do you like Picasso?"

It was a woman, an Indian with a husky British accent. She had bold good looks that challenged a man.

"Picasso?"

"That etching of a minotaur you were looking at is one of his 1930s works. Are you an admirer of the Spaniard?"

Peter glanced at the etching. "I'm so ignorant of art, the only thing that struck me was what a fine line there is between art . . . and bullshit. But I guess that's the same about many things in life."

The woman laughed, throaty and sensual.

She was a woman designed for a man. Her long fingernails were useless at a kitchen sink, her body language was too exotic for an office. She had that soft fleshiness useful only for cushioning a man on top of her.

"Many Picassos appear simple enough to have been drawn by schoolchildren," she said, "yet the price paid for the simple sketch is more than most people earn in a lifetime. There are men who would do anything for that kind of money."

"Women, too. Are you a friend of Zhdanov's?"

"I am a professional party person. I am paid to bring a little excitement and adventure into the lives of the rich, bored men who attend Zhdanov's parties."

Her voice was low and husky, an East Indian Lauren Bacall.

"Sounds more like a safari than a party."

"Perhaps it is. A little bestiality would not be unusual in my line of work."

She laughed at the look on Peter's face.

The thought that Tashi might be one of Zhdanov's party girls—high-class whores—sickened him. Young women with too much makeup and too few clothes were disappearing up the stairs with men who had more paunch than hair. There was enough cocaine scattered around to ski on.

"Are you rich and bored? Or perhaps a rising young statesman?"

"I'm with the CIA."

"How marvelous. There are two other CIAs here tonight, plus a couple of ex-KGB generals and a Napoleon."

Something in her body language didn't jive. He didn't find her sexy. The effect she had on him was the sense of erotic danger the male black spider might experience before mating with a black widow.

"I am Arju."

"Arju. Very pretty."

"It is actually Arjumand. I was named after the lost love the Mughal emperor built the Taj Mahal for."

A portly Hindu with a roll of battle medals on the breast of his black tuxedo grinned at Arju and winked as he walked by arm in arm with a young man who should have complemented his lipstick, wavy hair, and jewelry with a dress.

"That's Mr. Narja. Do you know him?"

Peter shook his head. "No."

"You should. He'd be a valuable contact for a man in your profession. He's the commissioner of police."

Peter shrugged. "I'll pass. I wouldn't want to make it a triangle."

"You wouldn't. You'd double both their pleasure."

She moved close enough to breathe on him. "There are rooms upstairs where you can experience all your dreams and all you've ever imagined. Spend the night with me and no woman would ever satisfy you again."

He spotted Tashi across the room. She was standing by the French doors leading to the rear garden. They were separated by fifty feet and two dozen people, but for a magic moment the sounds of the party died, the people faded, and they were aware only of each other.

She turned away, breaking the magic spell as she went out of the French doors.

"Sorry," he told Arju, "somebody I know." She said something but he didn't catch it as he hurried after Tashi.

Arju moved over to the spiral staircase. Bagora appeared from the other side of the stairs.

"I couldn't tell if he was armed," Arju said.

"He isn't. He's an amateur." He frowned at her. "You should have kept him out of the commissioner's sight. He might see a picture of Novak later and remember the incident."

Arju shrugged. "It was not of my doing."

"Don't make any mistakes tonight. You know your duties." Bagora leered at her. "Fail and I'll stuff your ass with hot coals."

Bagora left her and went through a door marked PRIVATE and down a flight of stairs. At the bottom of the steps he tapped a code into an electronic lock and entered a room after the door clicked open.

He took a seat at the control console for half a dozen small video screens fed by cameras that spied into every room and behind every bush on the island. He flipped from room to room, checking out the action until he found something that suited his taste.

The men were guests in a deluxe room of the villa. One man was an Arabian oil minister; the other, also male, was a U.S. senator, a dimple-cheek political whiz kid portrayed by the American press as a rising star with White House ambitions, in Calcutta as part of a Third World fact-finding junket.

The star became tarnished that night as the head job the whiz kid gave the oil minister was captured on video tape in living color and sound.

Bagora rubbed the bulge in the front of his pants as he watched the show. Reluctantly he switched to catch the action in the garden.

Peter found her in the garden, in the cool of the fountains and lush greenery.

"You shouldn't have come here!" she said.

"I was invited."

"You have to leave immediately. Go back to Calcutta now."

"Are you one of Zhdanov's party girls?"

"Go home, Peter, go back to America. This isn't make-believe. You can't rewrite the characters to make them what you want."

"Why did you run away?"

"I . . . I can't explain."

"Is all that"—he gestured back at the house—
"crazy dirty money so important? Where do you find
love? In Zhdanov's wallet?"

"You don't understand."

"How the hell do you expect me to understand if
you don't explain?"

She stepped close to him and gently brushed hair
from his forehead. "Peter . . . Peter, run from here, run
as fast as you can. I can't go with you. I can't explain.
You have to trust me. You and I can never be."

"Come with me. We'll work it out together."

She shook her head. "I thought I could direct my
own life, but now I know I can't change my path any
more than the moon can. The steps I take today were
set into motion a thousand-thousand years ago. It is
my kismet, my fate, and it is too terrible for you to
share."

He took her in his arms. She tried to turn away,
but he pulled her close and his lips found hers, touching, fire to fire, melting their bodies together until
their souls touched.

"Peter . . . Peter, we can't . . . we can never be—"

"Tashi!"

Her name exploded in the garden like the crack of
a whip. They broke apart and turned to face the in-
truder. Zhdanov had entered the garden.

Peter was startled by the man's looks. Zhdanov's
chilled good looks were not what he had imagined.

Zhdanov stared coldly at them. "You are letting
Mr. Novak monopolize your time, my dear. My
guests are eager for your company."

She hesitated, at the juncture of two roads.

"Don't go, Tashi." Peter tried to grab her arm, but
she slipped away and ran back to the house.

Peter stepped up to the man, his fists clenched, angry blood pounding in his temples.

"Why did you invite me out here?"

Tension filled the air like static electricity.

Zhdanov didn't reply but stared coldly at him, taking his measure. Peter had an urge to crack the man's handsome veneer with a right cross. Two guards hovered in the background, and he kept the urge in check.

Zhdanov broke the tense silence. "A short time ago in London Tashi passed a bag to you during a critical moment. We assumed you were an innocent party, that your presence on the street was purely coincidental, but we were obviously wrong. This is the last warning you'll receive from me. Get out of Calcutta—and stay out of my affairs."

Zhdanov's expression never changed as he spoke; his smile was frozen like the happy face morticians paint on the dead. Peter wondered if the man had got his face the same way he got his eyes.

"Let Tashi go," Peter said. "She doesn't want to be with you."

Zhdanov left the garden and a cold wind stirred in his wake. Dr. Poc oozed greed and violence, old-fashioned human vices Peter could understand. But Zhdanov was different. Jinnah was right—the man was as cold-blooded as a snake. A snake Tashi clung to.

"Screw it," Peter told a stone cupid peeing in a fish pond. "Screw everything."

Arju was waiting by the French doors as Peter approached. She looked around cautiously and whispered, "Tashi's my friend. I have a message from her." She handed him a glass. "Here. Drink this so it will look like we're having a good time."

The liquor tasted good but left a sweet, sticky aftertaste. He started to say something, but his tongue stumbled on the words. A hot flash kicked him and his whole body experienced an orgasm.

*   *   *

Tashi found Zhdanov watching his guests from a second-floor interior balcony overlooking the ball-room.

"Why did you bring Peter Novak here?" she demanded.

"To take a look at him, see if he is as innocent as you claim."

"And?"

"It was an unnecessary exercise. My conversation with him confirmed what I already had uncovered—he's in league with Poc."

"He's been used by Poc."

"I'm afraid for once I'll have to discount your usually keen perceptions about people. You're ignoring the obvious because you've become emotionally involved."

"No harm must come to him." She stepped closer to Zhdanov, her eyes searching his face for a clue to his intentions. "If anything happens to Peter Novak, you'll never see me again."

"He's playing a dangerous game and I have no control over the other players. My opinion is that Mr. Novak will not survive the next forty-eight hours in Calcutta."

"Why do you say that?"

He shrugged. "You've met Dr. Poc."

"He must not be harmed!"

"It's not in my control."

"You can protect him."

"Why should I do that?"

"Because he . . . he's . . ."

Zhdanov started to walk away. She grabbed his arm. "Please. I'll do anything. Just don't let him be harmed."

"Show me the way to Shambala."

"What?"

"Between us we can find it. You know we can."

"You're asking me to betray Shambala."

"Am I? Use some common sense. How long will it be until the Red Chinese stumble onto the valley?"

"Why do you want to go there?"

"Not for the reasons you think. There's something in that tomb that I want. When I get it, I'll leave peacefully."

She shook her head. "What you're asking me—"

"What are your choices? If the Red Chinese beat us there, if they get access to the power in the tomb, Shambala will not only be destroyed, but the rest of the world will also suffer. If we get there first, we can save Shambala."

"I don't know, I'm so confused." She hid her face in her hands.

"You want Peter Novak protected, those are my terms. If you don't cooperate he'll be found floating facedown in the Hooghly with his throat cut."

"I'll help you!" she cried. "Damn you. *Damn me!*"

Peter was naked on a bed. On each side were naked men and women. They rubbed warm oil on his body, caressing, their hands massaging his chest, stomach, sliding up his thighs, teasing his groin.

Arju knelt beside the bed, running her tongue up the contours of his neck, whispering in his ear. At a signal from Arju the group surrounding Peter suddenly lifted him into the air. His whole body exploded with pleasure. They lay him back on the bed. He laughed. He wanted to purr with pleasure.

Bagora quietly entered the room and Arju slipped away from the bed to talk to him.

"Is the rest of our entertainment for Mr. Novak arranged?" Bagora asked.

Arju grinned. "The girl could be Tashi's twin."

"I want his mind thoroughly polluted," Bagora said. "Confused. It will make the gherao easier. There must be no bruises on the body and no connection back to us. His death must appear an accident."

"All is arranged. You will be pleased."

Inside the bedroom the group around Peter faded back; the room went dark except for a light beaming down at the bed.

Arju mounted Peter, sitting on his groin. Peter stared up at her with drug-glazed eyes. On the wall to the right a giant video screen went on. Arju pointed at the screen and grinned lewdly at Peter. "I said I'd tell you all about your sweetheart. There she is, doing what she likes best."

On the video screen a girl was lying sideways on a bed. A man was belly to belly with her, another had entered her from the rear. A third man was kneeling over her face. He put his penis in her mouth. The man turned to the camera. It was the old, toothless beggar whose face was half eaten away from cancer and who had accosted Peter in front of his hotel.

Arju scooted up to Peter's face. She lifted her dress and shoved an erect penis at his face. Arju grinned. "I told you no woman would satisfy you after you had experienced me."

Peter exploded, smashing the transvestite across the side of the head with his fist. He got off the bed and swung his fists wildly at anything that moved around him in the dark room. He ran screaming at the wall video. He bounced off the wall, got up, and slammed into it again. He kicked and screamed as guards held him down and Bagora put a drug-soaked cloth over his face.

CHAPTER 20

Peter awoke with the sun scratching at his eyelids and an angry horsefly trying to slip between the corners of his lips. He was in jungle foliage next to a neglected dirt road. His head felt like a sore full of pus and ready to pop.

The road was surrounded by jungle on both sides, dense, green walls alive with the cry of strange birds and excited monkeys. He got to his feet, dizzy and nauseated. The air was thicker than the atmosphere in an oven. *Where the hell was he?* The last thing he remembered was Arju, a drink, his mind exploding. Then a nightmare? How had he gotten into a jungle? At least there was a road. It had to lead somewhere.

He started down the road, weak-kneed at first, forcing himself to walk faster as he tried to outrun the mosquitoes that swarmed about him like flies around a garbage can. His pace slowed; in minutes his clothes were soaked, his breathing hard.

He staggered off the hot-plate road to rest in the shade of a rhododendron tree. Something long and narrow slithered in the foliage, and he veered back onto the road, his heart pounding in his throat.

He didn't have the strength to run far. He was surrounded by rain forest and dying for a drink of water. He would have licked a mud puddle if he could have found one. *What was Zhdanov up to?* Why had he been drugged and dumped in a jungle? He suddenly realized he wasn't alone. Moving in the jungle along the road were men, poor Hindu farmers. He shouted at them but no one returned his call. They kept walking, eyes straight ahead. As if they couldn't hear him. As if he didn't exist.

It scared the hell out of him. He walked faster.

He couldn't speak the language, but they had ears. They should have turned to his shouts. They were deliberately ignoring him but seemed to be pacing him. *They were veering closer.* Each man carried a short, thick piece of bamboo. No one spoke a word or looked at him.

"What do you people want?"

They suddenly blocked his path, a wall of men surrounding him. They stared stonily back as his eyes went from one to another. His head swirled from the heat. "Why are you doing this?"

Peter started to approach the line and the bamboo sticks went up. He charged the line, head down. They blocked him and he fell to the ground while rough hands jerked the shirt off his back. He got up and came at them with fists and feet, but they beat him back with bamboo paddles.

He lost track of time, of the number of times he got off the ground to stagger against the line. Finally he collapsed on his rear, his lungs ready to explode from the oven air, the sun peeling the skin from his back and shoulders like a blowtorch. He dry heaved; he didn't have enough fluids left for a good puke. He sat helpless in the sun, melting to death, his life fluids soaked up by the dust of the earth until even sweating stopped and ringing began in his ears. The ringing turned into a harsh roar. He heard yelling, feet stampeded around him, and a car slid to a stop by his outstretched feet.

"Get in!" The man in the driver's seat was an elderly priest.

*   *   *

"*Gherao* is what they call it in India."

It's hard to explain to a Westerner, the priest told Peter as they drove toward Calcutta in a battered old Land Rover.

"The Hindus consider it a nonviolent method of persuasion or punishment. Usually the man in the middle of the circle has done something to annoy someone—made a girl pregnant and the other men are friends and relatives, students gathered around a teacher whose grading was severe, creditors punishing a debtor or forcing money from him."

"How long does the person stay in the circle?"

"Until the instigators get what they want or feel the person is properly chastised. Last year the director of the city's water department died in a gherao."

Peter shook his head. "I thought Hindus were humane. Many are vegetarians because they won't kill animals."

"Gheraos don't kill. The sun does."

Brutal logic. "The mountains kill," Peter said.

"What did you say? Mountains?"

Peter shook his head. "I'm sorry, I'm not working with a full deck right now. When you said the sun killed, something about mountains flashed in my mind."

Labor was cheap in India. A day's wages for all the men in a small village was probably little more than his air fare from London to Calcutta had been.

Someone had hired a whole village.

To let the sun kill him.

It didn't take much guessing to imagine who had done the hiring. But first Zhdanov had played with his mind. He could remember only bits and pieces of what happened after he was drugged—terrible incidents his mind balked at putting together to form a nightmare. He felt dirty, like slimy worms had slithered over him.

The priest's name was Father Decimus. His white collar had a yellow ring around it and his black suit was dusty. Brown blotches made his face look dirty. He looked a little worn and shabby, like the battered Land Rover. He talked very little on the drive back; he had been returning from a missionary hospital in the jungle when the good Lord had guided him to Peter.

There was something familiar about the man. "Have we met before?" Peter asked.

"I can honestly say this is the first time I have ever spoken to you."

It was dark by the time they reached the city and Father Decimus let Peter off in front of the Hooghly Hotel.

"I don't know how to thank you," Peter said.

"Our paths may cross again, my son. The Lord acts in mysterious ways. Who knows what He may have in store for the two of us?"

Lo Fat stepped out of the shadows as soon as the priest drove away. "You come," he told Peter, stroking the big .44 like a teat.

Honorable Cousin, the fat ball of humanity that owned the House of the Three Perfections, sat behind a haze of curling cigar smoke as Dr. Poc observed Peter with dangerous eyes.

"Did you enjoy your visit with Zhdanov?" Poc asked.

"Only slightly better than being murdered by Thugs."

Dr. Poc stroked his beard. "It appears fate intervened and the man who was to acquire the box defaulted in his mission. Pity. He was the best thief in Calcutta." He paused and sliced Peter with lizard eyes. "Though word came to us that you had been released from jail, you did not return to advise us about what happened in your attempt to obtain the silver box. This annoyed my honorable cousin, whom, I regret to say, is not a patient man."

Honorable Cousin stared at Peter as if he were taking measurements for a coffin.

"However, my honorable cousin is a forgiving man and will permit you another opportunity to curry his favor."

Peter grinned tightly. "That's nice of him not to hold it against me just because you set me up and nearly got me killed."

"Precisely. You may redeem yourself by completing the mission of the man who defaulted in obtaining the box."

"You can go precisely to hell."

"After you turn over the box to me you will be rewarded beyond your wildest dreams."

"That's what I'm afraid of."

"I fear you have, shall we say, no choice in the matter."

"Shall we say I've seen so many hatchets, guns, and knives since I arrived in Calcutta, I've lost faith in my fellowman. That's why I left a letter with Assistant Commissioner Jinnah of the Calcutta police telling him exactly who-and-what since I arrived. I have to call him once a day or he'll open the letter."

After some singsong between Dr. Poc and the Yellow Peril, Honorable Cousin's great mounds of fat quivered with rage behind the screen of cigar smoke.

"We don't believe you," Dr. Poc said.

Peter looked him square in the eye and said, "Precisely."

"Obtain the silver box and I will give you that which you most covet."

"You can't pay me enough to risk another stay in the Calcutta jail."

"Bring me the box," the yellow lizard whispered, "and I will tell you about your father. And the woman you desire."

A young man with his suitcase wrapped in a blanket joined the poor along the Hooghly for the night. He wore tattered white cotton pants, a shirt acquired from a street vendor in Calcutta, and black leather shoes recently resoled in London.

He couldn't have fooled anyone who cared. The poor didn't care. Not even about a young American who rubbed dirt on his face to look like an Indian.

Peter went to sleep by the river rather than risk getting his throat slashed in his hotel room. He lay on the ground and watched the moon.

The King of Tigers was still riding the moon, trying to get out of Calcutta, but finding himself back in the city each night because no one wanted a tiger for a neighbor.

Like the King of Tigers, he was between the proverbial rock and hard place: It was murder to go through with Poc's mad scheme and murder to refuse. He was the victim in either case.

Poc wanted him to rob a museum. The Marble Palace. The most beautiful building in Calcutta. A stately palace with graceful columns, it would have been in harmony beside the Colosseum in Rome or the Parthenon in Athens. Instead it sat right smack in the middle of the Chor Bagan—the Thieves Garden, the most notorious slum in the city.

A palace that once housed Indian princes, trimmed with acres of plush greenery, exotic plants, Neptunian fountains, and ancient statues, was surrounded by a "garden" that grew scum, ripened young boys into thieves, blossomed girls into whores.

Poc's simple little chore was for Peter to rob the palace museum of the silver box. "Bring me the box and I will tell you about your father," the Chinese had said.

His father. It always came back there to roost. The silver box, the skull, Tashi, Poc the Pox, and the shadowy Zhdanov. He wondered if bad karma could be removed surgically, like cutting out a rotten appendix.

The next day Peter found Saru at the Temple of Kali creating goose bumps among a group of women wearing badges of the Christian Missionary League of Cincinnati. The little con artist was spinning bloody tales of Kali meshed with an occasional choice tidbit about his own harrowing experiences with a mad American drug pusher.

Peter pulled him out of earshot of the missionaries. "I need your help."

Saru drew himself up to his full four-foot height and squared his shoulders. "You owe Saru forty rupee."

"Christ. I know a moneylender who could use your talent for arithmetic. You'll get your money—and more if you help me."

The boy pointed to the group of church women who by this time had correctly identified Peter as the depraved criminal. "Missionary women pay much baksheesh. Maybe they take Saru to America to work in their temple at Cin-Cin-Nat-Ee"

"And maybe hell will freeze over before you get a visa. Listen, kid, my life's all fucked up and I have to straighten it out."

The boy frowned. "What . . . 'fucked up' mean?"

"Screwed up, bad, ya know. My life's in a mess and I've got to unscrew it. Savvy?"

"Saru savvy. I tell church women can no go to America." He turned away, then spun back around with a crafty look on his face. "Saru's help cost much baksheesh."

"I figured that."

Saru ran to the women and announced he could no longer be their guide.

One of the women cast a suspicious glance at Peter. "But you give such interesting lectures. Is there"— she gave Peter a look church people reserve for white slaves and child molesters—"anything we can do to help?"

"No can help. My friend's life all fucked up and Saru have to unscrew. Savvy?"

Peter walked hurriedly toward the steps leading down to the river as he heard the outraged cries of the missionaries. What kind of perverted karma did he have when his actions could tempt devout, middle-age Christian women to tear him to shreds on the grounds of a pagan temple?

Saru caught up with him at the river.

"I've got a job to do and afterward I'll need a safe place to hide. Where I won't be at the mercy of Thugs, tongs, or thieves."

Saru shrugged. "Thieves everywhere in Calcutta."

There were half a dozen dilapidated dhows anchored upriver. Clotheslines were strung and he could see children aboard.

"Are those boats always anchored there?"

"Sometime go 'way and come back with fish."

"Can I rent one?"

Saru laughed. "Can rent police if have enough baksheesh."

He grabbed the boy by the front of the shirt and pulled him close. "Listen carefully because if you screw up, I'm going to peel off your dirty little hide, inch by inch. I want you to carry a chit to a policeman named Jinnah and get away without anyone knowing who sent it."

*   *   *

At midnight Lo Fat picked him up with a car. The car was a piece of junk. Poc told him it would be a prewar Plymouth, but he didn't say which war.

Lo Fat was to create a diversion by crashing into the front gates of the palace, then bribe the guards to forget the damage. Later he would return and demand his money back to create another diversion and cover Peter's retreat, then pick up him down the street and take him a few blocks away to rendezvous with Poc.

Lo Fat let him off at the southeast corner of the palace grounds. Poc had told him there were only two guards on the grounds and assured Peter there wasn't a single human being in the palace after it closed at sundown. Peter saw one of the guards when he cased the joint earlier. The guard was a Sikh, a member of the ancient warrior class of India the British recruited into the Imperial Indian Army; male Sikhs were trained as fighters from the time they could walk. The guard was armed with a .44 similar to Lo Fat's. Peter thought about what he had read about Sikhs and decided the guard had probably teethed on the gun.

Peter heard the crash and the Plymouth's blaring horn. When shouting erupted between Lo Fat and the guards, he chinned up and bellied over the wall. He landed in mushy turf and rolled to his feet, making it to the corner of the building without detection. He moved swiftly by the reflecting pool and down the line of marble columns. He had eight minutes before Lo Fat returned to the gate. A guard came around the west corner and Peter crawled into bushes. He had no contingency plan if the Sikh came crashing into the bushes with a blazing .44 other than dying of fright.

He felt something crawl up the inside of his pant leg, something long and skinny with tiny legs. Many legs! Centipedes, "thousand-leggers," grow a foot long in the tropics and are capable of clamping onto a person's skin until they're burned off with a hot iron. The Sikh's footsteps crunched in his ears while the creepy thing worked its way around his knee and crawled on the soft flesh of his thigh. *It was going for his balls.*

Peter wanted to scream. He grabbed a handful of pants at his crotch and squeezed. Something snapped, crackled, and popped.

When he heard the guard's footsteps fade he stood and shook out his pant leg. It was too dark to see what dropped out. He didn't care. He had had it with the most beautiful building in Calcutta. He wanted to rob the place and get back to the safe slums.

A shrill cry erupted and he slammed himself against a wall with his heart pounding. A mynah bird in a cage eyed him and cried out again. He moved quickly to the palace doors, praying the bird wasn't a primitive alarm system.

Flimsy French doors led from the courtyard to the interior. The wood was dry-rotted and separated like moist putty when he worked at the lock with a knife blade. Poc had said there were no burglar alarms. Peter was amazed at the naïveté of the Indians who permitted priceless treasures to be guarded so loosely.

He slipped inside, pulling the doors closed. He was uneasy because everything was going so well. There had to be a catch. He wondered why Poc's last emissary failed; what Poc meant when he said the man "defaulted." He went through a room displaying weapons from antiquity, stone axes to wide-mouth Chinese cannons, then down a long corridor to the Religions of the World display.

The silver box was in the religion section along with Buddhist prayer wheels, ancient Hebrew manuscripts, and gold statues of Hindu deities. Smaller than the proverbial bread box, it was engraved with monkeys riding winged tigers and reliefs that looked like mountains and valleys. He could see a piece of bone through slots in the side.

He pulled up his bulky sweatshirt and slipped the box into a sack hanging from a cord around his neck. Then he picked up a small box made of hammered silver and slipped it into the pouch as well.

Fear fanned the hair on his neck. He sensed someone had entered the room. He turned slowly, reluctantly. Poc had spoken the truth; there wasn't a single human being in the palace after nightfall. They turned a *tiger* loose!

Peter took absolutely the right action: He froze from shock. The animal was as big as a small horse; its mouth hung open and saliva dripped from between the cracks of inch-long teeth.

The tiger growled and moved toward him.

In the bravest quiver he could muster, he commanded: "Stop!" The animal stopped. It has to be a tame tiger, he told himself. How the hell else could they catch it each morning before they let the tourists in?

The tiger came at him again. "Stop!" he shouted, pointing a trembling finger at the beast.

It stopped.

"Sit!" he commanded.

Wrong command. The beast took another step toward him.

"Stop!" he screamed. It stopped, but he was running out of working space and he didn't dare show fear by backing up.

"Go!" He pointed at a door out of the room. "Go, damn you!"

The tiger slowly backed up, confused, not knowing whether it should eat Peter or obey him.

Peter took a couple of brave steps forward and stamped his feet. "Go! Go!"

The beast shied off and Peter repeated the command, stamping his feet. The tiger, growling, trotted into the next room. As soon as it was out of sight, Peter turned and ran toward the courtyard doors.

The tiger heard the retreating footsteps and overcame its indecision.

Peter heard the roar but didn't look back. Five hundred pounds of man-eating beast charged like a big yellow locomotive.

He crashed into the courtyard, almost running into the arms of a guard. The startled Sikh clutched at his gun and then gawked in terror when he saw the tiger. He ran for the reflecting pool as Peter was diving in headfirst.

The tiger ran up to the edge of the pool as the other guard came running around the corner. The guard fired a wild shot and ran, crashing through a full-length window with the tiger following him back into the Marble Palace.

Peter crawled out of the pool and raced for the front gate. Lo Fat had done a nice job of smashing them. Peter leaped through the opening and ran out onto the street. He tried to appear nonchalant as he hurried away, as casual as a man could appear wet, running from the scene of gunfire in the middle of the night with boot black dripping off his face and a bulky package hanging from his neck.

Lo Fat was waiting behind the wheel. Peter got in, pulling the door closed but keeping the handle down so it didn't click shut.

He knew trouble was coming but wasn't sure what direction it would come from.

It came from the backseat. A shifty-looking character popped up, an Indian with gaping holes between his betenut-stained teeth. He looked about on a par with the rodents Peter had shared a jail cell with for two days.

He put the rusty barrel of a .38 to the back of Peter's head.

"Is this Dr. Poc's payoff?" Peter asked.

Lo Fat giggled. "Look so, look so." Then he got serious. "Give box."

Peter sighed. "You want the box, huh?"

The rodent behind him cocked the gun. "Give box."

Peter worked the silver box out of the pouch of his sweatshirt with his left hand, his other hand still holding the car door closed.

"Give box!" the rodent repeated.

Peter handed it back to the man. "Here."

Rodent fumbled one-handed with the box and used the gun to help hold it.

Peter leaned against the door and bailed out with the hair-raising sensation of free-falling before he hit the pavement. He rolled as he hit, the silver box he had hidden under his sweatshirt gouging his stomach as he tumbled.

The Plymouth's brake lights lit up and the brakes screeched, then the tires burned rubber as Lo Fat surged ahead, apparently deciding Peter wasn't worth taking the time to kill now that he had the box.

Peter got to his feet and ran for an alley as the Plymouth rounded the corner. He stopped and leaned against a wall, heaving to catch his breath. His abdomen hurt like hell where the box gouged it. He could hear the tires screeching as Lo Fat hit the brakes and the crash of metal as the Plymouth failed to stop in time to avoid hitting the police barricade.

His anonymous tip to Jinnah had worked out nicely, he thought as he limped painfully toward the river.

He walked along the riverbank and followed it to where Saru was waiting with a rowboat. He climbed aboard and rowed himself and the boy to a waterlogged dhow anchored in the middle of the river.

Aboard the dhow, Peter took the silver box out of the sack from under his shirt and curled up in a corner with the box clutched close to him. He mumbled something to Saru before he fell into an exhausted sleep. The boy caught only the gist of it, something about keeping a sharp lookout.

The boy sat with his back against the transom and brought his knees in close to his chest. He looked up at the tiger moon and smiled. It had taken a lot of baksheesh to rent the boat, and his commission was very big. Life was good.

The next morning when Saru came back with an English-language newspaper damp from the ride in the leaky rowboat, Peter grabbed the paper and re-treated back under the dhow's awning. He half ex-pected to find the ugly mugshot of him taken at the Calcutta jail plastered on the front page.

Instead he broke out in howls of laughter.

The story related how a local Indian male with a long police record and a Chinese with a criminal rec-ord in three countries robbed the Marble Palace, caus-ing minor damage and much fright when the palace's guard tiger escaped onto the palace grounds.

The tiger, Sandra, was the mate of Sam who was caged after he killed a thief in the palace a few days before. Authorities say Sam became unmanageable after tasting human flesh.

Peter decided the tiger's dinner was Poc's "finest thief in Calcutta."

"The thieves were captured a short distance from the Marble Palace after they ran into a police trap that had been set up to capture suspects involved in a ma-jor drug transaction. Police had been advised of the illicit drug sale by an anonymous informer . . ."

Things had worked out nicely. He could walk down

the streets of Calcutta in perfect harmony with nature and the police. Except for the matter of a bloodthirsty Chinese tong and Zhdanov's assassins.

He sent Saru with a chit to Dr. Poc, setting up a time and place to meet that night—a time and place of Peter's choosing and under very strict rules.

CHAPTER 21

He chose 10:35 P.M. on the bottom step of the Kalighat, the stairway down to Trolly's Nullah, the tributary of the Hooghly River that dumped into the Bay of Bengal. At 10:35 the massive ocean tide was in full ebb and the river, backed up for a hundred miles by the earlier high tide, rushed back to the sea.

Much of the success of the night's mission depended on Saru being able to steer the dhow. Peter let the boat drift upriver with the incoming tide to give Saru some practice. Teaching him to push the tiller left to turn right was almost beyond Peter's thin patience. He finally grabbed the kid by the seat of the pants and threw him overboard, making him swim in the murky waters until he promised faithfully he wouldn't blow it again. The baptism worked wonders.

Peter stood at the top step and waited for Dr. Poc to make an appearance. He thought about the plan he'd concocted and wondered if the merciless Calcutta sun had baked his brains. Maybe it was the influence of the tiger moon in the brooding night sky. Full moons are reputed to drive men to strange acts.

A lone rickshaw came down the street. He could see the glow of Poc's white beard. His hatchet men had arrived earlier and crawled into the cracks. Saru's buddies had sniffed them out and reported back to Peter. As the rickshaw drew closer, Peter turned his back and went down to the bottom of the steps.

Poc paused at the top, then came down slowly. When he reached the bottom the Chinese scholar, expert on Oriental religions and skulduggery, bowed slightly.

"As you can see, I followed your instructions, shall we say, to the 'T.' " He started to put his hands up his sleeves.

"Keep your hands in sight!"

Poc looked offended but withdrew his hands. "I leave guns and fighting to those better equipped by nature to manage violence. I was reaching for the packet of money we agreed upon."

"Don't bother. The exchange isn't taking place here. I'm not a fool. I know the area is crawling with tong men."

"You brought the box?!"

Peter grinned. "Not exactly, but it's due any moment." Out of the corner of his eye he could see the dhow approaching.

Poc looked up the steps. "Where is your man with the box?"

"Coming right up, Doc."

The dhow pulled up to the steps.

"It's a trick! I'm not getting on that boat!"

Saru tossed a line so Peter could stop the dhow. "And I'm not standing here to get a hatchet in my back the minute I turn over the box," Peter said.

Poc suddenly realized the only person on the boat was a small boy. A whistle hidden inside his mouth popped between his teeth, and he turned around and blew a shrill signal.

Peter held onto the dhow line with one hand and grabbed the back of Poc's collar with the other hand. Both men were dragged off the dock and into the river as four screaming Chinese with tong hatchets broke over the top of the steps.

"I can't swim!" Poc choked. He clawed Peter's

clothes, getting a hold as Peter pulled hand over hand on the rope to reach the side of the boat. He hauled himself and the old man over the transom.

Poc puked green river water on the deck while Peter took the helm from Saru.

Bengal Bay was a watery desert under a burning sun, swarthy green, the color of sewer water, the sun's reflection a yellow oil slick on the surface.

Peter made Poc sit in the sun while he and the boy took shelter under the palm-leaf canopy. They were miles off the coast with the dhow bobbing in the swells. He raised the ragged sail, but there wasn't enough wind to fill it. The only way to propel the boat back to land was to be swept in with the flood tide, carried with the islands of garbage that went to sea with the ebb.

The box was lying under a bundle of rags. Peter kicked the rags aside.

Sunlight reflecting off the box cast a silver spray across Poc's face. "I had to make sure you had it," he told Peter. Poc took his hand out of his sleeve. Peter gaped with shocked fascination at a derringer pointed between his eyes.

Poc squeezed the trigger and Peter flinched. The firing pin tapped hollowly.

He knocked the gun aside. "You should have kept your powder dry." He found a long, steel needle up one of Poc's sleeves, a thin stiletto up the other. "Sweet bastard, aren't you?"

Poc said nothing. He slipped his hands back into his sleeves and drew his face into a blank mask.

Saru awoke and sat up, rubbing his eyes.

"Go back to sleep," Peter growled.

The boy looked from one man to the other and curled back up on the deck.

Peter turned a paper bag upside down and a chunk

of raw, red meat flopped out. He cut slices and tossed them overboard.

"Chumming for sharks," he told the stoical Chinaman.

"You are a fool to think I will grovel for my life. You could slice off pieces of my flesh and feed it to the sharks and I would not yield."

Peter sighed. "Yeah. I kind of figured that. You Chinese are big on face."

He sliced another piece of meat and threw it over. Poc tried to hide his curiosity, but his eyes followed every move. "Why don't we end this foolishness? You have what I want. I have your money."

"Bullshit. You had everything up your sleeve but the payoff—gun, knife, and hatchet men."

"What did you expect? You agreed to return to the House of the Three Perfections with the box. Instead you demand a meeting at the river. I suspected a trap."

There was a bump against the boat. An eight-foot gray shark swam away from it, then came back and rubbed again.

"Right on time." Peter tossed a chunk of bloody meat over the side and the shark charged it. "Hungry devil." He threaded steel fishing line to a hook and buried the hook in a slab of the meat. "Tell me about the box, about the puzzle, the pot of gold at the end of the rainbow, and my father." He tied a slipknot in the free end and held the line so the knot dangled back and forth like a hangman's noose swaying in the breeze.

Poc spat at Peter's feet. "I'll tell you nothing!"

Peter grinned. "I put the hook in this piece of meat because I'm going to use it to snag a shark. Now, it wouldn't do much good for me to reel that monster in because he'd eat us all. And you're so brave, it wouldn't do any good to throw you to him. So I thought of a different game to play.

"After I hook him I'm going to toss another piece farther out and he'll move away from the boat like a torpedo. If I kept hold of this line, it would cut my hand off. So I'm going to tie it to something."

Peter finally had Poc's undivided attention. Saru, no longer faking sleep, listened wide-eyed.

"First I'm going to tie it to your balls."

Dr. Poc looked puzzled. "Balls?"

"Your family jewels . . . dingleberries, your testicles, your goddamned nuts!"

"Ah, yes. Nuts. Go on."

Go on? The bastard apparently hadn't got it yet. "I said I'm going to tie the loop to your nuts, then—"

"Yes, yes, I understand. You tie a slip knot, throw the meat, hook the shark, it slices off my, shall we say, nuts."

Peter cleared his throat. "Next I'm going to tie it to one of your ears. And since I'm running a little short of bait, I'm going to toss your balls out there for him to chase."

Poc nodded. "I see. Then my other ear, perhaps my fingers one by one—"

"Precisely."

"Very good. A nasty piece of torture. Not as enduring as Chinese water torture, not as painful as bamboo slivers under the nails, but an interesting example of barbaric punishment." The Chinese scholar bowed. "You have a true Oriental mind."

Peter considered chucking his little game and throwing the bastard overboard.

"Don't be angry, Mr. Novak. You have accomplished your purpose. Shall we say . . . partners?"

Peter glared at him. Even in defeat Poc left the impression it was all part of his master plan.

"What's in the box?"

"It's a Box of the Dead, dating back to the old Bon religion, the pagan worship that predated Buddhism in Tibet. There's a piece of skull inside with markings on it."

"Sounds like some bones someone's been dropping in my lap. It's a treasure map, isn't it?"

"Precisely. Open the box and I will show you the pattern."

"We're going to need a locksmith unless you have a key. I've tried picking the lock."

Poc smiled smugly. "The lock is a red herring. A Box of the Dead is opened by manipulating the raised carving. Place your thumbs on the two monkeys and push outward."

The monkeys faced each other.

"Go ahead, Mr. Novak. Try it."

Peter hesitated. Something in Poc's voice—*eagerness*. His face betrayed no emotion, no motive, but not every snake rattles before striking. Peter set the box in Poc's lap.

"Open it," he told the man.

He detected the slightest hint of a smile on Poc's lips as the man used palm stems to push sideways against the monkey heads. The lid of the box popped open. At the same time tiny needle points popped out of the eye area of the monkeys.

Peter locked eyes with Poc. "You just tried to kill me."

"Precisely. The poisonous needles were designed to thwart . . . grave robbers?"

"Close the lid," Peter said.

Peter took the box. Poc's fingers lingered over it, brushing the raised silver relief.

Peter walked toward the stern; he tripped over a coil of hemp. The box flew out of his hands and went over the side.

Poc cried out and ran to the stern. As the box hit

the water the shark lunged at it, brushing it with its body and, determining it wasn't edible, let it pass. For a moment Peter thought Poc was going to dive in after the box.

"Fool!" He lunged at Peter's throat.

Peter kneed him in the groin. The old man went down and wriggled in pain.

"You didn't have any more pain when you saw that box sink than when I turned around and faced a tiger . . . or an assassin's blade." He grinned and nodded at Saru.

The boy pulled in a fishing net. The box glimmered in the net like a silver fish.

"That was a little bit of Oriental retribution," Peter told him.

The tide carried the dhow back toward the river's mouth as swiftly as it had swept them out to sea. The Tibetan Box of the Dead sat between the two men in the cockpit of the boat.

The day had taken a heavy toll on Poc's strength and energy. The flesh of his jowls dropped as if weighed by his great beard; his black oily eyes remained alive even as the rest of his system shut down.

"Where's the treasure located?"

"Tibet."

"Tibet! That's thousands of miles from here!"

"Hardly. Tibet borders India a few hundred miles from here though a journey there might seem like thousands of miles because it involves climbing the Himalayas and walking on the Roof of the World."

"Where in Tibet?"

Poc looked at him shrewdly. "If I disclosed that information, no reason would exist to ensure that I stay alive, would there?"

There was inescapable logic in Poc's deduction.

"What's the treasure? A golden Buddha or something?"

Poc shook his head. "According to Tibetan folklore, the people of that strange land are descendants of a Monkey-King who flew over the Himalayas on the back of a winged snow leopard and mated with a She-Demon."

Peter thought about the snow leopard pendant Tashi wore.

"Near the spot where they mated is a statue of a winged snow leopard with a gemstone for an eye. The eye is a midnight-blue sapphire as big as a robin's egg and worth a king's ransom. Beyond the statue is the tomb of the Monkey-King, a treasure room with riches no king since Kublai Khan has beheld."

Greed spread across Poc's face like garbage racing across the bay at the tide line. "The tomb of the Monkey-King holds more than worldly treasure. It shelters the secret of the ages. The man who unlocks that secret will be a king of kings!"

"Tell me about my father."

"Give me the skull," Poc countered.

"I'm hanging onto it. It'll keep me alive."

"Precisely."

Peter let the stalemate stand while the dhow floated back toward the Kalighat. He docked the boat at the foot of the steps and left Saru to watch it until the owner returned.

Saru was happy. His patron had wrangled much baksheesh out of the Chinaman and the boy was flush for the first time in his life.

Peter made Poc walk beside him and carry the silver box as they went up the steps of the Kalighat. He had cleverly deduced the Kalighat steps was the last place Honorable Cousin or Zhdanov would suspect he'd return. He didn't see Bagora weaving through the crowd on the steps, coming behind them and slipping a dagger out from under his coat. He went for the Chinaman.

Dr. Poc gasped and fell against Peter. Peter clumsily tried to hold him up, but the old man slipped out of his hand and fell, leaving blood on Peter's hand.

Bagora darted through the crowd, silver box in hand.

Peter started after him. As he broke over the steps he saw four of Honorable Cousin's men led by Lo Fat coming at him like the Four Horsemen of the Apocalypse.

A tong war cry pierced the air and hatchets came out from under black pajama tops. The crowd exploded with panic.

Peter saw the battered old Land Rover cutting through the crowd stampeding around him and he went for it.

The passenger door flew open and he dived head-first onto the front seat. The Land Rover roared away with screaming tires and a cloud of black exhaust smoke. The back window exploded as a tong ax crashed through.

Hours later two priests boarded a train at Howrah station, a young one who walked humbly with his head bowed and an older one with a ring around his collar and rust blotches on his face.

Sitting in a train rumbling across the gray-green world of the Bengal Delta gave Peter an opportunity to study the priest.

Father Decimus had a lonely face. His eyes were dark and urgent and spoke of burden. More than carrying a cross, the priest was nailed to one. As soon as they were seated, Father Decimus took a nip from a tin flask he pulled from his inside coat pocket. He smelled a little musty, a little ninety proof, like a stuffy old wine cellar.

The sun was setting and shadows filled the corners of the train compartment. The priestly clothes Father Decimus loaned him were too small and smelled of whiskey and sweat. Peter changed back into his own clothes as soon as the train left Calcutta.

"Dark days are falling upon the earth," the priest whispered. "I've spent forty years in a race with the devil to keep the power and might of Jehovah Himself from falling into the hands of the Forces of Darkness. Now the beast is rising and a battle is coming. Soon armies will march, nations will fall, the dragon's breath will scorch the green earth."

Peter wondered what the hell he had gotten himself into. The priest was Poc's adversary and had been dropping the skull in Peter's lap since London. That was about all he had learned since racing away from the Kalighat in the Land Rover. What he didn't know was whether he was dealing with a madman or a saint. He cleared his throat. "Tell me about the skull you've been dumping on me."

"The skull in the carpetbag was a fake I doctored to appear prehistoric. The skull in the silver box is the true map, the one you so cleverly spirited away from Poc's assassin."

Peter felt the piece of skull inside his shirt. Dr. Poc had not been happy about carrying an empty box, claiming Peter was using him as a decoy. He had been right.

"I figured the London skull was a fake," Peter said. "Poc didn't show any real interest in it."

"That's because he recently traced the skull-map to the museum. Had I know the silver box was in the Marble Palace, I would have braved the jaws of the tiger myself." He blew his nose with a handkerchief soiled the color of his rusty face. "A year ago I discovered that someone besides Poc and myself was searching for the skull-map. I decided upon a deception to draw out my enemy and see his face. I doctored a skull and spread rumors that I had the skull-map. I went to London because I was advised you were inquiring about the plane crash. The rats followed me."

"First you got the British on my back. You were in the room the night I was being interrogated by that bastard with the blue nose."

"The British would not listen to me when I told them another mission to find Shambala was necessary. They were more concerned about keeping you from embarrassing the government by discovering they had flown secret missions over Chinese territory with the cooperation of India. I found it necessary to keep you involved through my own devices."

"You kept dumping the bones on me as bait for your trap. I could have been murdered. Christ, I almost was murdered. Twice over. Not to mention arrested." Father Decimus didn't show any remorse at the suggestion he had used Peter as bait. Peter's gratitude for the priest pulling him out of the fire twice suddenly evaporated. He felt like a laboratory animal spared not out of mercy but to be used again in a more gruesome experiment.

"Did you know my father?"

"I met him at the briefing for the flight. The day the plane took off was the last I knew of your father until a few years ago when I heard a story in a remote corner of Tibet that a man with silver wings had fallen into the Vale of Shambala."

"What was he like? What type of person was he?"

The priest waved aside the question. His look said it was irrelevant. "I don't know. A young Englishman . . . Scotsman, RAF, reckless, I suppose, as young fliers tend to be. I don't remember much about him. He flew away and failed to return with word of Shambala. An expedition led by a noted mountain climber was sent overland to find him, but even those men failed to return. Since that time I've spent nearly three decades covering on foot the territory that plane flew over in hours."

"Who is Zhdanov?"

"The devil's own disciple." The priest took a long drag of the flask. "Over thirty years ago I teamed with that abominable Chinaman and a White Russian named Zhdanov in an expedition to a remote area of Tibet. We tracked down a skull-map to Shambala; it had fallen into the hands of a pagan tribe in ancient times and had been placed in a cave as an object of worship.

"I saw Zhdanov die in that cave, falling into a pit that carried him all the way to hell. The man who calls himself Zhdanov today bears no likeness to the man I knew other than the name and the fact he seeks the skull-map."

"Are you saying it's not the same man?"

"It's not the same face, but faces can be changed. It's the same evil."

"Is Poc a Red Chinese agent?"

The priest scoffed. "Poc merchandises his soul to the highest bidder of the moment."

"Where does this skull-map lead to?"

"To the source of the power capable of defeating the forces of evil. The ultimate power source that fuels the universe. The holder of that power will carry the day at Armageddon."

"I don't know what you mean. What power?"

The priest stared at Peter with burning eyes. Emotion choked his words as he spoke. *The bones of God.*"

He had fallen into the hands of a madman.

The priest wiped his face with the soiled handkerchief. "The story I'm going to tell you is as old as the earth itself. How is your Bible, Peter?"

"I've seen *Ben Hur* and *The Greatest Story Ever Told*. I'm not trying to be facetious," he added quickly, "but most of my Bible study came from watching old movies."

"Your story is not as unusual as you might believe. Television and sex have more impact on society's mores than priests and philosophers. Evolution, the theory that man descended from the ape, has blinded man's faith." The priest took another nip of brandy.

"When I put on the cloth of the Lord, I swore to save religion from the spreading rot of evolution. I set out on a mission, a crusade, to find the physical evidence that would prove Divine Creation beyond doubt and save Mother Church. I trained as a pale-ontologist, the discipline that traces the roots of man through fossils."

"A strange field for a priest." Peter wondered if the man did it to "see the face of the enemy."

"It is a test of my faith. Like the faithful who have themselves crucified at Easter to experience the suffering of the Lord Jesus, I have pierced my own flesh with spikes.

"Early in my training I began to suspect that there was not a contradiction between Genesis and Darwin. The Bible says the Lord created the earth and placed a mist in the sky to hold in the heat of the sun, turning the earth into a lush, green paradise. Into this strange new world He placed His most precious creation, made in His own image: man. Adam to be precise, and the gullible Eve.

"I won't bore you with the exact details of the feud that arose between the two sons born to Adam and Eve. I'm sure Cain and Abel have been adequately documented by Hollywood. After Cain murdered his brother, he became a wanderer until he settled in the

land of Nod, a place east of Eden. There he took wife
and begot children. But who did Cain take to wife if
no other people were on earth? One theory is that
Cain married his own sister or a niece. Either marriage would have been incestuous, and you can find
this theory footnoted in many Bibles. I reject this
blasphemy!"

"Then who did Cain marry?"

"The answer is found both in the Bible and science.
Life can be traced back millions of years, yet science
can only place Homo sapiens, modern man, on this
earth for about 40,000 or 50,000 years. But Homo
erectus, a man-ape, dates back a million years, walked
upright, buried its dead, employed fire, and had other
'civilized' pursuits. Modern man evolved from Homo
erectus, but there is a gap between modern man and
Homo erectus. That gap, which may be the greatest
scientific prize of all, is the *missing link*.

"What the Creationist and the Darwinist fail to appreciate is that there was a mating between a Homo
erectus female and a biblical being and the result was
a new species, Homo sapiens, just as horses mate with
donkeys to create mules. *The missing link is Cain, the
son of Adam and Eve.*"

Peter listened intently as the train slowly crept toward the great Himalayan Barrier, the largest land-
mass on earth.

"For forty years I have roamed Central Asia, that
part of the world east of Eden. I often heard tales of
a place called Shambala, a fabled land of magic and
mystery lost in the vast Himalayas."

"You can find Shambala only in the heart," Peter
murmured.

"What did you say?"

"Nothing. I'm sorry. Go ahead."

"Shambala is said to be warm and green in contrast
to the ice and rock that characterizes the Roof of the

World because a mist hangs in the air above the valley, sealing the sun's warm rays, creating a subtropical atmosphere. The people of Tibet believe that they, and all mankind, are descendants of the mating between a Monkey-King that came from the India side of the mountains and a She-Demon from Shambala."

"You believe Shambala is the land of Nod, Cain was the Monkey-King, and a Homo erectus female was the She-Demon."

"Exactly!" The priest's hands were shaking. "There's a valley hidden in the forbidden reaches of the Himalayas, a valley so high it survived the great Flood, a place where the miracle of the Lord is still visible in the form of the mist that once turned the earth into a garden paradise.

"In Shambala, in the holy mountain that guards the lush valley, is the tomb of the Monkey-King, the resting place of the man we call Cain, a being, like his father and mother, created in the *image of God*. To open the tomb is to see the father of the human race in his original form, man in the image of God before mating with Homo erectus polluted our bodies with the physical features of the ape.

"Because he was created in God's image, to look at Cain *is to see the face of God*!"

The priest leaned forward and whispered hoarsely. "The dark forces are gathering, my son. The final conflict is upon us. Zhdanov seeks the tomb of the Monkey-King to exploit it in the name of Satan. We must find the tomb first, unlock it, and use the power within, the power of the Lord, in the struggle to come. The power in that tomb has kept a valley green and warm for an eon in the icy reaches of the Himalayas. It is a spark of the universe. We must wield it in the name of Almighty Jehovah. Join me, Peter, as a soldier for Christ."

People and places without names slipped by the dark window next to Peter. He heard the priest talking, putting in the last jab, telling him that the woman he wanted was on her way to the mountains with Zhdanov to claim the prize, but he didn't turn and look at the man. His mind swirled. Shambala. The bones of God. His father. A trip to the Himalayas with a soused priest. Peter knew there was no turning back. The answer to his father, to Tashi, to his search for himself, was up there, on the Roof of the World.

CHAPTER 22

Peter had read about the Himalayas, seen pictures of them, but he was still unprepared for the awesome spectacle of the world's highest mountain range erupting violently from the Indian plains and soaring over five miles high. Majestic purple in the breaking dawn, capped with virgin snow, twice as high as the Swiss Alps, they were truly the Roof of the World. "And we're going up there," Peter said aloud, but to himself. Father Decimus was fifty feet away, negotiating for a four-wheel-drive vehicle and a driver.

My mountains, Tashi had called them. Shambala was up there somewhere, he thought. Shambala and answers.

Father Decimus yelled for him. The proper amount of arguing, haggling and arm waving had been conducted to form an agreement to rent a truck.

Peter sat in the back of the truck with the packs of supplies and equipment. Father Decimus had had the packs waiting at the train station in Calcutta, ready to go when the time was right. The time was right when I had the real skull-map in hand, Peter thought.

The truck rumbled up the Himalayan wall until the road tapered into a foot trail at a small village.

Peter stood by and watched while Decimus haggled with Sherpa porters there. The priest seemed to converse easily in whatever language proved necessary. With the porters carrying most of the packs, they left the village on foot and tramped through a region cultivated with terraced rice paddies that were soon swallowed by green jungle, a lush rain forest with bamboo as tall as three-story buildings and rhododendron trees as massive as oaks.

"You must carry your own sleeping bag, a knife, and enough food for a couple days," Decimus told him. "That way you can survive if we get separated."

As they climbed higher, the vegetation grew sparse and finally disappeared almost entirely. Peter discovered every muscle, ligament, and bone in his body as he fought back against the abuse. He carried only a small pack, his bedroll, a few clothes, and a canteen of water, but the way was all uphill, the air thin and cold, the days wearily long.

The pass over the mountains was more than sixteen thousand feet high; nothing grew at that altitude except rock and snow.

The east side of the Himalayas lacked the lush vegetation that covered the side facing India because the great range blocked the rain clouds that created the tropical jungles of India. The strange ecological system created snow-clad mountain peaks and dry, barren valleys laced with chilling winds.

"Are we in Tibet?" Peter asked.

Father Decimus shrugged. "The peaks of the Himalayas are a no-man's-land, so isolated and sparsely populated they belong to whoever claims them at the moment. To the west is India, Nepal, to the east Tibet and Red China. We're somewhere in between."

The priest was Peter's first exposure to a religious figure, and the man fascinated him. Father Decimus was a juicy novel to a people reader. His inner spark, his driving force (faith? fanaticism?) intrigued Peter. The man looked unhealthy but operated in the mountains like a four-by-four Jeep. Watching, observing, analyzing Father Decimus became Peter's obsession;

it helped keep his mind off his own aches.

He decided Father Decimus was unfit for human companionship. Decimus had spent so much time in the wilderness, so many years alone, he had forgotten the small amenities one person treats another with. It wasn't that he was rude—if asked, he answered, if Peter fell too far behind in the march, he waited, but he did so without warmth.

The priest was a man with a purpose. Friendship, sex, fine meals, sunsets, and soft music were distractions. In some ways Peter felt lost and confused and envied people with a sense of mission. Life would be so much simpler if he could devote himself to a cause, put on a uniform or wear a label.

Thoughts of Tashi were never far from his mind. She spoke of the strange realm called Shambala as her home, the place the priest claimed was the birthplace of Man, the place where his father's plane may have crashed.

What strange paths my life has taken, he thought. Maybe there is something to that kismet stuff. He had embarked upon a journey that took him to one of the great cities of Europe, one of the worst slums of Asia, through sweltering jungle, and now a bitter-cold Arctic-like region on top of the world. Not in search of the bones of God but in search of *his* own maker, his father. And along the way he had lost his heart to a strange and beautiful young woman.

He tried not to think of her, but it wasn't possible. His heart was with her.

The jet helicopter sped across the Roof of the World like a black bullet. Tashi and Zhdanov occupied the two seats attached to the right side of the bulkhead that separated the main cabin from the cockpit. On the other side of the cockpit door Bagora had taken out the seat divider and was sprawled across the double seat. He was asleep with a grin on his face. Even when relaxed in sleep the little man's face was sinister and ugly, his lips twisted in a sneer. Tashi wondered if the man's pleasant dreams were other people's nightmares. Ma was at the tail end of the copter, the big Mongol straddling a small jump seat like a gorilla on a stool. He dozed with his head rocking gently as the copter plowed through air currents.

Zhdanov was beside her, not asleep, but in a quiet, introspective mood. He had been like that almost from the moment she had agreed to help him find Shambala. He barely spoke to her, merely acknowledging her presence more than anything else, and had left the details of the trip to Bagora.

The "details" were the cases of equipment stacked down the right side of the copter and the six men in black uniforms on the bench seat attached to the left wall. Black-clad storm troopers. Black copter. Even the automatic weapons were black. Bagora liked black.

Six men with automatic weapons invading Shambala. The thought made her stomach wrench. There were hundreds of monks at the lamasery, but they would be helpless against modern weapons. A handful of Spaniards with muskets had conquered the Aztec civilization. Six men with machine guns probably could have conquered the Roman Empire.

Somehow she had to keep control of the situation. She had been so caught up with her feelings about Peter, she had not recognized Bagora was the real threat. Bagora had always been around, an evil little man hovering in the background, half servant, half doting assistant to Zhdanov, feeding Zhdanov's hate— and dreams of revenge. But Zhdanov had been the final authority. Now Zhdanov had retreated into a shell and Bagora had become openly more assertive. With Zhdanov she had hope that she would someday

penetrate his steel mask and calm the storms within.
Behind Bagora's sneering veneer was a worm.

She looked out the porthole, her mind's eye searching for Peter. Where was he? Calcutta? On his way
back to London to continue a fruitless search for his
father's family? In America, returning to his old job?
Zhdanov had promised to protect him from Poc, had
told her Bagora would be sent to Peter with money
and a plea from her to return home, but she doubted
he would take the money or heed her wish. He was
too proud, too defiant. What would he do when he
found out she and Zhdanov had left Calcutta? He
couldn't follow her. Zhdanov had planned the expedition for years and had been prepared to leave fully
equipped in a specially designed copter on short notice. Peter couldn't follow, not on foot, not across the
Roof of the World, not without months of preparation.
But a small doubt, and a larger fear for him, nagged
at her.

The world beneath the belly of the copter was that
of untouched ice and snow, ruggedly beautiful, fan-
tastic crystal peaks and sweeping drapes of snow, a
place without the edifices of man or even the foot-
prints. What had Peter said? White was the color of
innocence. The black copter was an alien invader to
this tranquil world, the roar of its engine and steel
blades shattering the peace and harmony, creating avalanches that raged down protesting mountains that
had never been disturbed by even a human whisper.

Catastrophic results from the mere roar of an engine. A hundred copters could fly over Calcutta and
not even rattle the city's dirty windows. What other
delicate balances of nature would she upset by leading
men from the Western Heaven to the Vale of Shambala? Love was supposed to bring joy, not catastro-
phe.

Doctor, lawyer, Indian chief . . . choices. She had

finally made a choice. To save the person she loved, she was bringing back to Shambala a man who had been driven from the valley, blind and in pain, his mind racked with hate and fear, his pockets stuffed with gems that were mere baubles in Shambala but amounted to a king's ransom in the rest of the world. Had she sealed the fate of the valley? Or had that been done long ago when man built bombs more powerful than legends?

Shambala, Vale of Gold. Of God. She had not seen the green valley since she went to the Forest of Lam to learn the secret ways of mountain ascetics and fell into a river canyon fleeing Mongolian brigands . . .

THE HIMALAYAS

It was still dark when Tashi crawled ashore, battered and half drowned. The river had punched and beaten her. Her body ached all over. She had no idea how far downstream she had been swept.

The night was frozen; chilling wind swirled through the river canyon, embracing her like a thing cold and dead, turning the wetness in her clothing to ice.

Her mind and body were stunned. She tried not to relive in her mind the horror, but it came back and she cried Lsong's name aloud over and over. Lsong— the only mother she had known—the monks, the Pathfinders, were all gone. She was alone for the first time in her life, alone and battered and freezing.

An inner spark, that same subconscious sense of survival that dragged her from the river, flamed and stirred her numb body. She sat in the lotus position in a space between two large boulders, meditating, her breathing in cadence with her chant, stirring the fires of her imagination, heating her blood and sending it pounding to her extremities.

Oṃ Mani Padme Hum!
O Jewel in the Heart of the Lotus!

The next day she began the climb out of the river canyon.

She was hungry, cold, and confused. She had no idea of the way to Shambala; the golden vale was lost in the twisted contours of the vast mountains. She needed a skull-map and a Pathfinder who knew the secret ways.

She walked upriver until she found a spot where she could climb out of the steep canyon. None of the terrain looked familiar. She stilled her hunger pangs with meditation and wrapped herself in thumo fires that night. She would have to find food and shelter before she lost the strength to keep herself warm.

She wandered aimlessly through forest and rocky badlands until a valley with scorched yellow grass stretched out before her. Moving across the valley floor was a tribe of people and hundreds of animals: yaks, horses, sheep. Men riding horses, men dressed like Mongols, rode at the front and back of the procession.

She threw herself on the ground. She had had a good education; she knew that the nomadic tribes on the Roof of the World were not Mongol, that the Mongol raiders had come from the deserts and steppes of the Sinkiang to the north. But Tibetan nomads, the Khampas, were cousin to the barbaric Mongol. Khampas riflemen had been the rear guard for the Dalai Lama's escape from Chinese hegemony and had kept up guerrilla warfare against the invaders that left the most isolated region in the world even more of a no-man's-land.

She waited until the nomads were a speck in the distance before hurrying down to the valley floor in the hope of finding food scraps left in the tribe's path.

She was a vegetarian, and a handful of grain would be a meal.

Vultures were lined up around a pit and circling overhead. She moved toward the pit cautiously; the birds were creatures from the place of nightmares and shadows.

A sound came from the pit. She froze.

It came again, a groan of pain.

Someone was in the hole!

The birds fluttered nervously. Tashi's heart pounded. The pit was the size and shape of a grave. She heard the groan again. Fear fought compassion as she forced her feet to the rim of the pit.

An old man was stretched out in the hole. He was ancient, wasted by time, life, or illness to little more than a skeleton with leathery flesh pulled tautly across bone.

He gaped at Tashi in shock.

Tashi's features were only vaguely Tibetan, and her silken sari, made from rich cloth provided by the Great Gomchen, was alien to the poor peasant. He stammered something about "demons" and passed out from fright and weakness.

The old man must have been abandoned by the tribe, left to have the flesh picked from his bones by birds and beasts after he died, she thought. It was different from the burial practice of Shambala, where friends waited until the person had passed beyond sorrow, then took the body into the forest and chopped it up, scattering the pieces for wild creatures to feed upon. Life went to perpetuate life, ensuring speedy rebirth for the deceased. Tsaral told her that in the Western Heaven the dead bore the insult of having their blood drained and chemicals pumped into the body.

The man in the hole was not dead, and she could not leave him for vulture bait. She strained to get him into a sitting position, then wedged herself behind him for leverage to drag him out of the pit. Even in his wasted condition he was heavier than she.

She was dizzy and nauseated by the time she had him half out of the pit. A wave of chills crawled over her. She closed her eyes. She could taste the nausea bunching up in her stomach, pushing up her throat. She sensed another presence and snapped alert.

She was surrounded by four horsemen. They were on her before she could run. Two men threw her to the ground and tied her hands. The other men dismounted and placed the old man back into the hole.

The horsemen remounted, with one of the men holding onto the end of the rope tied to Tashi's hands. They set out in the direction where Tashi had seen the people and animals moving earlier, dragging her behind when she fell and could not regain her feet.

They took her to their encampment where yurts had already been set up. Her arms and legs were tied to stakes in the center of the encampment and dirty blankets thrown on her to keep her from freezing during the night. Half her body was scratched and rubbed raw. Her sari was in shreds. Almost as agonizing as the fear and pain were the vermin that crawled out of the dirty yak-hair blankets during the night and attacked her body.

The next morning the blankets were removed and she was stripped to the waist. They handled her cautiously, as one might handle a poisonous snake. Men, women, and children, young and old, surrounded her, and none tired of staring at her, although they all kept their distance as if she carried some horrible plague. She heard them talking and understood much of their guttural Tibetan. She spoke to them but they ignored her questions and pleas.

Suddenly the earth thundered and the ground shook. Horse hooves pounded in her ears, inches from her face as horsemen circled, shouting, firing rifles in the air, waving swords wildly. The dirt and dust kicked up covered her like a brown blanket, clogging her throat, turning into mud on her face and neck where sweat melted the dirt.

The men jumped from their horses and formed a wide circle around her. They squatted, watching her, weapons at the ready, a heavy silence hanging in the air.

The ominous silence was more terrifying than the wild horse show. Fear crawled over her like a nervous rash. Circulation stopped and her body screamed to move. She could hardly breathe, but she had training that permitted her mind to reach every part of her body. She calmed herself, quieted her screaming joints.

A line of women carrying wood passed through the circle and stacked the wood in a heap to her right. It took her awhile to figure out why the wood was being stacked. They were building a bonfire to *burn her at the stake*!

They were waiting for the judge to arrive and pass sentence.

He came an hour later, riding a milk-white donkey, the sacred animal usually reserved for High Lamas and Incarnates. But this was not a prelate of the Church of Buddhism; he was of the Old Religion, a ngagspa, priest-magician of the Bon religion, the primitive, animistic faith of superstition and black magic that predated Buddhism. He was spiritual cousin to the ngagspa who choreographed Lubo's dance with the demon corpse.

The ngagspa wore a tall, conical hat with a grinning skull mounted on it; he had dirty red robes and shifty black eyes. He was magician, medicine man, healer, exorcist, soothsayer, and no doubt charlatan, feared and respected by the primitive nomads who practiced the Old Religion.

The circle of men widened, men shoving back against each other, as the ngagspa approached Tashi. No one wanted to be close when Exorcist met Demon.

The ngagspa gave a signal and flaming torches were thrown into the pile of wood. He pulled out a dagger with a magic formula etched on the blade and walked a wide circle around Tashi, chanting magic words, drawing mysterious signs in the air with his dagger. His assistant, an apprentice magician, followed holding open a large empty leather sack.

As the magician-priest chanted, the men forming the circle picked up the words and began to chant and stamp their feet.

Drums began to beat.

The ngagspa moved closer and closer to Tashi. As he did, the circle of nervous triggers tightened. He suddenly lunged with the dagger at Tashi. The knife stroke caught her across the stomach and blood oozed from a thin crack.

The moment he saw the blood the exorcist went into a frenzy. He danced in spasmodic jerks, stabbing the air with the dagger, screaming a torrent of gibberish and foaming at the mouth.

The crowd went wild. Men shouted and leaped in the air, firing their weapons, waving swords.

The ngagspa fell to his knees beside her. The heavy makeup on the man's face had smeared into a rainbow-colored nightmare. His apprentice knelt on the other side, holding open the bag. At the height of the clamor the ngagspa raised the dagger above his head with both hands and plunged it down toward Tashi's chest again and again. The apprentice suddenly snapped the sack shut, ran to the fire, and threw the sack in. A wild roar from the crowd shook the earth.

Tashi had stopped breathing. Her ears were ringing, her mind reeling. The ngagspa was trembling. Paint-colored sweat dripped from his chin. His eyes were wide open but unseeing.

The apprentice helped his master to his feet. The crowd parted again, respectfully, fearfully, as the apprentice led the ngagspa away.

A man cut Tashi loose and carried her to a place on soft sheepskin rugs near where the headmen of the tribe had gathered in a huddle before the chief. An old woman put a blanket around her and gave her a bowl of cool water to drink.

The men huddled with the chief of the tribe and haggled over her as if she were a beast of burden, not realizing that they were bartering over a young girl who was worshipped as a goddess. She was purchased by one of the headmen for a small bar of silver and a mare heavy with foal.

When the headman claimed his purchase, she stood up and faced him.

"I am Tashivaana of Shambala," she said proudly.

He slapped her with his open hand and she fell to the ground. "Chain her with the dog till we're sure she won't run away," he told the old woman.

There were eight yurts in the headman's clan, big, round tents of yak skins stretched across wood framing. Each yurt was home for a family of nomadic herdsmen. When the herds exhausted a pasture, it was time to move on; the yurts were disassembled and packed, ready to move to the new location.

Chained to a stake at the entrance to each yurt was a big mastiff, a shaggy-haired, snarly tempered beast of a dog with loose, fat lips and floppy ears. Each was a watchdog, alarm system, and garbage disposal. The dog stayed in front of the yurt day and night, winter and summer. When it snowed, a hole was dug that the animal could crawl into. Raised brutally, its vicious temper cultivated, the dog threatened to attack any stranger who approached its master's tent.

The dog tied to the stake in front of the headman's yurt had a chain a dozen feet long. Tashi's chain was shorter. The mastiff was jealous of the territory it dominated, the dozen feet of rock and parched dirt that was his kingdom. He growled and bared his teeth when the chain from the collar placed around her neck was attached to his stake. The old woman gave the brute a kick, and an uneasy truce settled between the two chained creatures. He roamed the length of his chain, but any attempt by Tashi to move a few inches was met with a snarl.

Later in the evening she heard laughter and talk and the smell of cooking coming from inside the yurt. Much of the talk was about her. The men who found her pulling the old man out of the pit thought she was an evil demon stealing the old man's body. The sick old man had been left in the hole because he could no longer keep up with the tribe. If he had been able to crawl out and join the migration he would have been welcomed. If he lacked the strength, the pit became his grave.

It was the way of the nomad: The tribe had to move to new pastures or the animals would perish and the tribe would starve.

The duel between the suspected demon and the exorcist was the most exciting event in years. The exorcist had chased the demon out of her body and into the sack before his apprentice flung the sack into the fire. All the yelling and shooting was designed to keep the demon at bay if it managed to slip away. The blood from the wound on Tashi's stomach had proven that she was merely possessed by a demon and not a demon itself. Demons had green slime in their veins.

After the talk had died down, the old woman came out and dumped a bucket of slop on the ground between Tashi and the dog. The dog attacked the garbage, growling and eyeing Tashi as it gulped down mouthfuls. She was chained for two days before she realized she was expected to grovel in the dirt with the dog for the slop thrown out each morning and night.

On the third night the old woman took pity on her. After tossing the garbage to the dog, she handed Tashi a palm leaf with a greasy lump of brown food on it. It had a strange and unpleasant taste.

"What is this food?" she asked.

"Hoshnogo," the old woman said. "The rectum of a sheep, stuffed and sewn."

Tashi spat the mess out of her mouth in disgust. The old woman slapped her across the face. Leaping forward, the dog devoured the remains of her "treat."

The days chained with the dog challenged her sanity and her strength. She drew upon her faith and the words of the Great Gomchen to survive. "Not all your needs are known nor all the tests you will face. But the mind is a powerful force. When you must be strong, draw from the inner well of strength that lies in the recesses of your mind."

She meditated. Under the burning noon sun. Under the black night sky. And she came to an inner truth: She did not want to die. It was not her right to die. These crude savages who called themselves Buddhists but ate meat and treated humans like dogs and dogs like worms were not worth her death. To survive she would have to adapt to her environment, flow in its current, and finally conquer it.

She started with the dog. She dug a rock bigger than her fist out of the ground. When the night's slop was tossed into the dirt, she leaped and smashed the dog across the nose with the rock. After the dog retreated with a yelp of pain, she carefully picked through the slop with her fingers, picking out bits and pieces of vegetable matter. The dog made a lunge and she hit it between the eyes with the rock. From that time on she was master of the dog run.

On the morning of the fifth day the headman cut her loose. "Work hard, guard your mouth, and you will be treated well. Try to run away and we will cut off your ears the first time. The second time we will cut off your head."

She moved into the yurt and learned the way of the nomads, a life of hard work and drudgery for women. Female slaves were treated as beasts of burden. Awake before dawn, she milked the yak cows, bringing home two buckets full of warm milk balanced on a pole set across her shoulders. She helped prepare the morning meal around the hearth that dominated the center of the tent, careful to stay to the right of the hearth, the women's side. Men entered the tent and stayed to the left. They never crossed into each other's domain except to sleep with their spouses at night.

After the men ate, the women ate, then Tashi took her turn with the rest thrown to the dogs.

Six people besides Tashi shared the yurt: the headman and his wife, referred to as the "old woman" even by her husband, the eldest son, and the son's wife, heavy with child, and the headman's other children, a boy about fifteen and daughter of fourteen. Animals made up the rest of the "family": the two dogs, the mastiff perpetually chained to the entrance and the one that herded the animals, and the herds—a hundred sheep, a dozen yaks, half a dozen horses.

Tashi spent most of the day picking up yak dung in the fields. The dung was stacked and dried as fuel for the cooking fires because wood was scarce. She also helped herd the animals, milked the yak cows again toward evening, and carried water from the stream to the house; on very hot days, she set out pails of water for the animals to drink. The stream near the yurt was the runoff from mountain snow. The water was so cold it had to be set in the sun to warm or the animals would get sick.

At night while the men sat in front of the hearth drinking and telling stories and the woman sewed and gossiped, Tashi sat in a corner and picked lice out of the family bedding.

The men of the yurts did very little work. They sat around talking about battles they fought, wished they had fought, or claimed they had fought, smoking tobacco, sharpening their swords, cleaning their old muskets, or riding off to hunt. Caring for the animals, the yurt fire, gathering food, preparing meals, weaving clothes, and all the other chores that made the harsh life in the nomadic camp survivable were performed by women. They bore many children, most of whom died close to birth or were swept away in one of the frequent epidemics that raged in a land where it was believed that sickness was caused by demons entering the body and exorcists were hired to perform cures. Children died young. Women aged quickly.

When summer came to an end, the yurts were dismantled and packed on yaks and the clan set out for the winter pasture in the lower altitudes, moving out of the mountains and roaming in the southern Sinkiang. The journey necessitated herding the animals across trackless desert from oasis to oasis. Along the trail Taq, the younger son and Tashi's only friend, told her stories about the desert.

"Never stray from camp while in the desert. If you become separated, always stay on the trail because there are demons hiding in the dunes. You can hear them singing and calling your name at night. If you follow the sound, they will keep calling from different directions until you become hopelessly lost. Then they will eat the flesh from your bones and you will wander the desert forever a naked skeleton!"

"The only demons in the desert are created in the mind."

He scoffed. "What does a mere girl know about demons? My father has heard the demon sing and call his name. Do you doubt the word of the headman?"

An expression of doubt would have gotten her a severe beating, even from Taq, and she humbly confessed her ignorance.

While the men herded the animals, she and the other women walked behind collecting dried dung for the night and morning fires.

The desert was incredible to a girl raised within sight of towering mountains in every direction. When they came out of the foothills the land was flat as far as the eye could see. She gawked at the sea of sand. It was a strange new world, and despite the joy of discovery she was saddened because she knew each step took her farther from Tibet and the green and gold Vale of Shambala.

It was often several days' journey from one oasis to the next. In the desert, water was life's blood. On their first morning in the desert, Tashi rose and went to the goatskin bags that held the small supply of water the family carried for drinking and cooking. The animals drank only at watering spots. She drank and then poured more to rinse her hands and face.

The old woman jerked the water bag out of her hand. "No! In the desert you don't wash like a fish. Do this." She took a swig of water, swished it around her mouth, spit it out into her palms, and used it to wash her hands and face.

Tashi decided she could go without washing during the days between water holes.

When they stopped at an oasis, the men would wander over to the other camps to swap stories and barter with the Chinese and Mongolian caravan merchants. Tashi wanted to ask the traveling entrepreneurs if they could tell her the way to the forest of Lam, where the skull-map showing the way to Shambala had been thrown into the river, but she didn't dare speak to a passerby.

At one oasis she saw a Chinese army patrol, and Taq told her with a laugh that the Chinese practice a religion called communism and were trying to convert the nomads. "They send their priests to teach us, but the priests go away quickly. The life of nomads is too bitter for Communist priests. They leave books and we burn them for the supper fire."

A week into the desert a caravan of donkeys passed. Children strapped to the donkeys cried out as the caravans passed in the night.

"Sho-ring children," Taq told her. "Children sold for the price of mother's milk because their families are too poor to feed them. The lucky ones will end up like you, sold to a good family of nomads or a Chinese farmer. The stronger boys will be sold to the salt mines in the Karakoram. The prettiest girls will go to a House of Delight."

"What is a House of Delight?"

Taq snickered. "A place where a man goes to experience the body of a woman who is not his wife. You need not fear. They would never take a turtle face like you."

Tashi threw a piece of camel dung at the giggling boy. She did not have a "turtle face," as Taq well knew. The boy followed her around the camp like a lovesick puppy.

The winter pastures were along the shores of a muddy lake in the middle of a great steppe. Through ancient custom and usage each clan knew exactly where to graze its herds. Disagreements were rare and usually were settled by the chief of the clans. Sometimes they were settled by gunfire.

As the months passed, dark winter fell upon the land and bitter winds blew down from the mountains and across the steppes.

At the winter pasture the daughter of the headman married amid a great feast that ended in a drunken brawl. Tashi hid with the other women in a gully while the men rode their horses, firing their rifles in the air and waving swords. One man was killed and two others suffered serious knife wounds. It was considered a good time for all.

The marriage left a bed empty in the yurt and the headman took another wife, the daughter of the chief, a vain, stupid girl who took an immediate dislike to Tashi. The old woman who bore the headman's children showed no emotion at the presence of the new, young wife in the conjugal bed.

The reason for the new wife's displeasure was obvious. Tashi was developing into a shapely young woman, a fact not lost on the new wife, the headman, or any of the men in the neighboring yurts.

Late in January, the last month of the Tibetan calendar, Taq came to her excited.

"Come, turtle face. The eagle huntsmen are here."

She followed him to where most of the clan had gathered.

"The tribe has hired hunters to kill the wolves who attack our sheep. Look at the great birds. Are they not amazing?"

Two hunters sat on their horses while a third stood talking to the chief and headmen about the price for the hunt. Each huntsman had an eagle perched on his arm. The birds were over two feet tall with a wingspan twice as great. Their claws, clamped around a heavy leather band protecting the arms of the huntsmen, were as long as a man's finger and as sharp as a razor.

"The men track the wolves across the steppe on

horseback, then let the eagles fly. The eagles will come down on the wolf pack, ripping the backs of the wolves into raw meat and clawing out their eyeballs. While the eagles distract the wolves, the men will ride up and shoot. Isn't it exciting?"

She had been trained to love and respect all animals, even wolves, but she didn't speak her thoughts.

"We are going to watch the kill. You can ride on the back of my pony."

She shook her head. "No, it is better you go alone. Kaama has instructed me to gather dung for the fires of next week's feast."

Taq grinned sourly. "She would instruct you to cut off your own head if she could. She hates you. But do not worry, little slave. I am almost full grown. Soon I will ask my father for permission to take you as my wife."

"Your father would never permit that. He would lose both a slave and the dowry a new wife brings to the yurt."

"Then I shall marry a rich wife and buy you from my father. You shall be my number-two wife!"

He was so earnest Tashi did not have the heart to laugh. When he leaped on his pony and rode off to join the men in the hunt, she yelled after him, "Ride with care, Taq. You are too daring!"

Rather than heed her warning, he dropped from the saddle and bounced his feet on the ground while the horse ran at full gallop. He leaped back into the saddle, laughing like a banshee. He was a good horseman and a better showoff. She worried about his antics. Taq had more heart than brain.

They brought the boy home draped across the saddle. Tashi and the other women ran out to meet the men when the horsemen appeared in the distance with one rider not in the saddle.

"He tried to chase a wounded wolf to the ground," Taq's father told them grimly. "His horse stumbled and Taq fell."

The boy was not dead. He had a broken leg and the jagged end of the bone had cut through the skin. He made no sound of pain as they carried him into the yurt. Had he uttered a single whimper, he would have shamed his family and lost the respect of the men in all the yurts.

The leg was set and the wound covered with moss and wrapped in palm leaves. Blood was drawn from the neck of a yak, curdled, and fed to the boy to give him strength.

"We must wait to see if demons enter the body," Taq's mother told Tashi.

As the days became weeks and the leg did not heal, it became obvious that a demon had in fact entered the body through the open wound. His body burned with fever and shook with icy chills.

Tashi mopped sweat from his head and shooed flies from the raw wound whenever she could. Even her acts of mercy seemed to infuriate Kaama, who gave her a kick at every opportunity or sent her on the nastiest chores.

A lamb was brought into the tent and staked next to Taq. Three days later the lamb was brought outside and beaten by the men, who believed the lamb had drawn the demons from the boy and now had to have them beaten from it. When the home cures failed, an exorcist was hired to rid the boy of demons.

The witch doctor, a dirt-encrusted old man with long black hair groomed with camel urine, spent two days chanting, beating drums, and howling like a mad dog to drive the demons from the boy. Nothing worked, not even the hours Tashi lay awake at night meditating, directing the power of her mind to close the wounds.

One morning Tashi returned from milking to discover the boy on the ground outside and the yurt being disassembled by the women. The headman and his other son were a dozen yards away digging a hole the size of a man's body.

"We are leaving this pasture," the old woman told her. "There is no longer enough grass to feed the sheep."

"Why do the men dig in the ground?" Tashi asked.

"It is for Taq."

"For Taq? But Taq is still alive!"

The old woman shrugged. "If he can walk from the grave to join us, he will come to the new pasture. If he cannot, his body will feed the animals of the steppe and his spirit will be reborn to a new and better life."

When the camp was packed and the herds rounded up, Taq was placed in the hole. Tashi knelt beside him and cried until the headman pulled her away and told her to join the march.

Taq did not have the strength to walk from the grave.

Tashi cried during the first day's march. Not even the blows across her back with a wooden rod delivered by the vindictive Kaama could make her stop. That night, after the supper fire cooled, the old woman pulled Tashi aside. The mother of Taq had grown more withered in her sadness.

"It is the way of nomads, little one. If we did not move the herds to new pasture, the animals would die and we would all starve. It is the way of nomads."

It was brutal logic and a savage land. That night for the first time Tashi cried for herself.

CHAPTER 23

She's a witch," Kaama told the family gathered around the supper fire at the spring pasture. "Was not Taq hurt and did demons not enter his body after last talking to her? Never in my lifetime has the winter pasture grown so thin we had to leave it months early. Never except the very first time she is there."

Kaama shot an accusing glance at Tashi, who was squatting nearby staring down at the dirt between her feet. Tashi didn't dare challenge the young wife of the headman with eye or voice. "Was not the well at the oasis bitter and didn't six of our sheep die from the demons in the water? Now one of our best yak cows has gone dry, a cow only in its fifth year. It is her, I tell you. She is a witch."

"Silence, woman," the headman told her. Tashi noticed he had not spoken the words as strongly this time as he had when Kaama had made the accusation against her in the past. Pastures fail to provide sufficient grass, wells turn briny, and reckless boys fall from horses, all without the aid of curses, but the milk cow in combination with the other disasters disturbed him.

The eldest son's wife, ripe with a second baby, had told Tashi earlier the motive behind Kaama's accusations.

"She has lain with the father of my husband for nearly twelve moons and is still without child. The father of my husband looks upon you with favor. She fears he will take you as his wife and send her back to her own father's tent, as is his right when a new wife is barren."

Tashi realized she would have to deny Kaama's accusations or every trivial incident that occurred would be attributed to her evil eye.

She resorted to the truth.

"Kaama spreads lies about me because she is barren and fears she will be sent back to her father's tent."

The headman beat her and chained her with the dog.

"Just for today," he told her, not unkindly.

After he left, Tashi squatted beside the dog and stared bitterly at the ground. She scratched the dirt with a stick.

Kaama stood at the entrance of the yurt and laughed.

"Two dogs squatting in the dirt. Like brother flies buzzing around a pile of dung."

Then Kaama saw the marks in the dirt and fled back into the yurt. The marks were as meaningless as chicken scratches. Meaningless to me but not to Kaama, Tashi thought. Kaama was so ignorant, her mind so bent by petty jealousy, she might really believe Tashi was a witch.

Tashi began to think about a little Unenlightened revenge.

That evening the old woman brought Tashi supper and a blanket. "It's the way of the nomad," the old woman said.

Tashi crouched behind a tall boulder in a grove of trees and watched Kaama. It was the gray hour before the fall of night, the time when Kaama returned to the yurt each day after tending the herd.

When Kaama was a hundred feet away, Tashi tossed a pebble to attract the woman's attention. Kaama turned to look, and Tashi pulled a string attached to a floppy-eared hat hanging in the tree. The hat danced in the limbs.

Kaama yelled from fright and ran.

That evening the old woman told Tashi, "Kaama saw a demon in a tree today."

"Kaama sees many demons," Tashi murmured. Then loud enough for Kaama to hear: "Perhaps the demon seeks revenge upon the one who named it."

The next day Kaama took a different route home from the herd. Tashi was waiting behind another tree.

"You vain, stupid girl," Tashi said after Kaama ran in terror again from the tree demon.

When Kaama returned with the headman and his son, both armed with rifles, the demon was gone.

"It was here! Hanging in that tree," she cried.

The headman had been playing dice with the other men, and the diversion put him in a foul mood.

A week passed and Kaama didn't see the demon again. There was general relief in the yurts.

Each evening when the sun went down wind gusts blew across the plains. Tashi waited seven days for the wind to blow in exactly the right direction.

As Kaama came in from the herds, she watched the trees cautiously. When Kaama thought she had made it, Tashi pulled the string and the demon popped up from the ground and into the tree.

Kaama screamed and ran. Tashi pulled the string loose; the hat fell to the ground and rolled like a tumbleweed in the wind.

Kaama looked over her shoulder and saw the demon racing toward her. Her blood-curdling screams roused the encampment; men ran out of the yurts with weapons at the ready, every dog in the camp went wild, leaping into the air and barking.

The headman led a group of armed nomads to battle the demon. Minutes later the men came back with the headman carrying the hat. He grabbed Kaama from where the women had huddled together for protection and pulled her by the hair into the yurt. The sounds of the beating and her wails were heard throughout the camp. In the days that followed Kaama wore the hat around her neck on a piece of rope.

It was the old woman who first recognized the hat.

"That was Taq's hat," she muttered one day as the women cooked the evening meal. "I wonder how it got outside the yurt."

Kaama glared at Tashi. The woman's eyes were still puffed and blackened. Tashi wondered what nature of demon she had created for herself by humiliating the woman.

In the early fall, just before it was time to move to the winter pasture, Tashi and the old woman returned to the yurt from collecting yak and camel dung in the fields to find Chinese traders had come to the encampment to barter. Kaama was talking to two of the traders. As the women approached the yurt, Kaama turned and stared at Tashi for a moment before turning back to the men.

"Beware," the old woman said after they stepped into the yurt. "The demon-spotter is up to no good. She is probably buying a potion to change you into a piece of mutton she can feed to the dogs."

Late in the evening, after everyone in the yurt had gone to bed, Tashi was awakened by a kick. She sat up to find Kaama standing over her.

"Stupid girl. My chamber pot is empty. Go to the river and fill it."

"But I filled the pot this morning!"

Kaama shrugged. "Then someone knocked it over. Hurry now."

Tashi left the yurt carrying the chamber pot. She trudged down to the river, more annoyed at Kaama with every step. If she were in Shambala, she'd have Kaama empty *her* chamber pot. And drink out of it, too, she thought with Unenlightened malice.

At the river's edge, she bent down to dip the pot in the water and someone grabbed her from behind, smothering her cries.

The two Chinese traders, a tall man and a wispy creature with watery eyes, squatted beside the campfire drinking whiskey and throwing dice. She heard their talk and knew that they were gambling to see which one would have the privilege of violating her first. "The first gets a virgin, the second a whore," one of them said with a sneer.

The fat man won.

He leered at her. He held the bottle of whiskey above her and very slowly poured it on her face, down the center of her chest, circling each breast so her blouse clung to her body, continuing down her stomach, and letting a puddle form on her skirt between her legs. When the bottle was empty, he threw it in the bushes.

He untied the string to his pants, letting them drop to the ground, exposing a huge belly, almost hairless, quivering like a big yellow sack with a pig inside. The fat hung from his abdomen, hiding his penis, giving him the appearance of a eunuch.

Tashi closed her eyes. She turned her face from him as he bent down and put his cold, rough hand up her blouse, fondling her breasts, pinching the nipples. He ripped open her blouse, smothering his laughter with one of her breasts, sucking till he drew blood.

His free hand tore off the rest of her clothes leaving her naked, unprotected, against his sticky, raw flesh.

His fingers probed her pubic hairs as they entered her, first with one finger, then two.

Her mind screamed in horror. She wanted to die.

He tore the bindings off her feet. She tried to kick him, but he stopped her with his body weight and positioned himself on her with his penis between her legs, probing. Too fat to get his hand between her legs to guide himself in, he bounced on her trying to enter with brute force, cruelly, without respect for the delicacy of her genitals.

Entering, he moaned with triumph.

As he raped her he snickered with the conceit of a bully on top. "Mine is bigger than any you'll find when we take you to the House of Delights."

She knelt before the altar. Seven butter lamps flickered on the polished brass plate inscribed with holy scriptures that hung on the wall next to the altar. She could see the reflection of a China doll in the brass, a girl with too much makeup, powdered cheeks, red, red lips, hair piled high and held with colorful pins, eyebrows as thin as a pencil line, painted fingernails so long they curled at the ends.

The reflection was that of a stranger yet it was her own.

She was in the House of Heavenly Delight in the City of Ying-su, a frontier outpost in the broad Sinkiang desert province.

She had her own small room, a cubbyhole used for both business and living. It smelled of cheap perfume and sweet incense, odors that permeated the entire house from the ground floor where Madam Wang held court, to the half-dozen individual cubbyholes on the second floor where the business of "pleasure" was conducted.

The door to her room opened without warning and an enormous black woman filled the doorway. It was

Zara, Madam Wang's Nubian slave. The Amazon had arms and legs as powerful as a Mongolian wrestler.

Zara sneered at her. "Madam Wang want to see the nun." Tashi knew the woman hated her, but not personally; she seemed to hate everyone but Madam Wang, whom she served as bodyguard, bouncer, and lover. She called Tashi "the nun" because of Tashi's pious habits.

Zara was the first black-skinned person Tashi had seen, but the Sinkiang had been the place of many firsts. Her previous experience had only been with the so-called yellow races, the amber Chinese, bronze Mongolians, and copper-skinned Tibetans. In the Sinkiang she had not only seen her first black, but many dark-skinned Indians and Afghans, people she thought had the complexion of mud, and a woman with white skin, a skin coloring Tashi at first perceived as unhealthy. The woman was a missionary from a far land, preaching a strange faith. She was known in the town simply as the Christian Woman.

Tashi followed the Nubian into Madam Wang's sitting room.

The queen of prostitutes spent her entire day and far into the evening holding court from a huge stuffed chair in the reception room, with a cup of tea, a bottle of velvety Chinese whiskey, and a plate of sweets within reach. The woman looked like a bloated China doll. As a young girl her feet had been bound in the old Chinese manner, leaving her with the tiny, crippled feet men of that day admired. With her legs swollen with fat, the little feet looked like knots on the end of sausages.

There were two men seated to the right of Madam Wang, a man in the crisp uniform and polished black boots of a major in the Army of the People's Republic of China and a scholarly looking, elderly Chinese in a white-and-gold brocaded robe. The men stared at

Tashi, and she looked down at the worn, dirty rug at her feet. A year in a brothel had not deadened the shame and humiliation of having her body sold for a man's pleasure.

"This is the girl I told you about," Madam Wang told them. While the two men continued to stare at Tashi, Madam Wang tore a leg from a live crab in a bowl next to her chair. The sand crab was on its back, drowning in sweet wine sauce, kicking frantically. Tashi tried to avoid glancing at the crab but was inexorably drawn to witness the torture and share its suffering. She sincerely hoped Madam Wang would be reborn as a worm in a cesspool in hell.

The woman licked dripping sauce from the leg, then cracked it between her teeth and noisily sucked the meat. She threw the spent leg on the floor and glared at Tashi. "She's been nothing but trouble to me. She's called the nun because she is more interested in being pious than in giving pleasure to my generous customers. Customers fear she is casting evil spells on them because they can hear her muttering incantations when they are tasting her flesh." Tears welled in Madam Wang's eyes. "She doesn't care that I starve myself to keep her fed." She broke another leg off the crab and licked it with her tongue.

"Tell us about the stories of the valley," the major snapped. "I don't wish to stay a moment more than necessary in this disgusting place. Get on with your story, woman."

Madam Wang wiped wine sauce off her face with the back of her hand and eyed the major coldly. "You are in the Sinkiang *Autonomous* Region, not China proper. In the Sinkiang we still respect honest, small business persons like myself who slave to bring a little pleasure into the lives of our courageous workers."

The major scoffed. "The Sinkiang is the crud on the bottom of the world's cup, woman, and you are

a whore-mistress, a leftover from capitalism. I realize
you are permitted to run this sinful, disgusting establishment because you bribe the—"

"Please." The major's companion held up his hand.
"Major, your superiors in Beijing ordered you to escort me on this trip to gather information, not to re-
form one of the last remnants of corrupt decadence
left in our society."

"Dr. Poc, please tell the major that there are officers
of much higher rank than he who are my regular customers," Madam Wang hissed.

Dr. Poc stroked his beard and muttered, "For a certainty, for a certainty."

Tashi observed Dr. Poc out of the corner of her eye
and quickly decided his scholarly manners and dress
were more a veneer than fact; he had the eyes of a
lizard.

"Tell us about the girl," he told Madam Wang.

Madam Wang shifted her great bulk in the chair
and frowned at Tashi. "This troublesome mountain
girl was brought to my door by two merchants who
trade with Tibetan nomads. Before they, uh, liberated
her from the nomads, one of the women in the camp
told the merchants the girl was a witch who casts
black spells and that the girl claimed to have come
from a green valley at the top of the Snowy Mountains," she said, referring to the Himalayas.

Dr. Poc stroked his beard and eyed Tashi.

Madam Wang sneered at the major. "When word
came that the authorities sought news of any stories
about a green valley in the Snowy Mountains, as a
patriot I knew it was my duty to report the matter."

The major didn't hide his contempt when he stared
back. "Of course, the fact a substantial reward was
offered didn't add to your patriotic zeal."

Dr. Poc chuckled without humor. "This is the third
time in ten years the People's generals in Beijing have

permitted me to seek out stories about Shambala in the Sinkiang and have sent an officer to accompany me. Each time the officer found it incredible that the glories of the People's Revolution have barely touched upon this forsaken region."

Tashi's heart pounded; she kept her eyes on the floor, not daring to look up and let them see the shock that hit her. Shambala! The Red Chinese government was searching for the valley. The Red Dragon was once again threatening the land!

The major said to Tashi, "Look at me, young woman."

Tashi continued to stare down at the floor.

"Teach her respect," Madam Wang told Zara.

The Nubian raised her fist to strike Tashi but held back at Dr. Poc's sharp command.

"Wait!" He stared at Tashi intently. "When I mentioned Shambala a moment ago I saw her react. Raise your eyes to me, woman."

Tashi slowly raised her eyes and met Dr. Poc's gaze.

"She's not pure Tibetan. Her eyes, her cheekbones, her nose, there's obviously a mixture," Poc said.

"What were the nationalities of your parents?" the major demanded.

Tashi replied so quietly it was almost a whisper. "I do not know. I was an orphan."

"Tell us about—"

"No." Poc frowned at the major. "Not here. I wish to talk to her alone."

Madam Wang chuckled lewdly. "Take the bitch upstairs if you like and taste her flesh while you question her."

"Silence, woman!" the major snapped. "I am an officer of the People's Army and I do not consort with prostitutes." Before Madam Wang had a chance to retort, the major spoke to Dr. Poc. "I will not permit you to speak to her alone."

Dr. Poc raised his eyebrows. "Permit me? My mission is sanctioned by the People's Counter-Revolutionary Security Bureau. You were sent here as my guide, not my superior."

"This woman may possess information important to the People's government. You are not an official of that government. It is my duty to ensure such information is retained by the People's government."

Dr. Poc bowed his head modestly. "I am a humble scholar that the People's Counter-Revolutionary Security Bureau has seen fit to, shall we say, bless with the endeavor of searching for Shambala. I would regret having to report to the bureau that valuable information was lost because you violated my need for secrecy. I hope that the army is not once again infringing upon the prerogatives of the bureau."

The major met his eye. Both men knew the bureau was the secret police and could override even the army, but the major didn't flinch under Poc's stare. "The bureau obviously does not have all the prerogatives in this matter or I would not have been sent to accompany you. I will have to radio my superiors for instructions."

The major checked his watch and then addressed Madam Wang. "It will take four or five hours to get a response. We are staying at the inn. Send the girl there to Dr. Poc's room at seven o'clock this evening unless you hear differently from me."

"Nonsense," Dr. Poc said. "We are wasting time. I demand to question the girl now."

The major stared at him coldly. "Seven o'clock."

Zara led Tashi out with a tight grip on her arm. When they got to the stairway she gave Tashi a slap across the back of the head. "Get to your room and stay there until I come for you."

Tashi went back to her room; she was shaking. It didn't matter why the mysterious old Chinese and the icy army officer sought word of Shambala; protecting the secret of Shambala had been inbred in her. She would protect the secret with her life, but she realized that might not be good enough. She had heard tales from the other girls that these barbarians who practice the religion called communism had drugs that could rob a woman of her mind.

She had been biding her time, waiting for the right moment to make her escape, and now there was no time left.

After waiting an hour, she sneaked down the stairs and out the back door. She went out to the dusty cobblestone street and hurried toward the town square.

She kept her head down, refusing to meet the glare of decent women and the leers of their husbands as she hurried up the street. There was an unwritten law that prostitutes stayed off the public street during the daytime hours, and she prayed no one would challenge her and drag her back to the house of ill repute.

The "incantations" Madam Wang's customers complained of was meditation. Faced with the humiliation of having her body used by men for pay, she retreated into soul-cleansing meditation each time she was violated. It had kept her from going crazy— or killing herself.

She had tried to run away soon after arriving at the House of Heavenly Delight, but Zara found her and brought her back. When the Nubian finished beating her and consuming her flesh with lust, Tashi tried to kill herself by tearing pieces of cloth from a blanket and stuffing them down her throat. Zara caught her and pulled the rags out. Then beat her again.

More than once she had damned herself a coward for not having tried again. One of the girls brought in after Tashi had waited until her customer had finished, then asked him to show her the knife on his belt. When he pulled the knife, she threw herself on it. Another, torn from the arms of her husband by brigands on the night of their wedding and brought to Madam Wang's, had waited day after day for her husband to rescue her. When he came for her and saw what she had become, he cut off her head. The brigands went unpunished.

As Tashi lay for days recovering from the beatings Zara gave her, she took a step closer to understanding her purpose in life. Her body was a transitory shell that could be abused, but her soul was not merchandise for a whore-mistress. She had to endure the indignities of the moment to enable her spirit to take the journey of an eon. To escape she had to bide her time and obtain the knowledge she needed to find her way back to Shambala.

She knew Tibet was somewhere to the south, across burning desert and rocky badlands. And somewhere in the shimmering mountains that made up the Roof of the World was a skull-map hastily thrown into a river to keep it from Mongol hands. She had to find that river, find the map, and use it to make her way to Shambala.

There was nothing between Ying-su, the dirty little village where Madam Wang's House of Heavenly Delight was located, and the mountains to the south except endless desert, a no-man's-land not even camel caravans dared cross. But she had a plan and an accomplice.

She found the blind lama sitting on the rim of the fountain in the middle of the town square. His ragged robe was almost as dirty as the cobblestones in the street.

"Your beggar bowl is empty, holy one." She dropped several coppers into the bowl the old man held in his lap.

"My bowl is full of the miracles of life, child, and now it is full of the necessities, too."

She leaned closer to him and whispered, "We go tonight, holy one. Meet me by the Gate of Sighs an hour after sunset."

He nodded, his eyes staring ahead unseeing. "Tonight, child. To continue the pilgrimage that has had neither beginning nor end. We go together, to mother Tibet and beyond to the green Vale of Shambala where I shall use my magic to get the golden gates to open so we may enter and dwell in paradise."

She hurried away. She had to make it to the house of the Christian Woman before she was spotted.

When she reached the other end of the square, she heard heavy footsteps behind her and started to turn when she took a blow on the head.

Zara grabbed a handful of her hair and nearly lifted her off the ground. "You've been a bad girl, little nun. I would teach you a lesson, but the major changed his mind and sent for you." She guided Tashi back across the square, keeping a cruel grip on her hair.

Zara took her to the inn and knocked on a door. The major opened the door and stepped aside as Zara gave Tashi a shove into the room. "If she causes you any trouble, send for me and I will teach her a lesson."

He shut the door. "I sent for you because I am the People's representative and am the only person authorized to receive information about this place called Shambala. Dr. Poc is well known to the People's Army Command as a criminal and opportunist. Do you understand?"

"I know nothing of this place you speak of."

He hit her.

The back of his hand caught her across the side of her face; she stumbled backward and fell onto the bed. When she started to get up, he hit her again. She blacked out for a second and lay in a daze, her head swirling and buzzing, the taste of blood in her mouth. She heard him speaking and he came into focus. He stood beside the bed and took off his trousers.

"Whores are a product of the exploitation of women by the capitalistic system. When I return to Beijing, I will take you with me and leave you at a center for rehabilitation of incorrigibles." He meticulously folded his trousers over the back of the chair next to the bed, carefully smoothing out wrinkles and aligning the crease. He took off his dress shirt and hung it from a corner of the chair. His underwear, neatly folded, was placed on the chair.

He stood beside the bed, staring down at her. His expression and voice were no different from what he would have used in a discussion with one of his subordinates in his office; the difference was the major was stripped down to his T-shirt and massaged his naked genitals as he spoke.

"It is well known that those at the highest levels of government seek information about this lost valley. The person who finds this valley will bring glory to the people . . . and himself."

He climbed onto the bed and knelt over her, straddling her between his legs, and ripped open the front of her robes, baring her breasts. He put his erect penis between them and pressed it back and forth against her. His body quivered with excitement.

She closed her eyes tight and retreated into the mind. *Om Mani Padme Hum!*

The door burst open and he sprang off her, cursing. Dr. Poc had entered the room.

"What are you doing in here?"

"I am, shall we say, protecting the investment of a lifetime," Dr. Poc replied.

The major shook with rage. "Get out of here! Get out! I am on official business. I'll have you shot!"

Tashi sat up and watched the two men.

Dr. Poc put his hands up the wide sleeves of his robe and slowly eyed the major, starting with the man's bare feet and moving up. "I'm sure your superiors will be surprised when they learn how you conduct your business."

The major went for Poc's throat with his bare hands. As the major grabbed him, Poc's hands came out of the sleeves with a knife in each, and he shoved the blades into the major's abdomen in an upward stroke.

For a moment the major and Dr. Poc stood toe to toe, grasping each other, like two lovers about to embrace.

Tashi stared in horror as blood poured down the major's bare legs.

Poc stepped back and the major collapsed to the floor. He calmly sidestepped the body and sat down beside Tashi on the bed. She stared at him wide-eyed. His eyes had the impersonal predaciousness of a snake, and she realized she had been stolen, not rescued.

He smiled at her. "For longer than your lifetime I have searched for the magic valley called Shambala. I saw your reaction when I used the name at Madam Wang's. You know of this place."

He pulled something out of his sleeve and put his hand to her bare breast. She flinched from pain. The point of a long hat pin was pressed against her nipple.

"Very quickly, tell me everything you know about Shambala. Each time you pause I will place a needle in, shall we say, the most sensitive places."

She cried out and pushed him away, sending him off the side of the bed. He grabbed at her robes as she clutched at the holstered gun hanging on the back of the chair, and she swung around and caught him across the side of the head with the gun. The blow made him stumble backward and trip over the major's body.

She dropped the gun and ran from the room.

CHAPTER 24

The Christian Woman lived in a house off the east end of the square. There was a simple wooden cross in front. Tashi had spoken several times to the woman about the faith called Christianity and the God-child Jesus. She admired the goodness and self-lessness of the God-child the Christian Woman worshipped but questioned the religion's emphasis of blind faith over the power of the mind.

Despite Tashi's refusal to convert to Christianity, the Christian Woman had befriended her, and Tashi went to the woman's house whenever she could slip away from Madam Wang's. She knew her prostitute's life ate at the very marrow of the Christian Woman's soul.

"I wish I could free you from the dreadful life you've been forced into at Madam Wang's, but I'm helpless," the woman told Tashi early in their rela-tionship. "I'm only tolerated in Ying Su because I've been here longer than the Communists, and the bu-reaucrats in Khotan know I can do no harm in this dust bowl. They even use me in their propaganda as an example of their tolerance of religion. Madam Wang owns this town, and her payoffs reach all the way to Khotan. If I antagonize her, I would be forced to leave. If you were a Christian I would have better ground to fight from. But how can I justify interfering between you and Madam Wang when you're a Buddhist?"

Tashi could not make false adherence to another faith to save her life when it could cost her soul. To prostitute her body was cruel fate; to prostitute her faith was truly worse than death.

The Christian Woman understood. "I'd rather rip out my heart and feed it to the lions than renounce my faith," she told Tashi.

Tashi enjoyed the brief and few sojourns she'd had in the woman's garden where peace and serenity seemed to grow along with the flowers. Now she sat in the garden for the last time as she explained to the Christian Woman and the woman's companion, Fatima, what had occurred at the inn.

The Christian Woman listened in silent horror. Fatima, a young woman about Tashi's age who had been converted from the Islam faith, wept as Tashi told the story.

Tashi's hands shook as she tried to drink the tea they served. "I leave the village tonight," she told them.

"Of course you must," the Christian Woman said. "I just wish you were journeying with a companion more reliable than a blind priest older than the hills."

"The lama has been from mountain to mountain in the Sinkiang," Tashi said, "and made the journey back to Tibet many times." Her lips quivered as she tried to smile. "He says he has eyes on his feet. He told me a demon stole the eyes in his head while he was crossing the Kunlun Mountains on a pilgrimage to Tibet. He is very eager to guide me back to the land of our birth because he believes he has learned magic that will defeat the demon and get back his eyes when we go over the mountains."

"I can tell you what happened to the lama's eyes," the Christian Woman said. "I took a look at them in the marketplace when I filled his begging bowl with rice. His eyes have been severely burned and the corneas scarred. They call the Kunlun the Mountains of Blinding Light because they're snow covered and the reflection can be fierce. The glare burned his corneas when he crossed without eye protection. It's as simple as that. But because he hasn't a scientific understanding of a physical phenomenon like snow blindness, he attributes it to demons."

Tashi tried to explain as the Great Gomchen would have explained to her. "It does not matter whether demons took the lama's eyes. As long as he believes it, the demons exist if no place other than in the lama's mind. When he dies his soul must go to Bardo and wander until it finds the path to rebirth. He believes as long as he is blind he will not be able to find his way through Bardo. He must battle the demon and get back his eyes or his soul will wander in purgatory forever."

"And how do you battle something that doesn't exist?"

"With the mind," Tashi said simply. "Perhaps when we cross the mountains he will come to understand his blindness."

The missionary sighed. "You have a long and arduous journey ahead. I have traveled the Sinkiang many times and, unlike the lama, I have both my eyes. The desert is filled with perils."

"We plan to—"

"No, no, dear, don't tell me your plans. If I am questioned, I must be able to state truthfully I don't know your route. Not that it will be difficult to guess. The only road out of Ying Su is the one to Khotan. When they cannot find you there, they will realize you were insane enough to attempt to cross the southern desert and return to your homeland. That route is so terrible, they may even decide to leave you at its mercy."

The Christian Woman shuddered. "It is one of the most barren deserts on earth. There are great distances between oases, and often when you get there the ponds are briny or have been covered by sand. The dunes are as large as mountains and shift with the great winds that roar down from the Kunlun. No matter how many times you travel through them, the route is different the next time."

"The Elephant Hills," Fatima said. "There are demons in the hills who sing and call your name to lure you off the main trail so you become lost and wander until you die of thirst. Then they devour your body. Or so my people say," she added hastily.

"Don't fill the child's head with such nonsense," the missionary snapped. "It's true there have been sounds reported by travelers in the dunes Fatima calls the Elephant Hills. Even Marco Polo wrote of them. But singing sands have been reported in the Arabian Desert, too. It's caused by the wind rolling across the dune, though I admit no one knows why one dune sings and another doesn't. I suspect it has something to do with the shape of the particular dune. But regardless, it's not the Sirens that call to you."

Fatima's eyes were wide at the thought of Tashi crossing the dreaded southern desert. "There is a wandering lake where salt creatures can grab you and pull you under, and the Swamps of Fire where fiery demons battle."

"Fatima! Stop speaking nonsense. The child has enough burden. The lake seems to move because the river that creates it takes a new route each summer and creates a different lake because the previous year's riverbed is filled with sand. Those salt creatures are simply mushy salt beds similar to quicksand. And fire demons are no more than will-o'-the-wisps, what

my people call 'foolish fire.' Combustible gases form
from rotting vegetation in the swamp and briefly flare
up. There are no demons. It's natural, physical phenomena."

Tashi and Fatima looked at each other with the
same thought. Singing sands? A wandering lake?
Killer salt beds and fire-fights in a swamp? The Christian Woman had a lot to learn about the demons that
plagued Central Asia.

The Christian Woman stared at the roses in the
garden for a moment. "I have heard of this Dr. Poc.
It was many years ago, back in the early days of the
revolution. The stories I heard about him convinced
me he is the right hand of Satan himself. I'm sure
you have not heard the last of this devil."

An hour later a slender boy left the house of the
Christian Woman for a rendezvous at the Gate of
Sighs with a blind lama. The Christian Woman and
Fatima watched the youth leave the yard.

"Go with God, Tashi," they whispered to the young
woman in disguise.

Before Tashi left the house, Fatima slipped a small
dagger into her hand. "If the Nubian catches you,
stick it in her heart," Fatima whispered.

The blind lama was waiting at the Gate of Sighs.

"Are you ready, holy one?"

"I have been a traveler in many past lives; my feet
and begging bowl will sustain me in the lives to
come. I am always ready to start a journey and to
stop one."

He carried a long, gnarled walking stick. The stick,
his dusty robes, and the begging bowl were his only
worldly possessions.

They went through the north gate of the city, their
steps softly resounding in the tunnel leading through

the thick mud wall, the sound effect giving name to the Gate of Sighs.

She walked in the darkness into an empty desert, guided only by the full moon and a blind man. For a long time she cried, washing the filth and humiliation of Madam Wang's from her system.

"Do not cry, child. You need not fear. My feet have eyes to see the road and I have magic to protect us from dangers."

"I am not crying from fear but for my soul."

In the hours before dawn, when the noise and passion of the customers of the House of Heavenly Delight had quieted, Zara went to the room of Madam Wang. The harlot queen was sitting up in a brass bed with silk pillows behind her back. She was naked and her great breasts hung like sacks of yellow mud.

"Have they found her?" Madam Wang asked.

"No. They have searched the village house by house. Dr. Poc disappeared also soon after reporting the girl stabbed the major. There is suspicion he and the girl fled together toward Khotan."

Madam Wang stared with half-closed eyes at the Nubian. "They are wrong. I don't know what crack that old weasel crawled into, but the girl would not flee to Khotan. Her heart yearns for the mountains of Tibet. To get there she must cross the southern desert. Go after her. Kill her and bring me back her head. The murder of the major has caused me much grief." Tears glistened in her eyes. "It will take all my money to save my own head. Bring me back her head so I can spit in her face."

Zara turned to leave and Madam Wang called her back. The harlot queen put a hand under each of her massive breasts and lifted them to show Zara.

"Hurry. I grow cold and my fires must be stoked."

*   *   *

As they walked the next day, the blind lama showed an amazing knowledge of the terrain.

"Your words are my eyes," he told her. "These feet have carried me many times to the holy mountains and now your words reveal to me that we are following the same path."

He knew the general route but had to be helped around the trees, rocks, and holes. It was impossible for her to practice lun-gom, the speed and endurance march taught to her by the hermit-wizard in the forest of Lam. The old lama could not move that fast.

The steppes were dressed in a colorful carpet of late summer flowers: yellows, reds, violets. They passed along a riverbank where prairie grass grew as tall as a man's shoulder. From a hillock above the river, she watched a herd of wild yellow donkeys swimming almost over their head in a sea of grass.

"After this river," the lama told her, "for the next day's journey there are only briny wells. The water is drinkable but will not quench your thirst. Then there is an oasis where the grassy steppes end and the desert begins. In the desert the oases are three days apart and it is sure death to miss one." He laughed. "But do not fear. This old holy man can find an oasis with the eyes on the soles of his feet. I will lead you across the Mountains of Blinding Light to the holy mountains of Tibet. After I wrestle my eyes from the demon, we will travel to the joyous land of Shambala. It is said that in Shambala the young gain wisdom and the old gain youth. It is said there is a tree whose leaves are always green whether the sun be hot or snow lay on the ground. On the leaves are written a holy message from the Enlightened One that says . . ."

The old beggar-lama rambled on about the wondrous sights that awaited them in the land of Shambala. She doubted that he had any serious belief that Shambala existed. To him it was a land of milk and honey, filled with powerful magicians and ruled by a living goddess who breathed fire, a legendary place many had heard of and none had visited, a land of mystery and magic somewhere in the Great Himalayas in northwestern Tibet. Ruled by mystic forces, Shambala could be entered only by those trained in the dark secrets of the Tantric arts.

She had tried to convince him that she was indeed the fire-breathing Tashivaana but soon concluded that the old man had a simple, almost childlike faith. To him Shambala was a place of mystery and magic and she was a young woman of flesh and bone; the two would not mesh in his simple equations about the world.

They found the sweet oasis at the end of the steppe and spent their last night with grass underfoot. Spread out before them was a vast, illimitable desert, a terrible, doomed wasteland where nothing grew but misery.

Tashi had crossed a desert with nomads, but the southern desert was a boundless empire of sand and rock. The blind lama did not share her lack of enthusiasm for the region.

"Those who say the desert is dead are people who have never crossed it but stay home and tell tales. Even I, a sightless one, can *feel* the life teeming in the sands."

The only thing Tashi felt teeming in the sand were hot coals.

Heat waves rising from the desert floor melted the horizon. She wiped sweat from her face and used the dampness to pat her dry lips. Life with the nomads had taught her water in the desert was life's blood.

"I will be happy, holy one, to leave this land of Mongols and Chinese and return to my mountains."

They slept the second night in the desert on a small plateau surrounded by faceless dunes. The next morn-

ing they fixed a breakfast of tea with butter and salt.
The tea warmed them in the morning and cooled them
as they sweated in the heat of the day.

As they rose from their morning prayer and were
ready to leave, Tashi spotted a black creature bouncing across the desert toward them. Zara! The Nubian
was homing in on their tea fire and moving at incredible speed.

"What is it, child? Your hand is ice."

"Trouble approaches. An evil person from the
house where I was employed in Ying Su. She will
make me return."

"But you cannot go back to Ying Su. We must go
and find the demon who stole my eyes!"

Tashi pulled on his arm. "Come! We must hurry."

She led the lama down the side of the plateau. No
trail was notched out, and the descent was slow and
tortuous because the plateau was covered with stones
and rain-carved gullies.

Tashi felt the dagger Fatima gave her. She told herself she would use it to take her own life before she'd
return to Madam Wang's; her fear was that Zara
would be cruel enough to leave the blind lama alone
in the desert.

The lama stumbled on a stone and she kept him
from falling. He sensed her panic. "Do not fear, little
one. I will not let this evil person harm you. I will
drive away the demon with my magic."

A shower of rocks and dirt flew down. Zara stood
on a ledge near the top of the plateau. Her feet were
spread in triumph, her sweat-soaked flesh glistened
like black snake skin. She held a tall spear with a
steel warhead. A gust of wind stirred the Nubian's
robes and hair, giving them an eerie animation. A
high-pitched cry came from her, the scream of a jungle cat hungry with rage before it devours a helpless
prey.

The lama turned and looked up at the direction of the scream, his ears seeing what his eyes could not. "The demon!"

Tashi pulled on his arm. "We must run! Run!"

She tried to pull him with her but he jerked his arm out of her grip, causing her to stagger back, the heel of her right foot locking against a boulder. She tripped and fell backward over an embankment and slid down the side of the hill.

The lama started up the hill, following the Nubian's cry, stumbling over the stones and ruts in the way. He fell and picked himself up, only to fall again.

Zara raised her spear, pulled back, and let it fly.

The lama struggled to his feet. He froze as his sensitive ears picked up the whistle of the wind parting before the razor-sharp warhead. The spear struck him in the chest, splitting his chest open, protruding out between his shoulder blades. He staggered back, dropping his staff, falling to his knees.

Tashi crawled up the hill on her hands and knees. She broke over the top of the ridge and ran to the lama. "Holy one! Holy one!" Blood squeezed out from around the spear in his chest.

"I can see the Light," he whispered. He collapsed against her, life and spirit escaping.

She tried to cradle him in her arms, but he was too heavy and he slipped from her. A shadow fell across her. Zara leered at her. "You have been bad, little nun." She kicked Tashi, bowling the girl over. Before Tashi could get to her feet, Zara kicked her again, sending her back over the embankment.

Zara was waiting at the bottom. She grabbed a handful of Tashi's hair and jerked her off the ground, holding her like a rag doll, a knife in the other hand.

"I'm going to cut off your head and mount it above Madam Wang's door."

Tashi pulled the dagger from her robe and struck

blindly at Zara's face. Zara screamed, letting go of her. The Nubian's left eye flowed with blood. Tashi backed away from the stricken giant, then turned and ran.

The desert unfolded as an endless waste.

Tashi moved swiftly in a lun-gom trance, her breathing, feet, and chant in cadence, the weight off her legs, her feet carrying her as if they were prancing on the wind.

Zara came behind her with long, gangling strides, each step two of Tashi's, but not as swift. A Cyclops with blood on her face and murder in her heart.

It was a race. A contest of speed, endurance. A test of discipline, will. A race to the death. No shade, no water, no rest. For Tashi to stop, even to hesitate, was certain death.

The sun was a flame that scorched her face until layers of skin peeled away, exposing pink flesh that sweated blood like rare meat turned over a fire. Her nose blistered and her lower lip split open and bled pus until the sun cooked the pus hard. Burning sand ate her sandals and fried her bare feet, cooking the flesh on the bottom of her feet until her soles dried and cracked and she left bloody prints on the sand.

She saw the Elephant Hills in the last light of day, dunes as large as mountains.

The wind began as she reached the dunes. It was a wind Tibetans had a name for: red wind. The Tibetans believe wind is caused by the gods galloping their horses across the sky. Red winds were caused by an angry race between the gods. The winds began in the Kunlun, high on the icy slopes, and swept down to the valley floor during the first hour of night, turning the sun-roasted sand frigid, creating a sandstorm that attacked her skin with the sting of a thousand bees and scraped coagulated blood off her wounds until her face bled red mud.

The storm blotted out the night sky for an hour before the gods slowed to a gallop and a wind without a name swirled through the canyons of the lonesome dunes.

An eerie moan floated on the breeze, as if the hills, as if the night itself, were in agony. She heard her name whispered and she cried out, not in answer. The spirits called her name, beckoning for her with a luring melody filled with promises: fresh water to cleanse her wounds and a soft bed to rest her aching bones upon. She had merely to step from her path and seek the comfort of their arms.

It was the song sea nymphs used to lure sailors to their doom on rocky coasts, the seductive melody Lorelei sang to Rhine mariners.

Tashi closed the window to her mind and sang her own liturgical tune. *Om Mani Padme Hum!* O Jewel in the Heart of the Lotus!

They raced through the night and through the next day, beyond the Elephant Hills and across sun-scorched salt flats, cracked and peeled, a scaly sore on the crust of the earth.

The southern desert. The bottom of the world's cup.

Two days without water, without food, without rest.

Her feet stopped bleeding only because the hot ground had fried blood, flesh, and sand into a hard cake. She had stopped sweating because the sun had drawn the last drop of moisture from her flesh. Her lungs ached from the oven-hot air she drew with every gasp.

Slowly, like a spring under pressure too long, Tashi began to wind down. She never looked back, but she knew the beast was closing the gap. She could hear the pounding footfalls, the labored breathing, could feel the hatred that was gaining on her, by inches, by minutes.

Tashi reached within herself, back to the Cave of the Spiritual Light, back to the Tantric arts. In her mind's eye she soaked in the crystal pond beside the cave, the clean, pure waters cleaning her wounds, washing the dirt from her pores and the caked mud from her mouth and throat. She stepped out of the pond and rolled in the virgin snow, giggling and shivering.

Her feet began to move, to wing, driven by the rapture of her imagination. And slowly she spread the gap between her and the Nubian.

The Swamps of Fire.

Foolish fires, the Christian Woman called them, fires that flashed capriciously, dancing, warring. The swamps stank, the morbid smells of the dead, the rotting flesh of the corpse Lubo danced with, the foul odor of the black rot on Tag's leg.

She sensed something in the swamp, something cold and slimy waiting in the murky waters for her to miss a step and stumble into the mire.

Behind her the Nubian ran along the water's edge, her good eye bulging in terror.

The driving force behind Tashi's lun-gom was mental conditioning that created physical endurance. The source of Zara's strength was her very primitivism—the woman was an animal. Like a camel or horse that will keep moving until it drops dead, Zara was driven by animal instincts.

Tashi could not outrun the beast, could not outlast Zara's reservoir of mindless energy. "Man is not as strong as the ox nor as swift as the antelope," the Great Gomchen told her. The difference was the mind. She had to devise a way to overwhelm Zara. Prehistoric man dug holes to trap beasts and beat them to death with crude clubs of wood and stone. Traps and clubs are inventions of the mind, Great Equalizers.

Tashi flew across the desert, her mind locked in a trance, but her inner consciousness inventing traps to bring down the beast that sniffed her tracks.

The Wandering Lake.

It was an ocean. A great sea without an end. It was nothing like Tashi had imagined. She had expected a small body of water, perhaps the size of the Lake of the Celestial Reflection at Shambala. Instead it was as if the blue sky had fallen to the desert floor. She had heard that somewhere there was a great sea filled with most of the water in the world, and she imagined this to be it.

She broke out of her lun-gom trance and staggered to the edge of the lake in utter joy. Dropping to her knees in the mud, she put her whole face into the water, drinking deeply. She recoiled, crying out in pain as the water bit into her raw throat and burned like acid on her wounded face.

The Wandering Lake was a great salt sea.

Pausing beside the lake cost Tashi the race. She ran along the shore, unable to cry because her body lacked the fluid to even tear.

Zara came relentlessly on, running naked, her clothes torn from her body by the red wind, her skin covered by layers of dirt caked on by sweat and baked hard by the sun. She looked like a creature that had crawled out of a crack in hell.

The shoreline changed to salt ponds and bogs. Lurking in the shallow ponds were marsh monsters, the primeval creatures the Christian Woman called quicksand.

Tashi tried to steer clear of the dreaded salt marshes, but the Nubian cut her off, forcing her deeper into the bogs. She waded in a shallow pond, as terrified of what might be hiding in the murky water as she was of Zara. Suddenly the mushy sand grabbed her, swallowing her to the knees in one horrible gulp.

She struggled frantically to kick loose from the sandy jaws, but lost her balance and fell forward, going under. Her feet broke loose of the suction of the sand as she went under. She splashed and kicked in panic, breaking onto the surface again, choking and coughing. Reaching out blindly, she got a handhold on a prickly bush and used it to pull herself onto a shallow spot.

Zara charged into the pond like a water buffalo.

Tashi turned to flee deeper into the marsh, but a cold hand touched her heart and she stopped. She swung around and stared at the Nubian. The beast was coming directly at her.

Between them was the marsh monster.

Shaking from fear, Tashi sank into the water on her knees and waited, bait for the beast. She closed her eyes and chanted. *Om Mani Padme Hum!*

She heard the splash of water, Zara's cry of panic and confusion.

Om Mani Padme Hum!

The shouting became screams and the water boiled from the battle between Zara and the marsh monster. Tashi chanted until long after the last outcry, long after the water had returned to calm. Then she opened her eyes. There was no sign of Zara. Blind animal drive had led the beast to destruction.

She sat in the lotus position on an icy ledge high in the Snowy Mountains. Thousands of feet below her, a white water torrent raged through a snaking canyon on its way west to the Land of the Rains where it joined other rivers to form the Ganges, the mother of holy rivers.

She was in a trance, her breathing in cadence with her chant, psychic energy flowing, bursting from her, ignited by the energy created by the million times a day the mantra was chanted by Tibetan Buddhists. Lsong was wrong; words were not carried on the wind. They rode on a bridge of psychic energy created by millions of people.

Om Mani Padme Hum!

She knew her heart and strength could lead her to Shambala, but instead of setting out for the elusive valley, she had sat on the ledge and stared at the river for hours, searching her very soul. "All rivers lead to the Land of the Rains," Lsong had said. The Land of the Rains, the hot, green place where the rains fell because not even the clouds could climb the great Himalayan barrier.

Since the day she had fled Mongol raiders, Shambala had not been far from her thoughts. Duty tugged at her, a stick prodding her home, but she hesitated at the juncture of two worlds, the sacred mountains before her, the river below, her own will battling the conditioning that she had been subjected to since she amazed three lamas by turning over a piece of wood with the word Tashivaana scratched on it.

She had discovered in the Sinkiang that she was a woman of flesh and blood, not a religious relic. She could not return to Shambala and become the object of worship for many and love for none.

There was a world beyond the icy reaches of Shambala, beyond the sand of the Sinkiang and the towering citadels of the Roof of the World, places and wonders the Christian Woman had told her about, cities wider than deserts, buildings as tall as mountains, machines that carried men to the moon.

More than the wonders of science, the Christian Woman had told her the Western Heaven was a place of the heart with family and love. Love. She had been worshipped, sexually abused, used as a workhorse, but had never experienced a man's love, a mating of heart and soul. Golden child but orphan, she had never experienced her mother's bosom or the strong arms of her father. Nor had she even spoken their names.

She couldn't return to Shambala, not without knowing herself. She felt as if much of her past were a series of doors she had never entered, doors shrouded in mystery and secrecy.

The man in the dungeon was an enigma behind those doors. He had been taken from Shambala, wounded in mind and eye. He was the first door to her past, and she could not return to Shambala without having opened it and looked in to see herself.

She left the ledge and made her way down the gorge to follow the waters to the Land of the Rains. And beyond, to the Western Heaven.

CHAPTER 25

CALCUTTA, INDIA...TWO YEARS LATER...

All the demons from hell were loose in the city. The very earth beneath Tashi's feet trembled from the pound of jackhammers, the roar of trucks, and the babble of voices as she walked barefoot down the street.

Demon machines destroyed shapely old buildings and reerected formless skyscrapers in their place, while on the streets, cars and trucks and motor scooters roared and choked out black clouds that turned the air foul and the skies ashen.

The pavements were filthy from the excrements of Man and Machine; not even the people crowding the streets had been spared the attack of demons: Everywhere she looked were sores and coughs, bloated bellies, and bloodshot eyes. And she recognized that even the most vicious demons—anger, greed, indifference—were running wild.

The city was hotter than the skin of the sun. Her heart ached for the heavenly skies and sweet air of Shambala. Her feet, blackened from street tar that the burning sun kept molten, longed for a cool mountain stream.

Calcutta was a vision of a frightening future, the worst of a bad past. Everything the monks of Shambala feared.

The hotel she entered was the best in the city. With

her worn robes and bare feet she would have been quickly and firmly escorted out the front door, but the name of the man she asked for intimidated the staff.

Zhdanov.

She gave the clerk a slip of paper with a single word written on it. The skeptical clerk sent a porter with the slip of paper and a request for an audience to the great man's suite.

The response was quick and surprising: The young woman was to be sent up immediately.

Tashi was met in the entryway of the suite by a short man with cruel lips and dark eyes. An enormous Mongolian bodyguard stood by.

"I am Bagora, Mr. Zhdanov's assistant. State your business."

"That can be revealed only to Mr. Zhdanov."

Bagora leered at her. The little man's look was both brutal and sexually suggestive. "For some reason my master will permit you to intrude into his presence. But heed my words: Waste his time and I will have Ma"—he gestured at the big Mongol—"cut off your ears."

Bagora showed her into the study and left, closing the door behind him. The room was cool and shaded, the only light spreading in from the window behind the desk. A man was seated at the desk, all but his shape lost in the shadows.

"Who are you?" he asked.

Her eyes adjusted to the dimness and she stepped closer to the desk.

The man who called himself Zhdanov was in his early fifties, slender, incredibly handsome, but with features that were locked tightly in place, as if they had been molded from the death mask of an emperor. Or a surgeon's scalpel.

"I am a traveler, a seeker," she said.

He studied her. She met his eyes and flinched; his

eyes were chill-green, violent, like the mad dog
storms that raged on the Roof of the World.

"Why have you come?"

She felt pain, as if a knife were shearing her soul,
pain worse than what she felt when her body was
violated. "I'm not sure," she whispered. "I have spent
two years tracking you, following a trail you left
many years ago. I'm not sure why. I only know that
I have come to Calcutta because . . . you are here."

He touched a piece of paper on his desk, the piece
of paper she had sent as her calling card. The word
scribbled on it was SHAMBALA.

"Do you know the way to Shambala?" he asked.

"No. I . . . I left many years ago and I do not know
the path back." Her mouth was dry, her throat con-
stricted. She needed a glass of water but dared not
ask.

He didn't say anything for a moment.

He stared past her, lost in thought, before his eyes
found hers again and he said quietly, "You look like
your mother."

CHAPTER 26

Two days' march north brought Peter and the priest to a village, a cluster of mud-walled houses built around a dusty town square. Decimus rented rooms in what he told Peter was a typical Tibetan residence, an awkward, two-story mud building. The bottom level was a stable containing a couple of yak and some scrawny chickens. The second level had three rooms separated by yak-hair curtains. The kitchen was black with soot from the cooking fire that burned without benefit of a stove pipe. A hole in the roof carried out some of the smoke.

Dried yak dung, scooped off the stable floor, was the chief source of fuel for the fire. The yak-dung smoke permeated food cooked over it with a scent and taste of rancid, roasted peanuts.

The toilet facilities were practical, if primitive. One room had a hole in the floor to squat over. The discharge fell into the stable below where no doubt some of it got recycled along with the yak dung to the kitchen fire.

The occupants of the house were three men, a woman, and a couple of kids.

"The three men are brothers," the priest told him. "The woman is their wife."

"Woman? Singular. One woman, three men?"

"They're heathens. In the most rural areas they

band together like this because so little land can be cultivated and the crops are small. If each male married and raised a family, in a generation or two there wouldn't be enough food to feed the population."

"It makes sense. Sort of. Hell, if a Muslim can marry several women, I guess one woman can have several husbands." Peter grinned. "An early version of women's rights. But what about the kids—how do they know which guy is their father?"

"The eldest brother is called father by the children. The others are called uncle."

"Do all the brothers get to, uh, share the wife?"

The priest wrinkled his nose. "If that question is intended to ascertain whether all the males engage in coition with the female, the answer is yes."

Something about the arrangement didn't compute with Peter. "What about the extra women?"

"What extra women?"

"If half the people are women, and one woman marries several men, what happens to all the extra women?"

The priest opened his mouth to say something, then shut it and walked off mumbling something Peter didn't catch, but Peter had the distinct impression it had to do with Peter's level of intelligence.

Peter shrugged and headed for the house. It still didn't compute with him. He wondered if they dumped girl babies in a river to see which sink or swim like farmers do with puppies.

He entered the house, making an unintelligible but polite response to the unintelligible but polite greeting from the woman of the house and one of her husbands. On his way to the back bedroom he wondered if it was the day that particular husband had been assigned coition (whatever the hell that was) with the communal wife.

He spread his bedroll on the floor and lay down.

A bed with yak-hair blankets was against the wall, but he had already discovered thirty seconds on it caused him to itch in more places than the bed touched.

The priest came in. "I paid off the Sherpas and hired Tibetan porters. We must be prepared to go on without the assistance of porters when the dangers of the journey cause these Godless heathens to turn back. There is a renegade Buddhist monk called the Bandit Lama leading a ragtag band of brigands, and the locals fear entering the region where his band is said to be operating."

"Why would a Buddhist monk go bad?"

"When the Red Chinese took over Tibet, hundreds of thousands of monks were turned out of lamaseries. The truly faithful followed the Dalai Lama into exile. A few took to the hills and became robbers. The Bandit Lama was once the High Lama of a small, isolated lamasery."

Peter was tempted to comment that some people— Voltaire, for example—might argue the transition from priest to thief was a natural one, but he kept his mouth shut. He rolled over and pulled the covers over his head. For a person raised with little formal religious indoctrination, the past couple of weeks had been an eye opener. Bloodthirsty Hindu goddesses, renegade Buddhist monks who rob and kill on the road to Enlightenment, a drunken priest searching for the bones of God in a pagan valley. He dreamed about finding the karma machine. And turning it off.

They left the village the next day, the taciturn priest in a hurry for his appointment with God.

It was a march across valleys, over passes, down into more valleys, a lost world of peaks and valleys hidden from the march of time. Even the name the people of India gave to Tibet revealed little about the region shadowed by mystery: the Land Behind the Snows.

Each day brought the threat of a snowstorm. The Tibetans told them snow did not fall in the mountains, it raged and howled like a mad dog.

They dropped into a narrow valley, plunging so deep they marched in shadows until noon before the sun peeked over the rim.

Peter was bringing up the rear when a commotion broke out among the porters. They dropped their loads and wouldn't budge. Father Decimus was arguing heatedly with the head porter when Peter broke in to ask the priest what was going on.

"They're trying to turn back. They're frightened because they've spotted tracks of a snow leopard. These ignorant mountain people believe a snow leopard is a djinni, a supernatural beast that can change shapes and take the form of a man or any other creature. They say the region ahead is a forbidden zone, an area ruled by the spirit of the snow leopard. The head porter also claims he's spotted hoof marks made by horses, an indication the Bandit Lama's men may be operating in the area. These fools believe the snow leopard will lead the brigands to us so we won't invade its territory."

"Maybe they know something we don't."

"Nonsense! Superstition has kept Central Asia centuries behind the rest of the world. Every phenomenon they can't explain—from an infection in a wound to off-season rain—they attribute to demons. It all has a scientific explanation."

"Sure. Like that skull you're using to guide us to a place no one has seen."

Peter sat on a rock and watched the priest and head porter argue. The words were strange to him, but the body language told the story. The priest was pulling all stops—bribery, threats, pleas, and no doubt the

Tibetan version of "God will punish you."

A horse neighed and Peter looked up. A group of horsemen had gathered on the ridge. They were a horde from the annals of Genghis Khan, as if warriors from the steppes of Asia had crossed a time warp into the twentieth century.

The riders came down the incline, firing from the saddle, sending the porters running in panic.

Peter and Decimus hit the ground. The priest shouted something, but Peter didn't catch it. Or move a muscle to respond. He didn't need the priest to tell him they had managed to stumble onto the Bandit Lama's men. Horse hooves pounded in his ears, inches from his face, as the raiders rode into the camp, firing in the air, waving swords and rifles wildly.

The horsemen rounded up the porters like cattle and herded them back to where the porters had dropped their loads.

The bandits were a hard-looking lot, with long, greasy black hair woven into braids, animal-skin hats, rough garments, and boots trimmed with fur; they carried rifles and had bandoleers crisscrossing their chests. Each man rode, ate, slept, and probably made love with one arm bare. In their occupation, bulky clothing encumbered a quick draw and could mean certain death.

They stripped Peter and the priest of everything but their clothes and lined the porters up, kneeling, hands on head, like POWs waiting for a bullet.

Brigands went down the line, forcing open the mouth of each porter and shoving something in. The reaction from most of the porters was to gag and vomit.

"What are they doing?"

"Making the porters eat dog droppings so they'll throw up."

"For the love of God, why?"

"Some of the porters swallowed their jewelry. They're making them vomit it out."

"That's barbaric!"

The priest shrugged. "It's more humane than slitting open their stomachs."

"Are they going to do that to us?"

"I suspect not. They could see we made no attempt to conceal anything. They're going to hold us for ransom. I heard the men who tied us discuss it. They assume that men from the Western Heaven are all wealthy."

"That's insane."

"Welcome to the twelfth century."

A guard stepped back from the ritual with the porters and kicked the priest and Peter.

They shut up.

The porters were stripped of their valuables—inside and out—and turned loose. The two men from the Western Heaven were thrown over the back of a horse and carried away with the rest of the booty.

The fortress of the Bandit Lama was a battleship-gray hulk chiseled out of solid granite a hundred feet up the side of a cliff. It was once a lamasery. The monks who built it must have been human flies, Peter thought.

He and Father Decimus were dumped into a cage that was hauled up like a bucket of water from a well. Unless you were a bird—or human fly—it was the only way in or out. Rough hands pulled them out of the cage and pushed and shoved them into the center courtyard.

Fifty men, some still dressed in the robes of the Buddhist priesthood, were gathered in the courtyard and the tiers above, drunk and rowdy with that bloodthirsty fever that has infected drunk and rowdy crowds since the thumbs-down days of the Colosseum in Rome.

The Bandit Lama sat on a stone throne, surrounded by bodyguards. He was priest, magician, medicine man, healer, exorcist, brigand, murderer, and thief. He wore a high, coned hat with a grinning skull mounted in it; his face was powdered red and black.

Peter and the priest were forced to their knees to wait their turn while a Chinese merchant brought in by another raiding party was being interrogated by the brigand leader. The merchant was trying to get across the point that he should be turned loose because there was no one to ransom him.

The Bandit Lama didn't look pleased at the prospect of having a nonpaying guest. He cracked an order and guards dragged the merchant away.

Frantic activity broke out among the brigands and Peter saw money exchanging hands. A moment later a long, agonized scream echoed into the courtyard. When the scream stopped, the men burst into another frenzy of money exchange and argument.

"What the hell is going on?" Peter asked the priest in a whisper.

"The Chinese merchant finally managed to convince them he didn't have any money. The devils were wagering on how long his screams would last before he hit bottom."

The blood drained from Peter's face. "They threw him off the edge?"

"It is in God's hands," the priest mumbled.

The Bandit Lama shouted for order, and the mob settled down and directed its attention to the new attraction.

A long discussion ensued between the priest and the renegade lama. Father Decimus didn't look any happier than the merchant.

"They're sending a message to a Nepalese military

outpost to be relayed to the British Embassy in Katmandu. They consider all white men British since the
British ruled India and once invaded Tibet. They're
sending another messenger to a Red Chinese military
outpost."

"Why?"

"They're going to hold an auction. Sell us to the
highest bidder."

"The British aren't going to ransom us."

"I don't think I'd mention that. The Chinese merchant had no one to ransom him."

The Bandit Lama eyed Peter for a moment, then
left his throne and came down the steps. As the man
got nearer, Peter realized the gaudy red smear on his
lips was lipstick; he smelled sweet and sour, like
cheap perfume sprinkled on a pig.

Two guards jerked Peter to his feet and held his
arms.

"What does he want?" Peter asked as the Bandit
Lama stared at him like a prize lamb.

"He says he has heard that men from the Western
Heaven have their penis clipped. He's referring to cir-
cumcision. He wants to see your penis."

"Jesus!"

The priest's voice trembled. "The heathen bastard
is a *sodomite*!"

The Bandit Lama bent down and reached for the
zipper to Peter's pants just as Peter's knee came up.

The last thing Peter remembered before a rain of
blows drove him to the floor was the squishy feel of
the Bandit Lama's nose against his knee.

CHAPTER 27

"Y ou crazy motherfuckers! Fuckin' yellow bastards. Let us out of here!"

No one paid any attention to Peter's curses. They were too busy enjoying the sport and wagering on the outcome.

Peter and the priest were in a pit with their backs to a wooden wall and their arms outstretched and tied to iron rungs. On the other side of the pit was a long, cylindrical-shaped mesh cage with two rats inside, one at each end of the cage.

In the center of the cage was a smelly chunk of ripe yak-milk cheese. Between the rats and the cheese were thick strands of hemp. The rats were in a race. The one that chewed through five pieces of hemp first would get to the cheese.

What made the race interesting to the drunken mob surrounding the pit was the result: When those razor incisors sliced through and a piece of hemp snapped, a spring-hurtled dagger flipped across the room.

Peter's rat gnawed through its first rope and the dagger struck the wall a foot from the fingers of his outstretched left arm. Decimus's rat was still working on its first piece.

When the dagger struck, the crowd went crazy. Bets were made, collected, or changed. Losers and winners broke into fist fights.

Decimus's rat broke through the hemp, and the

priest cried out when the dagger struck and cut the flesh of his right leg.

Peter screamed at his rat. "Stop chewing, you bastard!"

The rodent ignored him.

The priest's mumbled prayers, the cries of the crowd, his own heart beating, all merged into a deafening roar in Peter's ears. His rat cut through another hemp and a dagger bit into the wall beside his neck.

It was all part of the game. The first daggers were not set to be lethal. It was the last blade or two that would go for the heart. A quick kill would have disappointed the crowd.

Peter watched in horrified fascination as his superrat disintegrated another piece while the priest's rat slowly nibbled. He calculated the projection of the blade. It was aimed for his groin!

The crowd knew it and went wild. Years of illgotten gains were bet on the exact spot the dagger would strike. Peter frantically pulled himself up. The blade struck between his legs, quivering against his crotch.

A man who lost on the throw leaned over the rail and shook his fist at Peter. He shouted down Tibetan obscenities.

"Fuck you, you ugly bastard!" Peter screamed.

The man spat. His aim was better than the rat's. One of his buddies slapped the spitter on the back and shoved a mug of beer in his hand.

A commotion broke out as the Bandit Lama's bodyguards cleared the path to the pit and the brigand leader stepped up to the railing with a rifle. The lama took aim and fired. The priest's rat exploded. He fired a second time and the super-rat bit the dust.

No one offered an explanation for their sudden release as Peter and the priest were led across the courtyard and lowered in the cage. The answer was waiting on the valley floor when they stepped out of the cage.

"I am honored to be of some small assistance in, shall we say, extricating you from the clutches of cruel fate," Dr. Poc told them, bowing.

"You're supposed to be dead," Peter told him.

"A mere flesh wound. Painful, but not lethal."

Lo Fat stood by stroking his .44 with sweaty palms.

"I'm disappointed, Chinaman," Father Decimus said. "I found solace in the belief you were burning in hell."

"Precisely." Poc stroked his beard. "Do not thank me. I understand you are too overwhelmed by emotion. Suffice to say I could not stand by while a fellow scholar and his young associate suffer at the cruel hands of barbarians. It cost my meager life's savings to buy your freedom, but your gratitude is gold to this old man's heart."

"If this scoundrel was sure he could read the markings on the skull, he would have paid those thieves to cut out our livers for dogfood," the priest told Peter.

"You have the skull?" Poc asked.

"We have a long and arduous journey ahead," Father Decimus said, strapping his pack to his back. "Let's get started."

One fact of life was not lost to Peter as he trudged behind the priest in the darkness with Poc and Lo Fat bringing up the rear with two donkeys: He was excess baggage. He did not possess valuable knowledge as the priest did. Poc glared at him like an uninvited guest at a cannibal's dinner party.

Peter was curious as to why Poc ventured into the wilderness with just Lo Fat for protection. He asked Poc about it that night as they sat around a campfire. "I'm surprised you didn't bring along a few of Honorable Cousin's tong brothers."

Dr. Poc stroked his great white beard and smiled wisely. "It is said that an apple sliced thinly is not tasty."

"You're giving Honorable Cousin the shaft."

"Precisely."

"What about the Red Chinese?"

"Precisely."

Another day's march brought them to a gorge, a crack hundreds of feet deep formed by a primordial upheaval that split the mountain. A raging, serpentine river careened in the bowel of the gorge.

The only way across was a narrow log. Human hands had put the log in place, but moss and icy green slime coating the log indicated no one had used it often or even recently.

The two donkeys had come as far as they could. They were turned loose, bait for wolves.

The men could make it across by sitting and scooting—if the log wasn't so dry-rotted it broke under the weight. As usual, the clever Chinese had the solution.

"You go first," he told Peter.

"Screw you."

"You are the heaviest. If it holds you, it will hold the rest of us."

"And what if it doesn't hold me?"

The Chinese bowed. "We shall carry you in heart's memory along life's highways."

"Go precisely to hell."

Lo Fat's .44 settled the issue.

Peter straddled the log and slowly scooted along. He knew he wasn't supposed to look down, but that was as easy as crossing a street without looking for cars. He was almost across when a roar shattered the peace of the mountains.

A great cat stood on a ledge high above them. Its roar filled the canyon again. Peter realized he was witnessing something special, an animal only a few

Westerners had seen in the wild, a Stone Age beast with a long shaggy gray coat and black-coal spots.

A snow leopard.

He thought of Tashi, of the silver medallion she wore, of her in his arms. A shot rang out, its percussion ricocheting off the canyon walls like a volley of cannons. Lo Fat's bullet chipped rock a dozen feet below the snow leopard.

The beast let out another roar, the blood-chilling scream of a hungry cat about to devour its prey. No one moved. Even Lo Fat's finger froze on the trigger of the .44.

The big cat disappeared into the rocks, and Peter experienced a chill as he slowly scooted the rest of the way across.

They were in the forbidden zone.

CHAPTER 28

A fresh drizzle turned the walls of the Lamasery of Shambala the color of wet emeralds and caused the prayer flags to droop and the prayer wheels to grind to a halt. Not even faith could resist the elements.

Tashi walked into the room at the top of the tower, the classroom where Tsaral had tried to "shape" her into the proper image. The room was unchanged; even the dust on the books seemed like the same dust she had seen in her youth.

The lotus petal stool, carved from a single piece of rainwood, was still there. She had spent hundreds of hours sitting on the stool as her tutor tried to instill in her the mixture of duty, wisdom, and fidelity that the lamas of Shambala decreed for their Tashivaana.

Nearly twenty years had passed since she had last seen the room. What would she be like now if she had stayed in Shambala? The image of a caged bird came to mind, and she shuddered at the thought.

The sound of footsteps came from the stairwell, and a moment later the High Lama entered the room, dragging his feet a little. He was old and stiff and the climb up the tower steps had captured his breath. He had aged and shrunk until he looked like a green apple left to shrivel and brown in the sun. She helped him to a chair and gave him a kiss on the forehead.

He raised his eyebrows and she smiled. "For honey cakes when I deserved a spanking."

He chuckled. "I remember. So many years ago, but I remember."

"Where is Tsaral?"

"Tsaral is old, almost as ancient as I, I'm afraid. I gave him permission to return to the village of his boyhood to die among his memories." He sighed. "Soon I, too, will pass beyond sorrow. I will not miss this life. I look forward to the next." He looked toward the window. "Last summer I sat up here and imagined that in my next life I was a bird. Birds have small appetites to satisfy and can fly above life's troubles. But where do birds go when it rains?"

"They don't have to go to a special place. They're in harmony with their place in the world, and rain is part of their rhythm of life. We are the only creatures that shape the world to suit our fancy."

Eyes dulled by age and cataracts examined her. "You have seen many things, more than even these old eyes. You have been beyond the mountains, followed the rivers to the Land of the Rains and to the Western Heaven. You have seen demons and know they are terrible to behold." Respect underlined his words, as if she were now the master, he the student. "When you arrived last night the joy in the lamasery was greater than any I have ever beheld. No Tashi-vaana has made the journey since the days of old when the Monkey-King and the She-Demon fought the seven-headed dragon." His voice fell to a whisper. "You have much to tell us."

She shied away from the unspoken questions and examined the pattern of snow leopards in the thread-bare rug.

He sighed again. "You have come back bearing a great burden. There are words you must tell me that your heart does not want you to speak. Words about these strangers that you have brought with you."

She knelt beside his chair and took his hands in hers. His hands were wrinkled and thin. "Holy Father, the men from the Western Heaven who have come to Shambala will dig into the great mountain to find the tomb of the Monkey-King."

The shock of her words traveled from his heart to hers. His hands trembled and she kissed them.

"This cannot be. It is not meant for men to dig like moles for the secret of the tomb. The legend says the Monkey-King will rise when—"

"Legends are words!" Another jolt went through him and she gently squeezed his hands. "Forgive me, Holy Father, but I have been to the outside world, and the demons are more terrible than we imagined. They cannot be stopped with tales from the days of old."

He pulled his hands away. "You don't believe in the legend? What has happened to you? Have demons stolen your mind? Child, you don't understand. You can't change destiny. You can't unmake what you are or what you are to be. You must follow the Path. To change your steps is to . . . to court more terrible consequences than you can imagine."

"I know the consequences," she whispered. "There were times when I was beaten and violated and humiliated, when my body was sold to satisfy the carnal desires of men. I believed there could be nothing worse that I would ever have to face. But now I have been forced to look within and see the truth about myself . . . and another. To know the truth about one's self is the most frightening demon of all."

"I am sad, sad. I want to leave behind the sorrow of this life," he said. "I am not an oracle, I cannot read the future from a man's ashes or from the ripples of a lake. But I knew the day we found you, the child we had secreted away and erased from our memories, that the time had come."

"Why me? The spirit of the Tashivaana has passed through women for an eon, and none have had to look into their own soul and see . . . see . . ."

She went to the window and looked to the great mountain that guarded the green vale. "When I was a little girl, I stood here and asked Tsaral what was beyond the mountains. He never really gave me an answer because he didn't know. It was like asking a blind man to describe a sunset." Her heart searched for the pulse of the man she knew was climbing the highest mountains to come to her side. "I will never be able to explain to you why I had to come back this way," she whispered. "But I promise you that I will give my life to defend the secret of the tomb."

THE HIMALAYAS

CHAPTER 29

The forbidden zone.

The region even Tibetans dared not enter.

It was like the dark side of the moon, a bitter, unfriendly place peopled with strange ice formations that glared down at the men invading the territory. The sky was ashen; swirling fogs of ice crystals, like the dust devils that wander the western plains, haunted the frozen wasteland, creating an eerie animation that fed the imagination with the unimaginable.

It was a place of no life except their own, of no sounds except their footfalls and labored breathing. Bitter cold wrapped around them, freezing their outer layer of clothing and beards, turning them into ghostly white snowmen. Their breath froze in midair and rained to the ground as ice crystals; their eyes were swollen almost shut from snow blindness.

Two days into the frozen wasteland they entered a great glacier field, scaling mountains of ice and crossing ice bridges over chasms so deep the bottoms were lost in shadowy gloom.

Peter realized they were making prints where no other Westerner had trod, that they were on an exploration no less daring than Peary's, no less dangerous than a walk on the moon. But he was too damn miserable to appreciate his good fortune.

There was nothing to build a fire with and the food

they carried had been gone for three days. No food and no fire had not driven them to comradeship. Lo Fat took the deprivations the worst, staggering behind them like a frozen yellow scarecrow, muttering to himself in Cantonese. The first few days he had complained loudly to Poc, only to be rebuffed; finally Poc simply stopped listening and Lo Fat began talking to himself.

Peter was sure the man's pea brain had cracked from the cold. Lo Fat's arguments with himself were getting louder and his delusions more dangerous. Several times he fired shots from the .44 at imaginary enemies. Even Poc was uncomfortable with Lo Fat bringing up the rear with a blazing revolver. He tried to take the gun away only to have the man threaten to use it on him.

On the fifth night in the ice fields, Peter, Decimus, and Dr. Poc huddled together and watched Lo Fat. The skinny hatchetman had fallen into a troubled, broken sleep in a sitting position with the .44 in his lap. When it became obvious Poc was not going to make a grab for the gun, Peter got quietly to his feet and started for Lo Fat. His footsteps made crunching sounds on the ice and Lo Fat jerked awake, staring about wildly. Peter turned and staggered off to the right, pretending he was on a call of nature.

When they resumed the march the next morning, Lo Fat brought up the rear with a new glint in his eye: His enemies finally had substance.

At midday they paused just below the ridge of a glacier to catch their breath while Lo Fat slowly struggled up behind them. Peter, Poc, and the priest had made their way up the slope with great care, fearful of starting an avalanche.

Peter sat wearily in the snow and watched Lo Fat heavy-foot it up the slope. Peter's lips were split into double harelips, he had lost all feeling in his feet, and for all he knew his toes were bouncing around in his boots. He never removed the pack on his back, not even when he slept. There was nothing in it but some underwear he couldn't put on because he would have frozen to death trying and a metal canteen full of frozen water he was too tired to throw away.

Peter nodded in Lo Fat's direction. "Have you seen the way he stared at us? He's thinking our clothes will keep him warm."

Dr. Poc stroked his frozen beard and shrugged. "One of us must fall first. Lo Fat is the weakest link. The clothing from his back can help others survive. There are even stories of men who survived on the flesh of their dead companions. If you could disarm him . . ."

"Jesus," Peter said to the priest, "can you believe what this maniac is proposing?"

The priest stared woodenly at him.

Peter shook his head in disbelief. "This must be what hell is like. Frozen and miserable with assholes for company. Look at me, priest. Do you even know where those goddamn scratches on that skull are leading us?"

"God is directing us!"

"Then goddamnit, tell Him to direct us somewhere warm!"

"You'll burn in hell for using the Lord's name in vain."

"Being with you bastards is hell! You people are crazier than Lo Fat. Neither one of you gives a damn about people. You'd sell our flesh for your fuckin' treasures and bones of God and . . ."

"Forgive him Lord for—"

". . . your fuckin' souls for a fire!"

"He is a sinner who knows not—"

"You'd warm your feet in hell if Satan offered!"

"Strike him down, O mighty Jehovah!"

"Silence!" Poc snapped.

Lo Fat was a dozen yards below them, waving the .44 and screaming.

"He thinks we're plotting against him!"

Poc was already moving as he spoke the words; the spry priest was on his heels.

The cannon boomed and the snowpack trembled from the concussion. Peter threw himself flat as another shot thundered. The snow beneath him trembled and began sliding down with a roar that shook the mountains. Wind and ice ripped at him as he rode the avalanche down. The great mass of snow broke up at the bottom of the slope, creating snow boulders as big as houses. Peter came in with the last of the debris, a bolt of pure terror electrifying him as snow covered him. He pushed up, breaking through the snow with his back as he clawed and dug his way out, collapsing breathless on the hard pack.

The mountains were quiet. Lo Fat was gone, buried under a million tons of snow and ice, no doubt stroking his .44 all the way to hell. Decimus and Poc were not on top of the hill looking anxiously for sign of their fallen companions. They had not even glanced back before pushing onward. The only sound that disturbed the serenity of the moment was the sharp rasp of his breathing, a rain of ice crystals drizzling every time his breath hit the frigid air.

He was hungry, lost, and abandoned. Also angry and scared. It was the latter two emotions that got him moving up the mountain with more crawl than walk. As he struggled, he realized what it was about himself that enabled him to match the fierce drive the priest drew from belief in a higher being and the Chinaman from greed. It was faith and belief in himself: *If those two shits can make it, so can I.*

Tashi was out there somewhere, in that valley green and warm he had to find. He shivered with the

anticipation of holding her in his arms in front of a
roaring fire. She probably already knew he was coming. There was something mystical about her, like that
Druid princess. She had probably sent out mind
waves to find him. He laughed hysterically at the
thought. No one was going to save him. He had bad
karma. The end was just going to be stretched out a
little to make him pay for all those bad things he'd
done in past lives.

CHAPTER 30

The holiest place in Shambala was the Temple of Ice, the legendary gateway to the tomb of the Monkey-King. It sat atop the glacier that clung to the side of the great mountain; carved from ice as hard as marble and polished until it sparkled like the facets of diamonds, the temple had pillars mightier than those of the Colosseum and a dome that dwarfed the Duomo in Florence. The back of the structure melted with the glacier itself.

A hundred steps led up to the entryway where a huge beast stood guard, a snow leopard carved from ice as pure as crystal; its spots were gems more precious than those adorning the Peacock Throne. The eyes of the beast were star sapphires, the blue of the Lake of Celestial Reflection. From their depths came a fire, a teardrop of the sun. Beyond the snow leopard the temple was cloaked by a darkness steeped in the chill of the unknown.

Zhdanov's men were inside the temple, searching for the hidden door that led to the tomb.

Monks acting as bearers carried Tashi up the glacier, following a path hacked from ice. She would have preferred to walk rather than be transported on the palanquin but allowed herself to be carried because the monks considered it an honor to man the poles.

When they reached the temple, Zhdanov came down the steps to meet the palanquin. A chill went through her and she pulled her white fur cape snug.

The monks shied fearfully away as Zhdanov approached. He was dressed in a space-age foul-weather suit that would have permitted the wearer to maintain normal body temperature on either side of the moon. He had brought enough suits to equip his own men and the cadre of monks expected to help, but no monks of Shambala were among the workers. The monks would have sooner danced with a demon than don one of the suits and desecrate the holiest of places.

She looked to the folds of the green valley, the lake, and the lamasery before turning to meet his eye. "Have you found the entrance to the tomb?"

"No. But we will." He didn't say it, but she knew he suspected she could have shown him the way. He was right. She remembered the secret doorway from her visits to the temple when she was a child.

"I overheard Bagora talking to your pilot. Men have been spotted in the mountains, and the helicopter has gone for them." She had not overheard anything but had been told by Ma.

"I hate to disappoint you but it's the old Chinese and the priest. The copter radioed that it had picked them up a few minutes ago."

"Only those two?"

"You're wondering what happened to your Mr. Novak. The last time his two old friends saw him he was riding an avalanche on the other side of the mountains."

"Is the copter searching for him?"

"The copter is bringing back those two old fools so they can help me unravel the mystery of the temple. You can forget about your friend."

"If he's out there—"

"He's buried under snow and ice."

"I must talk to Decimus and Poc when they arrive."

"I've given orders that neither man is to speak to you. Go back to the lamasery. Stay in your room until I send for you."

"Please . . ."

Zhdanov motioned at one of the guards. "Escort the palanquin back down the mountain. She is not to leave the lamasery without my permission."

He watched Tashi's palanquin until it disappeared around a bend in the trail leading down to the valley floor. Bagora was waiting for him at the top of the steps.

The little man smirked. "How did Tashi take the news of her lover's death?"

"Don't call Novak her lover." Zhdanov stared at him coldly. "You were supposed to have taken care of Novak in Calcutta. You're lucky the mountains stopped him."

Bagora shrugged. "He's finished now."

"You had better hope so."

The High Lama and a group of elder monks were standing by the main gate when Tashi returned to the lamasery. They looked away as she stepped from the palanquin and walked by, her head bowed.

Monks followed her with their eyes as she walked through the courtyard. One monk, a small, thin old man with purple thread showing on the collar of his red robe, met her eye for a moment as if he wanted to speak to her, but he suddenly turned and hurried away. She had seen him before, hovering in the background, staring at her as if he had something to say but feared to do so.

The purple thread was a sign that the man was a Pathfinder, one of the special breed of monks trained to cross the mountains. She wondered if he had been one of those who took her to the Forest of Lam so long ago.

Ma was standing guard at the door to her room. She knew the big Mongol would willingly give his life for her and that Bagora would just as willingly take it if he found an excuse. She realized what she had to do. She was going to sneak out of the lamasery and cross the mountains to find Peter. It was a frightening thought. No one, not even the most venerable High Lama, had crossed the mountains without the assistance of Pathfinders.

From the valley side the mountains were sheer cliffs and there appeared to be only one pass, a narrow cleft in the side of the great mountain beyond the lake. The cleft disappeared in the mist that covered the upper region. The monks believed that a giant snow leopard crouched in the mist, waiting to grab with huge jaws foolish souls who attempted to leave the valley.

Tashi smiled affectionately at Ma. "I don't want you to sleep by my door tonight. Go down to the courtyard and sleep with the rest of Zhdanov's men."

The big Mongol shook his head. "I stay—"

"No, not tonight. I know why you stay and I appreciate it, but if you truly want to help me, you'll do as I say." She stood on tiptoes and kissed him on the cheek and hugged him. She felt safer with Ma by her door, but she knew Bagora would implicate him in her escape if he spent the night there.

Inside her quarters, she sat on the edge of her bed and rubbed her face with her hands. *Peter was in the mountains.* Lost. Perhaps buried by an avalanche. No, she was sure he wasn't dead. She felt *oneness* with him, as if the beat of her heart were united with his. He was still alive and she had to find him.

She went onto the balcony. One of her earliest memories of Shambala was Lsong scolding her for imagining a snow leopard on the balcony. The passage up the mountain, the cleft, was a jagged saw blade that cut into the mist near the top of the mountain. Shambala was a land of mystery and legend, and what lay hidden in the mist was one of its greatest secrets. All legends were a mixture of fact and imagination. She wondered how terrible the truth could be about what lay in wait for those trying to escape the valley.

She left her quarters after midnight, sneaking like a wraith beneath the front gate while a yawning guard stood watch on the wall above. The gate was open. Not even Zhdanov's men could close the doors frozen in place for centuries.

She moved in a fast, urgent lun-gom pace choreographed by the cadence of silent chant and the rhythm of breathing. She had to make it to the mountain by the break of day. When Zhdanov discovered her missing, he'd have his helicopter and men search for her.

A sound from the rear caused her to break stride and stop to listen. Only the rustle of leaves in the night breeze disturbed the silence. She went on, but the feeling that she was being followed stayed with her.

She reached the base of the mountain before dawn and started up the narrow trail that soon became a high-walled crevice in the mountain's face. Practicing even modified lun-gom was impossible there. She spotted the man following her when she paused to catch her breath.

Bagora entered Tashi's quarters after she failed to answer his knock that morning when he came to check on her.

He took one look at the unmade bed and cursed. "Just as I thought. The bitch has fled."

He spun around and found the doorway blocked by Ma's huge frame.

"Get out of my way, you fool. The woman is gone. I have to tell Zhdanov."

Ma didn't budge.

"Move!"

The big Mongol's eyes narrowed. The elephant had taken abuse from the mouse for too long.

Bagora's eyes suddenly lit up. "Zhdanov!"

Ma swung around, but there was no one behind him. When he turned back, the little man shot him between the eyes.

Tashi sat in the lotus position and waited as a monk made his way up the crevice. From a distance he looked like a red ant crawling between the rocks. When he got closer she recognized him as the Path-finder who had been giving her the curious looks at the lamasery.

He stopped a dozen feet away and bowed deeply. Small, brown, wrinkled, and a little gray, he had the quick, spry movements of an old chipmunk. Her heart was pounding, but she realized he was even more frightened of her.

"Tashivaana." He spoke in little more than a whisper.

Tashivaana. The She-Demon. Guardian of the tomb. Wielder of magic.   "Why have you followed me?"

He blinked a few times like a nearsighted owl and seemed to struggle with himself before answering.

"Tashivaana, I am Hying." He spoke as if she were expected to recognize the name. She said nothing and waited.

"Tashivaana cared for me when I was ill."

It was her turn to blink. She had left Shambala as a child. Then she realized what he was talking about.

"My mother cared for you."

"Tashivaana cared for me."

Tashivaana was her mother. Tashivaana was her. She realized that in his eyes *she was her mother*. Tashivaana was a spirit that possessed a succession of women, the earthly body changing but the spirit remaining the same.

She waited for him to say more and prompted him when the fountain didn't flow. "You are a Pathfinder."

"I am a Pathfinder."

"You have been here before with my mo . . . with Tashivaana."

"The High Lama say take Tashivaana to the mountain. The Council of Elders had spoken. I and another took Tashivaana there." He pointed to where the trail disappeared into the mist and she understood. Her mother had not been banished from Shambala, she had been given a death sentence. The Pathfinders had been instructed to steer her into the danger. But she had made it over the mountain and Tashi realized why.

"You showed Tashivaana the way over the mountain."

He nodded vigorously; a line of sweat ran down from his temple and dropped off his cheek. He was sweating from fear, not heat.

"I slipped away and returned to Tashivaana. I led you around the jaws of the leopard and over the mountain."

"Over the mountain," Tashi repeated.

"Over the mountain. To the man from the Western Heaven."

"What? What do you mean?" She spoke so sharply he looked ready to bolt. "Hying," she said soothingly, "tell me what you remember about the man from the Western Heaven. Was it the one from the dungeon? The man who flew over the mountains?"

He shook his head. "Men from the Western Heaven searched for man who flew over mountains."

An expedition had been sent to find Duncan MacKinzie, she thought. The authorities must have sent out teams of searchers in all directions from the last position the plane had been reported.

"The spirits of the mountains killed all but one man," Hying said. "The spirits had sucked most of the life from his body and made his blood cold."

Starved and frostbitten. Escaping from the problems created by a Westerner, her mother had found another Westerner and more problems.

"We took the man to the cave Pathfinders use when crossing the mountains and Tashivaana cared for him."

"Tashivaana saved him? The man lived?"

"Tashivaana stayed in the cave with the man for many weeks. I brought firewood and food many times. Tashivaana breathed life back into the man from the Western Heaven, and soon he was able to leave the cave."

"Where did they go?"

"We went south toward the nearest village. Many days' journey. Terrible storms came and the mountain spirits again attacked the man." Hying pounded his chest and coughed.

Pneumonia, Tashi thought. The man was probably still weak and his condition got worse.

"What happened after the mountain spirits attacked his chest?"

"The man from the Western Heaven passed beyond sorrow."

"What happened to Tashivaana?"

"Tashivaana sent me back to Shambala. You go." He waved in a vaguely southern direction. "Tashivaana go."

She went, Tashi thought, until she stumbled into a

farmhouse months later, ill and heavy with child. For a moment Tashi felt her suffering, her desperation, the swelling in her belly, a living person inside her demanding food and warmth, the icy chill of the Roof of the World wrapped around her like the cold fingers of the dead.

The silence was broken by the rasp of Zhdanov's helicopter. It was racing toward them.

"We must hurry," she said. The Pathfinder picked up on her sense of danger and shot by her, not in panic, but to show her the shortest way through the maze of boulders and brush. They were less than half a mile from the mist line. Once they slipped into the mist, the copter would not be able to follow.

She moved fast but was barely able to keep up with the little man. She had to make it into the fog and over the mountain. To fail was certain death for Peter.

Like the mindless whine of a rabid dog on their heels, the screech of the copter grew louder behind them. She didn't look back. It wasn't necessary. There was noplace to go but up.

Popping sounds from an automatic rifle were audible over the roar of the helicopter.

"Hide, Hying!" she screamed.

A bullet caught the old man on top of his left shoulder and ricocheted through his body like a hot knife. He staggered and crumpled on the ground.

The copter dropped lower to the ground and its roar filled the ravine as Tashi knelt next to the monk, an image of another fallen holy man flashing in her mind.

"Hying!"

The monk's robes were bloody at his abdomen where the bullet had exploded out, leaving an ugly hole.

"Leave me." He pointed a shaky finger at the mist.

"The leopard's jaws ... the breath ..." His eyes closed and he went limp.

"Hying!"

The copter hovered overhead, creating a maelstrom of wind and dust around her. The copter's belly opened and a black-uniformed trooper with a machine gun strapped over his back descended on a line.

Tashi dashed up the hill. No fire came from the copter or the man descending. The orders were to bring her back alive.

The storm trooper jumped free of the line before his feet hit the ground; and he shot up after her. The man was small, lithe like the old monk, but only a fraction of the man's age and even faster. He hadn't been climbing for hours and entered the race with a bolt of energy Tashi had already spent.

Her only hope was to lose him in the fog, but that maneuver was fraught with more danger than the man himself. Something even the monks of Shambala feared was waiting in the fog, and she was racing toward it.

The fog swallowed her; it wasn't just a heavy mist but was luminous, creating a whiteout, a shapeless, shadowless realm of nothingness. She tripped over a mound of snow and fell. The mound was two feet high and she hadn't seen it; she wouldn't have seen a twenty-foot wall. Helplessness increased her fear. She could see the dark shadow of the man behind her and that meant he saw her, but the next step she took might take her into a wall or over a cliff. She remembered Peter's comment about taillights in the fog. She was a beacon for her pursuer.

She moved forward slowly. Behind her the man fell and cursed. He had found the two-foot mound. He was plowing ahead at full speed, forcing her to move faster into the unknown. She walked into a solid wall and bounced back. Her body stung but she kept moving, following the curve of the wall to the left. She realized she was going through a passageway with another wall a few feet to her left. A breeze within the mist pushed at her back. The grade underfoot suddenly became a downhill slope. With the breeze at her back and the grade sloping down, she began to move faster, putting her arms out in front of her in case she ran into anything. The Pathfinder's words came back to her: "The breath . . ." Hying had said. The leopard's-breath. *The breeze must lead into the jaws!*

She threw herself to the ground. She could hear the crunch of the boots of the man behind her. He was coming down the slope full speed ahead. She wanted to keep running but her mind rang with alarm—a gentle slope, a little breeze to nudge you along, it was all too convenient.

She crawled on hands and knees, fighting the urge to get up and run from the man behind her. A few feet ahead the gentle slope ended in a sheer cliff. The edge of the cliff was jagged. *Like a leopard's jaw,* she thought. What had Hying said? Something about leading her *around* the jaws?

She sank onto her belly in the snow and rolled, covering herself with a coat of snow, becoming a part of the whiteout. She was tired of being a taillight. The man chasing her could lead the way from now on.

The trooper's boots crunched snow beside her head as he stamped by. He uttered a startled cry as he stumbled over the cliff. The cry became a scream of terror as he began to free-fall.

Shaking, cold, her mind fighting fear, Tashi got back onto her hands and knees and began feeling her way around the pit.

*   *   *

Kismet, kismet, kismet.

The word ran around Peter's mind, chasing itself like a dog after its own tail. He didn't have the strength left to formulate a more complicated thought. He was operating on nervous energy, a snake with its head cut off, too stupid to know it was supposed to curl up and die. Each time he dropped exhausted to his knees in the snow, he thought of Tashi and fire stirred within him, driving him on, higher and higher up the mountain.

Finally a storm came, the kind of raging tempest Tibetans call a mad dog, pushing him deeper into the jungle of ice. When the blizzard stopped, he stopped, sinking to his knees in the snow, looking like some abominable thing that had crawled out of a crack in the ice.

He saw the cave, but there was nothing he could do about it. The cave was a hundred yards away, but it might as well have been a hundred miles. He didn't have the strength to make it. The only thing keeping him upright was the coating of ice hugging his clothes. The storm had driven him to his knees, taking the last bit of his strength.

He stared numbly at the opening to the cave, trying to piece it all together. A hundred yards. Shelter. Someplace warmer than the subzero snow he was wading in. He tried to tell his knees to unbend, his feet to start moving, but the road down his spinal cord to his extremities was closed due to stormy weather and the message couldn't get through.

And then horror began. He saw someone—something?—come out of the cave and start down the hill for him. He wanted to get up and run, but all he could manage was a little shudder. He couldn't make out what was coming down the hill for him, didn't know if it was man or beast. He never even really looked at what was approaching. He just knew *something* was coming for him.

It was almost on top of him when he heard the words.

"Peter, Peter, I love you."

Tashi brushed ice from his face and kissed him, then rubbed her own face against his. He said something, nothing coherent. She helped him to his feet and he came along with her, ambulating mindlessly, like a zombie.

She built a fire from the supply of dried foliage Pathfinders had stockpiled over the years and spread her robe next to the blaze. Peter knelt on the robe and stared at the fire as she fed him from a bowl of tsampa gruel. "Barley and melted snow," she told him. He swallowed a little and then, as if the fire had melted him, he slowly sank onto the bed.

"I found the cave last night," she said, "just before the storm hit." Her eyes swept the walls and ceiling. "The moment I walked in I felt as if I had been here before. I . . . I sensed something."

He didn't answer. He had not spoken a word except the dribble that came out when she had found him. He had tried and she hushed him to save his strength. She removed his damp clothes and spread herself naked over him to share her body warmth with him.

"There is fire in each of us," she whispered, "but you have to find it. Breathe deeply, Peter, breathe in, and each time you exhale imagine your breath is a bellows fanning flames around you . . ." And she began to chant softly, timing it with her breathing.

Om Mani Padme Hum!

"O Jewel in the Heart of the Lotus!"

She rubbed herself back and forth over his nakedness, her body sizzling, her fires roaring, her hot sweat bonding her to him, driving her own body heat into him. She knew she had won the battle when his arms went around her, not tightly, but gently as he whispered her name.

Her breathing and chanting created a high that permitted her mind to flow freely. She imagined herself on the ceiling of the cave, staring down at the two of them lying naked beside the fire. *But it wasn't them.* The two people in her mind's eye were not her and Peter but two other people, strangers yet familiar. *Her mother and another man from the Western Heaven, a mountaineer sent on a rescue mission.*

As she watched the two people making love next to the fire she realized that she was watching her own conception.

CHAPTER 31

Peter's mind was surprisingly clear when he awoke. His body felt as if it had been left out on a freeway for the rush-hour traffic to trample, but he came awake fully alert, not from a sense of danger but because he was excited to be alive—alive and with the woman he loved.

Glare reflecting from snow outside the opening washed the interior of the cave, and he could see the rugged pattern of the rocky walls and ceiling as he lay on his back. Yellowish tongues of light flickered on the walls. He turned to look at the source—the small fire Tashi had built near the opening to the cave. She was beside the fire, in the lotus position, eyes closed, her long black hair delicately lacing her face. Sleeping? Meditating? Light and shadows from the fire danced on her face, and for a moment he imagined them in the backseat of a taxi in London, her face caressed by light and shadows as the taxi passed street lamps.

His mind switched off almost as quickly as he had awakened, and he fell back into a deep sleep. When Tashi checked him a few minutes later she found him sleeping with a smile on his face.

Hours later he came alive again and found her nestled in his arms. For a long time they lay together, naked, breast to breast, communicating only with the beat of their hearts. Finally the unanswered questions became too pressing and they had to break the rapture to talk.

"We're on the west side of a mountain bordering Shambala," she told him.

"Why did you lead him to Shambala?" There was no need to identify "him." Zhdanov was a shadow between them even in a forgotten cave on a lost mountain.

"To save you. He would have had you killed."

"To save me." He repeated the words as if he were trying to decipher some hidden meaning in them. "For two people who fell in love at first sight, we've spent an amazing amount of time just trying to be together." He wanted to tell her she had been foolish, that she should never have turned Zhdanov loose in Shambala, not even for him, but the words wouldn't come. He would have done the same thing to save her.

"What's this strange hold Zhdanov has on you? At first I thought it was money, that you were a trophy, but I didn't want to believe it."

"I thought he was my father."

"Your father?!"

"The priest, Father Decimus, what did he tell you about Zhdanov?"

Peter shrugged. "Not much. He left me with the impression that you were Zhdanov's woman. He knew very little about Zhdanov. Apparently the priest knew someone else with the same name years ago."

"Zhdanov is not his real name."

"Why is he using someone else's name? What's his name?"

She looked away and didn't speak for a long moment. Her features exposed no emotions when she turned back. "Zhdanov is the name I have always known him by."

"Why did you think he was your father?"

"It was something I was told."

"I don't understand." He took a deep breath and let out a long sigh. "I'm getting the distinct impression you're keeping secrets again."

"What did Father Decimus tell you about Shambala?"

"Legends. A search for the bones of God. The old man is whacked out from ninety-proof vapors. He knew nothing about my father except rumors that a plane had crashed in the valley. I always suspected Decimus and Poc were holding out on me, that both of them knew more but were keeping it for a rainy day." He gently caressed her cheek with his fingers. "God, I love you. But . . . what is it, Tashi, what are you holding back?"

She kissed his fingers, then held his hand tightly against her naked breast. "I was born in a village several days' walk from here and taken to Shambala when I was four. I was little more than a child when I left Shambala."

"Is what the priest said true? Did my father's plane crash in Shambala?"

"I . . . I was told a story by the woman who raised me that an airplane had crashed in Shambala before I was born.

"Tashi, I love you."

"And I love you."

"Then why are you lying to me? This isn't Calcutta, we don't have Zhdanov and his goons breathing down our necks. This is you and me, and for all we know, we're the last two people left on earth. There's no reason for secrets."

She kissed his forehead, his chin, each of his shoulders, and the nipple of each of his breasts. "I love you, Peter." She put her arms around his neck and hugged him tight, her tears wet against his cheek. He knew she was lying to him, not with malice but to protect him. But from what?

Tashi rubbed her hands on his shoulder and arm. "You're getting goose bumps."

"My kismet's tripping over my karma," he said.

Another day passed before she would let him sit up and feed himself. The food was plain and simple—hot barley tea and tsampa, a hot, mushy concoction made with melted snow water, barley grain, and yak butter. The food was left behind for the rare trips that the Pathfinders of Shambala made over the mountains. The trips were spaced years apart, and the food stock had to be nonperishable. "Barley lasts fifty years or more in a dry cave," she told him. The dried, frozen yak butter was almost as durable.

They spent three days in the cave and Peter slept almost all of it. His body told him he could sleep for another week, but the small store of barley and firewood was nearly exhausted. He hated having to leave. His bones were weary, but unless they went back down the mountain and found a village, they faced starvation.

"We'll never be apart again," he told her.

She smiled and kissed him softly on the cheek. "We will unless you cut this beard."

He rubbed the beard tenderly. "It's a good thing I have it. My cheeks would have frozen and cracked." He grinned. "It's one of the things that make men superior to women."

"I'll try to grow one before I rescue you again."

He laughed and hugged her. He was on an emotional high. Questions still hung between them like a clothesline of dirty laundry, but the answers would have to wait. They had survival to worry about.

They were not going back to Shambala. She had had a powerful urge to return immediately, to save the temple from desecration, but Peter had talked her out of it. "We can't fight Zhdanov's army with our bare hands." He convinced her they should make their way to the Indian side of the mountains and contact the British. "They've been searching for Shambala since Father Decimus convinced them decades ago that it existed. A planeload of British commandos would take care of Zhdanov's storm troopers."

Frigid air outside snapped at him as they left the cave. His clothes were dry and warm, but a chill slipped through and he shivered. "When we make it back to civilization, we're going to Hawaii and bury ourselves in hot sand up to our necks. I never want to see another snowflake as long as I live."

They started down the mountain. It had not snowed since the mad dog storm that had driven him to his knees; the snowpack was hard and icy, making the going slow. They were headed back the way he had come, but the terrain was all new to him. He had not done any sightseeing on the way up.

By noon they had made it to a great reef of snow and ice that extended for miles before them. The going was easier, and they smiled and held hands as they walked.

Peter felt her hand suddenly tighten on his. "What's the matter?"

"I hear something."

His ears picked up the sound before they saw the black killer bee angrily buzzing down the mountain.

Zhdanov's helicopter.

They couldn't outrun it and there was noplace to hide. The idea of digging a hole and covering themselves with snow occurred to him, but it was too late. They had been spotted—the copter was already bearing directly for them.

He held her close as the helicopter landed nearby, whipping up a fierce wind of needle-nose ice slivers. Three storm troopers armed with machine guns leaped from the copter and surrounded Peter and Tashi.

A moment later Bagora stepped down from the copter. He grinned at the two lovers. "It would give me great pleasure to kill both of you, but unfortunately my orders are to bring *one* of you back alive."

"Move, Tashi." Peter tried to push her out of the line of fire.

"Kill him!"

"Stop!" Tashi screamed. She hung onto Peter as he tried to push her away. *"He's Zhdanov's son!"*

The man who called himself Zhdanov was standing at the window when Peter and Tashi were brought into the room. It was the same room Zhdanov had once been nursed in by Tashi's mother.

Guards held Peter's arms. Bagora was behind Tashi, a gun to her spine. He made little pretense of not wanting to pull the trigger if he got the opportunity.

Peter stared at his father. *His father.* The secret Tashi had been keeping. The man he had journeyed halfway around the world to find. "Why are you doing this?" he asked the man his mother said was a warm, caring person.

Zhdanov spoke without turning to face his son. The son no one had told him about until his son—*his enemy*—had been brought to the lamasery. "This was once my room. They brought me here after the crash. They put most of the pieces back together"—he slowly turned—"but some of the parts were missing, and those I replenished in Calcutta."

A storm erupted in the green-ice eyes. "I was battered and crushed, but my eyes were not lost in the crash. They gouged them out"—he gestured at the door behind Peter—"that pack of ignorant monks with their religious mumbo jumbo. I was the fulfillment of the legend, but they tried to poison Tashi's mother against me. They thought I was a *monster*.

They knew I had been injured in the crash, that . . . that I was no longer . . ." He choked up. "They knew I could not have sex like an ordinary man, but they accused me of raping her anyway. They wanted to get rid of us. She remembered too much of her past life, yearned too much to be a real woman. They figured that if I didn't turn her head, some other man would."

"So you came back for revenge."

"I came back to claim what is mine."

"Just as you stole another man's eyes."

"The man was scum. His brains were fried by drugs."

He looked beyond Peter, bitter memories flowing. "They blinded me and threw me in that dungeon to rot. When they sent me out of the valley they gave me a bag of jewels, conscience money that had small value here but was a fortune to the rest of the world. Those jewels gave me back my eyes, a new face, and the wealth and power to return here." He glanced at the small man holding a gun on Tashi. "Bagora helped me. I assumed the name of a man who had died searching for a Shambala skull-map, knowing that it would draw the other searchers to me and from them I would learn the route to Shambala."

His eyes were green cesspools. "The power source is in the mountain. Thirty years ago I sat at this window watching mist rise from vents near the top of the mountain, and I knew that behind the legend was a machine that had been operating for an eon. The ponds in the courtyard gave me the clue. There were ponds for nine planets, but the ancients didn't know about *nine* planets.

"That fool priest, the monks with their gods and demons, none of them understand. The planet Pluto wasn't even discovered until a few decades ago. Only a space traveler could have known that nine planets circled the sun. *The Monkey-King was an ancient as-*

tronaut. The power source may even be the engine of his spaceship. The man who controls power like that will have the universe in his hand."

Peter's heart pounded in his throat. "The priest's trying to find the bones of God. Poc's hunting for a pot of gold. And you're looking for some screwy machine jockeyed by a spaceman. Three greedy, crazy bastards trampling everything in their way for a chance to play God."

He had crossed continents and climbed the highest mountains to find his father, and the man had not even given him the slightest recognition as his son.

"Did you love my mother?"

The question jolted Zhdanov. For the briefest moment his mask cracked, but his too-handsome face quickly resumed its frozen countenance. His answer was the most brutal of all. "I don't remember your mother."

Peter leaped at him. The guards grabbed him and he took two of them to the floor with him in a tangle of arms and legs.

"Don't let them hurt him," Tashi screamed. "Don't let them hurt your son!"

Bagora grabbed her arm and cruelly jabbed the hard steel barrel of his gun against her spine.

"We're going into the mountain to find the tomb," Zhdanov told Tashi. "You and . . . Peter Novak are coming."

"I'd rather die than show you the secret ways," Tashi said.

"Poc and the priest have found the entrance inside the temple. Once I have the power source in my hands, I will claim not only Shambala but the world."

Peter was angry, but most of all, he was sad. "They were right, the monks who blinded you. You *are* a monster. They should have killed you!"

*   *   *

Two hours later Zhdanov gathered his hostages and his henchmen in a corridor of the lamasery. Two of Zhdanov's storm troopers brought Peter out of a room where he had been held. He smiled at Tashi as they brought him into the corridor where Zhdanov, Bagora, three more storm troopers, and the most venerable Dr. Poc and Father Decimus were waiting.

Neither the Lord's Servant nor the Devil's Disciple showed any guilt or remorse at having abandoned him to Lo Fat and an avalanche.

"Eat any of your friends lately?" Peter asked.

He didn't get even a blink out of either of them.

"We're going to the mountain," Zhdanov said. "Kill anybody who steps out of line," he told the storm troopers.

Peter avoided looking at the man. His father was a wonderful memory. His gut wrenched at the reality.

"The monks weren't happy when Tashi was brought back a prisoner," Zhdanov told Bagora. "There may be trouble when we go through the courtyard."

"If they're aroused over treatment of the woman," Dr. Poc injected, "would it not be wisdom's path to treat her with reverence? Perhaps have them carry her in a palanquin?"

Zhdanov stared at Poc for a moment, then said to Bagora, "Keep a tight grip on her arm. She'll walk with the rest of us."

Poc and Decimus exchanged looks as the procession followed Zhdanov down the corridor. Zhdanov wanted to arouse the monks, not pacify them.

They moved in single file past walls richly veined with gold and treasures of an eon. Peter ignored the historical artifacts and focused his mind on their predicament. He had to save Tashi, and he wasn't going to be able to do it with his bare teeth. His hope was in the monks. If there were enough of them, they might be able to overwhelm Zhdanov's thugs by sheer numbers alone. But how many were enough? Zhdanov and each of the black-clad storm troopers carried an assault rifle, and Bagora had one automatic pistol in hand and another in a shoulder holster. Didn't some Spanish conquistadors conquer the entire Aztec Empire with a fraction of that kind of firepower?

As they came down the wide stairway leading to the courtyard, monks poured out of the orifices of the lamasery like files of army ants, red robes flapping.

A wave of the small brown men massed in front of the gate as a hundred others pressed to the side and back of the procession.

Chanting.

Om Mani Padme Hum!

O Jewel in the Heart of the Lotus!

It was not the melodious chant of morning and evening prayers but the angry rasp of a buzz saw. Peter realized he was probably one of the invaders earmarked for annihilation, but he didn't give a damn as long as Tashi was saved.

"Out of the way, you bastards!" Zhdanov screamed. Rage erupted from him as the wall of monks kindled ugly memories. He flipped the safety off his assault rifle.

Peter yelled to the monks, "Save Tashi!" but his shout was drowned out by the angry roar of the chant.

Tashi broke from Bagora's grip as Zhdanov raised his assault rifle. "Don't! I'll help—"

"*You took my eyes!*" The machine gun burst to life in Zhdanov's hands, shaking his whole body as a murderous line of fire ripped into the wall of monks, wiping away lives, splattering blood on holy ground.

"You took my life," Zhdanov screamed.

Bagora and the others opened fire.

Peter stared open-mouthed, his mind frozen by horror. People were *dying* around him. Monks were running. Bleeding. Dead and dying. Slaughtered.

He was pushed ahead by someone, one of the storm troopers. The route to the gate was open.

The acrid smell of gunpowder invaded his nostrils.

Some monks were sobbing. Crying out in pain. Agony.

Two of the Thugs had Tashi between them, almost dragging her. Her head was bent low.

Peter saw everything, the monks, Tashi. Heard the moans. Tasted death in his nostrils. But none of it registered.

A grunt came from the Thug holding onto his arm and the man fell at his feet, his head caved in by a huge rock dropped from the walkway above the gates.

Stones crashed down around them and they ran, Peter with them, running from the rain of death.

He stumbled over someone, another dead storm trooper, as he ran out of the gate.

Out of range of the rain of stones, Zhdanov turned and fired back at the lamasery until his clip was empty. He was clumsily inserting another, his hands shaking, his rage still unspent, when Bagora shouted to him.

"They're attacking the copter!"

Little brown men in flapping robes swarmed the huge helicopter, Stone Age men attacking a metal pterosaur with their fists and clubs.

With the copilot leaning out the window, trying to knock off attacks with the butt of his rifle, the helicopter lifted off. Two monks still clung to the landing rails and a third had got his legs over the long tail and sat upright. The monk riding the tail slid back, unable to gain purchase on the fuselage as the copter soared skyward.

Tashi screamed and turned away as the little man slid into the tail propeller and a spray of red blew from the whirling blades.

A piece of the propeller blew off with the blood and bone.

For a second the copter hesitated, then it spun wildly out of control and hit the ground, exploding on impact.

Thunder from the explosion pounded the circle of mountains, loosening avalanches.

The ground trembled beneath Peter's feet as a dozen avalanches roared down the surrounding mountains, too far away to threaten them but filling the valley with resounding thunder.

Someone gave him a shove and the troop was pointed toward the big mountain.

Peter felt that he was experiencing a prelude to the end of the world.

They went up the mountain to the temple of ice, Peter and Tashi, the priest and Poc, hostages of a madman commanding three storm troopers armed with twentieth-century weapons in a land lost in time.

They paused at the foot of the temple to put on foul-weather suits and for Zhdanov's men to treat their weapons with a solution to keep them from jamming in the subzero temperature expected in the passageway beyond the temple.

Near the lake below ugly black smoke still curled up from the wreckage of the copter.

No monks had followed. The fate of the invaders was in the hands of whatever harm awaited those who desecrated the temple.

They untied Peter's hands at the foot of the temple. Tashi moved to his side and he held protectively onto her arm. He felt her trembling and gripped her arm tighter. "Are you all right?"

She tried to smile. "I feel strange, as if I have led a thousand previous lives and in each I walked this very path, yet each step brings a new discovery."

"Tashi—"

She sealed his lips with her fingertips. "I know you don't believe in anything except the world you see, but believe this, Peter. No matter what happens, no matter what harm is done to our bodies, if our love is true, our kismet will bring us together, if not in this life, then in the next."

"Tashi, I love you so much."

"I'm sorry about the lies, about the way I treated you. When we were on the beach and you told me about your father, I thought that your father . . . was *my* father."

"Stop talking and get moving!" Bagora snapped. The little man had grown more arrogant since killing Ma. He even bridled at Zhdanov's orders.

The priest dropped back and whispered to Peter as they went up the steps of the temple. "Poc has filled Bagora's mind with promises of wealth and power. Poc is a pox. He could get a dog to bite its master."

The secret doorway leading into the heart of the temple was a narrow opening in an interior wall. It was in plain sight yet not visible. Father Decimus and Dr. Poc had overlooked it a hundred times before discovering it. Like a magician who hides his props in plain sight on stage, the builders of the temple had used an optical illusion to conceal the doorway. As the members of the expedition lined up to follow the priest and the Chinaman through the secret doorway and into the hidden recesses beyond, Dr. Poc stroked his beard and chuckled as he gestured at the door.

"It's all done with mirrors."

The group went through the opening in single file, with Zhdanov's storm troopers bringing up the front and rear. Peter stepped in front of Tashi to make sure he faced any danger first. They passed through the door and into a small chamber chiseled from ice. A stairway carved from ice led from the chamber.

"We've stepped into the glacier itself," Father Decimus said. "The stairway is leading us down."

"Down to the bottom of the mountain," Poc said, picking up on the priest's thought. "The legend says the tomb is in the mountain. It doesn't mention the glacier. The legend may be older than the glacier."

Peter's heart pounded as he started down the steps. Into the unknown. Every step took Tashi into greater danger. He had survived a frozen hell with Poc and Decimus; he'd take his chances willingly against Zhdanov. That was how Peter thought of the man. Not as Duncan MacKinzie, a handsome young RAF pilot his mother had pined over. Not as his father. But as Zhdanov, a man without a face, a past, a country. *Or* a conscience.

Peter could hear Father Decimus quietly counting the steps as they went down. He noticed the priest made a mark on the ice wall at the top before they started down the stairway. He was marking the path back. Dropping bread crumbs.

Seventy-eight steps brought them into an ice cavern, a netherworld of crystal and white; a forest of ice formations rose from the floor like pine trees. Ice-crystal stalactites sparkled like clusters of diamonds in the frozen heaven above them. Tashi came up next to Peter and he put his arm protectively around her waist.

"Have you ever been in here?" he whispered.

She shook her head. "No, only to the temple. It's incredible."

Father Decimus shook his head in wonderment, in memory. "I was once in a cave of ice in a desert valley, but this is a piece of heaven trapped in the heart of a glacier."

"Or hell," Dr. Poc said, remembering the swarm of vampire bats that attacked them in the desert cave.

"What's creating the light?" Peter asked.

The cones of ice emitted a glow like low-wattage neon, illuminating the cavern with soft and shadowy light.

"A fungus with illuminant cells," Decimus said. "It's not uncommon in caves."

Hand in hand with his goddess-lover, surrounded by a glittering, white-gold world, Peter had the sensation of walking through a dream.

The walls were silver, etched with hieroglyphics that told the story of the Monkey-King and the She-Demon, the battle, the final conquest. The Monkey-King was presented in robes that hid his features, but the drawings excited the priest and Dr. Poc.

"The Monkey-King was shorter than the She-Demon," Decimus said. "You can tell from the drawings that his head is larger proportionately than the rest of his body."

"Yes, yes," Poc said, stroking his beard. "Larger than the human head. But why are his features masked?"

Tashi volunteered the answer. "My people believe that giving him the features of a man or beast would be blasphemous."

Poc and the priest jabbered excitedly as they went from drawing to drawing. Peter pretended to be listening to the two scholars, but he was paying more attention to a guard who was too preoccupied gaping about at the awesome caverns to realize Peter was almost behind him.

Peter watched the guard out of the corner of his eye. The man had hand grenades on his belt. An exploding grenade would bring the caverns down on them. With one of those in his hand, he would be in a bargaining position with Zhdanov.

Peter tensed to make his move when Bagora suddenly shot in front of him. The little beast jabbed a 9mm automatic at Peter's face.

"I'm watching you," he hissed. "I want to kill you. Do something to give me an excuse." He waved his gun at the others. "Keep moving! Keep moving!"

A guard nudged Peter with the butt of his rifle. Peter turned his back on the man and gripped Tashi's arm firmly, keeping her close to him. "Don't be afraid," he told her. "We're going to get out of this."

"I'm not afraid," she said softly. "Not for myself. I'm afraid for you."

"We're getting out of this, both of us. We've got a date, for a candlelight dinner on the Champs-Élysées. It's our destiny, remember?"

The expedition moved slowly through the forest of ice, the unknown before them.

They crossed an ice bridge and entered a long tunnel that took them out of the world of dazzling ice and into a realm of frigid shadows, of mists and fog, a dismal, spine-chilling cave tunnel filled with strange shapes and twisted contours. The passageway was lighted, but the fungus glowed gray in the dreary place.

Peter could see that Zhdanov's men were not any crazier about the place than he was. The men walked stiffly, weapons at the ready; Peter could imagine the white knuckles inside their gloves. Mere money, even the big booty Zhdanov paid or promised, didn't buy the kind of loyalty that would last long in this primeval jungle of ice.

The tunnel broke into another great cavern, a place of the dead tombstoned with statues of women. A ghostly haze of ice coated the statues, giving them an eerie animation.

Peter stared at one of the statues. The eyes stared back. He shivered. "They're so . . . lifelike."

"We're in the catacombs, the burial place of the Tashivaana, the She-Demon-Goddess of Shambala," Father Decimus said.

"They're wax."

"No, they're mardongs. Mummies preserved in an ancient Tibetan process using salt and yak butter. In this cold, dry atmosphere they could remain unchanged for an eternity."

The eyes of goddesses dead a thousand years followed them as they made their way through the ghostly catacombs. It was a place of the dead, but each of them could sense something alive, some dynamic energy that remained kindled long after life left the body.

Tashi's face was pale and drawn. Peter held her close as he guided her though the graveyard.

"Keep moving," Bagora growled, not at the prisoners but at two storm troopers who lingered behind.

They're ready to bolt, Peter thought. That or open up with their cannons when something spooks them.

"Precisely," the old lizard told him, catching Peter's thoughts as he slithered by, his long white beard hanging out from under his protective mask like the tail of a yellow jackal. "They'll bring the place down on us if they panic and use their weapons."

The energy-charged atmosphere created a storm in an unexpected source. Zhdanov's frigid-handsome face had changed: The frozen smile was cracking, as if his own memories were being ignited in this chamber that stored the memories of an eon.

Bagora sensed the change in his master and the dog strutted taller.

Peter briefly caught his father's eye and the encounter left him confused. He thought he saw a human emotion in the man's eyes: pain.

Peter slowed his pace, letting others pass until Zhdanov was abreast. He walked side by side with his father, a lump in his throat. He bristled with pride and anger but had to approach the man for Tashi's sake.

"Send Tashi back," Peter said.

Zhdanov kept his eyes straight ahead, not meeting Peter's eye, not replying.

"You've found your way inside, you don't need her. Let her go back." His voice cracked.

Bagora was suddenly there, pointing his pistol like an accusing finger. "Get back to where you were!" He pointed the gun at Peter's temple as Peter moved by him. "I want to kill you," he hissed.

"Leave him alone." The command from Zhdanov seemed to rattle Bagora.

As Peter moved back to his position in the line, Tashi gave him a questioning look. He avoided saying anything by shaking his head and gesturing behind him, signaling her that he didn't want to tempt fate by further antagonizing Bagora.

They left the catacombs, the eyes of the dead following them, and marched single file through a narrow valley with a dark and brooding ceiling sky.

Ahead the cavern was filled with a mist so dense it seemed as impenetrable as the icy walls. The expedition slowed down—no one was in a hurry to be first to plunge into the heavy mist.

"Night in the lonesome October," Peter said aloud, to no one. In answer to the question on Tashi's face, he said, "Something I read by Poe. A search for the tomb of Ulalume, 'In the ghoul-haunted woodland of Weir . . . ' through an alley Titanic, roaming with his soul." He shook his head. "I'm getting fruity."

"It can feel us," the priest whispered. "It's an organism, a giant ice machine, inanimate but alive, built by some devious genius in primordial times. Ice kept frozen never changes form. It doesn't deteriorate like steel or stone. Traps created in ice will last for eternity. In that terrible fog before us is a trap. Or it's hiding the prize we seek. We must not let this veil of Satan stop us."

Despite the brave talk, the priest stopped short of the fog, leaving the path clear for a more daring—or stupid—soul.

Two reluctant storm troopers hung back again and Bagora paraded in front of them like a banana republic general. "Keep moving, you cowards. I am not afraid. Follow me!"

The little man started strutting ahead, glancing back to see if the two men were keeping pace. The two had slipped back farther. Bagora yelled and the two men suddenly bolted, turning and running back the way they had come.

Bagora drew his weapon.

Both Poc and Decimus shouted a warning but it was too late; the noise of the little man's 9mm automatic pistol resounded off the ice walls like a cannon shot.

The ceiling above the fleeing guards came down, millions of tons of ice hitting with the shock of a megabomb, sending a fury of snow and ice down the caverns like an avalanche in a storm drain.

Tashi was torn from Peter's grip as the storm hit and swept him off his feet. He thought it was the end and shouted Tashi's name.

He hit the cavern floor hard and was knocked breathless by chunks of falling ice. He experienced one pregnant moment of absolute silence and then his ears began to ring. He was belly down and it felt like someone—a lot of someones—were standing on his legs. He broke his left leg free and twisted around. His right foot was trapped under a block of ice.

A great noise sounded in the caverns, the shuddering groan of a million-year-old glacier collapsing within itself.

The caverns trembled and ice debris rained from the ceiling and tumbled from the collapsing walls. The floor itself was slowly breaking into great chunks that crunched and battered against each other like waves in a pounding sea.

He heard Tashi scream; the sound came from the rear of where he lay trapped. He twisted around, but debris blocked his view. Using his left leg, he kicked and pushed at the ice trapping him.

CHAPTER 32

The priest rose awkwardly on trembling legs. The explosion had blown a hole in the wall separating the glacier from the mountain, exposing a startling new world. The great mountain was a hollow volcano, a vast cavity large enough to hold Manhattan.

A sea of crimson lava filled the bottom of the mountain.

The explosion blew away the insulation between the fiery guts of the mountain and the icy glacier, and the two elements, hot and cold, went after each other like rabid pit bulls, subzero chill reacting against molten lava, creating flash-clouds bristling with electrified charges. Lightning flashed in the overcharged atmosphere as the underground maelstrom grew, sending hurricane winds through the caverns.

The priest held himself erect against the force of the wind; ignored the flaming bolts of lightning.

The miracle was before him.

A pyramid of ice stood near the gaping hole that led into the mountain. On top of the pyramid was a coffin of dark-blue ice, the midnight blue of the star sapphire of the snow leopard.

He stared at the coffin. For forty years he had searched and struggled in the Wilderness; forty years of sacrifice, dedication, doubt.

His heart had not deceived him.

Before him was the tomb of the Monkey-King. The answer to the creation of mankind.

Lava bleeding out of the mountain threatened the magnificent throne of ice and the tomb atop it.

He ran for the tomb, tripping over boulders of ice, picking himself up and pushing on against the howl of a mad-dog storm.

Dr. Poc twisted and turned, burrowing like a worm to free his skinny body from the debris.

He saw the tomb, saw the priest running for it. His quest, too, had been that of a lifetime. The cost had been everything he had ever possessed. He was not going to let another man have the victory. He unzipped the right arm of the foul-weather suit and pulled a dagger from up his sleeve.

Peter kicked with his free foot at the ice boulder holding his leg. Chunks broke, but he couldn't slip his foot out. He heard Tashi cry out again and he struggled with a strength born of panic, gasping in pain as the jagged ice cut his leg. Breaking free, he got to his feet, swaying to keep his balance as the ice pack beneath him shook and violent winds assaulted him. The walls of the cavern were compressing and collapsing, leaving a small island of flooring that was quickly breaking up as lava undermined it.

He ran and fell to his knees as the caverns gasped again in death throes. Daggers of ice rained from the ceiling and were hurtled by the wind.

As he came around the mound of ice debris, he saw Tashi lying near the edge of the remaining reef of ice. A guard was standing over her, working the cocking lever of his weapon in an attempt to unjam it.

Peter charged the man, giving it everything he had,

the sound of his pounding feet drowned out by the storm gripping the caverns.

The guard spotted him and spun around, aiming the machine gun from the hip. Peter threw himself at the man in a wild body block as a burst of lead ripped by. He hit the man and they both went down with Peter flying past him and skidding to the edge of the ice floor.

A great block of ice slammed next to Peter, cracking the slab of ice he was hanging onto. Lava boiled up from between the cracks like blood gushing from wounds. Tashi grabbed at his clothes and helped him scramble back as lava devoured the ice beneath him.

The guard was already on his feet. He yelled something savagely incoherent as he leveled the machine gun at them. Peter shielded Tashi with his own body as a single shot boomed. The guard recoiled, dropping the gun, clutching at his chest as he staggered and fell.

Zhdanov stood to the right, a pistol in hand. His frozen countenance was gone; for the first time he looked at Peter as a father seeing his son, seeing the woman whose seed was in Peter, the woman he had waltzed with on a rooftop when he was a different person in a different world.

A narrow path of stony ice led across the growing sea of lava to the pyramid. Father Decimus reached the base of the pyramid and paused, his chest heaving as he tried to catch his breath and keep his feet beneath him at the same time: wind and lightning created a tempest around him, threatening to sweep him into the fiery molten sea growing about the pyramid.

Someone was behind him, but he never looked back. The hair on the back of his neck told him it was the Chinaman, but it didn't matter. The quest of a lifetime was over. He was the chosen one of God. Nothing could stop him.

Lightning flashed above the pyramid. The ice of the pyramid was as flawless as the most precious diamond; the dramatic colors of the Frost of Heaven spread from the ice-gem as the flash of lightning bolts exploded overhead, turning the pyramid into a giant prism. The heavenly light from the prism sprayed the priest; youthful strength rippled through his body. He laughed from joy as he started up the steps leading to the top of the tomb.

Poc hurried behind him, fueled by rage and greed, a dagger in his claw.

A hundred steps led to the top of the tomb, and the priest took them with the vigor of a young man. He reached the top and stood before the coffin, so mesmerized he paid no attention to the shouted threats of Poc huffing up the stairs. Life and death were the concerns of mortals; he was in the presence of God.

He stared at the coffin, the answer to the mystery of life before him. *Angels or apes?* Was mankind the creation of God or a hairless freak that wriggled from the womb of a hairy ape? Forty years in the Wilderness had brought him to this moment. Now the answer lay before him.

Lightning exploded overhead as he placed his hands on the coffin lid. He felt *power* and he cried out, in joy, in fear, in ecstasy.

Dr. Poc, his face convulsed by rage, came up behind the priest, lifted his dagger in triumph, and plunged it between the man's shoulder blades.

Father Decimus gasped and fell forward against the coffin; he pushed himself back up and turned to his attacker. Poc screamed something as the priest grabbed him by the throat.

A bolt of lightning arced down, striking the top of the tomb, bursting into a tornado of fire, blowing the two men from atop the pyramid, sending them to the lava that was erupting from the fiery bowels of the earth like a belch from hell.

Balls of fire from the lightning bolt ricocheted off the tomb and into the ice cavern.

The ice underfoot shifted violently, throwing Peter and Tashi to the ground. A flaming blue ball of electric fire flew through the cavern and exploded at the far end.

Peter helped Tashi to her feet. He heard Zhdanov yell something but didn't catch the words. Machine-gun fire exploded and Tashi slammed against him. She tried to say something, but the words didn't come. She went limp, and he lowered her to the ground behind a slab of ice as machine-gun fire raked around them.

Bagora was on the tall mound of ice between Peter and the entrance to the mountain. His hair was disheveled and his foul-weather suit ripped and torn; wide-eyed and babbling things understood only by the insane, he fired the machine gun from the hip, barely holding himself erect against the force of the storm at his back.

Peter darted out, diving and rolling to the side as the man fired wildly.

Suddenly pistol shots rang out and chopped ice at Bagora's feet. Zhdanov had opened fire. Bagora turned to the new threat, returning the fire twenty to one as Peter raced up the mound of debris. He couldn't see what was happening between Zhdanov and Bagora as he crawled frantically up the mound, chunks of ice from the ceiling exploding around him like artillery rounds.

He was almost to the top before he realized Zhdanov had also been scaling the hill. He caught a glimpse of the man off to his right, taking cover from a spray of machine-gun fire.

Peter was a dozen feet away when Bagora spotted him. Bagora turned from the diversion Zhdanov had created and smiled broadly as he brought the machine gun around to Peter's direction.

Zhdanov suddenly stood up, yelling at Bagora, jerking off 9mm rounds as quickly as he could pull the trigger. Bagora hit him with a blast of the machine gun, rounds pelting him like a boxer's fists slamming a punching bag. Zhdanov fell backward and tumbled down the mound of ice.

Peter was breaking over the top, almost in grabbing range of Bagora, when lightning exploded somewhere behind the hill Bagora had made himself king of. Peter heard a sizzle and saw a ball of blue fire shooting out from where the lightning bolt had ricocheted off a wall of ice. He threw himself back down the hill as Bagora turned and gawked in horror at the fireball. It exploded as it struck the top of the mound, consuming Bagora in the inferno.

Peter spotted Zhdanov lying on a slab of ice that was breaking away, threatening to throw him into the convulsing sea of ice and lava. He made his way down the mound to his father's position.

Zhdanov got slowly to his feet. The left side of his foul-weather suit was bloody. The slab of ice he stood on moved farther away from the solid flooring as the caverns shuddered again in death throes.

Peter ran to the edge of the crevice and leaned out, offering his hand to Zhdanov as the ice beneath their feet was melting into the lava.

"Take my hand," Peter yelled.

Duncan MacKinzie reached out and touched the tip of his son's fingers with his own.

"Save Tashi," he said.

"Take my hand!"

Duncan shook his head. "It's too late for me. Save Tashi. Peter, I . . . I loved your mother."

The ice under Duncan's feet heaved up and turned over as if it had been disturbed by a primeval beast, flinging Duncan off. Peter cried out for his father as the man was swallowed by the lava.

Numb and operating off nervous energy, he went back to where he had left Tashi.

She had been beautiful in life; she was serene in death.

Crying softly, he knelt beside her and gathered her in his arms. He had crossed three continents to find something only to lose it again. He felt empty, lost. The caverns were disintegrating around him, but he felt no urge to run for safety. What was there to live for?

Tashi didn't belong in the bowels of the caverns, buried beside crazy Bagora and killers. She was a queen. He carried her back up the passageway, defying the death storm of ice and snow.

In the burial chamber of the queen-goddesses of Shambala, he gave her a place surrounded by the women who had defended Shambala for a thousand-thousand years.

He knelt beside her for a long time, holding her in his arms. Thoughts of joining her, and his mother and father, crowded his mind. Why take even one more step when everyone he loved was gone?

But Tashi had told him that no matter what happened, no matter what harm came to their bodies, if their love was true their kismet would bring them back together.

He had never believed in anything before.

But now he believed in love.

It was the only hope he had.

He brushed a strand of hair from her forehead and

kissed her. Holding her close, he whispered something meant only for her to hear.

Then he said good-bye and left the burial chamber, following the passageway back up to the temple.

Peter paused at a fork in the trail on the mountainside. He was leaving Shambala.

The mist that hid the valley and kept it warm was almost gone, exposing the path around the leopard's jaw. He followed the path, dressed in the foul-weather suit that made him impervious to the chill.

Ahead of him on the trail were two young monks, boys really, and an aged Pathfinder, his purple thread stained with blood from a wound. They were going over the mountain, too. Like him, there was nothing left in Shambala for them.

The great mountain was frothing in volcanic eruption. The death of the glacier had spread to the heart of the mountain, and the storms within were tearing it asunder.

Ice was forming on the Lake of Celestial Heaven, and flowers were already withering from the bite of the cold. The priest would have said God damned the valley for not protecting the tomb. A scientist might claim that the freak weather conditions had been created by the steam-radiator effect of a mountain filled with lava at the highest elevations in the world. Whatever the reason, the delicate balance wrought by God or Nature was gone and soon the green vale of Shambala would be another winter-bitter Himalayan valley.

The golden rays of the setting sun speared the remaining mist, and for the last time the celestial gems, a gift from the maker of stars and universes, sparkled in the silver sky—the Frost of Heaven.

He heard the cry of a wild beast. High on an icy ledge of the glacier hugging the mountains, a snow leopard stood, proud and majestic, its cry echoing the death throes of the valley it guarded.

She had told him that Shambala is found only in the heart. Now he realized what she meant. It wasn't a place, it was a feeling: the greatest gift of love one could give another. He turned and took the path that led over the mountain, back to the world he knew.

EPILOGUE

When the train pulled into the station, the old woman tapped Peter on the knee with her cane. "Young man, young man."

He jerked awake.

"You asked me to wake you when we reached Paris. If you're getting off, you had better hurry. The train will be leaving shortly."

He sat up straight and rubbed the sleep from his eyes. "Thanks. No, I'm not getting off. I just wanted to see the train station."

She raised her eyebrows. "Old memories. Perhaps a *liaison amoureuse*?"

He laughed. He liked her. They had boarded together at Calais and shared the compartment with her niece. The niece was an attractive young woman who made it obvious she was interested in Peter, but it was the maiden aunt who drew his attention. Miss Austin reminded him of Agatha Christie's Miss Marple; she had the charm and simple elegance of a more graceful time, the days when the Orient Express rumbled through the Balkans and tea was served only in silver.

"Nothing so glamorous, I'm afraid. Just ... memories."

"It must be so exciting to be a foreign correspondent. Are you on your way to Zurich to cover the summit? Or a juicy Mideast crisis we civilians haven't heard about yet?"

He smiled. "Something like that." He couldn't tell her, but the story he was covering would be bigger news than the summit. He had got wind of a cover-up in the New York financial district, and the tracks led to Zurich. Money was being funneled out of South America to New York via Swiss banks. Dirty money. Huge amounts of dirty money. And the people involved read like a who's who of the financial world. The story was going to blow the roof off Wall Street—if Peter didn't get his head blown off first.

He looked out the window. The platform was crowded with travelers getting off and on and saying good-bye in both directions. It was a train station like so many others, a rush of anxious people, with newspapers, gum wrappers, and cigarette butts scattered underfoot, trash bins overflowing.

His eye picked up a woman standing alone near a pillar that was beyond the press of the crowd by the train. The collar of her trench coat was pulled up.

She was the missing face in the Degas painting, the face the artist left blank because he couldn't brush features exquisite enough to satisfy his dream.

For a heartbeat their eyes met and time stood still.

A baggage cart moved between them, and Peter jumped up and pressed against the window for a better view. Like the sweep of a magician's cape, when the cart passed she was gone.

"Someone you know?" Miss Austin asked.

He answered her as he grabbed his overnighter off the rack and flew out of the compartment, but she didn't quite catch what he said.

The train was slowly moving out of the station when her niece returned. "The strangest thing," she told her aunt. "That young man sharing our compartment nearly bowled me over as he rushed by a moment ago. He leaped off the train and ran like he was on fire."

"It is peculiar, my dear. He was sitting here looking out the window and with a never-you-mind he jumped up and ran." She gazed out the window, smiling her thoughts. "I wonder who he saw? Perhaps he's on his way to some adventure. After all, he is a *foreign* correspondent. Mystery, romance, intrigue, oh, how exciting it must be for him!"

The pretty young thing sniffed. "I doubt it. Frankly, I found him a bit light-headed. I asked him why he was hurrying so and he shouted the queerest thing as he flew by. Just a single word."

"Really? What did he say?"

"Kismet."

"Kismet, my dear?"